PAS

Morgan's kiss w‥‥‥g, and Faith trembled. His arms clasped her more firmly, and the heated thrust of his tongue bent her backward in his embrace, forcing her to cling to his shoulders. She tried to deny the excitement of this closeness, but she had denied his touch too long. Heat rushed over her, and her struggles died as quickly as they were born. Even the flames of hell couldn't keep her from him. Sensing her surrender, Morgan let his gaze slowly devour his newly acquired wife, and then he was laying her down against the bench and kneeling over her.

''Don't,'' he warned. ''Don't let me ruin your life as I have all the others. Run from me just as fast as you can, Faith. . . .''

DEVIL'S LADY

DEVIL'S
LADY

by

Patricia Rice

AN ONYX BOOK

ONYX
Published by the Penguin Group
Penguin Books USA Inc., 375 Hudson Street,
New York, New York 10014, U.S.A.
Penguin Books Ltd, 27 Wrights Lane,
London W8 5TZ, England
Penguin Books Australia Ltd, Ringwood,
Victoria, Australia
Penguin Books Canada Ltd, 10 Alcorn Avenue,
Toronto, Ontario, Canada M4V 3B2
Penguin Books (N.Z.) Ltd, 182–190 Wairau Road,
Auckland 10, New Zealand

Penguin Books Ltd, Registered Offices:
Harmondsworth, Middlesex, England

First published by Onyx, an imprint of New American Library,
a division of Penguin Books USA Inc.

First Printing, September, 1992
10 9 8 7 6 5 4 3 2

Dedicated to those who have allowed—
and still allow—past hatreds to supplant the hope
of future happiness.
Forgive them, Lord,
for they know not what they do.

CHARACTERS

Faith Henrietta Montague—daughter of George Henry Montague and Leticia Carlisle Montague

George Henry Montague—Methodist evangelist, younger son of the Marquess of Mountjoy; Faith's father

Leticia Carlisle Montague—only daughter of Lady Lettice Carlisle; Faith's mother

Lady Lettice Carlisle—Faith's grandmother on her mother's side

Henry (Harry) Montague, Marquess of Mountjoy—father of George and Edward, uncle of Thomas; Faith's grandfather on her father's side

Edward Montague, Earl Stepney—elder son of the marquess; Faith's uncle

Thomas Montague—cousin of Edward, nephew of the marquess

James Morgan O'Neill de Lacy III, Earl de Lacy—disenfranchised Irish earl, also known as "Black Jack"

Sean and Aislin de Lacy—deceased brother and sister of Morgan

AUTHOR'S NOTE

The 1700's were a fascinating transition from the richly embroidered tapestry of Renaissance life to the rigid Victorian era of black and white. People who were just beginning to learn to eat with forks instead of knives lived side by side with generations who developed elaborate place settings requiring twenty-eight pieces of silverware at each plate. At the same time, people who were accustomed to giving full rein to their lusts in the most public of places (since privacy in Elizabethan households was at a minimum) were hindered by a new morality that confined their desires to hidden chambers.

In a lusty era that could produce such masterpieces of sexual literary fantasies as *Tom Jones* and *Fanny Hill*, highly moral tomes and simpering platitudes could be equally popular in novels like *Pamela* or Hannah More's morality essays. In England, perhaps the turning point can be documented with the Marriage Act of 1753 (which actually didn't come into effect until 1754), when the failure of earlier attempts to force marriage into a legal state was finally ended with an Act of Parliament. No longer could a drunken sailor get off a ship and wake up married to the prostitute he had bedded the night before. Marriage became not only a sacramental state in the eyes of the church but also a legally documented requirement in the eyes of the law.

I hope my readers will not be offended if I try to portray some of the lust of the period along with the religious forces that tempered the times. I make no attempt at giving a panoramic view of all the forces at work, but offer only those affecting one couple living during the center of this fascinating century.

One postscript for those already familiar with the thief-taker general: the character in this story is only a pale imitation of the original who operated a decade or two ear-

lier. All real-life characters have their imitations somewhere, and there is no doubt there were many who attempted to follow in the general's footsteps in the years after
his ill-fated demise.

PROLOGUE

1750

The November sleet bit more bitterly than a January blizzard into Faith's thinly clad shoulders, freezing any lingering hopes of autumn warmth brought about by the last Michaelmas daisies seen earlier in the day. Clutching her bundle, she pulled her meager cloak tighter, but the icy wind swirled between her legs and up her back, and her chilblained hands ached all the way to the bones.

The sudden storm had obliterated what remained of the afternoon's gloom. Darkness shrouded the trees ahead, mercifully disguising their threatening height and depth. The blight of miserable landscape on either side of her was no more comforting than the dreaded forest, however. The land rolled away in endless mud flats without sign of habitation or even life. Faith shivered and briefly closed her eyes against the blinding sting of wind and snow. Her lashes turned to painful shards of ice against her skin, and she moaned softly at this new punishment.

Her stomach felt as if it were flat against her backbone. The emptiness inside hurt even more than the numbness growing in her fingers and toes. The pitifully thin pieces of leather that had never adequately protected her feet were now worn into holes as large as the ones in her torn wool stockings. Unable to lift her feet, she tripped on the hem of her overlong homespun skirt and heard the worn material rip, but it scarcely seemed to matter anymore. Her mother was no longer there to scold or lecture on the proper attire of young ladies.

An ancient stone wall rose up alongside the rutted road, and Faith tried to imagine what it would be like come spring. The thorny briars spilling over the top would fill with scented roses, and perhaps larkspur and campion would sprout along the mud-covered base. If she could just remember the hope of spring, she might find the strength to keep moving in the direction of London.

At least Faith hoped she was still walking in that direction. She could no longer remember when she had seen the last signpost, or where. She wasn't at all certain that she remembered why she needed to get to London. The notion had been a nebulous one from the first, born out of desperation and a need to have some direction. Now the idea of London was no more than a spark against the blizzard, and in danger of dying completely.

If only she could sleep, just for a little while. There had been no barn to rest in the night before, and the ground had been cold and damp. And now it looked as if there would be no protection again this night. Exhaustion blurred her senses and froze her mind more thoroughly than the ice did her toes.

As the gloom of the forest rose up around her, Faith clung to the sight of the wall traveling along the road with her. The stones rose higher now, and the thorns had become thick brambles beneath which mounds of dirt concealed ideal burrows for rabbits and other creatures of the forest. Faith tried to imagine herself as a rabbit covered with fur, snuggled warmly deep inside that cozy bank of earth, and envied the animal its home. If only she could do the same— snuggle close to that wall and sleep until the cold and the night passed.

As she tripped once more, it became increasingly evident that she would have to lie down and sleep somewhere. She hadn't the strength to move her feet or lift her head, and even keeping her eyes open was a struggle she had begun to lose.

Just a little while, she vowed. She would curl up beneath the bank for just a little while. Sleep was impossible to find anymore, but she had to rest, and perhaps if she pulled her toes up beneath her cloak she might begin to feel them again. The thought became more appealing as the sleet came down harder and the barren trees offered little cover against the wind. If only she could burrow down on the far side of the wall, where the wind couldn't reach . . .

The pale glimmer of broken stone offered the opening she needed. Someone or something had broken through the ancient rock, leaving a littered trail of debris and a cut through which one small, forlorn waif could wriggle. Faith never hesitated. Perhaps the Lord had sent this blessing as a sign that things would get better. She didn't believe her father's ecstatic promises anymore, of wealth beyond her dreams to be had in the kingdom of heaven, but she had to believe there was Someone still looking after her, or she couldn't go on. She had lost all else in the world; she would not give up her beliefs.

As she wrapped her mud-colored cloak around her and knelt behind the barrier of the wall to say the prayers she had said every night of her life, the wind blew over her head and left her frozen body alone. For this, she gave grace, then, thoroughly exhausted, rolled up in the slight indentation of earth between wall and forest floor, placed her small bundle of possessions beneath her head, and closed her eyes and prayed for sleep.

It never came easily. To keep at bay the horrifying images that haunted her dreams, Faith tried to pursue the future. She had mistakenly thought she could find employment somewhere along this road, to help her goals. She knew herself for a hard worker, but there didn't seem to be a Christian soul in all of England willing to part with a few coins or even a hot meal for a day's work.

Had it not been for the aid of her father's parishioners, she could not have come this far. She closed out thoughts of her father, for they only led to that ugly morning . . . Faith squeezed her eyes tighter and tried to concentrate on where her plans had gone awry. If she could only find her faults, perhaps she could correct them and things would improve on the morrow.

She knew her father's parishioners had offered her coins only to hasten her way out of town. She was too young to know whether it was their own guilt they tried to ease or if they truly wished the best for her, but those coins had kept her from the workhouse, at least. She tried not to judge them too harshly for not offering a home instead of money. They were poor, desperately poor, with more mouths to feed than any one human being could provide. Her father had tried to show them the way out of poverty, the road to righteousness through the methods of hard work and discipline taught by John Wesley, but it was hard to give up the gin on a Saturday night, and work was not easily come by these days. Faith knew all that, and she tried to keep her father's lessons in her heart.

But it was damnably difficult to feel kind toward others when your toes and fingers were numb and your belly was empty. So she mulled her thoughts through the days since her money had run out. At first she had sought out other Methodists. Wesley had taught to give until it hurt, and her father had followed these precepts, sometimes to the detriment of his own family. She had discovered other followers were not quite so eager to accept this particular lesson. They were almost always poor, and they seldom offered more than a crust off their table, if that.

After a few days of starvation, Faith had not been quite so choosy in her search of employment. She applied at houses large and small, to the good Church of England believers and to nonbelievers alike. There had even been a few secret papists, but she had come to realize religion was no indication of Christianity. The few Good Samaritans who had actually given her food or money or a place to sleep came from all ranks, and they were few and far between.

She sighed as her stomach gave a hollow rumble, and she tried to find a more comfortable position amid the rocks and mud. Exhaustion wasn't enough to ease her mind to sleep. Every night she lay still and watched the procession of these ghastly weeks parade through her head. Should she have been humble? More proud? Should she have begged for work? Insisted? Should she have cried and told her tale of woe? Should she have lied and given some tale of her wealthy family in London?

She never found an answer. She simply quit confronting anyone. By now she looked like every beggar on the road. If people hadn't cared before, they would care even less now. She had learned that much in these last few weeks. People might help for a moment or with a coin or two if they thought that sufficient to help an unfortunate out of their way. But let the specter of permanent poverty rise before them, and they closed their eyes and turned their heads and pretended the ghoul didn't exist.

She refused to cry. The tears would freeze, in any case. She would make it to London somehow. Surely, in all that great city, there would be room for one small girl willing to work her fingers to the bone for a right to live. Perhaps, when she was strong again and could buy good clothes, she might inquire about the families she had never known. Perhaps. They had turned their backs on her parents, so there seemed little hope that they would acknowledge her, but she so desperately wanted a family again. . . .

The tears were gathering beneath her lids, and Faith forced them away with images of the rabbits in their burrows. She would be snug and warm again someday. She had not come this far to cry in her sleep. Mayhap London was just the other side of the woods.

The rattle and creek of the coach racing dangerously over the frozen, rutted road jarred Faith back to wakefulness sometime later. It must be earlier than she thought for the coach to still be abroad, but the darkness of the storm had the same effect as nightfall. She curled tighter in her cloak and wished she could be squeezed on the wooden bench between all those warm bodies packed into the lumbersome vehicle on its way to London. Undoubtedly there was an inn somewhere down the road where they would stop for the night. The innkeeper would bring them big mugs of hot toddy and steaming bowls of soup and seat them before a roaring fire. She could almost feel the heat of the flames, and her eyes closed drowsily at the warmth creeping through her veins. Tomorrow, perhaps, she would reach that inn and apply for a position. . . .

The sound of gunshots and screams, neighing horses, and violent curses jerked her awake once more. Fearing the nightmare had returned, Faith forced her groggy senses to search the darkness, but the shout of "Stand and deliver!" roaring through the wind's wail raised the specter of all those whispered tales of the road. Highwaymen!

She heard their voices carried on the wind: the whining complaint of women, the angry and helpless protests of men, as the deep and resonant orders of the thief stripped them of their belongings. She had known these woods concealed the dregs of society, but she had thought herself safe enough, since she had nothing they could want. It had never occurred to her that she might act as witness to their illegal acts.

Faith gulped as another shot rang out and a woman screamed. If only there were something she could do, but she knew there was not. Her fingers wrapped in the wool of her cloak as she tried to shut out the sounds. They could not be too far away. There could be thieves all along this wall, just waiting for some movement to betray her presence. She had no gun, no strength, no means but prayer of fighting their depredations. She prayed fervently, if not coherently. Please, God, do not let those poor people be harmed, deliver them from their enemies, let me live another day.

The sound of racing hoofbeats came closer, and Faith stared wildly at the wall, praying its shelter would conceal her from the horrors of the road on the other side. The wind wailed through the trees above, rattling the barren branches, and the icy sleet began again, pelting her with tiny shards that pierced like knives where they hit her face. The coach rumbled off, and she began to breathe once more, when the hoofbeats seemed to pound just beside her head and a huge beast flew over the wall mere inches from where she lay.

She closed her eyes and curled inside her cloak like a frightened hedgehog, but she couldn't shut out the sight of the black cape billowing like a thundercloud behind the alarming shape of a giant beast, half-man, half-horse, as it flew over her head. The hoofbeats thundered into the distance, but the image was engraved indelibly behind her eyelids.

The horse had to be huge, bigger than anything she had ever seen in her life. If it had breathed fire, Faith wouldn't have been surprised. And it had been blacker than the night sky, so black the man on its back had blended in until they had seemed one heaving, flying projectile of muscle and blood. She would remember the sight of them lunging over that wall until the day she died.

And that day could be today, should the highwayman discover she had seen him. Huddled quietly in her cloak, Faith tried to discern the sound of hoofbeats on the forest floor, but she heard nothing. She would have to leave this haven from the wind and hurry on as soon as she knew it was safe to scamper from hiding. The idea of walking a dark road infested with thieves and murderers held no peril compared to the possibility of the highwayman discovering her presence. Better the evils of her imagination than the very real terror of that beast bearing down on her again.

When she finally raised the courage to lift her head from her hiding place, she looked blindly through the icy sheets of rain, and at the sight revealed, screamed until insensibility overcame her.

The huge beast loomed overhead, cape flying backward

in the wind, the icy, masked visage glowering down with eyes of fire. Murder flared in those eyes, and his curse was deadly as he reached for the miscreant who dared witness his nighttime depredations.

1

JAMES MORGAN O'NEILL DE LACY III stood in the crumbling shadows of his home and choked back tears of shame and rage. Although he had not yet achieved his full manhood, his fists were large and murderous as he clenched them tightly at his side, straining not to raise them to the heavens and rail at his fate, straining not to let the hot, furious tears cascade down his face.

The man watching these struggles from behind stayed silent, his lined visage an etching of pain as raw as the boy's, but more ingrained. His own black hair was streaked with gray, and the shadows of his beard did not disguise the deep creases of suffering in his weathered face. He had a legacy of anguish to pass on, and it twisted in his heart as he watched his elder son's shoulders shake with just this first sample of it.

"You're the eldest, Jamie," he said. "And not to put too fine a finish on it, you're the one with the fists and the fire to be a grand soldier. Your grandfather would be proud of you. The day will come when you will ride in here with Charlie's men and drive the murtherin' redcoats out, but until that day, we must see you safe. Your brother will hold the lands for you. Sean can be trusted, and he's not the sort to be a soldier."

Sean was meant to be a priest, but neither of them spoke of that. Priests had been outlawed, along with everything that made them Irish, Catholic, and proud. Sean would become a Protestant, and hold the lands against the day the Irish rose again. It churned in Morgan's gut, and the red rage of hatred rose in him again. For years they had been teaching him patience. He had hidden in the hedgerows with the other children, learning from the outlaw priests, soaking up his heritage, and being told the day would come when he would ride his lands as unfettered lord again. And this was what it had come to. Exile.

"I should have killed the bloody bastard. At least he would not have Queen Maeve now." He mourned the horse almost as much as the forthcoming loss of his home. He had been there at her birth, trained her since a filly; they had been a part of each other. The lovely black mare was the only thing of value he had ever owned, and the damned English robbers would take her from him too. And they called it the law!

Though his son still spoke with the loathing in his heart, de Lacy knew his heir had gained control of himself again. He clamped his eldest's shoulder and shook it slightly. "He'll not keep her. We'll see to that. And you damned well did near kill the lad. That's why it's time for you to go. They'll be wanting your head if you stay."

Morgan knew that with his mind, but he could not reason with his heart. This was his land. *His.* He knew every acre, every leaf, every life that stirred in these rolling emerald hills beneath the wide Irish skies. He belonged here, not with the soldiers in France. His grandfather had died over there, a fugitive from his own home because of the bloody, dishonorable British. James de Lacy I, along with all the other brave Irish patriots, had volunteered exile in the promise that the British conquerors would not punish those who remained. And look what that promise had come to!

The first thing the conquering British had done was ban their religion. Then they had taken away their schools, their professions, their government. They were forbidden even to trade or sell in order to live. It seemed the only thing the British laws now allowed a Catholic to do was to starve in the hills. They weren't even allowed to die in the cities, for they had been barred from most of them.

But the law burning in Morgan's chest right now was the one causing his fists to curl and his bile to rise. A Catholic could not own a horse worth more than five pounds. Queen Maeve had been worth a hundred or more and he would not have sold her for a thousand. But when the bastard redcoat offered five pounds for her, he had to sell or leave their lands liable for confiscation if his refusal was reported, as it surely would be. Morgan's shoulders slumped as the humiliation of that defeat ate at his insides. Even though he had beaten the insulting bastard to a pulp, he had been forced to surrender the mare when the man pulled out a five-pounder and waved it in his face.

The loss of Maeve would bring tears to his eyes for weeks to come, but his father had promised she would be saved from the spurs of that inept idiot. He would have to be satisfied with that. For now.

He was being selfish, he knew. His father was sacrificing his lands to give his sons a future. Sean was sacrificing his beliefs to protect that future. The least he himself could do was give up his home to learn the trade needed to save them both from a lifetime of misery. He would become a soldier in France, and someday, he vowed, he would lead an army straight through the heart of Ireland, and the redcoats would pay for their treachery.

That day was in the far-distant past now, just another black moment in a long line of such anguished memories. Jack didn't know why it had come to mind, other than that he must have been as young then as this child was now.

He lifted the lifeless body from the ditch, shocked by the slightness of her weight. She scarce weighed more than a sack of flour. He couldn't leave her here. The sleet had turned to snow and she would freeze to death before morning. He shouldn't have terrified her into fainting. He could have sent her on her way then.

He ought to send her on her way now, but the memories held him back. His little sister must have been this size when she died. He hadn't been there to protect her then. No one had been. Why should he try to protect one of theirs when none had protected his? But he couldn't throw this bedraggled bundle of bone and cloth back into the ditch. Conscience warred with logic. Conscience seldom won, but he was weary this night, and cold, and the memory of his family broke loose shreds of heart he hadn't known in years.

Jack hoisted her into the saddle with him and gave the stallion the signal to move on. He couldn't linger longer to argue with himself or he'd have the sheriff to argue with too. It had been foolish to attack a coach so close to home, but it had been such an easy mark, he couldn't resist the temptation. The gold riding in his saddlebags eased that much of his worries.

The creature in his arms stirred, and Jack clasped her more firmly about the middle. She was but a child. There could be no danger there. In the morning he would put her back on the road, and there would be an end to it.

He did not mistake this one good deed as paving his road to heaven. He was doomed to hell for his life of crime, but he had no intention of dying anytime soon. He had a lifetime of vengeance to mete out, and he had scarcely begun. If he were going to hell, it would be for plenty of good reasons. There was scarce any point in going for just one infraction of the rules. He might as well break all of them.

A white smile flashed through the dark at the thought. There were lots of rules he had yet to break, but he was young. He would get to all of them soon enough. He would be in good company by the time Satan came for him.

The child moaned, but he could feel the rumbling in her belly even more than the sound from her throat. The road to London crawled with beggars but he seldom encountered little girls. Perhaps she was lost, but from the look of the rags she wore, no one would reward him for her return. She was just one more lost soul in the system of British injustice. It did not relieve his hatred to know the system was as unkind to its own as it had been to his.

When he reached the cottage, he dismounted with the child under one arm. He felt her stiffen into wakefulness, but apparently one glance at his fearful visage was sufficient to send her into slumber again. Patting the stallion, he carried the child's limp form into the darkness of the hut and deposited her on the bed. She could come to little harm there, and he had to see to his horse.

When he returned and lit the lantern, Jack discovered his unwelcome guest had curled into a ball in the center of his bed and fallen sound asleep. He was hungry and cold and impatient for his supper and a fire, but he raised the lantern just for a moment to examine his hostage from this night's evil deeds.

He was no judge of age, but her pale face was clear and unlined and very young. The hood of her cloak had fallen back to reveal a tumble of tangled brown hair that flickered occasionally with a hint of red. The high, almost aristocratic cheekbones reminded him painfully of his sister, and the knotting in his stomach was not entirely from hunger.

Jack turned away. Memories did not sit easy on an empty stomach. He resisted the urge to reach for the bottle of rum on the shelf. He knew the dangers of drink. It was better to use those dangers for his own gain and someone else's detriment. He would not rot his own wits with the liquor. He needed every ounce of brain and brawn he possessed to accomplish his objectives.

The child had not stirred by the time the fire had warmed the room and his supper boiled in the pot. He wondered if she were dead and wandered back to check the pulse at her throat. Her skin was icy to the touch, but he could feel the thread of life still beating beneath his fingers.

He wasn't a man who cared about anything anymore. The child could die and he would dig a grave and bury her out back and not think about her again. But as long as she was alive, he supposed he ought to do something to keep her that way.

The fire cast flickering shadows over the wattled plaster of the walls and the rough-hewn beams overhead as he sought a spare blanket and prepared a pallet by the hearth. A single table, chair, and bed made up almost the entirety of the room's furniture, and the wide plank floor had room enough to spare for one small pallet. Removing the child's muddy cloak, Morgan covered her with an old one of his own.

He stared awkwardly down at her tiny form beneath the enveloping material and wondered what in hell else he was expected to do to keep her alive. He had never taken care of another soul besides himself, unless he counted his horses. He wasn't at all certain that he wanted to start now.

Adjusting the pallet a little farther from the stone hearth and the fire's menace, he straightened and scowled and went to check on his horses again. He had been a damned fool idiot to bring her here, but as the snow hit his face as he opened the door, he knew he could have done nothing else.

The image of her frail face lying white and still against his rough cloak traveled with him into the winter darkness.

Faith stirred and moaned softly, then, remembering herself, tried to stretch her cramped legs. She ached in every fiber of her being, and her legs protested the movement, but she had grown accustomed to the pain. She was warm. There must be work to do.

Darkness did not deter her from rising. She could not remember where she was or how she got there, but a lifetime of habit forced her out of the cozy cocoon of her covers to stir the fire.

Next she needed to heat water, but if she had been shown

the pump or well, she could not remember it. Ignoring the emptiness in her middle, she used the fire's meager light to search out pail and kettle on this strange hearth. Unable to locate her own cloak, she donned the one that had covered her. It dragged along the plank floor as she sought the door, but it was warm, and she was cold as soon as she left the hearth.

The snow had stopped, leaving a crystalline covering that crunched beneath her feet as she wandered in the dawn's gray light, looking for stream or well. A large structure loomed against the midnight black of the trees, and her feet carried her in that direction. Barns meant animals, and animals needed water.

She found a trough frozen and covered in snow, and she broke the ice. A whinny from inside the barn reminded her that the animals would need to drink too, and she filled her pail and carried it to the closed door of the barn. Opening the massive panels almost proved too much for her limited strength, but her parents had taught her that the weak must come first, and the animals were always weaker than humans.

Her head spun dizzily as she forced an opening large enough for her to pass through, but she rested just a moment before picking up the pail and stepping into the darkness. Perhaps if she worked hard enough, the owner of this grand barn would allow her to stay.

To her surprise, the only inhabitants of the structure were four horses, a cat, and a few hens. The horse in the last stall was a magnificent beast so large as to be terrifying, but he only whickered gratefully as she offered the pail of water. Timidly she patted his long, soft nose, and he pushed against her hand, searching for treats. She smiled and wished she had aught to offer, but she did not.

She had always wished for a pet of her own, but they had moved too often, and her parents had protested the nuisance of yet another mouth to feed. Memories of the hatred that had marred the days of her life rose up inside her, and Faith knew any pet would have been victim to that passion. Her parents had known too, but she had been too young to understand.

Petting the scrawny cat that curled around her ankles, Faith went in search of the hens' nests. She hadn't had eggs in months. Would the owner mind sharing his breakfast if she cooked it?

The thought made her mouth water and her legs tremble as she carefully tucked the precious ovals into her skirt pockets. In her haste to return to the cottage and fire, she almost forgot to close the door, but she tripped on her trailing cloak and remembered it when she caught herself on the latch.

Closing the door and refilling her pail, she stumbled hurriedly through the growing dawn to the tiny cottage. It was smaller than the barn, but the snow gleaming on its thatched roof and the ice frosting the tiny windowpanes made it somehow part of a fantasy world coated with sugary icing. Or perhaps just her hungry stomach turned to thoughts of food.

She crept softly through the doorway, hesitating to wake whatever inhabitants there might be. She had slept in so many strange places these last weeks that she had grown accustomed to making her own way around other people's houses and lives. The peat she had thrown on the fire had begun to burn, and the warmth greeted her as she slid off her wet shoes and neatly hung her cloak on a peg by the door.

She was still shivering in her torn stockings, but she hung the kettle over the fire and took the eggs from her pocket and looked around for the larder. A few pots and skillets hung on the mantel, and a crude cupboard in the corner uncovered the bare rudiments of a meal. Whoever lived here did not spare much time or money on fancy food. There was nary an herb or spice of even the most common kind. A sack of meal, a tin of tea, a rasher of smoked bacon, a stale half-loaf of bread, and a pot of lard constituted almost the entirety of the pantry.

But that was enough to make a breakfast that would fill her stomach, if allowed. Since no one had come to hinder her actions yet, Faith boldly set about making the kitchen her own. Surely no one would complain to find a meal waiting when he awoke.

She conscientiously avoided looking toward the bed cupboard in the far shadows across the room. She had never seen a bed quite like that, but she recognized it for what it was from the soft snores within. At one time it had possibly possessed doors to keep out the cold drafts of a winter night, but not even a curtain blocked the large opening in the cabinet now. It nearly filled the entire wall, and if she thought about it, she would have to wonder what kind of giant needed that size of bed. But she didn't think about it. She merely kept working.

The smell of bacon cooking made his mouth water, and Jack conjured up steaming pots of coffee and fresh cream and baking bread to go with it. His stomach rumbled, and he awoke enough to know that last night's greasy stew wasn't sufficient to fill his ever-empty belly. He would have to ride down to the inn and sweet-talk Molly out of a bowl of porridge.

The idea of a bowl of Molly's lumpy porridge did not quite satisfy the image of Jack's dreams, but it would have to do. He had learned the bare necessities of cooking to keep from starving, but he didn't enjoy it or have the patience to learn more. And he was too hungry to plunder his larder for its meager contents now.

Swinging his long legs out of bed, Jack realized he had slept in his shirt and stockings last night. What imp of hell had caused him to do that?

Nearly bumping his head on the cursed bed roof as usual, he swore irritably and groped for his breeches. Only then did he realize that the floor was almost warm, and he wasn't shivering with the predawn cold of a dead fire. The smell of cooking bacon became more than a dream, and as he donned his breeches, his gaze sought suspiciously the source of this miracle.

The impact of seeing that frail figure bending over a flaming fire in his own hearth almost sent Jack back to his bed. He hadn't been drunk in years. He couldn't be hallucinating. When was the last time he had seen a feminine form over a fire, cooking his breakfast? Not since Ireland, he was certain. Was she a faerie from his lost past? A *bean sidhe* to haunt his soul?

She turned then, and the slim shadow became a child with a glimmering mat of waist-length hair, prosaically setting a skillet on the table. Jack released a pent-up breath of relief and emerged from the corners of the bed.

Faith nearly dropped the skillet as the lean form rose from the shadows, but as he walked forward with the steps of a man, fastening his breeches, she shoved her fears back in a box and faced her host. She did not recognize him, though she searched her memory for his presence.

He had to be over six feet in height, for he was much taller than her father. His hair was coal black and curled in disgraceful disarray about his collarless shirt. His eyes were hidden in the dawn light, but she could see the black stubble of beard on a long masculine jaw that squared with a stubbornness she had learned to recognize in others. This one would be no easygoing farmer who jested and produced a shy wife and half a dozen children. Faith gulped with a small measure of fear as he approached and she noted the strong breadth of his shoulders. She had thought him on the skinny side at first, but she could see now that he was all lean sinew and muscle—a formidable adversary if she ever knew one.

It was then that she remembered the prior night and the nightmare of the highwayman, but she couldn't piece the two together. A highwayman didn't offer beds to his victims. Perhaps he was some farmer who had stumbled across her in the snow and carried her here. She wondered where his wife was, and she threw an anxious look to the loft ladder at the rear of the room. Perhaps the rest of the family would be down in a little while.

"Bean sídhes do not remain after dawn,'' Jack commented casually at the child's stare. Coming closer, he could see her eyes were remarkably large saucers of a clear gray. He could almost see himself in them, but he could see nothing of her—no fear, no laughter, no tears. He had little acquaintance with children, but he remembered them as being normally open with their emotions. This one revealed only a pale, cold face with magnificent eyes behind cheekbones too sharp for her frail skin.

"Banshees?" Faith mouthed the word tentatively. He had a curious accent, a soothing lilt that drew her attention instantly. His voice was a deep, resonant baritone pleasing to the ears. She found no reason to distrust him in these few words.

"Faerie women. Do ye know naught of the faeries?"

Was he teasing her? Faith knew little of jests other than the mocking taunts of children. She stared at him with incomprehension, then ducked her head politely. "No, sir." She waited for him to abuse her for making free with his larder or to issue orders for the day's chores. She just prayed he would allow her to eat first.

When he didn't answer, those wide gray eyes came back up to stare at him silently, blankly, without a hint of laughter or mischief. He had always imagined forest faeries to be laughing creatures, and even human children should know how to smile. She would have him believing in witches and hobgoblins shortly.

Jack sniffed the air hungrily, then glanced toward the table. "I don't suppose you've made enough for two, have you? I'm that starved I could eat the hearth."

She could very well imagine this giant chewing stones, but the mention of the size of the meager meal brought a lump of fear to her throat. She was so hungry she was almost ready to fight him for those two eggs, but a lifetime of her mother's teachings warred within her. They were his eggs. She had no right to them.

Even as her nose and throat filled with the delicious scents of those lightly fried eggs and finely sliced bacon, Faith bobbed her head briefly and replied, "I fixed what I could find, sir. I'll eat when you are done, if you do not mind."

No child he knew ever spoke like that. Jack ran his hand through his hair and stared at her suspiciously. He and Sean had used to fight ferociously over the last crust of bread, and he had wrangled with half the county at one time or another when he was a child and tempted by a found fish or apple. Perhaps girls were different. Aislin had been too young then to fight, but he vaguely remembered some other strapping lasses pinning him down when he tried to filch their lunches. And this one, no doubt, was hungrier than he had ever been.

"There's plates in the cupboard. We'll share," he answered gruffly. Leaving her to divide the bounty, he started for the door and his boots.

"The horses have been watered, sir." She spoke softly, almost timidly, and he turned to scowl at her.

"People around here call me Jack. I'll just take a look for myself, shall I?"

Faith jumped, startled, at the slamming of the door. Then, glancing hungrily at the food simmering in the skillet, she allowed some of the tension to drain out of her. For all his gruff manner, he didn't look like he would eat her for breakfast.

She went to the cupboard and found a few tin plates and mugs and brought them to the table. Carefully she divided the eggs and bacon between the two of them, giving him the larger portion, since his appetite would have to be so much larger than her own, with his size. Then, keeping the plates warm on the trivet by the fire, she sliced the stale bread and soaked it in the skillet grease and heated it over the fire until it grew soft again.

The expensive tea had finished brewing by the time Jack returned, and she poured the steaming beverage as he shook the snow off his boots. She did not know what kind of house had tea and not food, but she didn't intend to question.

The room possessed only one chair. Without a thought, Jack scooped up one of the plates at the fire and threw himself to the floor, picking up a slice of bacon with his fingers and biting into it.

Faith regarded him with a mixture of dismay and outrage. "You cannot sit there! And that is my plate. Yours is here." She picked up the plate with the larger portion and set it at his rightful place on the table. "Where are your forks?"

Jack finished chewing his bacon and tilted one arrogant black eyebrow at her. "The bacon is sliced too thin. A starving man likes something substantial to bite into. Give me some of that tea. I hope it's strong."

Orders, she understood. Faith handed him a mug. "I did not find cream or sugar," she apologized.

"And you will not, for there is none. Sit. Eat." He gestured at the table. "There's a fork in one of those drawers somewhere, but the bread works just as well." So saying, he scooped his egg onto his toast and filled his mouth hungrily.

No lack of manners could appall her any longer, but being ordered to sit at the table while the owner sat on the floor went against all she knew. Uneasily Faith searched for the errant fork; then, seeing he didn't mean to move, she looked at the plate of mouth-watering food. With decision, she took the fork, plate, and mug and sat on the other side of the hearth.

He didn't raise an eyebrow as she bit into her thick slice of bread. They ate in harmonious silence, Jack with his legs sprawled across the floor, and the delicate girl with her skirts primly smoothed around her. Through narrowed eyes Jack appraised her look of ecstasy as she dug into the food with discreet but eager manners. Not only did she not talk like any child he knew, she did not eat like any child he had ever seen. Despite the fact that she was obviously starved, she neatly cut every bite with her fork and chewed it thoroughly before cutting off the next piece. He felt downright ashamed of his own abandoned manners by the time she was through.

With eyes closed, she sighed in a quiet enjoyment as she consumed the last bite of bread, and Jack was startled by the bolt of pleasure he received just from watching her. It had been a long time since he had felt anything akin to emotion, and he wasn't at all certain that he enjoyed the sensation.

Before he could find an opening for conversation, she leapt to her feet and poured him another mug of tea. She then took the heavy iron kettle from the fire and poured steaming water over the skillet and efficiently began scrubbing their eating utensils.

To Jack, who had unconcernedly left his dirty dishes to accumulate enough grease to feed the field mice, this efficiency was nothing short of amazing. Unwilling to admit his astonishment, he sat and sipped his tea and watched her work.

She could do with a good bath. Although it was obvious she had made attempts to scrub at face and hands with regularity, her hair was a tangled nest of filthy curls and her neck looked none too clean. The hem of her tattered skirt was caked with filth, and her frayed cuffs were grayer than the rest of the dingy fabric of her bodice. The bodice itself hung in wrinkled folds about her slender body, and he winced at the rail thinness of the wrists sticking out beyond the cuffs. She was little more than a dandelion wisp to be blown off in the breeze.

While he pondered her presence, Faith gathered her courage. She had never worked for a man living alone, but it was obvious that he needed her. The skillet hadn't been scrubbed clean in years, and the floor was coated with the filth of accumulated neglect. She knew from his expression that he appreciated her cooking. She knew without immodesty that she was a good cook. And she was good with her hands too. She itched to repair the worn hole in the front of his shirt. He didn't have much, but what he had seemed to be of good quality. That linen would last another few years if tended properly. How could she convey her usefulness to him?

"I'll slice your bacon thicker on the morrow, if you like," she offered timidly, hating herself for her lack of assertiveness. Only desperation could have forced her to say that much.

He raised those heavy black brows and regarded her calmly. "The snow has stopped. You would do better to be on your way. I'll see you to the road."

Pain twisted at Faith's insides, bringing tears to her eyes. She hadn't realized how high her hopes had risen. After all this time, she should have known better, but the fear of returning to that eternal trudge along icy roads with an empty belly and nowhere to go had obliterated common sense. She would do anything to stay in this cozy cottage just for a little while.

"I'm a hard worker," she answered with the defiance of desperation. "I can scrub your floors, cook your meals, mend your linen, keep your horses. I don't eat much. I can even sleep in the barn, if you prefer."

Had she been the most beautiful woman in the world, Jack could have told her no. He didn't need any interference in his life. He had his goals, and a partner was not one of them. Not yet, anyway. He had women when he needed them and solitude when he wanted it. A woman in his life would be a damned nuisance.

But she was a child—an oddly well-behaved child, to be sure, but a child just the same. She certainly didn't need the taint of his life, but it could scarcely be worse than the deprivations of the road. Jack found he couldn't say the words that would throw her out.

"Have you no home? No family? This is no place for a child." That was as firm as he could be.

She didn't look back at him, but continued scrubbing the skillet, fighting back the tears. "There's no one will be missing me. You needn't fear that. I've been looking for a position, but there's none to be had. I won't ask for pay, just room and board. What could be fairer?"

What, indeed? Jack sighed and stretched his legs and rose to his full towering height. He didn't have time for arguing with stubborn little girls. Rubbing his hand over several days' worth of beard and his ill-kempt hair, he wondered she hadn't run in horror from him. Did she even realize he was the apparition who had nearly frightened her to death last night? He suspected not, and he had no wish to enlighten her.

"This is no place for a child. I'm not here much, and these woods are full of villains. I'd recommend you look elsewhere. I'll be off now." He pulled his cloak off the peg, swung it around his shoulders and stomped out into the snow.

A few minutes later Faith watched his lithe figure ride off on one of the smaller horses from the barn. The old cloak billowed out around him, but he rode like a centaur, as one with his beast.

And beyond the shadow of any doubt, she knew she had just broken her fast with a highwayman.

2

SHE HAD NEVER done anything remotely rebellious in her life. Her father's religion had demanded obedience, and to retain his approval, Faith had learned to do as told. Not without question, perhaps. Her father hadn't been an unreasonable man, and as a scholar, he had allowed intelligent questions. But he would never tolerate direct refusal of an order. She could question, as long as she obeyed.

But she wasn't obeying now.

Faith watched furtively out the window to the winter landscape, then glanced back to the kettle beginning to boil on the fire. She had waited patiently all the morning for Jack's return so she could plead her case further. She had swept and scrubbed and tidied. She had found a chest with his meager assortment of clothes and pressed them with a flatiron she had found beneath the coal scuttle. It seemed an odd place to keep a flatiron, but Jack obviously had little notion of tidiness. She hadn't been able to find needle or thread, for example. She mourned that fact, and wished for her lost bundle, but she hadn't stirred outside to look for it.

She didn't want to know where she was or how far from the road. She didn't wish to venture forth in that snow and ice again. The wind still howled about the chimney, and there was nothing promising in the heavy gray clouds that practically sat on the treetops. If she went out, she might never find her way back. And she wasn't ready to face that possibility yet.

So she sacrificed her small bundle of possessions lost somewhere in the ditch last night to stubbornly remain in this cozy haven where she sensed she was needed. Or she convinced herself she was needed. The truth was, she needed this cottage more than it needed her, but she didn't want truths right now. She needed food and a roof over her head, and this one night's comfort had given her enough

strength to fight for both. Or she thought she would fight.
Jack hadn't returned yet to put the lie to her convic-
tions.

But now that she had made his home clean, she wished
to do the same for herself. Perhaps if she were a little more
presentable, he wouldn't object too strongly to her staying
just a little while longer, just until the weather cleared, perhaps.

It would not do to consider Jack's occupation while she
contemplated his home. She didn't know for certain that he
was a highwayman. She hadn't actually seen the coach
robbed. She didn't know that he was the man on the horse
or that the man on the horse was actually a highwayman.
She didn't know anything at all, in fact.

Confident in her ignorance, Faith poured the hot water
into the large pan she had found tucked under the bed. She
added snow to cool it off and picked up the sliver of soap
that she had found in the pan. He might protest if he discovered she had used the last of his soap, but she would
have the satisfaction of being clean.

As she scrubbed, Faith produced visions of scavenging
for soapwort plants and doing his laundry, or if she saved
the ashes and he could provide some lye, she could make a
year's supply of soap for him. There were so many ways she
could help. Surely, if he would just let her try, she could
convince him of her worthiness. This time, she would fight
for the right to stay.

She should have fought for her right to stay weeks ago,
and then she wouldn't be at the mercy of strangers now. But
she had never been forced to fight before, and she knew
little of it. When the adults around her urged her to do
something, she did it. She was beginning to understand that
that was a mistake, but it was too late to go back. It wasn't
too late to fight for this place, however, this small niche of
comfort in the cold vacuum of the world. He hadn't ordered
her out. She would stay.

As the day grew darker, Faith threw anxious looks at the
window and hurried a little faster. Once clean, she couldn't
bear to don her dirty clothes again. Without her bundle, she
didn't even have a change of linen. That thought gave her
pause, but, determined now, she rummaged in Jack's trunk
for an old shirt and wore it while she scrubbed her clothes

in the pan. She would lack linen anywhere she went. That was no reason to give up this one chance of work.

She wrung out her clothes and hung them over the mantel and chair to dry before the fire. Her comb had been lost with her other possessions, but she had found a brush in Jack's chest. It was old and elaborately engraved with the initials JML, and her fingers lovingly traced the etching as she drew the brush through her hair. Someone rich and aristocratic had once owned this brush. Could it be Jack? The first initial fitted, but nothing else did. She had seen very few nobles, but she rather suspected they didn't sport three-day beards and unkempt black hair. As a matter of fact, if she recollected rightly, they wore powdered hair and silk and red heels with clocked stockings. That was the epitome of a nobleman as she knew one.

She smiled with her daydream of elegant gentlemen, ladies in wide, sweeping skirts, each making polite bows and curtsies to the other. She had never owned an elegant skirt with hoops and panniers, but she knew how to curtsy in one. Her mother had taught her all manner of frivolous things such as that, to the amusement of both of them. She missed her mother dreadfully, but there had been years to become accustomed to her death and learn to live with her absence.

Not so her father. That had been too sudden, too violent, and Faith could not face it yet, might never face it. It had been senseless. Her father was a sternly religious man, a scholar, a gentleman who had forsaken his heritage for his beliefs. What manner of madman would hate him enough to kill him?

The pain of that morning stayed with her, growing with each passing day. She couldn't bear to think of it, but there were times when she could think of nothing else. He had been so cold and still when they carried him in; she had known he was dead without asking. They hadn't even allowed her to stay for the burial, but hurried her off with her small bundle of possessions and the collection of coins they had gathered between them. So many coins in a community where they were sparse beyond words had stunned Faith into belief when they insisted she go find her family, and set her out on the road.

One of the men had taken her in his cart as far as the toll road and given her the direction of another Wesleyan along the way. But by nightfall she had discovered that family had moved, and she had put up with a neighbor of theirs. After that, she had been on her own.

She should have turned back then, but she had been frightened and alone, and the urgency of the neighbors and friends she had left behind stayed with her. They wanted her gone, so she stayed away. There really was very little left there for her, anyway. They hadn't lived there long, and she had no close friends. Her family had little in the way of possessions. Even the house and furnishings had been rented. There had been nothing worth staying for.

The sound of a horse neighing outside returned her from her reverie, and Faith leapt from her seat and hurried to add fuel to the fire. Jack would in all likelihood be home soon. She didn't know what she would feed him, but she would think of something. She was accustomed to making do.

With her hair still damp from washing, she donned her own mud-splattered cloak and went outside to dispose of her washwater and draw fresh. She checked on the horses and found Jack had fastened a pail to the stall of each one and given them fresh hay. She rubbed their noses and murmured soft words in their ears, petted the cat and scratched behind his ear, then hurried back to the warmth of the fire.

With the flour and lard she rolled out unsweetened biscuits and set them to bake in the heavy Dutch oven over the fire. She had found a square of hardened cheese in a dark corner of the cupboard and scraped some of that into the dough before she set the biscuits to bake. Now she fried more of the bacon and added flour to the grease for gravy. She wished she had some onion root or even a potato to help fill Jack's stomach, but he would have to settle for what she could find. Perhaps he would bring back a rabbit to cook. The thought stirred her empty stomach into growling. The slice of cheese she had eaten for lunch was scarcely sufficient to last all day.

While the bread baked, she hastily braided her long hair into a single length, then tied it with a broken shirt string she had found in Jack's trunk. Then she tested her clothes, and finding them sufficiently dry, she scurried into them, apologetically stacking Jack's shirt and stockings in a pile to be washed another day.

As the room grew darker, she lit a lamp and waited. The

tea steeped and the biscuits finished baking and the bacon—cut thick—was good and crisp. And still he didn't come.

Faith looked longingly at the steaming hot food, went to the window and searched the darkness, and wandered restlessly back to the fire. It didn't seem right to let it go to waste. She didn't know what time he would return. She could always cook more later if it got cold.

She rationalized herself into the chair with a plate of biscuits and gravy and broken bits of bacon. The tea needed sweetening, but she gulped its strong warmth gratefully and gave the proper blessing for the meal. She had forgotten to do that this morning, and she apologized in her prayer now. The Lord had provided bountifully this day, and she was more grateful than she could put into words.

Perhaps she had no right to be here. Perhaps he would put her out in the morning. But for right now, right this minute, she was warm and dry and clean and sitting before a plate of hot food. She was learning to appreciate each minute as it came, without complaining of the past or worrying about the future. In soulful gratitude she bit into the steamy bread.

When she was done, she cleaned up and put everything neatly back in its place. The tea kept warm at the back of the spacious fireplace. The remaining biscuits stayed in the pot at the edge of the fire. They would dry out some, but the gravy would soften them. It was time to let the fire die down anyway. She shouldn't rashly use all Jack's fuel.

She wrapped a few warming bricks in flannel from his trunk and placed them at the foot of his bed. They would stay warm for quite a while there. If she had more soap, she could wash his sheets, but that was a subject she would broach another time. First, she must convince him to let her stay.

When she had done all she could to make Jack's home welcoming, Faith removed her newly washed bodice and skirt and spread the blanket she had used the prior night out on the hearth. Jack had taken the old cloak she had used for cover, but she had found the fine black one in his bed cupboard when she made the bed. It was of a rich, thick wool and lined with a lovely satin. She wondered why he hadn't taken it if he were to be out in the cold all day, but she wouldn't question his actions. She could only be grateful for the warmth.

She snuggled beneath the warm wool and rubbed her face appreciatively against the sensuous satin. Were she rich, everything she owned would be of such fabulous material. She closed her eyes, and within minutes she was dreaming of satin sheets and wide gowns and laughing gentlemen.

When Jack entered the cottage some hours later, he knew instantly that he was not alone. Instead of being greeted by the icy cold of a long-dead fire and the stench of his dirty dishes, warm air and the scent of something delicious welcomed him. He had stopped at an inn to eat earlier, but his stomach still rumbled with hunger for the bread he had desired just this morning.

Dropping his bundle, he cautiously approached the hearth, finding the bedding just where he had left it the night before. He frowned at the sight of his black cloak wrapped around her small figure. Had she made the connection yet? If so, his hiding place could be in danger. This was the best billet he'd had in many a year, and he was reluctant to sacrifice it for one wayward wench.

His frown didn't last long as he discovered the bacon and gravy waiting for him and opened the black pot on the fire to find the biscuits. He would wager all his wealth that the chit went to bed hungry so that she might leave him his fair share of the meal. He felt guilty as hell for having enjoyed that meat pie earlier.

Jack tried to maintain his irritation at this unwarranted interference in his life, but the smell of the bread made him grin. He helped himself, piled the biscuits on the plate with the congealing gravy, and scooped up the delicious mess with his fingers. The taste of cheese intermingled with the bacon startled him, and he savored the flavor. He couldn't remember ever eating anything so good.

He sat down in the chair beside the warm embers of the fire and cleaned his plate, then poured a mug of strong tea. He preferred coffee but hadn't bothered to supply the grounds lately. Tilting the chair back and sipping the hot beverage, he stared at the small bundle of bedding on his hearth. She must be exhausted, not to hear his clumping boots and his ungentle clanging of the pots and plate. He could just barely see her pale face against the black of his cloak. She had it pulled up all around her, as if she were still freezing. Apparently she had done something with her hair, since none of the rebellious strands crept around her face. Instead, he watched the thick length of her dark lashes curled against her velvet-soft cheeks and wondered at the innocence of such sound sleep.

He hadn't slept like that since his youth. Military life had taught him to sleep with one eye open, and his occupation now relied on it. He had no keen desire to be caught in his sleep and hauled to the gallows.

That thought made him scowl as he watched the sleeping innocence of the child. If he were not careful, he would drag her down with him. He'd have to send her on her way, perhaps when the weather grew warmer. Until then, her presence would allow him to wander farther afield, and she shouldn't be in as much danger. It would be convenient to have someone available to look after the horses while he was gone. He could make good use of her that way, without causing her harm.

With that decision made, Jack removed his boots and encountered another problem. Glancing from his bed to the hearth, he pulled his brow down in another black scowl. He hadn't slept in nightshirts since he was a callow youth, but he couldn't very well sleep in the raw with a child under his roof. Cursing that unforeseen development, he crossed the room to his bed and unfastened his breeches. He'd be damned if he slept in them. Her modesty would simply have to suffer the indignity.

He left the breeches on the floor where they fell, and rolled up in his bedcovers. The lingering warmth from the bricks was a pleasant surprise, and he stretched wearily to fill the bed. The shirt and stockings were a damned nuisance, but having his stomach full for a change almost compensated for it. Leaning his head back against his arms, Jack closed his eyes and slept.

Faith jumped awake with the first light of dawn. Her gaze instantly went to the bed, from whence soft snores could be heard, then traveled to the dirty plate on the table. He was back, and he'd eaten her meal.

Smiling, she jerked her bodice on under the covers; then, throwing a surreptitious glance to the sleeping man on the bed, she hastily scrambled into her skirt. Today was the day she would convince him to let her stay.

She hastened to do her chores as quickly and quietly as possible. She nearly stumbled over the heavy bundle by the door, and, breath catching in her throat, she stared at it wildly, fear pumping through her veins as she imagined the contents torn from their rightful owners. She had not overly concerned herself with a highwayman's ill-gotten goods, but that was undoubtedly what she had encountered now. She had never known a thief before. She could not imagine stealing for a living. Perhaps she was making a desperate mistake by wishing to stay here.

But when she walked out into the icy cold of the crystalline air, she knew she was not yet ready to travel on. The snow seeped through the holes in her shoes, and her ungloved hands reacted with pain to just the brush of the wind. If she had the choice of dying for pride or living with the devil, she would have to choose the devil. Her father might be ashamed of her choice, but she had discovered a deep desire to live.

Carrying the pail of water back to the house, she straightened her shoulders and prepared to face the devil. He was still asleep when she stepped in, and she tried to be as noiseless as possible as she set the kettle on to heat and rummaged through the larder for something edible. The hens had produced no new eggs, to her disappointment.

The sound of a deep voice behind her caused Faith to jump and swing around.

"Why don't you use what's in the sack? It's at least fresh, and I would rather have the coffee."

He emerged from the shadows of the bed still tucking his shirt into his breeches. It was the same shirt he had worn the day before, Faith noted. The hole was in the same place. This irrelevancy entered her mind as her tongue froze in her mouth. All the fine arguments she had stored away yesterday disappeared, and she could only stare at his imposing figure as he drew closer.

Jack gave her frozen stance an impatient glance, then bent to lift the sack onto the table. He produced the pouch of coffee beans and threw them at her. "Do you know what to do with them?"

He had shaved and had his hair trimmed, although it still hung loosely instead of being bound in a queue. Faith caught the pouch awkwardly and tried not to stare. He was much handsomer than she had imagined, albeit in a rough fashion. Broad cheekbones jutted to shadowed cheeks and a straight, thin nose that did not quite match the rather sensuous curve of his lower lip. When the square chin beneath that mouth tightened, she jumped and stared at the beans helplessly.

"I . . . I don't know what they are, sir."

"Jack. Call me Jack." He grabbed the pouch, rummaged about until he found the flatiron she had neatly set in his barren cupboard, and proceeded to crush the beans with a few vigorous hammers between iron and table. Then he handed her the flattened but more savory-scented pouch. "Just cook them like tea."

Wide-eyed, she nodded and accepted the pouch. She sent a sidelong glance to the large sack remaining on the table, and her stomach rumbled in harmony with her thoughts. Jack grinned.

"Take what you need. I'm seeing to the horses."

The grin almost made him human. It was lopsided and gleaming white and it deepened the little dent in his cheek. Aghast at this discovery, Faith stared blankly after him as he went out the door. Highwaymen weren't supposed to be human. She should be shivering in fear of the devil, not admiring his smile.

Fearing for her almighty soul, she dived into the bundle of goodies and nearly crowed with delight at each discovery. Far from being a highwayman's stolen bounty, the sack contained all the ingredients of a well-stocked larder. She nearly cried at the package of scented soap, and her imagination jumped recklessly to the immense cake she would make with the sugar.

She hastily whipped together a quick batter to cook in the skillet, set some of the smoked sausage into another pan, and put the coffee on to boil. It was a rather crude breakfast, but better than she had known for some while. With the pot of honey Jack had brought, it would fill their stomachs painlessly. Tomorrow, when she had more time, she would try porridge and muffins.

Jack returned with a barrel from the barn and set it on the opposite side of the table from the chair. Without questioning, Faith set out the newly cleaned plate he had used the night before, placed the fork and mug beside it, and poured his coffee. Jack gave a sigh of appreciation as he sipped the strong liquid.

He took the barrel, and after setting the food on the table, Faith reluctantly took the chair. He made her uncomfortable, and she tried not to look at him as she tasted the bitter brew he preferred. She made a face and pushed it away and began to tackle her bread, when his big hand caught her cup.

"Try it with sugar." He cut off a small chunk of brown sugar and dropped it into the hot liquid before pushing it back to her. "I didn't think to get milk. Children ought to have milk."

Faith lifted smooth rounded eyebrows at this assertion, but she silently took another sip. The sugar was an improvement, but coffee was definitely an acquired taste, she decided.

"I have seen children die of the fever after drinking tainted milk. I'll only drink what is boiled first." It was a daring thing to say to this big man who could snap her in two, but his insulting reference to her age demanded some response. Her mother had been the one to admonish her about cleanliness in food as well as body and hearth. It was ironic fate that her mother had been the one to die of the infectious pox, caught from a family she had tried to help who did not know her maxims of cleanliness.

Jack's mouth tilted at one corner as he observed the solemn waif who issued this proclamation. "Remind me never to feed you fine wine, then. Eat, or I shall finish this all myself."

He seemed quite capable of doing just that, and Faith hastily began nibbling at the honey-smeared pan bread. Jack watched her tiny bites with annoyance and tore into his own bread with great gusto. In the morning light he could see that she had pulled her hair into a single braid that glittered with red highlights when the sun caught it. She had a redhead's fine white skin, and now that it was clean and uncovered by the dirty mat of hair, her throat glowed with the same pearly translucence. Coupled with those delicate cheekbones and wide gray eyes, her features would soon develop into a face of arresting attractiveness. She might never be a true beauty. There were too many angles and planes for softness, and those eyes were more disconcerting than lovely, but a man would look twice, just the same. It should be interesting to see what a few years would add to her pitifully slender figure, but Jack didn't intend to be around to find out. He finished his bread and sausage and sat back from the table to finish his coffee.

"You say you're looking for work."

Faith watched him warily, but nodded her head.

He gave her slightness a scornful appraisal. "You're scarce big enough to do much. Those horses out there would pull your arms out of the sockets. Can you ride?"

Not as he did, but she could stay in the saddle. She nodded again.

He looked skeptical, but continued his interrogation. "I'll not have some family after my neck for corrupting and abducting their precious darling, will I? This is no polite place for a proper lady to be, and you have a lady's speech about you."

Her faint eyebrows went up again, but she replied calmly. "My parents are dead and there is none other to know of my existence. My parents were gentry, but we did not live any differently than this. I can cook and clean and sew and tend your animals. I can read and do sums, if you have need of that."

When she spoke, she ceased to be a child, and that worried him. Jack squinted warily at her carefully neutral expression, but he could see nothing in her to change his opinion of her age. She had the mind of an adult and the body of a child. A precocious combination, but sufficient for his needs. He wouldn't be here enough to make a difference at any rate.

"I can read and do my own sums. I need someone to water, feed, and exercise my horses while I am away. Can you do that?"

That caused her a moment's consternation. She knew nothing at all about horses but how to stay on one if necessary. She wasn't afraid of them, by any means. So couldn't she in all honesty answer yes? She had watered and fed all sorts of animals in these last weeks. It shouldn't be too difficult. To avoid lying outright, Faith nodded her head.

Satisfied, Jack set his mug down and stood up. "Then let us begin. I have need to be in Kent tomorrow. You will start your chores immediately."

Faith looked down at the dirty dishes, up to the man striding impatiently toward the door, and hurried for her cloak.

Her mother's precepts of cleanliness would have to wait. It seemed she was about to learn to be an ostler.

3

IT DIDN'T TAKE LONG to discover that the chit knew the next best thing to nothing about horses, but Jack had fastened onto this possibility and refused to let it go. She would learn, and he would ride farther afield and they would both be the richer for it, come warm weather.

He laughed at her horror when he insisted she ride astride and showed her how to pull the back of her skirt between her legs and tuck it in at her waist. She was the most squeamish child he had ever met, but then, he had already decided she was an oddity that he could use for his own purposes. And in addition to the truth of her claim that she was hardworking, he discovered she had a natural affinity with animals that was nothing short of miraculous.

Faith walked the smallest mare through her paces as directed, gritting her teeth against the insult of Jack's flashing grin every time he turned to see if she followed. Her skirt was torn and muddied again from the falls she had taken trying to mount on her own, but she refused to make any complaint. Only a man would be fool enough to take the perfect housekeeper and cook and turn her into a groom and ostler. She could see right now that his priorities were all cock-a-hoop, and she might as well become accustomed to it.

There was little enough area to exercise the horses in, and with the snow, they could not be walked long, but she was near to fainting with exhaustion by the time they had unsaddled and rubbed down the last two. The work itself wasn't so hard, had she her normal strength, but weeks of near-starvation, exposure, and exhaustion had collapsed all her usual reserves.

Faith grabbed the stall door and tried to steady her spinning head as she stood up. The healthy Irish giant was whistling contentedly to himself, and she had a mind to cosh him over the head with one of his riding crops for being so exuberant. Glancing down at her ruined skirt, she gave a small moan of dismay.

Jack was instantly at her side, his swift gaze taking in her white face, her desperate grip on the wooden stall, and the expression of pure exhaustion on her thin features. With a disgusted curse he caught her by the waist, lifted her nearly weightless form into his arms, and tramped through the snow to carry her back to the house.

The sudden movement caught Faith off-balance, and she clung to his shoulders in fear of falling until she realized how safe was his hold. Then, with embarrassment flooding her cheeks, she buried her face against his broad linen-covered shoulder and closed her eyes in hopes of shutting out this humiliation.

He dumped her on the chair before the fire and began systematically rubbing her chapped hands between his to bring the blood back into them. "You'll need gloves and something warmer than that gown. Did you come away with nothing at all against this weather?"

"Only my bundle, and I lost that the night . . ." She hesitated to mention that night, not knowing how to describe it without mentioning the highwayman.

"The night I found you?" He gave her a sharp look and saw her face draw tight with fear. So she knew. Or suspected. He nodded curtly. "In the ditch? I'll find it. I don't suppose it has gloves or a warmer gown, does it, now?"

Faith shook her head and tried to draw her hands free. Even kneeling, he was nearly of a height with her, and his magnetic energy seemed to encompass her and make her smaller. She had never been this close to a man who filled a room with vibrant life just with the sound of his voice. She had seen and heard John Wesley speak, and thought him to be the most powerful and impressive man she knew, but just this highwayman's physical presence could overawe a company. Should he ever take to the platform, the world would be his.

The thought of what a waste he made by devoting his life to crime instead of religion returned a small part of Faith's equilibrium. Stiffly she managed to straighten in her seat and take command of her hands again. "I traded what I did not need for food. This gown will be sufficient. Now, if you will excuse me, I will prepare your luncheon."

Dancing lights turned hazel eyes to almost green as Jack watched this girl-child struggle for her maidenly composure. She would make a lady to be proud of someday, if the streets did not wear her down. He would have to find her a real position when the weather grew warmer.

"Sure, and you do that, lass. I'll be seeing after that bundle of yours. I won't be long."

He rose abruptly, giving her a close glimpse of legs like young tree trunks encased in tight buckskin as he strode away. Faith closed her eyes and prayed for deliverance from evil as she heard him rustle around the room. When the door shut firmly behind him, she slumped briefly in her chair, then forced herself to rise and start the meal.

He knew she had witnessed his crime. She had seen it in his face. What would he do with her now? Would he hold her prisoner? That was absurd on the face of it. She had begged him not to let her leave. She was a prisoner by her own words, her own weakness. What did that make her? An accomplice to crime?

She had taken all her father's lessons to heart. She knew Jack was a thief, and as such, she was obligated to report him. She tried not to think of the pistol shots that night. For all she knew, he could be a murderer. It was enough to know that he had harmed innocent people, perhaps taken their life savings. He should be punished so that he could repent and be saved. But she could not imagine bringing him to that, even at the point of a gun. He would laugh in her face and snap her in two.

Short of running away to find someone in authority, there was nothing she could do but feed the fire and put on the kettle. Whatever Jack's occupation, he was the first person on this road to offer her food and shelter and a place to work. Surely God would excuse her this once for turning her head at his crimes. He could not be all bad, and perhaps she could make him change his ways without resorting to the finality of the law. That thought made her feel slightly better, as long as she did not think too hard on how she would go about turning a full-grown male from the life he had chosen.

Not for the first time, Faith glanced down at her reed-thin seventeen-year-old figure and sighed. She had no vanity. She was perfectly aware that because of her diminutive height and undeveloped figure, she looked thirteen or less.

Upon occasion she had looked with envy at the more buxom dairy maids and flamboyant village girls with their strings of beaux, but her parents had made it very clear that she was not for the likes of them, even had she the looks to attract their eye. She was educated far beyond the means of a farmer's life.

That was small consolation to a lonely female adolescent, but she had been kept too busy to worry about it more than in those few minutes of darkness before sleep claimed her after a hard day's work. The Lord would provide, she had always been taught, and so she had believed. Until now.

It was becoming quite apparent that the Lord wasn't going to provide her with breasts anytime soon, and for that she ought to be properly grateful. She had the certain feeling that had Jack realized she was more than a child, he would never have taken her in. Faith wasn't certain what he would have done with her, but she didn't intend to consider the notion long. She had a roof over her head and food in her stomach, and if she had to share it with a thief, she would not quibble.

By the time Jack returned with her muddy bundle of meager possessions, the cottage had filled with the rich aromas of boiling coffee, barley soup, and a cheese pie she had created with the one egg she had found and her memory of a recipe a sailor's French wife had taught her. Faith was quite proud of how well it turned out, and smiled to herself as she took it out of the old Dutch oven. The smile spilled over to include Jack when he entered, bringing with him the outdoor scents of cold air and horses.

The smile startled him, but he returned it gladly. The solemn child had been unnatural, and a friendly face was always welcome. The perfect white evenness of her teeth revealed as much of her upbringing as her other habits. There was no doubt she came from gentry trained in the niceties of bathing and the necessities of keeping teeth clean. She was no foul-breathed, teeth-rotted maid from the gutter. A vicar's daughter, perhaps. The profession of a younger, unendowed son of the gentry, it was notoriously underpaid and subject to the vagaries of both society's and the church's benevolence or lack of it.

Satisfied that he had found the source of her solemnity and origins, Jack threw the tiny bundle on the table. ''There you be, milady. It cannot contain much, but then, the faeries are said to make much of nothing. Let it not be said that I deprive you.''

The smile wavered at his appearance, but the eagerness in those wide gray eyes was sufficient recompense. A vicar's daughter would have difficulty thanking a popish thief, but at least she did not express her disdain. On the contrary, he could gather from the aromas greeting him that she was grateful for his humble abode and showed it in the only means available to her.

While her fingers flew on the knot in her bundle, Jack inspected the source of the aromas. He gave the pie a skeptical look, but he had to admit he had given her little to work with. He would have to see about that before he left.

When she gave a small cry of triumph and produced a little leather case from the large handkerchief of her worldly goods, he turned to see what had so excited her. The realization that it was no more than a sailor's mending kit made him snort with surprise. A child should crow over sweets and baubles, not sewing kits. Mayhap she was a changeling, after all.

''Is this ready for eating or shall I go mend my tack?''

As if suddenly reminded of his presence, Faith guiltily dropped the case and removed her possessions to the corner by the hearth where she had folded her bedding. ''It is ready, sir. I thank you most kindly for fetching my bundle. If you will take a seat, I shall serve you immediately.''

Jack caught her frail arm, his hand easily wrapping around the wrist almost twice over. Her wide eyes flashed up at him with a trace of fear but also with that unnatural stoicism he had seen the first night. ''I'm not a 'sir.' I think you know what I am, so we need not enlarge on it more. I have no need of servants to wait upon me hand and foot. I'll provide the food. You prepare it. Together, we'll share it. Is that understood?''

For a moment she saw the flaring cape, the ethereal man and beast flying over her head, breathing fire and smoke from an icy mask of stone, and then the moment was gone. He was but a man with harsh features, an Irish lilt, and a smile that could shatter hearts did he use it more. Faith nodded, and he released his grip. She breathed easier and hastened to bring the plates to the table.

Jack watched her with curiosity, wishing he knew her thoughts. It grew lonely out here, and he was by nature a gregarious man. It would be pleasant to have someone with whom to talk, but he had no notion of what girl-children thought or spoke about. It would have been much better had she been a boy. He shrugged and brought the coffee to the table and served himself from the pans she set before him.

"I'll bring you some meat for the stew pot this evening before I leave." He broke the silence casually.

Faith glanced up. Finding nothing in his dark features but interest in his food, she reminded herself of her Christian duty and asked, "Is that not poaching?"

Jack flashed her solemn features a look of surprise at this first controversial question from her mouth, but he answered with a grin. "This patch of land here is mine. If the creatures choose to come to me, who am I to deny them?"

She knew he was disguising the truth for her benefit, but uncertain of the technicalities of the law, she dropped her gaze back to the plate. He had finally tied his hair back in a neat queue, and with the long plane of his jaw shaved, he was easily the most handsome man she had ever seen, if one preferred devilish rogues. She most certainly did not.

"Shall I bake some bread for you to take on your journey?" She had no idea how far away Kent might be, but it sounded as if he might be gone more than a day, at least.

She didn't see the thoughtful look in Jack's eyes when they looked upon her bent head. He only replied, "That would be agreeable," and continued eating.

He left that night after dark, taking his massive stallion, wearing his satin-lined cloak and a dazzling white jabot of lace, buckling on a sword and scabbard Faith had not discovered in her housecleaning efforts. She tried not to stare at his imposing figure as he strode to the door, but her heart was in her throat the entire time. Only when he grabbed up the parcel of bread and meat she had prepared for him and tipped her a jolly wink did she relax to any degree. She lifted her hand in farewell, but she wasn't certain he noticed as he walked out, slamming the door behind him.

The cottage felt colder without him, and she shivered at the sound of hoofbeats disappearing into the distance. For the first time, but not for the last, she wondered what would happen should he not return.

Not wanting to contemplate that flashing smile going to the gallows, Faith turned back to the fire and began to scrub pots.

* * *

It was three nights later before Jack returned. Lying on her pallet beside the hearth, Faith heard him whistling as he brushed down his stallion. She was glad she had left the barn in pristine condition, all the horses well fed and groomed despite the fact that it had taken her the better part of the day and the ache of every muscle in her body. She hadn't minded filling the loneliness with work, and the hope that she had pleased him kept her awake as she waited for him to enter.

He did so quietly, trying not to wake her. When she sat up, wrapping the blanket around the chemise and petticoat she wore to bed, he grinned and flung his cloak across the chair. It felt good to have someone waiting for him.

"Hello, *bean sídhe*. Did you miss me?"

A tentative smile slipped across her face, almost hidden by the shadows of the dying fire. "Shall I make some coffee for you?"

"That won't be necessary. I have my own brand of fire right here." He reached up to the top of the cupboard and brought down the bottle of rum hidden there. He ignored the disapproval on her face and poured a fingerful, gulping it down to ease the chill from his bones. Then, carefully corking the bottle, he returned it to its hiding place. "That will do till morning. Would you like to see what I brought you?"

Her face lit with such amazement and eagerness that it could have warmed his bones without the rum. Jack lit the lantern to better watch the glorious expression on the child's frail features. Even though she rapidly tried to hide it, her eyes reflected the glow of expectation, and he felt a peculiar warmth growing within him. Perhaps that was the reason people had children. He reached for the sack he had thrown down by the door.

Those wide eyes suddenly grew fearful and wary, but he had nothing to hide. He was no fool to keep his stolen goods on hand to incriminate him. She would learn that soon enough. He drew out a string-wrapped parcel and tossed it to her.

Faith fumbled and caught it, relieved at the gift's wrapping—bought, not stolen. With trembling fingers she tore at the paper, aware that Jack watched her as he moved about the room, discarding scabbard and pistol and removing his boots.

She drew out a bodice and skirt of deep green wool of so fine a weave that it felt like soft fur beneath her fingers. Even her best Sunday dresses had never been so grand.

She didn't dare look at him. It was highly improper for him to have bought this for her, but she knew he thought he was pleasing a child. Yet the gown had obviously been bought from stolen funds, and she could not balance the wrong and right of it. She wanted to please him with the gratitude he expected, and she was properly grateful, but she could not possibly wear the proceeds of crime.

Jack watched the confusion warring on her usually impassive face and frowned. Of all the thieves and beggars in these woods, he had to pair up with a righteous vicar's daughter. Well, he had no intention of enduring pious suffering in his presence. Gruffly he ordered, "You will wear it before the other falls off your back. There're some frilly things in there to go under it. And stockings. And shoes. I'll not be carting you to a quack if your toes freeze off."

Faith gripped the gown against her and stared at him uncertainly. He was given to ordering her about, and she was accustomed to obeying orders, but she felt the first vague stirrings of rebellion. She glanced down to the rest of the contents of the package, and her heart ached to try them on, but her conscience reminded her of her Christian duty.

"I thank you very much for thinking of me," she offered timidly, "but I don't think I should accept. I have repaired my gown while you were gone, and I am quite healthy now, thank you." At the dark look forming between his black brows, she hastily added, "Perhaps you could give these to someone who needs them more than I do."

Jack stared at her with incredulity. She was pale in the lamplight, her single braid providing the only coloring she possessed, her childish form concealed beneath a swathe of thin petticoats and gray blankets. Yet there was nothing childish about that wide-eyed stare meeting his gaze. He had seen her delight in the gown, the first true emotion he had dragged out of her, and now she wanted to make him believe she didn't want it?

He stalked toward her, his shadow drowning the flickering color in her hair as he came between the girl and the lamp. She stared up at him without flinching, although she read the fear well enough in her eyes. He grabbed the remainder of the package and shoved it into her arms.

"You'll wear it and not be ashamed of the source, or you'll leave. I'll not waste my time on a creature so self-righteous she'd freeze before accepting what's offered her. Those kind weren't meant to live in this world, but the next."

He walked out, slamming the door after him. Shivering, Faith stared after him. He hadn't even taken his cloak. He would freeze. Setting aside the gift and the decision until the morning, she took the tongs to the heated bricks in the fire, and wrapping them in towels, carried them to Jack's bed.

He had tried to do the Christian thing. Shouldn't that count for something?

When the lamplight caught on the silver of a papist crucifix nailed in the high corner of his bed cupboard, Faith nearly dropped the bricks. Then, turning to glance thoughtfully in the direction of the door through which Jack had left, she wondered if she had not underestimated the highwayman. Perhaps he had some code by which he lived, and she had not yet understood it. She would very much like to know his story.

With that thought, she returned to her task.

4

"IT'S BEEN THREE bloody weeks, bigawd! Why the deuce did no one come to me before this? I know you for zealous idiots, but I did not think you to be inhumane! Where the hell is she?"

The soberly garbed man in simple broadcloth long coat and round uncocked hat held respectfully in his hand waited for the tirade to finish before defending himself and his fellow believers. The man screaming his curses as he paced the elegant library was very much a creature of this time and place. His ramillies wig was highly powdered, his expensive brocade waistcoat came to his knee and glittered with gold buttons and embroidery, and his buckram-stiffened scarlet frock coat had the sheen of silk. He wasn't wearing powder on his face, at least, but it would have been useless against his choleric coloring of the moment. His time-lined features still had the harsh angles of his youth, and with temper, his visage was formidable indeed. The soberly dressed man maintained his silence until he was certain he could be heard without shouting.

"I personally traveled to Cornwall to determine the true events of what I read in the paper. If you have any familiarity with that area at all, you know it is cut off from the rest of the world by centuries of suspicion and distrust. They took it into their own hands to handle matters without consulting any of us. That goes against my methods, as surely you must know, but your son could not change centuries of behavior in a few short months."

"I know nothing of your methods, nor do I care to hear your heresy! You are a scandal to the name of your parents, a revolutionary, a destroyer of the church and society! I want to know what happened to my son, and I want to know the whereabouts of my granddaughter!"

The man in black very much feared the old man would

suffer an apoplexy, and he tried to ignore his own anger at the ignorance of his lordship. This was not the time to explain that his teachings were within the framework of the established church, meant to strengthen and not to destroy. The fact that he chose to preach to the poor and encourage them to rise from the mire seemed to invoke nothing but wrath from the upper classes. Or perhaps it was the spontaneous emotion evoked by their meetings which revolted the blasé *ton,* but he suspected fear was behind it all. But this was no time to let the matter of religion come between them.

Satisfied the nobleman was prepared to listen, he replied, "Your son behaved with exemplary fortitude. He had developed a goodly sized following in those few short months, not an easy task in the face of the odds. He preached to the miners before they went to work in the early hours of the morning. He was a good speaker, and they listened."

The irate noble knew his son was a good speaker. George should have been in the Commons, not pettifogging with filthy dunderheads. His own rage over George's choice of professions had never dimmed. He could never forgive him for throwing away his breeding, his education, and his promising career to teach Methodism to village yokels. Never. Not even now that George was dead.

The man in scarlet silk lifted a crystal paperweight from the table and heaved it at the cold stone hearth. The glass cracked and shattered, and the man's shoulders slumped, suddenly weary with age. "What happened?" he demanded without emotion.

"The usual fear of anyone or anything different. My methods and those of my followers are not generally accepted by the local clergy. They are offended and revolted by the emotion generated by our speakings. They preach their disapproval in their churches, and it falls on ears eager to hear it. Forgive me, but the landed gentry are none too pleased to see their servants and tenants band together. It breeds fear and distrust. The riots are nothing new. You have read of them before. It's just in Cornwall . . . Well, the level of emotion rose higher than elsewhere. It was foreseeable, perhaps, but your son insisted that he could deal with it. He was a strong man, a fighter. He could not foresee that they would attack him with more than fists."

Lord Mountjoy turned a shade grayer, and his fists

clamped the library table as if he would tear it in two. "Do they know who did it? Have they been caught yet?"

"It was a riot, milord, an early-morning riot, before dawn. Undoubtedly there are those who know the men responsible, but they are a closemouthed lot. To keep their families safe, they will say nothing. It is a great tragedy, but that is the way of the world." The sober man in black remained aloof. There was nothing he could say to the gentleman to ease his pain. The gentleman had cast his younger son aside years ago. It was too late to mourn what might have been.

"And my granddaughter?"

This time, it was not the elegant man in scarlet who spoke, but a frail woman in black sitting in the far corner, almost out of sight. She was so pale and dainty and immobile as to be easily mistaken for a valuable porcelain doll clothed in silk.

The man in broadcloth bowed in her direction. "The villagers feared she would come to harm and smuggled her out of town. She was given money and directions, but we are having some difficulty locating her. She seems to have missed the road she was to have taken."

"She could be no more than seventeen, sir." There was reproach in her soft voice, but her fingers remained carefully still in her lap, unlike those of the man who now stalked the floor again.

"Lettice, go home. Let me handle this. There is no use in your making yourself ill." Mountjoy stopped before her and held out his hand.

She ignored it. "I want my granddaughter, Harry. She is all I have left. You and my late husband drove our children away. I'll not be content until I have my granddaughter back. I hold you responsible for this, Harry. You knew where they were, and you never told me."

Mountjoy rubbed his eyes and turned away. "I had no idea where they were, Lettice. I never looked for them. I had thought it better that way."

She turned paler, if that were possible, and then she rose with dignity. "I should hate you for this, Harry, but I can see that it is my own fault for relying on you. I'll not make that mistake again. Mr. Wesley, if you'll excuse me?" She nodded slightly and walked out.

The stricken man in scarlet stared at the broken crystal

on the hearth and spoke almost as if the other man were not there. "Her daughter was just seventeen when she married my son. She was an only child. We'll have to find the girl."

"She knows her daughter has been dead these last three years?"

Mountjoy bowed his head. "She knows. My son wrote to her. I refused to acknowledge his letter or her pleas. I was not thinking of the child at the time."

Wesley frowned and returned his hat to his head. "We will find her, but the young woman does not belong here. I will not keep her from you, but I'll see she has other alternatives."

Mountjoy ignored him, and taking this as dismissal, Wesley left. Neither man was known for compromising. They could never work together, but each had resources the other needed for this task. Closing his eyes, Mountjoy pulled a rope summoning a servant. If naught else, his wealth would pave the way.

Faith leapt down from her new sidesaddle, spread her green skirts and starched petticoats in an elegant curtsy, then stood up to offer a mischievous grin to the gentleman in shirt sleeves and buckskin. "It is most ladylike, I'm certain, but I was growing used to riding astride."

Jack grinned. Her cheeks were twin spots of color in the brisk winter breeze, and her unruly hair was already escaping her prim braid to curl in wisps about her striking face. A child's face ought to be round with baby fat, but hers was all angles and hollows, and only the wisps of curls softened it. He had the urge to cup her cheek and stroke the velvety texture of her skin, but he had already learned she shied away from even the most impersonal of touches.

" 'Tis a lady you'll be someday, my *cailin*. I'll not let you forget it. I'll rub the mare down. You go play with your pots and pans." Jack took the bridle from her hand.

A shadow passed across Faith's face. Not shying from his proximity as usual, she glanced diffidently to his face. "Why do you not name the horses?"

Jack's fingers clenched the harness, but he did not allow his anger and hatred to spew over her innocence. He merely tugged one of her curls. "They're all the same to me, lass. One's worth slightly more than the other is all the difference. They go to market when the time is right. Someone else can name them.''

Faith was slightly more perceptive than he gave her credit for. Daringly she touched the knotted fist on the bridle, and with a small smile bobbed her head and darted toward the cottage before he could misinterpret the gesture.

In the month since she had been here, she had learned Jack to be a man of many complexities. She had never come to know another person so closely, and he fascinated her. It was a dangerous fascination, she fully realized. He rode abroad at night with sword and pistol at his side. No man did that without the stain of blood upon his hands. She never saw the coins or jewels he stole, but she knew that the food on their table, the roof over their head, and the clothes on her back came from his stolen bounty.

She was living in sin as surely as if she had taken abode with the devil. She threw off her cloak and hung it on the peg and reached for the apron Jack had bought for her. Come warmer weather, she would have to leave. The memories of her icy tramp of a month ago were too close to create any desire to try it again soon. She had to stay in this haven for a while longer. She might as well make the best of it.

The sun beaming through the window taunted her, but Faith resisted responding to the mockery. It could turn wet and cold at any minute, and she had no notion of how far away London might be, or where she would go when she got there. Sometime she would have to ask Jack.

He came in just as she removed the heavy iron kettle from the fire. The first time he had seen her wielding those heavy pots, Jack had been tempted to take them from her. But she had a perverse pride in producing their meals without aid, and he was not one to add insult to injury. The pain in her eyes had dimmed, but seldom did he see the light of life either. He could only congratulate himself that she seemed stronger, and her hands seemed to be healing.

Remembering his reasons for staying home this night, Jack grinned and threw off his gloves. ''How would you like to go out tonight?''

Thinking she had not heard his words aright, Faith set the pot down and gave him a curious look. ''Go where?''

He poured himself some ale from the small keg he had brought home the previous week. ''Go out. You have seen naught but my miserable face for this month or more. I thought you might wish to see others, although I cannot promise you other than more ugly mugs.''

Faith stared at him in confusion. ''Where would we go? I thought you had no neighbors. I thought . . .'' She stumbled over the completion of that sentence. She had thought a highwayman would prefer staying hidden, but that was blatant nonsense. He had to stop somewhere for the goods he brought home. People knew him somewhere in the outside world.

Jack knew the rest of her sentence and ignored its implications. ''There's an inn at the crossroads. Admittedly, it is not the kind of place for a young lady to visit, but 'tis the holiday season, and it seems a shame that you must spend it with just me. Perhaps there will be a coachload of interesting people on their way to London for the holiday. No one need know you. It will be harmless amusement.''

Faith's lips curved softly at the corners as the idea began to take hold. Before she gave in to the seductive simplicity of it, she forced herself to ask, ''Is there no church hereabouts? I should think Christmas would be better observed in a place of worship.''

Jack kept a grip on his patience. She was but a child. A tavern might appeal to the likes of him, but she knew naught of such things. ''There's nothing so holy in these environs, lass,'' he admonished gently. ''And I'm after thinking the church would not be liking the presence of a man like me.''

To her surprise, she saw pain in his face at this admission, and she sought to assuage it. ''I should think if Jesus welcomed Mary Magdalen, he would welcome you. Have you ever been to a Wesleyan meeting?''

That caught him by surprise, and Jack had the grace to grin. ''Mary Magdalen, is it? I should turn you over my knee for such impudence. Cut me some of that bread before I starve.'' He pulled up the barrel and sat down to fill his plate. ''What do you know of Wesleyans? A ragtag lot of wailers is all I see.''

''There is something wrong with expressing joy?'' she asked calmly. ''Wesley is only trying to teach what the established church fails to make clear. It does little good to preach Oxford sermons to people who cannot even read. They need to bring order into their lives, find methods of salvation. They do not need the debates of John and Paul.''

The father's words tripped easily from the daughter's tongue, Jack observed wryly, hiding his astonishment at the content of those words. Vaguely, he had known many of Wesley's disciples were among the educated gentry, as was Wesley himself. He had just not associated this obviously very well-bred child with her precise speech and disciplined manners with the followers of that sect that were causing riots all across England.

"You are very likely right, lass. I am not partial to the Church of England myself, but riots don't seem to be a godly manifestation either." Jack saw her face suddenly pale, and the knife of her pain twisted in his gut too. What on earth had he said to the child that could cause such anguish?

She picked up her fork and stared down at the plate. "I think perhaps I should just stay here and pray. Do go without me, Jack. I'd not be in your way."

That was not at all what he wanted to hear. He reached across the table and forced her chin up until her watery gaze met his eyes. "I'd hear your reasons, Faith. I've not asked your story, as you've not asked mine. In this place, it is better not to know. But we have months of winter left to share, and I do not wish to watch you wither into an old crone before your time. You must get out or you'll waste away. Why will you not go with me?"

An inn where she would do naught but eat and drink and watch the people could not be sinful. She didn't think Jack would take the child he thought she was anywhere bawdy. For one brief moment he had made her forget her father's death, but she could not hope to be free of it forever. Faith shook her head from his grip. "It is not seemly to go about in public after a parent's death," was her only reply.

His own church taught that, but it didn't mean he had any faith in such niceties, any more than he had patience with a law that could steal from the poor and give to the rich. "You will go with me," Jack commanded. "I have lost brother and sister as well as mother and father, but I will not pretend to be dead because they are."

She stared at him then, saw the ravages of old anguish in the subtle hues of his eyes, and felt their shared pain. It was an odd feeling, this sharing with a stranger what she had kept to herself. A bond seemed to be forged between them that had nothing to do with the strong fingers now lifting to caress her cheek. Something inside her reached out to him, and blinking away her tears, she nodded.

Jack relaxed and returned his hand to his side of the table. "Will you tell me of your father?"

"If you will tell me of yours." Faith watched the sudden wariness leap to his eyes, then dissolve with his smile. Odd, the trust between them. Odd . . . but wonderful.

"I'll buy you an ale and we'll weep in our cups tonight if you like."

The curve of his chiseled lips promised better than that, and Faith felt her spirits lift in anticipation.

It would not do at all to become enamored of a rogue like Jack, Faith thought some hours later as the thick atmosphere of the local taproom enveloped her. Her ire at being introduced to the company as Jack's niece still rankled, but she had held her tongue still at the laughter that had ensued. It was apparent that many of these men were acquainted with "Black Jack," as they called him. She had no wish at all to know what they thought of her. The square-necked gown and kerchief that Jack had bought for her covered her with all modesty. There was naught there to indicate she was more than a child. At Jack's request she had merely pinned her curls beneath the scrap of lace he had presumed to call a cap, but she did not fool herself into thinking this made her look older. There were children in this room right now who were taller than she.

So she sat politely silent at the planked table by the hearth where Jack's friends and acquaintances came and went, and enjoyed the sight and sound of other people without thinking a single comprehensible thought. She felt almost numb from the barrage of sensations. The smoke-thickened air bore the odors of dirty hearth, ale, boiled beef, and unwashed bodies. The din of several dozen voices lifted in talk and argument bombarded her ears. Upon occasion, someone sawed on a fiddle or whistled through a mouth harp, and drunken song would erupt. She disliked the bitter ale Jack bought for her but savored the hot chocolate and meat pie he ordered later. She would have liked to recommend more onion, salt, and thyme in the pie, but the saucy maid who served them intimidated her.

Faith watched as this "Molly" bent daringly over Jack's shoulder to pour his ale. She could see straight down the odious servant's loose bodice, and she averted her eyes to escape the sight of plump white breasts. Jack, on the other hand, seemed to enjoy the view immensely, and she could have kicked him for his laughing chatter.

Amusement still lit Jack's eyes as Molly flounced away and he turned back to see how his diminutive companion fared. She barely reached his shoulder, and he smiled down at the little lace cap perched on a reckless tangle of titian curls. One could almost think it a halo, until he noted the angry snap of icy eyes beneath the fire-streaked tresses. His dark eyebrows raised, but he spoke calmly enough. "Is there something the matter with your chocolate, lass?"

Faith refused to respond to his charm. She lifted her cup and took a sip and watched the boy trying to pop chestnuts in the fire. "It is quite grand, thank you."

Her polite use of his usual demonstrative adjective made his eyebrows go up farther. "Grand, is it, now? Shall I call Molly to bring you another?"

All manner of naughty things were suddenly on Faith's tongue. She was horrified at the answer she almost gave, but the appearance of one of Jack's friends halted her in time. When he slid onto the bench across from them, she merely set her cup down and donned a sweet smile.

Jack gave her smile a suspicious look, then turned his attention to the curly-haired youth who beamed across at them. The red-haired sprout could not have seen his nineteenth year, but, a product of the city slums, he had a worldly cynicism behind that deceptive smile that would frighten a much older man. Jack hid his frown as the boy turned his beaming gaze to Faith.

"Aiee, an' it's a piece o' the sun ye 'ave, Jack! Where did sich a bounder as yerself find sich fairness?"

Jack sent a scowl at the lad's exaggerated accent but grudgingly made the introductions. "Faith, this imp from Satan is known as High Toby, and from the name alone you should know to avoid the scoundrel."

Startled, Faith gave the boy a second look. He couldn't be much older than herself. Surely he could not . . . But she saw the flash of irritation in his eyes at Jack's words and hastily revised her opinion.

"The name's Toby, miss, Toby O'Reilly. Pay no attention to Black Jack. He's just jealous of my charms and talents."

"Pleased to meet you, Mr. O'Reilly." Faith sent a glance

askance to Jack. They had never exchanged last names. There had never been a need to do so and several reasons why they should not. It seemed almost improper to know this boy's name. In this den of thieves and rogues, surely it could not be wise practice.

"You'll hang for a tongue as loose as yours, O'Reilly," Jack replied mildly. "You should tell by her name that Faith's none of us. She's a proper lady, and I'll see you treat her as such. Now, shut your mug and have a pint and pretend you're a gentleman."

A lady! Not a child, but a lady. That comment alone took away Faith's tongue. She knew Jack to be a man full grown, one with a vast amount of pride and confidence in himself, to the point of arrogance, but justifiable, for he was more than competent in everything he set out to do. That he treated her with the respect accorded a lady made Faith sit a little straighter beside him. He didn't treat Molly as if she were a lady.

"Ahh, she's with you, Jack. If she ain't peached on you, she'll not peach on any of us. Give us a smile then, Faith, and don't listen to this sod."

The situation made her uncomfortable, and she looked to Jack for guidance. Her parents had always protected her from the "unsuitable" elements, and she'd really never had much opportunity to talk with people her own age. She was much more comfortable in the company of adults, where she need only be silent and do as told. She didn't know the proper response.

Jack's attention was elsewhere, however. She followed his gaze to the tavern door, where a bull of a man swaggered in. As tall as Jack, but heavyset, with the build of a barrel, he had the close-set eyes and pudgy features of a brute and a bully. There were other large men in this room, mostly scattered about at the far tables in the shadows, but none had the disturbing presence of this one. Faith glanced nervously for the proprietor and found him equally nervously swiping glasses. With a room full of paying guests from the London coach, he had reason to be nervous.

"Who is he?" she whispered to Jack. Toby, too, turned to watch the new arrival.

"An old acquaintance." Jack lifted his mug and nonchalantly took a swig.

The gesture seemed to rivet the bully's attention on their

corner, and to Faith's dismay, he began elbowing his way across the room in their direction.

"Well, now, if it ain't my old friend Jack." The enormous belly came to rest at eye level from where they sat.

"You didn't stay away long, Tucker. What brings you back?"

"There's the matter of a debt I owe. Want to step outside awhile so we can talk about it?" He leaned forward over the table, breathing heavily, and his narrow eyes caught a glimpse of Faith hiding in Jack's shadow. He grinned, revealing a missing tooth and several rotted ones. "Molly ain't good enough for you anymore, you bring your own? Toby here can handle her while we talk."

Jack stretched his long legs beneath the table and disdainfully lifted his mug again. "We have nothing to discuss, Tucker. This is my territory now. You're trespassing. It's Christmas and I'm inclined to be generous. Don't push me any farther than that."

A flash of silver and Toby's gasp brought sudden clarification to Faith's dazed interpretation of this encounter. She stared in astonishment and fear at the evil-looking dagger in the man's hand, and the meat pie in her stomach churned and turned to lead. But then she felt Toby relax and grin, and she strained to see around Jack. It wasn't until the innkeeper hurried toward them and Jack shifted to greet him that she saw the reason the bully had suddenly gone quiet.

The huge black pistol in Jack's hand was pressed directly against the man's belly, while his finger rested easily on the trigger. She hadn't even known Jack wore the weapon, and she gave a small gulp of fright and sank back into the corner at the cold malevolent look in Jack's eyes. Nothing her parents had ever taught her could prepare her for this situation.

"I don't want no trouble," the innkeeper intruded anxiously. "If you two would just carry the argument outside . . ."

Jack's pleasant response belied the black fury in his eyes. "There's no argument, Nate. Tucker was just wishing us a happy holiday, weren't you, my friend? He'll be leaving now. It's not sporting to make his wife a widow on Christmas."

"You'll swing one of these days, Jack. Just see if you don't," the man spat angrily, returning the dagger to its hiding place.

When he turned and strode out, Jack ordered another

pitcher of ale just as if they had never been disturbed, but Faith had seen another facet of his character that she had only suspected existed before.

She shrank back in her corner and said nothing further. With her, Jack was all that was charming and kind, but she had known a highwayman had to be ruthless. Until tonight she had not known what ruthless meant.

Now she did, and she could not prevent a shudder of horror. What would happen did he turn that hard side of his nature on her? She would stand no chance against him.

She lifted her eyes to search his familiar face and found the icy glitter of his gaze staring back.

5

"YOU WILL LEARN it or I'll turn you over my knee and paddle some sense into you!"

"I will not! Guns are horrid. Take that awful thing out of here."

Faith backed away from the long-barreled pistol in Jack's outstretched hand. Ever since Christmas he had been rude and abrupt and impossible to talk to. Now he had come home with this new weapon and a determination to teach her its use, and she wanted no part of it. She could see anger in the taut pull of his jaw, but her fear of the gun was even greater than her fear of his anger.

"I cannot leave you here alone with no way of defending yourself. You learn the pistol or leave. I'll not be responsible for any more deaths." Jack spoke curtly, throwing the heavy weapon down on the table between them. He didn't have the time or patience to play guardian angel to babes. She offered too many complications in return for the small comforts she provided. Were it not snowing a blizzard out there now, he would turn her out.

Faith turned terrified eyes to the sheets of white beating against the window. She couldn't go out in that again. She was stronger now, but not that strong. Her gaze fell on the deadly weapon on the table, and she shuddered.

The memory of what another such weapon had done roiled bloody images in her mind, images she had forced from her consciousness for too long. They came back crisp and clear now: blood and death. Her gaze turned once more to the blinding snow and an equally unspeakable fate, then drifted unwillingly back to the man holding the weapon of death. He loomed closer, unnaturally large, forcing a decision, and with a whisper of protest on her lips, Faith slumped to the floor.

Cursing, leaping forward, Jack caught her before she fell.

She was still practically weightless in his arms, but she had added a little flesh in these last months. His hands closed over soft shoulders as he lowered her to the floor. In the interest of privacy, he had prepared a pallet for her in the loft some weeks ago, and he cursed its absence now. He grabbed a linen towel on the rack before the fire and folded it beneath her head.

Before he could wonder what to do next, Faith jerked and tried to sit up, grabbed his arm, and wailed "No!" in a cry that set the hackles at the back of Jack's neck on edge. It was useless to hold her down. Instead, he scooped her into his arms and let her struggle against his chest, where she could not hurt herself.

"Hush, lass," he crooned softly. "I'll not harm ye. Be still now. It's all right." He felt the violent shudders of her slight figure against his chest and stared blankly at the wall. Had his sister suffered these nightmares before she died? Had her world become such a torment that she shut it out rather than face it? Remembering the small child he had last seen when she was but four, he could very well imagine it being so. What chance had a girl-child against the world with no man to protect her? He had not been there to save Aislin. Had he been given Faith as a second chance?

She was weeping into his shoulder now, her slight frame shaking with the force of her sobs. In these months since she had been here, she had never once cried, although the intensity of her unhappiness had always been just below the surface. Perhaps it was a good sign that she let it out now. He knew nothing of these things. He simply crossed his legs and held her in his lap and let her cry. It was rather like holding a soft kitten, and he smoothed her hair down her back as he would stroke a pet.

When the sobs broke down to hiccups, Jack lifted her chin so he could see into her tearstained face. "I think it's time you tell me your story, lass. I'll not be made to feel such a bully again." He lifted a corner of her kerchief and carefully swabbed at her eyes.

"It leaves such an awful hole," she gulped incoherently. "I cannot do it. I cannot."

Not one to look at words metaphorically, Jack didn't let his mind wander to where these words led. He shifted her to a more comfortable position, and to his startlement, his palm brushed against a slight curve where he had expected none. She was still too lost to sobs to notice, and he carefully avoided repeating the gesture. Molesting children was not one of the crimes he intended to indulge in.

"What leaves a hole?" he questioned gently. "What do you fear, my *cailin?*"

"They shot him," she whispered in horror. "Shot him! He did nothing but speak, and they shot him! How can they do that?"

The image her horrified words painted was an unsettling one. Jack wrestled with his conscience and reluctantly pried some more. "Your father? Someone shot your father?"

A quick hard nod was his reply, before those wide gray eyes turned up to his and he could read the terror in her soul that she had kept trapped there all these months. "They said there had been a riot, that some of the ruffians got out of hand. But rioters don't hold pistols, do they? He was only speaking. He had nothing. Why would they want to shoot him?"

He didn't know. He didn't know why one man lifted his fist in hatred to another. He only knew it had been going on since time began and was not likely to end anytime in his future. Not if he could help it. Sighing, Jack stroked her braid.

"Perhaps it was an accident. Men are like that sometimes. They get all boiled up with anger and don't think what they're doing. I've seen it happen too many times, Faith. I'm sure your father was a good man. He was just in the wrong place at the wrong time." He didn't want to imagine what she had seen if she had seen her father's body. A pistol hole at close range was one of the ugliest sights he had ever seen, and he had seen many. Jack held her a little tighter, squeezing out the memories.

Faith finally became aware of where she was and what she was doing, and her cheeks flamed hot against Jack's shoulder. She tried to extricate herself from the tangle of legs and arms, but perversely, he continued to hold her. Her head filled with the masculine aroma of his skin, lightly covered by only a loose shirt, and she was acutely aware of the male hardness of all those surfaces she touched. His arms were heavily muscled and strong around her. Perhaps they had been comforting, but now they made her exceedingly nervous.

"Is there ever a right place and a right time?" she murmured. Pressing a hand against his broad shoulder, she indicated her wish for freedom.

Those words were too adult for a child. Before he could run his hands over the slender creature in his arms to test his suspicions, Jack let his hold fall slack so she could slide out of his lap. He watched carefully as she settled herself cross-legged in front of him just like a child, but her modest gown and kerchief revealed little of what was beneath. He knew she wore no corset. Beyond that, he couldn't say. Child or woman? He'd rather not know.

"I suppose, if we recognize it, there must be a right time for everything. But like everything else, it's difficult to know opportunity until too late. Hindsight is a marvelous thing."

Faith nodded her head in understanding but refused to look at him. With his thick black hair pulled back with only the one lanky strand falling across his forehead, and the fire flickering across all the angles of his face, Jack had the harsh looks of an executioner. Sometimes she had difficulty remembering that he was a criminal without a heart. It could very easily be a man like Jack who had aimed his pistol at her father's heart.

"I can't use a weapon," she whispered hastily. "I would rather die than know I killed. I'm sorry, Jack. I'm a coward. I couldn't do it."

If his suspicions were correct, instant death would be the least of her worries. How in hell had he got caught up in this? Irritated, Jack climbed to his feet. "You must have relatives somewhere you can go to. Give me their names and let me take you to them."

Hope flared briefly in Faith's eyes as she tilted her head back to look up to him. Then she shook her head and turned to stare at the fire. "My parents' families disowned them when they joined the Wesleyans. I have never met them or heard from them, though I know my father must have informed them when my mother died. There is no one. If you wish me to leave, I shall need to take a position somewhere. Perhaps you could write a reference for me."

Jack wanted to laugh at the thought of scrawling "Lord Morgan de Lacy III" across the bottom of a proper reference. It would have all the good folks scrambling for their genealogies of the aristocracy.

"Give me the names of your parents. It won't hurt to try."

Faith cast his dark features a quick look. "And will you tell me your name too? Must I always know you as Jack?"

She was quick. He would grant her that. Making a formal bow though she sat at his feet, he introduced himself. "James Morgan O'Neill de Lacy, milady. I'll answer by any and all of the above. May I have the pleasure?"

She smiled at this game and scrambled to her feet to offer a proper curtsy. Morgan. She rather liked the name Morgan. She'd known he couldn't be a plain ordinary Jack. "Faith Henrietta Montague, sir. Shall I call you Morgan? I like that much better than all the rest. I fear my name is bigger than myself, but yours fits very well."

Jack chuckled, and the world seemed to shift back to normal. "Yours is a mouthful, but no more so than my own. Morgan is the name I was known by most often. Your father was French?"

"A descendant of the early Normans. He once said his father's title traced back to William the Conqueror."

Title. That discovery would be almost laughable if not so close to heartbreaking. He had already figured her father to be the younger son of gentry, but he had not imagined a title into the picture. So here they both were, the blue-blooded descendants of the world's most civilized countries, living in a hovel with only his sword and pistol to provide for them. God had a wicked black sense of humor.

"A Lord Montague should not be hard to find. When the weather clears, I shall look into it. You may have grandparents looking frantically for some trace of you." And if they found her here, they would have him hanged. How damned blind could any man be? He was imagining his twelve-year-old sister instead of recognizing an aristocratic female of uncertain but quite possibly marriageable age. They would emasculate him before they hanged him.

She looked disbelieving, as very well she might. If her relatives were truly noble, he could find them easily enough, but she had no reason to know that. She did have every reason to belive that he might hold her for ransom once he discovered them. An excellent idea that was, too, if he were certain he could keep her safe. With the return of Tucker, he couldn't guarantee any such thing.

"Until then," he announced firmly, "you will need to learn to protect yourself. This house is not so well hid that none know of it."

The terror returned to the wide eyes swinging up to him. "I'd rather die," she replied almost as firmly as he.

Exasperated, Jack glared down at her obstinate features. "Just how old are you, Miss Faith Henrietta Montague?"

Her bottom lip went out stubbornly as she placed her hands on her hips. "That's for me to know, Mr. Jack Morgan de Lacy. Do I ask you such personal questions?"

He almost laughed at this typically female response from his normally docile housekeeper, but the matter was too serious to encourage her rebellion. "If you're old enough to be taught what being a woman means, you're old enough to know that it is not your death a villain will seek. You might only wish you were dead when he is done with you, but you will have to live with the black memory of that humiliation for the rest of your life. And so would I." This last he added more softly as he watched first the puzzlement, then the horror, cross her face.

Jack's—Morgan's—face was almost as pale as hers against the black shock of his hair as he gazed down on her. The anger and pain in his eyes made his warning explicit, and Faith felt the truth of it somewhere deep in her bones. She might look a child and be treated as one, but she had ears and a mind of her own. She had heard the tales, the whispers, and knew somewhat of the relationship between the sexes. She did not know the physical details, but she knew enough to expect them to be unpleasant. And here was Jack telling her that it was worse than death. Imagining a physical assault by someone like the bully Tucker, she felt revulsion and disgust, but she shook her head. Nothing was as final as death.

"I could just pretend the gun was loaded, couldn't I?"

"No!" The word exploded out of him in fury. "If you point a gun, you had better intend to use it, or you'll be worse off than if you had not." At the pain in her slight face, Morgan ran his long fingers through his uncombed hair and tried one more argument. While her gaze was fixed on his face, he pleaded, "If you cannot do it for yourself, lass, think of me. I would not have your harm on my conscience. There is enough there as it is."

That shocked her even more than his earlier statements, and Faith stared at him in disbelief. It would matter to him if something happened to her? Surely the hardhearted highwayman did not expect her to believe that. Did he think her a simpering fool?

At the wry quirk of Morgan's lips and the suddenly bleak expression in his eyes, Faith caved in. As he turned away, she touched his arm. "I will try to learn, for your sake. But you must remember, if it were not for you, I would not be alive today. Whatever may happen in the future, you have given me more time than I would have had otherwise."

That was true, and Morgan tried to comfort himself with that, but somehow it was no longer enough.

Strange, to develop a conscience at this late date. He shrugged and showed her how to load the pistol.

"The girl escaped, you say?" The man leaned back against the rough tavern wall and sipped leisurely at his tankard of ale. Sated by the hours in the wench's bed upstairs and having just finished a full meal and a pitcher of ale, he was inclined to be genial. "Didn't know there was a girl. Old bastard never tells us anything."

The rough-looking character seated across from him shrugged and buried his unshaven face in his own tankard, drinking deeply of the dark brew. Coming up for air, he wiped his mouth on the back of his tattered sleeve. "Women don't count for much. Ain't likely she'll get far in this weather."

"Quite true. But her father's dead, you say? You're certain of that? I'll not be having another obstacle placed in my way when the time comes."

"Aye, he's dead, right enough. Bloody great hole where his heart should be. Shoulda heard the likes of what he was preachin'. Bloke deserved to be killed, if you ask me. Weren't no trouble at all."

"Ahh, well, he always was a puffed-up bastard. There's a certain justice in ridding the world of troublesome creatures, don't you agree?"

Since the gentleman was buying, the rogue nodded silent agreement and signaled for another round. Perhaps he ought to apply his wits to the subject of the missing girl again. It would fatten his purse if the gentleman decided to pursue her too. But the thought of tracing a lone girl on the highways between here and Cornwall in this weather was too chilling to consider long. He let the subject drop and eyed the approaching ale with hunger.

Despite his relaxed attitude, the gentleman pursued the complication of a female Montague awhile longer in his thoughts. If she had friends, she might show up in London at any time. He needed to be prepared for that eventuality. Despite his companion's words, there was some difficulty in having a female claim to this family. He wondered how old she was. A mere child was easily dealt with. A young woman—that was another matter entirely.

He would have to pump his companion for further information and plan accordingly. Turning his cool gaze back to the drunkard across from him, he let his thoughts play over the possibilities as he began his questioning. A young girl of marriageable age could very well suit his plans nicely. And if not, he could always have her killed.

The unusually bad winter kept Morgan in more often than usual, or so he told himself. But by the beginning of February it was time to try one of his more audacious plans. It could easily take a fortnight to carry out, and he had need to carry it off while Faith was still here to look after his horses. She had some rudimentary knowledge of guns now. He could not protect her more than that. When he came back, he would have to start his search for her kin. It would not do to keep her here much longer.

He ignored his reasoning for that as he strapped on his scabbard and watched the pale gleam of round bare arms as Faith scrubbed at the ancient kettle. The bit of chemise ruffle at her elbow was worn and patched, but she somehow managed to keep it white and starched, as she did his shirts. Miraculously, she had cured the holes and frayed edges of all his linen, saving him the necessity of returning to the tailor anytime soon. He would miss her housewifely attentions, but it was dangerous to both of them to have her linger.

She looked momentarily dismayed, then resigned when he explained the length of his absence. Ever obedient, she offered no word of complaint or protest. Morgan almost wished she would, so he could feel irritation or anger at her nagging presence. Instead, he felt a cloud upon his soul with his departure.

He left her with more than enough fuel and provisions for a fortnight, but fire and food could not feed her soul. Faith pressed her face against the window and watched

Morgan go, his cape billowing around him in the breeze as the stallion galloped off into the night. His absence was like an emptiness inside her, and she did not know why it should be so. He was only her employer, whatever he might say.

The days passed in a monotony of tasks. The cottage was still Faith's pride and joy, and she kept it scrubbed and glistening. The animals were her companions, and she secretly named them all, spending hours grooming and exercising and talking to them. The nights were longest, when it was too dark to do more than sit by the fire and wish for Morgan's vibrant presence. Even when he was silently mending his tack, the room was always full of him. He would look up and give her a wink, or grin and call for a piece of her cake, and she would feel good all over inside. When he wasn't here, she was empty.

Faith washed and mended their limited wardrobes and the sheets upon their beds. With a length of fine cambric Morgan had brought her, she cut out a new shirt for him, knowing it would never be as fine as the ones he had, but hoping he could wear it around the cottage. Carefully she gathered a ruffle from the scraps of the same material and hoped that would look gentlemanly enough.

For she had decided that James Morgan O'Neill de Lacy had to be a gentleman, despite his occupation. Even though he wore no wig or red-heeled shoes, he had the manners and speech of a gentleman when he chose to use them. Perhaps he had not needed these polite niceties for a number of years and was out of practice in their use, but they were still there, under the surface. She had seen them on more than one occasion. He could charm the sparrows out of the tree when he chose. The combination of charm and ruthlessness could be a fatal one to anyone so foolish as to be attracted to it, but she had no fear of that. He thought her a child and would not bother to expend his charms on her.

Faith banked the fire and climbed into the loft to undress. Her childish chemise was beginning to pull too tight across the bosom. She cupped her hands beneath the growing curves of her breasts and wondered if she would ever be half so lovely as her mother had been. More food than she'd had in a lifetime and the constant exercise of the horses and her other manual tasks had added some flesh in the right places, finally, but not enough. She would certainly never have the bounty of the curvaceous Molly.

Remembering how Morgan had eyed the tavern maid's ample bosom, Faith sighed. He would never look at her like that. She should be thankful for small favors, she scolded herself, but still, it was a serious blow to her pride. She was tired of being a child.

She put herself to sleep trying to imagine what it would be like to find her grandparents. Visions of silk gowns and enormous mansions filled her dreams easier than smiling faces and welcoming hugs, and all of them gradually faded before the picture of Morgan in frock coat and cocked hat, helping her down from a grand carriage.

Faith woke with a start to a sound in the room below. Remembering all Morgan's dire warnings, she felt her heart begin to pound noisily. Surely any intruder would hear it and know her presence. Pressing a hand to her chest in hopes of muffling the sound, she groped around for the pistol Morgan had insisted that she keep with her.

A chair scraped, and a muffled curse or groan drifted through the open loft door. Fear instantly became panic, and Faith threw herself face-downward over the opening to find the intruder.

The banked fire gave no light, but she could see his silhouette framed against the window as he reached for the hidden bottle of rum atop the cupboard. Morgan!

Without thought to her state of undress, Faith hastily placed her bare foot on the top rung of the ladder and climbed down.

6

MORGAN TURNED AND SAW a ghostly white figure fly down from the ceiling, and for a moment he almost believed in angels again. Then he staggered against the cupboard, felt the pain rip through his thigh, and reality returned.

"Morgan!" The cry broke from her lips as he lurched unsteadily for the chair.

What could he say? Feeling a fool, Morgan lowered himself to the chair and closed his eyes. He didn't know why in hell he had insisted on riding all the way back here like this. There was a brothel in London where the whores would have taken him in and nursed him in the most pleasant of ways. He could be there now with all that voluptuous beauty hovering over his fevered head and cooing in his ear. Instead, he had a hysterical child in patched cotton chemise wringing her hands and gazing at him with damned wide gray eyes and tears.

"Heat some water and tear up that cloth I brought home the other night. Then go back to bed. I can look after myself."

Her heart skipped a beat, but obediently Faith stoked the embers and added kindling beneath the pot of water she kept in the fireplace. The bolt of cloth was now a shirt, and she hesitated over this command. He would be angry, but there was naught she could do about it. Silently she climbed back up to the loft and from her small store of possessions drew out the old chemise she had carried with her when she first arrived. It really didn't fit properly anymore. There was no sense wasting hours of work and perfectly good cambric when a rag was available.

Morgan paid little heed to the scrap of cloth she held when she came down. Knife in hand, he attempted to saw through the thick buckskin of his breeches. The crude bandage he had tied about his thigh earlier lay in a filthy ruin upon the floor, and the blood was beginning to flow again. He cursed as his head spun dizzily and his hand slipped. He should have kept a closer eye to that guard. He was getting careless.

Soft fingers curled about Morgan's, and he gladly surrendered his weapon. She smelled of the fragrant soap he had brought home to please her. He leaned back his head and closed his eyes as the pain throbbed through his leg. He was aware of her gentle hands holding him there while the cold knife blade cut along his breeches, but he was beyond absorbing anything other than that he was home. It was an odd feeling, this sensation of belonging somewhere, but it wrapped around him as warmly as the heat from the fire. He was home, and in the morning everything would be all right.

Faith's fingers trembled as she cut through the last of the breeches leg. She could see the long, bloody gash across the outside of his thigh, but she was not at all certain whether the gash or the tree-strong limb it marred made her more nervous. She had never, ever touched a man's leg before. The hair-roughened skin covered rippling lengths of muscle that dwarfed her own meager limbs. Desperately she applied warm compresses to the wound and tried not to think of what lay concealed at the top of his bare thigh beneath the remains of his breeches.

"Just wrap it up, lass. 'Twill be fine in a day or two." Morgan's voice was weary, and he spoke as if from a distance.

Faith looked dubiously at the gaping wound, but the bleeding was not such that it required more drastic measures. At least, she didn't think it would. Remembering her mother's strictures on cleanliness and the treatment of wounds, Faith reached for the bottle on the table. She had a better use for the alcohol than rotting his stomach.

Morgan roared at the unexpected rush of stinging liquor across his leg. His eyes flew open, and he glared at Faith with ire at this betrayal, but she ignored the daggers he looked and proceeded to tear her thin shift into long lengths.

It took a moment before Morgan realized that she tore a garment and not the bolt of material he had specified. He grabbed a strip of the threadbare linen and found the suspicious remains of a bit of lace and a button, and he growled ominously.

"What is this? Can you not follow the simplest of orders? Bring me the bolt of cloth, and I'll do it myself. I'll not go about with lace dangling from my leg."

Faith jerked the scrap from his hand and pushed his palm hard against the padding she had folded over the gash. "Hold this still. I cannot work when you wiggle about." She removed the offending bit of lace and the one button and carefully set them aside for other use. "Unless you intend to go about as God made you, no one will know what you have on. There is no sense in wasting perfectly good cloth."

"It is my perfectly good cloth and I'll waste it as I wish," Morgan growled. "If you had other plans for it, I'll buy you more later. I'll not have you tearing up your garments for my sake."

"Did you think I could sit here for a fortnight and do nothing but comb my hair? Your cloth is already made up into a serviceable garment. I saw no reason to render it into rags. I apologize if you are offended, but you did not say you meant to set up a hospital."

Odd, he had never heard that tone of defiance in her voice before. It quavered slightly, as if from disuse or as if she were waiting for the blow to follow, but he could not raise his hand even if he wished to. Closing his eyes again, Morgan gave no reply. He could not begrudge her a new shift or two if that was what she wanted of the cloth. The one she had on was a child's loose bodice buttoned to the neck, without the frills and furbelows he was accustomed to seeing when he undressed his women. It didn't suit her.

That wasn't a particularly coherent thought, and he shook his head groggily, trying to recover his senses. The slim figure in white beside him rose to carry away the bloody water and bandages. Her waist-length braid glistened in the firelight, and he caught a glimpse of a well-rounded calf and dainty ankle, and he groaned at his fevered imagination. He refused to open his eyes again when she returned. He would not let his fever turn a scarecrow child into a full-grown woman to suit his lust.

"You need to be in bed." Her voice was almost seductive to his fevered mind, and Morgan growled at the thought. To his surprise, the sound almost came out as a groan.

Rejecting her offer of help, he pushed against the table and staggered to his feet. He needed to rid himself of his sweat-drenched clothes, but he could not offend the child's modesty by mentioning this. He attempted to remove his coat and felt himself falling before small but strong hands caught and steadied him.

With much tugging and pulling, both coat and waistcoat fell to the floor. Morgan lurched for the bed and caught himself on a slender shoulder conveniently placed by his side. Her bones were more frail than a bird's, but she held his weight as far as the bed.

She managed to remove his boots without his help. The ride had been eternally long, and he knew he'd lost a lot of blood. A little rest would bring him around. Gratefully he swung his legs into the bed and allowed the covers to be pulled up around him. A little rest, and he would be fine.

Faith brought her blankets down from the loft and curled up by the fire, where she could be close should Morgan call for her. She doubted that it would ever occur to the man called Black Jack to call for help, but she wanted to be there if he did. He was so perversely self-sufficient that she was little more than a convenience to him, but he was too intelligent to throw away any convenience he could make use of. He could have bandaged his own leg, got himself to bed, and undressed, but it saved energy to allow her to do it. She didn't fool herself into thinking he would be grateful that she was there. It would be nice to be needed, but Morgan had made it plain that he didn't need anybody.

But he liked her cooking. He wouldn't throw her out as long as she could cook. Holding that thought, she slipped into slumber.

Morgan made an impossible invalid. The next morning, still groggy with fever and pain, he tried to stumble outside. Faith caught him, pushed him back into bed, and handed him the cracked china chamber pot from under the bed. She then absented herself to feed the horses.

When she came back in, he was asleep. She emptied the pot and started a light broth cooking from the last of the dried meat. When he woke, he refused to eat it, demanding something more substantial. She gave him bread and poured the broth into a mug and he drank it as if it were coffee, too fevered to know the difference.

The next day was a repeat of the first, only Morgan's fever had subsided slightly and he was a little stronger. Faith had a harder time keeping him in bed and forcing nourishing liquids down him. She knew in another day or two it would be impossible to control him, and she fretted over the slowly knitting wound in his leg as she bandaged it. Too much movement would reopen it. How was she to make him lie still or even listen when she scolded him? Why should he listen to a child?

By the fourth day, Morgan was aware enough to clearly see the slight figure garbed in the overlarge gown she had worn when first she arrived. She had apparently taken it in and hemmed it and made it fit a little more respectably, but it was a woman's gown and required curves and a corset to fill it out properly. She covered the lack with a large kerchief and a chemise with large ruffles and succeeded in almost creating the illusion that she was more than a child.

Deciding that lying in bed was sapping his brain, Morgan swung his legs over the bed's edge. The figure in drab brown placed her hands on her hips and glared at him. He gave her his best grin and dragged himself to his feet. She braced herself for his fall. He stepped forward, staggered slightly, and gratefully grabbed her slight shoulder.

"Get me to a chair and fetch me a stout stick, Faith, me lass. I'll not be a burden to you for long."

"Don't try your blarney on me, James Morgan de Lacy. That leg shouldn't be moved until mended. I'll take the stout stick to your thick head should you try to go farther than that chair."

Morgan cast his small maid a look of astonishment as he sat down, then chuckled at the grim expression on her delicate face. "Hit a man while he's down, will you? Just remember, I'll be up again soon, and then I'll seek my revenge."

At his chuckle, Faith managed a quivering smile of relief and dipped an impudent curtsy. "Yes, master," she replied solemnly. These small freedoms to speak her mind were wondrous new, and she still felt intrepidly daring when she allowed her thoughts to blurt out. It never ceased to amaze her that he did not take offense, at the very least. "I have made a vegetable soup. Will you have some?"

"No meat in it, I suppose." He stretched his leg and considered that fact gloomily. He needed to be up and about.

"You will not miss it." Faith ladled the soup into a cracked bowl and carried a loaf of bread to the table with it. She was dying to hear the story of how he had injured his leg. At the same time, she really did not want to know. She could be serving a meal to a murderer. It would be much better if she simply ignored everything that went on outside this house. Spring could not be much more than a month away. She would leave then. Surely he would not stop her.

Reminding herself that it was her Christian duty to lead Morgan to the path of righteousness, Faith perched on the barrel at the table rather than avoid him by cleaning the pots, as usual. She watched as he savored the soup, reading the pleasure clearly on his broad face as he tasted the meal she had made for him. Were it not for the harsh angles of his bones and the occasional glint of ice in his eyes, he would almost be a handsome man. Surely he could do better than this life of crime.

"Have you ever thought to seek a less dangerous occupation?"

Morgan choked on his soup and glanced up at the ingenuous child perched with her tiny chin cupped in her hands as she met his gaze with all seriousness. The subject of his "occupation" had been carefully avoided these last months. She must be feeling brave indeed to mention it now. He had been much too lenient with her. He should have barked and yelled more and terrorized her into silence.

"This one suits me," he answered curtly, hoping to discourage further incursions upon his privacy.

"It suits you to nearly lose your life, or at best, your leg?" Faith ignored the ire leaping to his eyes. If her father could face a mob, surely she could face one maimed highwayman.

" 'Tis my business what becomes of me, not yours. I'd rather die with sword in hand than perish of starvation."

"You are far from starvation," she pointed out accusingly. "You can buy a cow and some more chickens and start a garden, and you will have all that you could possibly need."

"And you think that's all a man wants?" Irate, Morgan struck back. "You think I should be grateful for a puling little acreage and a cow? Do you wish to spend the rest of your life gathering eggs and stirring pots over an ancient hearth?"

Dreams of silks and lace briefly swept through her

thoughts, but Faith resolutely cast them out. Happiness wasn't silk and lace, but a lifetime such as he described did seem a trifle tedious. "It is far better than hanging from the gallows," she replied tartly. "Have you no trade? You could sell this land and move to the city if country life does not suit."

"Oh, country life suits fine enough." He sneered. "I could be riding my thousand acres of rolling hills, taking my horses to Newmarket, overseeing a tenant population of hundreds, but a papist is not good enough for such as that. Your fine English parliament leaves me no other career but that of thief. This land is mine only through an Englishman's unlucky gamble. Should it be discovered what I am— not a thief, mind you, but a papist—I would not hold title long. One fine day I'll have all I want, but it shall be at the expense of the bloody Sassenachs who cost me all I owned."

His bitterness soured the food on the table. Faith had nothing to say in reply. The Wesleyans had been jeered and set upon by ruffians across the country, but they had never been persecuted as had Catholics. She knew little of the penal laws, but surely they could not be so cruel as to deprive a man of a proper living. She sighed and rose to clear the table.

"I think it will cost you your most precious possession should you continue this course," she said slowly.

"My life is none too precious, even to me, if it must be lived forever this way." Ignoring the pain in his leg, Morgan rose and stomped toward the door. If she would not find him a walking stick, he would do so himself.

Faith heard the door slam and lowered her trembling hands to the table. She was a fool to think she could change him, but he was a fool not to change. If only she could make him see—but he was blind, blind from hatred and perversity. Where was the good in fighting that?

Remembering the man who had taken her in when no other would, Faith straightened and vowed to try again. Somewhere inside that hardened shell waited a good man needing to get out. She would have to show him the way.

Morgan returned with a rabbit for the cookpot and using a stout tree limb for support. Faith shook her head at his stubborn foolishness, but held her tongue. From the lines of exhaustion on his face, his pride had cost him enough this day. She brought him a cup of coffee and found a keg to prop his leg on, and resumed paring potatoes for their evening meal.

"When my leg heals, I will go into London and find what I can of your family. You need to tell me what you can of them." Morgan sipped his coffee gratefully and followed the motions of Faith's slender back. She was still angry, he could tell by the set of her shoulders. It seemed odd to have anyone reprimand him or care what became of him, but he would not succumb to her weakness. She would be gone in a few weeks' time and there would be none to care whether he lived or died. The English had seen to that, damn their murdering hearts.

"There is naught to tell," she responded curtly. "My grandparents disowned my parents when they accepted the Wesleyan way of life. I have never met them, and their names were never mentioned in my presence. My father's name was George Henry Montague and my mother's Leticia Carlisle Montague. Other than knowing that they came from good families and were well-educated, I know nothing."

If Montague was truly from the nobility, it would be a simple matter to discover him. Returning the long-lost child to the fold might be another matter entirely. She would not easily give up her father's beliefs, and judging by the glimpses of temper she had shown him, her family might not find her particularly obliging in any other way. Still, she was a child, and she did not belong in these realms of the deprived.

"That will give me somewhere to start." It was more pleasant to pacify her with promises than to delve into his criminal activities again. He didn't wish to earn her hatred.

"It would be better could you find me a position," Faith responded defiantly. "I have no desire to be anyone's poor relation. I can earn my own way."

"That's a damned foolish thing to say," Morgan answered irritably, forgetting his desire for peace. "You are much better off in the protection of your family than working for strangers. You know nothing of the world out there."

Faith threw down the knife and glared at him. "I know never to trust what a person says he is. I'd thank you to mind your own business in the future."

She stalked out of the house, leaving him to pare his own potatoes. She didn't know why she ached so at the thought of being forced to leave this isolated cottage to join a family she had never known, but it cut more cruelly than any knife.

She had no home, she told herself, but when the hay-scented warmth of the barn struck her, an overwhelming feeling of grief reached out to suck her in. Never would she see the ginger cat again, or pet the mare, or feed the mighty stallion, should she go away to London. She did not know if she could bear to be torn away.

They dined in stony silence that night and went to bed without the quiet exchange of the day's events that they had come to share. Faith climbed into her loft with her back taut and pretended she did not hear Morgan reaching for the bottle above the cupboard. Let him drown his evil tempers. It was none of her affair.

Only later, when she had drifted into a restless half-sleep, did Faith hear the quiet sounds of someone creeping about the room below. She willed herself to sleep, but the shuffling footsteps pried on her nerves. Morgan never crept or shuffled. Even in pain, he stomped and swaggered. Something was not quite right. The hour was much later than she had thought, judging by the cold enveloping her. The fire was long since banked.

Her hand slid beneath her pillow to the pistol she had not touched since Morgan returned. The hated metal burned her palm, and she almost dropped it, but a muffled sound from below forced her fingers to close around the butt.

Quietly she slid to the loft hatch and peered down. At first she could see nothing, but as her eyes adjusted to familiar shadows, she stifled a gasp.

A hulking silhouette that could not be Morgan filled the center of the room. A flicker of moonlight through the windows caught the point of silver in a massive hand. Even as Faith watched, she could see Morgan staggering from the bed, reaching for the scabbard left dangling from a nail in the wall, and her hand clutched convulsively around the pistol as Morgan's bad leg seemed to give out beneath him.

The intruder's hand swung downward with a club bigger than Morgan's head, and stifling a scream, Faith tightened her fingers on the weapon in her hand.

7

SHE DID NOT even remember pulling the trigger. She certainly did not remember aiming the gun. She only remembered complete terror and anger as the deadly club flew toward Morgan's head and she knew he did not have full use of his limbs to recover himself. The explosion that sent both men rocking backward stunned her as well as them. Morgan grabbed the bed and reached for his sword. The intruder crumpled to his knees and fell sideways to the floor.

Suddenly it was no longer a puppet show in make-believe. Faith felt the horror creep upon her as the pistol scorched her hand. She dropped it, and the noise of it bouncing in the silence below seemed almost sacrilege. Her stomach cramped, and she wanted to retch, but she could not bring herself to go down the ladder to find the bowl.

Morgan glanced upward, and at the sight of the white face framed in the loft entrance, he ignored the body on the floor and started up the ladder. The bastard wouldn't be going anywhere soon, and the child in the loft was a thousand times more important. The wrenching pain in his leg went unnoticed as he grabbed Faith and lifted her frozen form against his chest.

Awkwardly he lowered them both to the ground, thanking the heavens that he had not toppled them from the ladder. Faith shivered uncontrollably in his arms, and when Morgan would release her, she buried her face in the curve of his shoulder. She felt more frail than a newborn filly in his arms, and he gentled her as he would any injured animal. Somewhere inside, a fire stirred, but his tenderness was only for a terrified child.

He carried her to the bed and pulled a blanket around her, and uncurling her fingers from the hairs on his chest, left her huddled in the protection of the massive cupboard where he had been sleeping.

It took only a moment's work to verify what he had already guessed. Morgan had killed before and knew the gut-wrenching horror of seeing life disappear in a puff of smoke. He had grown hardened to death, however, and felt no sympathy for the blackguard who would have taken his life had he been given but a minute more. From the shape and size of the body, he knew it to be Tucker. The man had evidently come to steal and kill as he had done before. Perhaps news of Morgan's injury had made him brave. Whatever the reason, the villain had died more quickly than he deserved.

But the knowledge that it had been that delicate creature in his care who had done this set something loose inside Morgan's chest. Faith should never have been subjected to this kind of terror. No one, male or female alike, should know another man's blood on his hands, but for a gentle female to come to this was even more horrifying in scope. He had to get Tucker out of here. Then, somehow, he had to make it all seem an unpleasant nightmare to be forgotten. He might as well reach for the moon.

Normally, removing Tucker would have been little problem, but Morgan's injured leg could not bear the extra weight. To his disgust, he was forced to drag the body from the room. The ominous silence from his bed did not bode well.

He went back to don his shirt and boots, but did not dare look in on Faith. His first task must be to hide the body. She was a murderer now, like the rest of them in these dark shadows of the forest. If brought before the law, she might cry self-defense, but she would die inside before she ever reached a courtroom. Morgan had seen the insides of enough prisons to know a gentle female could not survive. It little mattered if she were a child. Half the occupants of Newgate were children. Justice only went to the survivors. It was no wonder the gibbets dangled with hardened criminals. They were the only ones who lived long enough to see justice served. It was rather like the witch hunts of the prior century: if they drowned, they were innocent.

Reflecting bitterly on the British system of justice, Morgan managed to haul Tucker over his smallest mare and lead it out of the clearing. No one would mourn the dead man's passing. Even had he wife and children somewhere, they would certainly be grateful to see the end of his abuse. Faith had merely saved the law the necessity of erecting still another gallows. But Morgan rather thought this rationality would not impress a child who was terrified of guns and had never killed before.

When Morgan returned, Faith was still sitting wrapped in the blanket where he had left her. At least this time she had not fainted, although oblivion might be preferable to the horror etching those wide gray eyes. His leg ached abominably, and he sat down beside her, easing it full length to keep from disturbing the knot of pain.

There was nothing he could say. He took her in his arms, and when she did not protest, Morgan leaned back against the wide mattress, carrying her with him. His feet were still on the floor. His intentions were of the purest. There was none to know how they spent this night. He nestled her slender warmth against his side, stroked her hair, and prayed to a God he had long since deserted.

It was dawn before she finally whispered, "I killed him, didn't I?"

Morgan considered denying it. She was quite capable of believing anything he told her, particularly if she wanted it to be so. Perhaps it was callousness that made him tell the truth. If so, he chose the gentlest words he knew to cover it.

"It was Tucker, lass. He meant to murder me in my bed. It would not have gone well for you had he succeeded. You did the only thing you could have done."

"I did not mean to do it," she wailed softly. "I did not mean to shoot at all. It just happened. How could it happen like that?"

Morgan cradled her head against his shoulder and pressed a kiss to her unruly hair. "I do not know, my *cailin,* but I am glad for it. He would have coshed my head and carved my heart and thought no more of it. I was a fool to think myself so safe that I need not keep my firearm at my side. I'll not let it happen again."

Morgan's voice was as thick and soothing as warm honey, and his strong arms made Faith feel safe and protected. As long as she did not have to open her eyes or leave this haven, she could pretend it never happened. She wanted to stay here forever. She wanted to feel more of his kisses.

That thought startled Faith into looking up. She could see

the harsh jutting angles of Morgan's profile, and the gentle curve of his lips. He was such a contradiction, even in his features, that she never knew what to expect of him. But she knew she was growing overwarm in his arms and that she could not stay here forever, much as she would like to.

A feeling of coldness stole over Faith's heart as she pushed from his side. Morgan let her go without any sign of reluctance, but there was a questioning curiosity in those dark-lashed hazel eyes as he followed her movement.

"I will have to go away now," Faith announced matter-of-factly. "They will come looking for me. I cannot shame my father's name by allowing it to be known in this manner."

A grin began to spread across the highwayman's mobile lips. "You have a high opinion of English justice, lass. Even should Tucker be missed, which is doubtful, do you think it is written on the air that one Faith Montague perpetrated the crime? Nay, lass, I think it best you stay with me awhile. When you leave here, it shall be as Lord Montague's grand-daughter, and no one will dare accuse you of anything other than foolishness."

"Foolishness!" Faith glared down at his blasted laughing eyes. "Of what foolishness do I stand accused?"

"Of trusting an Irish papist highwayman, my lass. But how's a child to know a rogue from a knight? I'll ransom you in return for my good name, or keep you here in do-mestic bliss forever, or until my neck is stretched, which-ever comes first. Do you think we might have a morsel to eat?"

Fury flared through her, a white-hot fury Faith had never dared to free in all her life. A man had died this night—at her hand—and he made jests! He talked of hanging and asked for food! Was he insane? Had she found shelter with a madman?

She struck his arm, knowing she hurt her hand more than the iron-clad muscle she abused. "There is a dead man out there, with family somewhere. They could be left to starve. I could hang for protecting your worthless life. We should be praying for our immortal souls. And all you think of is your stomach! How could you?"

She leapt from the comforting shelter of his arms and fled toward the door. Morgan could not follow so easily. His leg had grown stiff during the night, and the pain in just sitting up was excruciating. He cursed himself, he cursed Tucker, and he cursed the little imp from Satan who made him feel the biggest fool alive. He had spent nearly a decade denying his conscience, inuring himself to the kind of life he must lead to win back what had been taken from him, and this little imp would smite him with feelings he didn't want or need. Tucker was a damned murderer and deserved to die. Morgan refused to mourn his death. It was a little more difficult to deny Faith's cry for help, for that was how he saw her anger. He didn't know how to assuage her fears or remove the awful blot from her memory. Only time could do that.

He found his stick and dragged himself to the hearth to start the morning fire.

By the time Faith had sorted through her confusion enough to remember Morgan's wound and return to the cottage, he had set the fire roaring, burned a pan of bacon, and filled the air with the aroma of overcooked coffee. He was contentedly scorching toast in the bacon grease when she entered.

He looked up but said nothing at the sight of her bedraggled chemise-clad figure. Her braid had come partially undone and fallen across the overlarge folds of her unadorned bodice in tangles. Her bare legs and feet bore the scratches of her flight. He noted their length and shapeliness but politely turned his eyes back to the fire. She was terrified enough for one day without imposing his lustful wanderings on her.

He really did need to find out how old she was. She kept herself buried in linen and wool and kerchiefs big enough to tent an army, so that it was impossible to gauge her age by looks alone. But this glimpse of her in the morning light revealed a perfectly proportioned filly of small stature, not the gawky child he had imagined. Perhaps she was not amply endowed, but that did not mean those weren't a woman's curves beneath that threadbare shift. He remembered children as being all bony knees and elbows and awkward gaits. He was just beginning to realize how blind he was.

When she came down, she was properly clothed in her old brown dress that safely disguised everything but the rounded curve of her arm. There was nothing bony about that creamy limb, and Morgan once more averted his eyes to the fire. This could become exceedingly awkward. A child was one thing. He could pamper a child and send her on her way when the weather cleared, without a moment's qualm. A young virgin was quite another kettle of fish.

Morgan turned his crisp toast with his knife. "Will you have a bite to eat?"

She wasn't hungry, and the unappetizing mess he called a meal scarce appealed, but she politely took her seat at the table. "Just some toast, if you do not mind."

Setting his jaw, Morgan pried a piece of toast loose and dropped it on the table before her.

Faith quivered a little inside at the return of the taciturn stranger, but she bravely took her toast and ignored his silence. It was time she left here, whatever he said.

Swallowing a lump in her throat that had little to do with the wretched toast, Faith managed to speak. "The weather is more favorable now. If your leg does not bother you too much, I had best be on my way. By the time you are well enough to travel, it will be warm enough to let the horses loose. You will not need me any longer."

Munching the tasteless slop that he had survived on for years, Morgan contemplated this offer. She was quite right. It was time for her to leave, but he didn't think either of them was ready for it yet. He didn't want to go back to tasteless meals and a house that echoed empty when he came home. She wasn't strong enough or cynical enough to survive alone in this harsh world. That she would have to leave eventually, he knew, but now wasn't the time.

He shook his head and swallowed a sip of the thick coffee, grimacing at its bitter taste. "You'll not be leaving until I can go to London and find your family. You would not even make it safely through the forest on your own."

Knowing now the kind of men who lived here, Faith could understand the truth of his words, but still, she watched him warily. He did not meet her eyes. Did he mean to hold her for ransom, after all? That would be foolish indeed. He would be stuck with her for a lifetime if that were the case.

"I have no wish to be a burden to you. I have made it across the breadth of England without your help. Surely London cannot be much farther."

Black brows pulled together in a thundercloud as Morgan glared at her. "You will stay and I will hear no more argument. Have the horses been watered?"

Faith blinked, felt a lightness in her chest, and nodded.

She might be three kinds of a fool, but she didn't want to leave. Gratefully she offered, "Shall I fry some eggs for you? You could see to your leg while they're cooking. The water should be warm by now."

Morgan hid his relief and nodded curtly. He had no sense at all, but he didn't want her to leave just yet. There would be time enough later, when the weather grew warm.

"What do you mean, there is no trace of her? Is the country so large that a child can disappear into it? Do we harbor red Indians who will carry her off to their camps? Have the Gypsies declared her queen and spirited her back to their homeland? Do not give me your faradiddle, Watson! I'll have her whereabouts or your head."

The rotund man with wisps of hair around his gleaming bald pate struggled nervously with his unaccustomed cravat as the tall lord paced the library like a hungry tiger. He should have worn a wig, Watson decided as he eyed the aristocrat's lanky grace. A wig would have made him a gentleman, and his lordship would not speak to a gentleman thus. He would do well to learn the manners of his betters if he were to get ahead in his profession.

Mountjoy swung around and glared at the silent runner. "Well? Have you nothing to say for yourself?"

Watson drew in his stomach and tried for a portentous voice. "There are many things that might befall a child on such a journey. This has been a harsh winter. It is possible we might find her bones in the hedgerows at some future date. We can continue searching for as long as you require, my lord."

Mountjoy's color turned choleric, and he lifted his arm as if to bodily fling this purveyor of bad news from the room. "Get out! Get out before I have you thrown out, you damned excuse for a man. I'll box your ears if you linger! I'll report your impudence to Fielding. I'll see you drawn and quartered should you show your face in my presence again."

Paling, seeing all hopes of promotion fly out the window, Watson turned and scurried out. Far be it from him to report that a girl resembling the subject in question had been seen at a wayside inn known to harbor some of the countryside's worst criminals. That remark would undoubtedly cost him his head. Let someone else tell his high-and-mighty lordship that his granddaughter may have fallen among thieves and harlots.

In the library, Mountjoy paced the jewellike colors of his newly acquired Persian rug. He condemned all the incompetent idiots of the world. He vilified his son and the Wesleyans. He cursed Lettice and her tear-filled pleas. Then he rang the bell and summoned a servant to bring his elder—and now only—son to him.

If something weren't done soon, his title would die with this foppish macaroni he called heir, or go to that blasted arrogant nephew of his. Mountjoy glared at the oil painting hanging above the mantel and shook his fist at the cherubic face of the heir to Mountjoy.

Perhaps he had better summon his lawyers. There had to be some way of passing on this accursed title. A granddaughter, indeed! Damn George, he couldn't even manage to produce a grandson for him. Neither of his sons had been able to do anything right. Always he had to do everything himself.

The poker-faced servant bowed stiffly at his lordship's command, then backed out. He wouldn't be the one to tell the marquess that his heir hadn't returned yet from his night's carousing. Not when his lordship was in a temper, at least. Let him simmer in his own juices for a while.

8

FAITH STARED AT HIM in disbelief as Morgan settled his tricorne firmly on his thick hair, threw back his cloak to check the fastening of his scabbard, and strode toward the door with a still-noticeable limp.

"You are mad! You cannot go out like this. Your leg is not yet healed. The ride will tear it open again."

Morgan turned impatiently. "It is mending. That's all that is necessary. See to the horses and I'll return in a day or two."

It had been nearly a month since he had ridden out. Faith had hoped that might mean an end to his marauding. She could see now that she had been a fool to think so, but even shattered hopes were hard to give up.

"Please, Morgan, don't go. We have enough provisions to last for months. I can start a garden. With Melisandra in foal, you could make a tidy sum at the fair. You needn't go out."

One black brow went up. "Melisandra?"

Faith had the grace to blush, but didn't lower her gaze. "She needs a name. That's what I call her."

Melisandra. Morgan covered a grin. That was a dramatic name for the pretty black mare, but no more so than Queen Maeve, he supposed. It wouldn't do to encourage her, though. She was growing far too bold to protest his nighttime forays. Against the firelight she was no more than a slender wraith, but a crackle of red glimmered in her russet curls, and those damned wide eyes were enough to haunt a man's dreams. He forced his expression to a glower.

"Call her what you will. She'll be sold come fall. I'm going now." He strode out without giving chance for further protest. She might as well learn that he had no intention of changing for her sake.

Faith stared at the closed door and fought back tears. She

had tried to divert him from his villainous ways. She had hoped to atone for her crime by returning Morgan to the Christian life. If he could not see the path of righteousness, she could not lead him to it. It was time she took steps toward her own salvation. She could not live off the proceeds of sin forever.

She did not dare borrow Morgan's horses without permission. So in the morning, after she had set the house to rights and seen the animals fed and watered, she set out on foot. If nothing else, she knew there was an inn nearby. Inns had need of cooks and tavern maids and maids to do the cleaning. She was quite accomplished at all those chores. Actually, she acknowledged to herself with a wry grin, she could fill the position of ostler, if required. Perhaps she ought to garb herself in Morgan's clothes and offer her services in the stable.

It was well after noon before Faith found the inn. It looked shabbier in the daylight than she remembered. The faded sign of a rampaging bull dangled from only one link. The ancient leaded glass in the tavern window was so filthy as to make it useless for letting in light. The mud and wattle between the half-timbered siding was chinked and moldy and hadn't seen whitewash in a century, if ever.

Refusing to be discouraged by this unprepossessing appearance, Faith stepped inside the dusky interior. The brisk March wind outside had done nothing to air the reek of ale and cooked cabbage inside. The odors of unwashed chamber pots mixed insidiously with other noisome stenches that she had not noticed the night she had arrived on Morgan's arm. Morgan had a way of waving his hand and making the unpleasant disappear. Or perhaps it wasn't his hand but his charming smile. He could drop a squirrel from a tree with that smile.

Drawing her frayed cloak more closely around her, Faith searched for some sign of the proprietor. Whether he knew it or not, he needed her services. Somehow, she had to convince him.

When he finally waddled out to inspect his visitor, the innkeeper was taken aback by her soft-spoken request for employment. Ladies did not work in public houses, and certainly not ones like this. When she pulled back her cloak to reveal the tender features of youth, a head of russet hair capped in a scrap of lace, and the wide eyes of innocence, he nearly choked—until he remembered that same delicate face in his taproom some months ago.

She had been with Black Jack the last he had seen of her. His narrow eyes swept suspiciously down her slender figure, but the cloak concealed any sign of a swelling belly. Well, if Black Jack had tired of her, then his patrons would enjoy a new face, especially one so young and tender as this.

Nodding his head and wiping his sweaty hands on his apron, the innkeeper agreed. "Ye can begin with the linens. T'night, I'll set ye to the taproom." Her smile of pleasure quelled any further doubts. Wait until the boys saw the surprise he had for them tonight!

Faith frowned at the tightness of the bodice stays Mrs. Whitehead had insisted that she wear. She knew maids were expected to wear uniforms, but she had scarcely expected one so indiscreet as this. Her small breasts were pushed up until they resembled melons ready to pop. The tightness of her lacing made her gasp, and she wondered how she was supposed to work in such binding.

She had no mirror in which to see herself. Nervously she tried to adjust the stomacher higher, but it would not budge. She wished for a brooch to keep her kerchief securely fastened over her bosom, but she had to be satisfied with tucking the ends inside her bodice and praying they would not work loose. Without the kerchief, she was nearly naked.

The skirt and petticoat were too long, thank goodness. The last maid must have been of taller stature. Mrs. Whitehead had eyed the length with displeasure, but she had said nothing. It would be a nuisance trying to walk with skirts trailing the ground, but it would be better than revealing any more of herself than the gown already did.

Changing the linens and emptying slop jars was tedious work, but Faith was experienced and efficient and accomplished it with little instruction. Proudly, she discovered she had time to scrub the jars, and performed this task with alacrity. There was nothing worse than the smell of a dirty chamber pot.

She was offered a tankard of ale, a bowl of stew, and a chunk of stale bread for her supper. Sitting in the kitchen, Faith eyed the grease-coated hearth and utensils with doubt and an itch to scrub them thoroughly, but no one had mentioned a need for a kitchen maid. She would have preferred working here rather than in the smoky, male-populated taproom, but she was content to have any employment at all. She would not complain on her first day here.

She wondered what Morgan would do if he came home tonight and found a cold hearth and an empty table, and her stomach twisted nervously. She had hoped to find a position to occupy only her daylight hours, but surely he would understand if she must work the evenings too. He never considered what it must be like for her to sit alone by the fire and watch darkness fall and wonder where he was. And since he didn't exactly offer her a paying position, he could not object if she tried to earn her own way.

Or she didn't think he could. She'd rather not think about it at all if she had a choice. She had finally found work and was well on her way to independence. Let him put that in his hat and lump it.

She wasn't feeling quite so confident a little while later when she stood behind the bar washing tankards in a basin. It was early yet, and the room was nearly empty, but the smoke and the dimness and the male laughter made her edgy. Molly had already made it clear that the tables were her territory, and Faith gratefully agreed to that. She tried to keep her back to the room as she washed and dried, but the occasional shout from behind her made her start and jump often enough.

The cheap, high table that served as bar between kegs and customers was never intended for more than overflow from the tables, so Faith held back uncertainly when two of the customers strode up and demanded refills. That was Molly's job, and she sent the other girl a questioning look. But Molly was squirming on the lap of one of the gentlemen in the corner and took no heed of her plight.

Shrugging her shoulders, deciding there could be little more to this than treating a guest with respect, Faith took their tankards and filled them at the keg. Instead of returning to their table, they lingered, their gazes following her every moment, their whispered words not so quiet that they kept her ears from burning.

Faith had no illusions about her looks. She was small. She had the height of a child—and nearly the figure of one, when compared to Molly. Her eyes were too large for her face, her nose too small. Her hair looked like the forest floor in the autumn. Brown matted leaves had the same charm as her unruly curls. She had braided them tight and wrapped them around her head, but she could feel the wisps escaping and sticking to her brow as the heat increased from the steamy water and the huge log in the hearth.

The words of the two men at the bar made no sense when looked at in that light. It could only be the blamed bodice that they were seeing. She was so nipped in at the waist and pushed up at the bosom that they must see her as something she was not. In this light, it was more than possible.

A familiar voice rang out behind her, and Faith swung around in surprise and the beginning of a smile. The red-haired youth Morgan had introduced to her was working his way toward the bar, and from the grin on his angular jaw, he remembered her. It was good to see a friendly face. More than good. The two customers who arrived first turned to watch Toby's approach with disfavor.

"Why, an' it's little Faith I be seein'!" he exclaimed with a grin at his own jest. "Did Jack decide he might share ye with us lesser mortals?"

Faith carefully drew him a tankard and placed it on the bar. "Jack has no say over me. How have you been keeping, Toby?"

He raised a puzzled eyebrow but did not question her quiet words. Casting a glance askance at the two black-guards slavering over her, Toby decided it was in his best interest to linger. He raised his tankard and grinned. "To independence, then, lass."

The tavern began to fill, and Faith moved nervously before the crowd beginning to swarm around the bar. Molly was giving her filthy looks, but Mr. Whitehead seemed to beam approvingly as she quickly filled cup after cup. Since Molly wasn't paying her, Faith had to assume she was doing something right. She just wished the men weren't so blatant in their personal comments. Perhaps she ought to teach them that wasn't polite.

"She's a shy 'un, Matt. Maybe we ought to break 'er into the traces."

Faith recognized the voice as one belonging to a black-bearded individual who had been particularly loud in his admiration all evening. She ignored him as she scrubbed at the latest lot of tankards Molly had dumped into the basin. The water was no longer warm, but that didn't seem to bother anyone.

'' 'Ere, girl, bring us another,'' the man named Matt shouted.

Faith dried her hands on the soaked towel and reached for two clean mugs. They seemed to find that remarkably funny, but she did not intend to abandon her mother's strictures on cleanliness. It seemed a filthy habit to refill a dirty mug, as she had noticed Molly doing on several occasions.

She felt their hot gazes eyeing her exaggerated bosom as she brought them their drinks and accepted their money, but she was unprepared for the heavy hand reaching over the bar to grab her arm as she took the coins.

"There's some in that for you, girl. Just give us a kiss now." The black-bearded man leaned over the bar and jerked her forward.

Faith gave a scream and swung the heavy pewter tankard instinctively upward in an attempt to defend herself. The tankard caught Black-beard on the jaw and he gave a yelp, but his companion found it immensely funny and reached to join the game.

"Let's give her a welcome, boys. She's a feisty one, but I take my turn first." With a burly arm, the man called Matt grabbed Faith's waist and lifted her bodily from the floor.

Faith struggled, but the bar between them kept her from kicking, and the tight binding of her laces didn't allow much movement. She felt a heavy hand squeezing at her breast, and she screamed in outrage as Matt's foul breath flowed over her face.

"Leave 'er alone, mate. She belongs to Jack and 'e'll 'ave your skull if you touch 'er." Toby spoke sensibly, although his change of accent warned of a change in mood, and his right hand rested on the hilt of his knife.

Matt scoffed and dragged his victim onto the bar. Faith's skirts wrapped around her legs as she tried to kick free, and her hands beat futilely against impervious shoulders. The kerchief covering her breasts came loose with the mauling, and she nearly expired with fear as the man's nasty mouth came down to close over hers.

Other hands grabbed at her skirts and legs, and her screams filled the air, drowning out Toby's warnings.

Morgan patted his winded stallion as they cantered down the last stretch of road before they reached the cottage. The night was brisk, but there was just a touch of spring in the air. He inhaled it deeply. He had no right to this feeling of well-being. The haul he had taken had been small, the fence had been particularly niggardly in his payment, and his leg ached like hell.

But he imagined the fire awaiting him, Faith's petite figure sitting beside it with her hands full of her perpetual sewing, and a steaming hot supper in the kettle, and his other concerns vanished. He remembered the newly sewn cambric shirt he had found in his trunk, and his smile grew even broader. He had found a treasure, better than any fey faerie, even if she had a temper beneath that docile demeanor.

When he rode into the clearing and discovered the darkened cottage, Morgan frowned. Perhaps it was later than he thought. Quietly he led the stallion into the barn, fed, watered, and rubbed him down. Even if Faith had gone on to bed, he knew there would be something keeping hot over the coals, and his sheets would be warmed with heated bricks. The cottage would be cozy and his coffee would be fixed just right. Never had he lived in such luxury, even when he had thought himself heir to a thousand acres. His crumbling home had boasted only the most slatternly of servants willing to work for a moldering roof over their heads. Never had he known such comforts as Faith introduced to him. He had half a mind not to part with her. Her unfeeling grandparents didn't deserve such a gem.

Remembering the surprise he had brought for her, Morgan rummaged in his bag and tucked a package under his arm before returning to the house. He would have to wake himself up early in the morning to catch her eagerness. Faith loved surprises, he had learned, and it was so very easy to please her. Wait until she saw what he had found on this trip.

When he opened the door on icy darkness, Morgan's insides clenched, and his hand instantly went to his sword. No lantern burned on the table. The fire had died completely. No smells of cooking food perfumed the air. And the room was empty of Faith's presence.

That sent him hurriedly across the floor to the loft ladder. She had to be here. There was nowhere else for her to go.

Finding her empty pallet, Morgan felt an icy knife drawn through his heart.

She had left him. She had put on that ratty cloak and

walked out of his life. He should have expected that. Nothing good ever lasted long in his care. Everyone left him eventually. He didn't know why he should be so surprised at this desertion.

He slowly lowered himself down the ladder and went to light the lantern for himself. He had no stomach for his own cooking. Perhaps there was some cheese in the cupboard.

He wondered if he ought to go after her. She couldn't get far on foot. He'd likely find her sleeping in the hedgerows again. That threadbare cloak of hers wasn't enough to keep out the cold night air. She would be prey to every thief and panderer in the shire. She would never make it to London on her own.

As the lantern light spread across the hearth and table, it caught on a glimmer of silver on the shelf by the fireplace. That was where Faith always left her precious sewing kit. He ought to have bought her a new one. Her scissors were old and dull and her one needle must be blunt by now.

Morgan wandered over to examine the source of the light. He exclaimed at the discovery of the little leather case lying open, waiting for its owner's return. Faith would never have left that behind. Grabbing the lantern, he returned to the loft.

Her few meager possessions lay neatly stacked by the pallet on the floor. Only the green gown and petticoat he had bought for her were gone. She hadn't left him. His heart began a furious pounding as he climbed back down.

She had gone out and not returned. That she had meant to return was a fact that Morgan had difficulty grasping, but the sight of Faith's few precious possessions drove it home. She hadn't left him. Therefore, she must be in trouble.

Cursing vividly, Morgan reached for his cloak and ran for the door. There was only one place he knew of to start searching. In this darkness, he might not see her if she were lying huddled in some ditch, but if anyone had seen her this day, it would be the villainous patrons of the Raging Bull. He might have to knock a few heads together to get any information, but he'd skewer them all if necessary to find Faith. She was too young and inexperienced to take care of herself. She was his responsibility, like it or not. He did not take responsibility lightly.

He didn't take the time to saddle a horse, but took the nearest to hand, and grabbing the mare's mane, kicked her into a gallop. She sprang forward eagerly, and the wind swirled around them as they fled down the lane.

It seemed to take a thousand hours to reach the brightly lighted inn. There was no London coach this night, Morgan could see at a glance. That meant the worst scoundrels in the shire would be here, carousing and raising hell. Whitehead made them behave when the coach was in, but he let them amuse themselves otherwise. If it were early enough, he might still get some sense out of the best of them.

The roar from the taproom was louder than usual as Morgan entered. Swearing violently at the bad luck of arriving during a brawl, he strode in with a thunderous look across his face, his hand already at his sword. He would beat the bastards to the floor and put his foot across their necks until he had questioned them all. He was in no humor for drunken tempers. He had seen the drink drown too many good men, his father among them. It was a temptation he generally avoided, for very good reason.

A woman's screams momentarily caused Morgan to freeze. He had been ignoring the bulk of the crowd at the bar in the favor of finding a few sober heads at the tables, but the screams drew his attention to the riot currently in progress.

Toby's furious cries of protest barely overrode drunken laughter. A shifting of the crowd gave a glimpse of a long white limb kicking furiously from beneath an unfamiliar mustard-yellow skirt; then the crowd closed again, cutting off his view.

He had seen enough to drive fear and fury through his soul. With a roar, Morgan jerked his sword from the scabbard and leapt to a table. The first arc of the steel severed the shirt from one man's back. The next swing sent an upraised tankard flying through the air and caused a scream of pain as the hand bearing the tankard spouted a stream of blood.

The crowd began to fall back then, but Morgan had no patience for their terrified expressions. Sword swirling, he sent men staggering backward, knocking down their companions who foolishly did not retreat fast enough. The livid expression on Morgan's harsh face was sufficient to send the less intrepid scurrying for the door. The whine of steel and flash of silver drove the remainder from their prey as surely as if a whirlwind had descended in their midst.

Only Toby remained, and he was busily helping the terrified female on the bar to her feet. The red-haired youth ignored Morgan's black expression in favor of supporting the slender sprite in his arms, helping her to gather together her torn bodice and to right her long skirts.

Looking up, Faith nearly fainted at the sight of the rigid pull of muscle along harsh cheekbones and the black scowl along Morgan's high brow, but she only grasped desperately at his coat when he jumped down from the table and reached for her. She clung to the rough wool, burying her face against the heat and strength of him as his arm wrapped harshly around her. The fierce possessiveness in his dark features as black eyebrows drew together warned all and sundry of their trespass.

Finding the innkeeper huddling in a far corner, Morgan pointed his sword and his wrath in that direction. "I'll have your heart out for this, Whitehead! And if you ever let another of these filthy beasts touch her, I'll remove those parts you prize more dearly than your stone-cold heart."

"For the devil's sake, Jack, get her out of here!" Toby fingered the pistol in his hand nervously. His knife had been lost earlier in the melee, and the one shot the pistol allowed was not sufficient to hold back a mob.

Growling something incomprehensible, Morgan swung his cloak around Faith's trembling shoulders, then gathered her easily into his arms and strode for the door. "Come along, Toby. Leave the vermin to their amusements. I'll not be back to pull your hide from the fire later."

That was probably as close to an expression of gratitude as Jack would ever offer. Toby hurried in the taller man's wake. He was young and small and did not pack the muscular strength of many of the men back there, but he was wiry and quick and possessed the cockiness of youth. He might have stayed to argue the point, but he obeyed Jack's greater wisdom. Jack had looked after him more than once. It would be the height of foolishness to ignore him now.

Faith was weeping against his shoulder, but all Morgan could think of was the sight of those lovely breasts revealed for all to see, the same breasts pressed tauntingly against his side now. Rage ate at his insides, but Faith's slender feminine form in his arms created another disturbance that nearly had him paralyzed. He stalked toward his horse, unheeding of the youth who followed.

A look of worry flashed across Toby's face at the livid expression in Black Jack's eyes as he threw Faith atop his horse and climbed up behind her. Daringly Toby planted himself in front of the dancing mare. "She's had enough trouble, Jack. You take care of her."

There was a bleakness in the older man's expression as he glared down at the interloper, but without a word Jack whipped his mount around and started down the road, leaving Toby to stare after them.

9

MORGAN MAINTAINED HIS SILENCE all the way back to the cottage. Faith dried her tears, and, thoroughly wretched, clung to the highwayman's closeness without thought or pride. His black cloak engulfed them both as the rise and fall of his mount carried them faster and farther from her disgrace. The humiliation reached deep down inside her and clutched at her spine and ravaged every ounce of courage it had taken her to walk out into the world this day. She wanted nothing more than to curl into the safety of Morgan's large body, never leave again, to be part of his midnight booty.

The fact that he was so furious he couldn't speak didn't terrify her, oddly enough. He was a brutal man, one who could wield sword and pistol without a qualm, as he had done this night. But the arm around her now was the only shelter she knew, and his silence comforted her better than words.

He rode the mare into the barn and dropped Faith to the hay in the nearest stall. When she hastened to fetch brush and water, Morgan caught her arm roughly.

"Get back to the house. I'll take care of that."

Her eyes widened at his harsh tone, but Faith hurried to do as told. She would never be disobedient again. She would scrub his floors and polish his boots. But right now she had need of warm water to scrub away the feel of filthy hands, decent clothes to cover herself, and a dark hole to hide in. She had not missed the sudden gleam in Morgan's eye when his gaze fell on the pale curve of her breasts beneath the torn bodice. She didn't want to know the meaning of that gleam.

The fire was dead and the water cold, but Faith carried a pail to her loft and hurriedly ripped off the hated mustard gown. She mourned the loss of her beloved green wool, but she would never go back to claim it. She would never leave

Morgan's home again. If he let her stay. She prayed he would let her stay.

The terror of being turned out into that cruel world again made her ignore bruises and pride as she hastily scrubbed and donned her old drab gown. She would make it up to Morgan. Surely this one transgression would not convince him to throw her out.

His silence began to take on new and ominous meanings as her fingers trembled over the lacing. Not bothering to secure the cloth ties that completed the bodice, Faith hastened back down the ladder to start the fire, her mind worriedly cataloging the contents of the cupboard for an easy meal. She must at least make his coffee ready.

When Morgan came in, she had the coffee almost boiling, but he ignored the slight figure silhouetted by the fire and reached for the rum. Cursing at finding the bottle empty, he drew himself some ale and drank deeply. Faith made no sign that she saw him, but concentrated on the smoked meat she was slicing. His sharp eyes caught the trembling of her fingers, and his gaze rose to study the rise and fall of her breasts beneath the bulky gown.

She was slender, no doubt, but the creamy curve of her throat dipped to feminine hills and valleys beneath the unfastened ties of her gown. In his mind's eye Morgan could see the firm mounds of young breasts lifted for all to see and grab, and his anger frothed and foamed inside his chest. Gad, he had been a bloody idiot.

"Go on to bed. You needn't do that for my sake."

These first gruff words cutting the mounting silence startled Faith into dropping the knife. She scrambled for it on the floor until rough fingers caught her arm and dragged her upward.

She found herself staring into Morgan's impassive expression, her body pressed firmly along the length of his as he held her arm in a tight grip at his side. Hazel eyes became a smoky green in this half-light, and, terrified, Faith watched his chiseled lips turn up in a mirthless curve.

"How old are you, Faith Montague? And don't be giving me any of your witty answers. I want the truth."

Nervously she licked her lips, and the grip on her arm tightened. The gleam in his eyes smoldered, and hastily she gave him the answer he sought. "Eighteen this month, if it's March now."

"It is." Morgan stared down at her, held in the grip of some fascination he didn't even try to understand. Eighteen. Not a child. The words danced in his head with little licks of flame like imps of hell. His gaze returned to the glimpse of skin at her throat.

"Eighteen, and no more sense than to enter a taproom after dark." He forced the words out, throwing scorn as a shield between them. He watched her flinch but didn't let go. There would be bruises on her arm no doubt in the morning.

"I couldn't refuse employment when it's offered," Faith protested. Somehow, the anger in his steely grip was giving her courage. "I cannot live off charity forever."

"Charity, is it now?" Morgan couldn't keep his gaze from straying. He tried to focus on the fear in her face, but he saw only the luminescence of those long-lashed eyes and rose-hued lips moistened by a small pink tongue. If he lowered his gaze from those temptations, he found himself mentally stripping back that ghastly brown wool from skin the texture of cream satin. His imagination could easily carry him farther, and he allowed his tongue to act as barrier to his thoughts. "It's not charity I offer. You work for me and I'll pay you in coin. The kind of service you offered tonight pays well. I'll meet whatever price Whitehead offered, and double it to keep you exclusively mine."

She didn't even need to understand the words. The insult in his tone spelled it out quite clearly. On the edge of breaking already, Faith made no attempt at control. Her free hand flew up to smack hollowly along his high-boned cheek.

Morgan's head jerked back at the blow, but a grin began to form on his lips. Violence put them on a level that he understood. With a tug, he pulled her up against him, his arm around her waist forcefully pressing Faith's struggling frame firmly where he wanted her. Without consulting her wishes in the matter, he bent to taste the lips that had been beckoning him for longer than he could remember.

Faith gasped at the shock of Morgan's hard mouth slanting across hers. She could smell the fumes of ale on his breath, but other, more arousing odors confused her senses. He always smelled of horses. Tonight he had the smell of perspiration from his long ride. The lacy jabot tickling at her throat still had the faint odor of clean linen. But beyond all that there was a strong scent that was all Morgan's own, a musky masculine smell that overpowered her, just as the touch of his body in so many places overwhelmed her ability to think. She didn't even try to fight the lips moving across hers. They belonged there, he seemed to say, though he said nothing, but merely tasted of her mouth.

She had never been kissed before. The feeling of intimacy was so shocking it took a moment before she realized she was expected to respond. Some tiny fraction of intelligence warned that she ought to struggle, but she longed for this physical comfort after the harrowing events of earlier. Morgan wasn't hurting her; he offered a form of tenderness. She responded to that more than the harsh grip around her waist.

When her lips finally moved beneath his, Morgan felt the fierce flame of desire and excitement leap through him. Usually he sought out London's whores or Molly's favors when he grew bored and restless and needed some release for his energy. The heat of passion might rise during these interludes, but there was no thrill of the chase or anticipation of the future. What Faith offered with her childish kisses was so much more that Morgan could scarcely rein in his desire, although he knew he must do so to obtain the fullest measure of her passion.

Morgan felt her body soften in his arms, and he explored Faith's eager lips thoroughly until they parted with pleasure. His loins grew thick and heavy at the ease with which she gave way to him, and his tongue responded intimately to that tempting hollow opening beneath his kiss. She stiffened at his unexpected invasion, and though he knew he could press on, Morgan slowly withdrew, nuzzling tiny kisses along her lips and across the satin smoothness of her cheek to nibble delicately at her ear.

Her blood seemed to flow with fine wine, and her head spun dizzily as Faith clung to Morgan's broad shoulders and allowed him these freedoms she had never before dreamed of. She knew she should stop him, but she could not see the harm in what he was doing to her. She felt like fire and smoke in his arms, and she ached to explore these sensations to their ultimate conclusion.

But at the same time, she was terrified at the depth of her emotions. When his tongue touched hers, a shock of pure electricity shot through her, and she tried feebly to break away. His caresses reassured, and she bent her head to his shoulder as his kisses grazed through her hair.

"Ahhh, Faith, ye're like a long draft of cool water after a summer's day. It will be a pleasure to know you," Morgan murmured against her ear.

Whether it was the sensuous vibrations of his husky voice or the phrasing of his words that warned her, Faith couldn't say, but she suddenly stiffened at the implications of his words and actions. He was seducing her, just as her father had warned that a boy would do should she be alone with one. And Morgan was far more than a boy. He was a man, with a man's strength and desire. She wouldn't stand a chance against him now that he knew she was not a child.

Faith jerked free of his hold and hastily caught the collar ties of her bodice and overlapped them, glaring at him furiously as she did so. "I'm not your harlot, Morgan de Lacy. I'll be your cook and housemaid and groom, if you wish, but I'll not live in sin with the likes of you."

Amusement wrinkled his eyes at this return of her spirit. "You would live in sin with the likes of someone else? What are your preferences, Faith, my sweet faerie? A gentleman? An honest farmer? A merchant? I'll be whatsoever you wish. You need only wave your magic wand."

He exuded virility and male confidence, and Faith was seriously tempted to smack him again. The fine lace at his throat was rumpled from their kiss, but the black coat and stark white waistcoat beneath bespoke a gentleman's attire. He was too many men at once, and he suddenly frightened her. He could do anything he wanted to do with her, and she wouldn't have a chance against him. Not knowing perfectly what seduction meant, but understanding clearly the humiliation of brutality, she stared at the upturned lips in his chiseled face with something of awe. Why would he do this to her?

"I'm no faerie," she finally whispered. "I'm a plain, ordinary working girl. You could have beautiful women by the droves. If I cannot just be your housekeeper, let me go on to London. I think I could earn a living with my needle."

Those huge eyes could easily slay dragons. Morgan felt her innocence smite his heart and he flinched inwardly, even as he raised his hand to release her russet curls from the cap and pins. Thick tresses tumbled to her shoulders and beyond, catching the fire's light and playing tricks of red and brown in the glow. A plain, ordinary wench, indeed, but one who gleamed like a candle in the darkness.

"You'll come to learn there's no such thing as plain, ordinary working girls in London, my *cailin*. Sooner or later you will end in some man's bed, willing or no. The city preys on the unprotected, and you're as unprotected as they come. It is time I looked for your grandparents."

The relief and happiness in her eyes sent a wave of guilt through him, but Morgan made no effort to discount her hopes. He had spent seven more years in this world than she had, but all his years had been ones of hardship and hatred. He saw the world through eyes of cynicism so thick it distorted even the loveliest of angels. He could see this enchanting creature in a few years, worn by the toil of fourteen-hour days, nursing a bastard babe at her breast from some man's rape. He could see her cold, noble grandparents turning up their aristocratic noses at this odd Methodist daughter with the sullied reputation of having spent the winter months in a thieves' den. And he saw no hope of happiness for her at all in either place.

But he wouldn't tint her world with the grays and browns of his. Gently Morgan caressed her silken hair and let her hold her dreams a little while longer. "I'll leave for London on the morrow. Tonight, why don't you open the surprise I brought you? I thought you deserved some reward for all your hard efforts."

Faith watched him warily, unsure of his suddenly gentle demeanor. A minute ago he had been holding her in passionate embrace and offering his bed. Now he was treating her as a child again, offering her trinkets. Her gaze strayed to the package he indicated on the table, then back to Morgan's deceptively peaceful smile.

"You have given me room and board. I did not bargain for more."

"Very good. You're learning to be suspicious." Morgan leaned over and grabbed the bundle and dropped it in her hands. "But you'll accept it anyway, in the nature of a bribe. I'd not have an unhappy maiden crying my name and occupation to the authorities, should you leave here. I'm willing to pay for your silence."

He didn't mean that, of course, Faith fully realized. He knew quite well that she would never give him away. But if it made him feel better to say it like that, she would not argue. Strangely reluctant, she picked at the package strings. Morgan's blade quickly ended this excuse for dallying.

The paper spilled open to reveal a shimmering sea of yellow silk. Faith gasped at the striking beauty of it as the delicate folds caught and reflected the firelight and danced and blew in the draft created by the cold and heat combining. Her fingers stroked the feather-light fabric covetously, and she drew it from the folds of the package to billow before her.

Faith sighed as if she had died and gone to heaven. The yellow silk overskirt was lined with white satin, and the elbow-length sleeves had a waterfall of white lace. The delicately embroidered white satin stomacher was modestly adorned by a sheer fabric so fine it could not be compared to a kerchief. It was a lady's gown, and not for someone like her, but just to be able to touch it was worth the having.

Morgan smiled at the ease with which she could be won. Like any woman, she could be charmed with pretty baubles, but hers wasn't a greedy reaction so much as the gentle admiration for something of beauty. She hadn't even imagined herself wearing it yet, had not noticed the lace-edged petticoat or the satin corset and silk stockings beneath it. He had thought to prove her a woman. He had succeeded in proving she was an innocent.

"I do not know if the fit is right. You will need to try it on in the morning. Right now, I think you had best go on to bed. There are shadows under your eyes."

Faith clasped the silk against her and stared at him as if he'd gone berserk. Then Morgan's glance down to the remainder of the package caused hers to follow, and she blushed a bright red. He had bought her intimate garments, as if she were already his mistress.

Where had that thought come from? Startled, she threw him a wide-eyed look and blushed brighter. He could not possibly . . . But he could. Those green eyes said he very definitely could. Her color faded as Faith once again registered the elegance of Morgan's attire, the contrast of fine lace to harsh visage and callused hands, and remembered the seductive tenderness of his mouth. He chose not to, but he very definitely could think of her in the way he thought of Molly.

That knowledge sent a tingle all the way to her toes that had little to do with fear. Laying the precious silk back on the table, Faith carefully walked the distance to the loft. She could feel his gaze boring into her back, but she refused to be intimidated. Things didn't have to change just because he knew she was a woman. She would show him they could remain the same.

As her foot touched the first rung of the ladder, she could hear Morgan's deep voice call softly, "Pull it up behind you, lass, for your own good."

The color rushed to Faith's cheeks and heat raced through her blood just as if he had crept up behind her and kissed her ear again. What had he done to her to make her feel like that with just a word or two?

Understanding the wisdom of obedience in this case, for the first time since they had shared the cottage, Faith pulled the ladder up into the loft with her.

Morgan was gone in the morning before Faith had time to come down or to try on the yellow silk. She tried not to look at the empty cottage with dismay. He had gone to London as he had said he would. Last night was no more than a wicked memory. Morgan wouldn't try to take her to his bed. What need had he of her—a female so small and unformed as to be thought a child? It was absurd to even think of it.

But the bruises on her arms and breasts were very real and marred her skin in places revealed by the gown's décolletage. Faith stared down at herself as she pulled the fine white muslin over her breasts and tucked it into the stiffly embroidered stomacher. The gauzy fabric did not conceal the livid bruises, nor did it disguise the high curve of her breasts pushed up by the corset. Faith took a deep breath and watched the high white curves move with her.

She could feel the silk of the gown rub across her uncovered nipples, and she shivered with some strange longing. She would have to make a chemise to go under this. It was indecent to feel her nakedness beneath the satin corset and silk bodice. Indecent, but very exciting.

Shocked at her wickedness, Faith hastily removed her elegant garments and returned to her old wool ones. They would never feel the same again, and she sent a longing glance to the silk. She knew it was her place in life to wear heavy, coarse wool and work for a living, but she couldn't help dreaming of wealth and elegance. Her mother had given up such a life in return for love. She would have to hope for the riches of love too.

Glancing at the highwayman's cloak hanging beside the door, Faith felt the blood rush to her cheeks once more. What hope of love would she find there? It might be easier to seek wealth.

10

March, 1751

LORD MOUNTJOY'S VALET adjusted his lordship's wig and added a dusting of powder. Behind his face cone, the marquess coughed, and growing impatient with the process, he waved aside the valet and threw down the mask.

His scowl grew blacker at the scuffle of feet and restless rustle of silk behind him. Glancing in the mirror, he could see his son and heir lounging across the settee, sipping at wine, while his nephew stalked the dressing room like a hungry tiger. The two men could not be more unlike, and he could not stifle the unbidden hope that it would someday be his handsome nephew and not his portly son who would take the title.

Made even more irritable by that thought, Mountjoy rose and allowed the valet to remove his dressing robe and bring his coat. He glared at the indolent man sprawled across the chair. "Wine at this hour, Edward? Do you never let your liver rest?"

"The pickling aspects of alcohol have never been thoroughly pursued." Edward raised the crystal to the light and admired the rainbow of colors. "What did you want of us at this ghastly hour, dear pater?"

The man at the window swung around and waited impatiently for the answer to his cousin's question. Dark whereas Edward was fair, lean whereas Edward was rotund, Thomas was a direct antithesis of his cousin, but both held a common interest in this question.

Not for the first time, Mountjoy wondered if he had been wrong to keep them on such short purse strings. He had hoped to teach them financial responsibility, but he very much suspected he had taught them to pray for his early departure from this mortal coil. Well, it was much too late to change his habits now.

He shrugged into the coat the valet held for him. "It has

been over four months since my granddaughter disappeared. The fools and babbling idiots I have paid to trace her can find nothing. It is impossible that a well-brought-up child can disappear from the face of the earth. I want the two of you to find her.''

Both men managed to look bored. The one at the window stared out into the street, evidently intent on some fascinating sight below. The one on the settee reached for the decanter.

"I cannot honestly see the point, dear pater. She is bound to be an uncouth country bumpkin with sharp tongue and pious airs given to hysterics at mention of fire and brimstone. Damme if I can think what you would want with the likes of that.''

"I'll be damned if I can think what I want with the likes of you, either!'' the marquess exploded. Shrugging the valet away, he gestured curtly for the servant to leave, then reached for the decanter in his son's hand. "If you do not find her, I'll leave all that is not entailed to the institution at Bedlam. Bigawd, if they wouldn't know better what to do with it than you.''

The man at the window turned around and lifted a disdainful eyebrow. "That is quite an encouragement for me. I wonder at your calling me here at all. Should this personage be found, Edward inherits everything. Should she not, Bedlam gets half. I rather favor the second option myself.''

This wasn't going at all as the marquess had planned it. He had meant to offer rewards, dangle rich plums before their indolent noses, inspire a little action and concern for their niece and cousin, but as usual, their arrogance had got the better of his temper. Mountjoy growled, "Find her and wed her and you can have Bedlam's share. That way I'll know the line will perpetuate, something neither of you seems eager to do presently.'' He threw his corpulent son a look of disgust.

"That sounds as much punishment as reward,'' the man at the window murmured, turning back to his observation of the street. A lone horseman at the corner caught his eye, and he watched the man's progress as the marquess rattled their cages behind them.

"Then marry someone decent and I'll split the inheritance between both you and her, should she be found. All I want is to see the line carried out and my granddaughter located. That task should be none too difficult.'' The marquess reached for the jewel case on his dressing table and removed the diamond-encrusted ring he favored. The sight of such wealth should set their juices flowing.

The dark-haired cousin concentrated on the interestingly garbed gentleman stopping before the door below. Black was favored only for mourning, but somehow, the man didn't appear to be very mournful. His rugged face did not have the soft features of an idle gentleman, nor bear the wig required of fashion, but the expensive lace at his throat and wrist had the quiet elegance of both. A very interesting character, and about to knock at the door, if he did not mistake.

Smiling, the Honorable Thomas Montague turned and made a brief bow before his uncle and murmured words of departure. Searching for the lost Henrietta was a singular waste of time as far as he was concerned. The chit could not inherit the title and would only dilute what remained of the wealth. No, he had far better plans than marrying a holier-than-thou antidote who was too stupid to find her way out of the woods.

He trotted down the stairs in time to catch the butler opening the front door.

Morgan stared up at the quietly elegant limestone town house, then let his gaze drift down the bank of windows that indicated the number of apartments within. The only Montague he could trace was a marquess, and one wealthy enough to own nearly half a block of London property for his own personal use. The upkeep alone would house half the inhabitants of London's slums for a year. A man did not give up a life like this for something so intangible as religion. Faith's father had to be a liar.

The fact that the marquess was known as having only one son proved Morgan's theory. Even a deceased son should have been mentioned. Unless her father's name was really Edward and not George and he was actually heir to all this magnificence, Morgan very much suspected George Montague had glorified his name and origins. Morgan needed to verify that the heir still lived, but he was uncertain how to go about it. He belonged to none of the gentlemen's clubs and had never made any attempt to take his small place in a society that despised his upbringing. But if Faith were the only daughter of the marquess's heir, he would have to return her to her family for her own good.

Perhaps at the cost of a little ransom. Morgan grinned up at the blank windows. He didn't want to part with his little faerie, and he thought it doubtful that she belonged to so noble a house as this, but just in case . . .

His boots rang out on the stone steps as he climbed up to lift the knocker. What he found within would determine his words, and he waited impatiently for an answer. A few discreet inquiries first, perhaps.

The butler answered the door, but the tall dark gentleman lounging in the foyer behind him was the one to come forward at Morgan's first careful question.

"Mannering, what is this? Do you always leave gentlemen to idle in the streets? Have you an appointment with the marquess, sir?"

Morgan's eyes narrowed as he took in the very proper young man in fashionable cadogan wig and expensively tailored gray silk coat. The aristocratic arrogance of his sharp features and air of authority labeled him the heir, and Morgan didn't know whether to feel relief or disappointment for Faith's sake. He felt certain she would not be happy with a stiff, proud bastard like this one.

"I am searching for the family of George Montague, sir." Morgan refused to offer the obsequious "milord" the man obviously expected. "I have news of some importance to bear. Have I found the right household?"

Thomas had known this was his lucky day. The half-deaf butler had removed himself from hearing, and there was none but himself to deal with this development. Smiling inwardly, he took careful study of this bearer of bad tidings. The visitor was insolent to an extreme, and though garbed in a gentleman's attire, he was no gentleman. The jeweled flash of those green eyes was hard and cold, and the knowing sneer forming on his thin lips deserved a set-down. Thomas obliged.

"I am sorry, sir," he replied coldly. "The name is unknown to me."

Morgan had lived in a world of deceit and lies for the better part of his twenty-five years, a world created by Sassenachs such as this one. He recognized their lies when he heard them. He had been prepared to hear lies. It was no more than he had expected. Faith wouldn't be welcomed here. But glancing over the man's shoulder to the gleaming tiled floors dotted with priceless carpets, the gilded framed oils of Montague ancestors, and the heavily polished mahoganies of an earlier decade, he couldn't help feeling that Faith was being robbed. She deserved some portion of this wealth.

Morgan removed his hat from beneath his arm and adjusted it to his head. "That's a pity. Then I suppose I shall have to visit a solicitor. Perhaps you would recommend one?"

Thomas sucked in his breath and glared at the insolent cad, then took Morgan's elbow and started down the steps to the street with him, discreetly closing the door after them. "I don't know what you want," he ground out between clenched teeth, "but this is a house of mourning. The marquess's health is failing. He can withstand no further shocks. A solicitor will avail you nothing and would only hasten the marquess's departure. Unless that is your intent, I would advise leaving the matter alone."

Morgan caught his horse's reins and pitched a penny to the lad holding them. He gave his companion's nervous features a shrewd look. "What is it worth to you?"

Stunned by this audacity, Thomas glared at the man. With a little careful manipulation, it would be just a matter of time before dear, darling, obese Edward departed this world. The old marquess would be so terrified of losing his only remaining heir that he would gladly grant Thomas everything he wished. Why should he share the proceeds of this hard-earned plan with any mousy Methodist? He could think of no other reason why this thief in black would be blackmailing him.

"The price of your silence will be your health and that of anyone who would make false claims against the estate. George Montague never existed, for all the world knows."

Morgan smiled mirthlessly at this typically British arrogance. The world would no doubt suddenly remember the twenty-year-old scandal of George Montague were its memory jogged. What it would cost Faith was another matter entirely. He mounted his horse and met the heir's gaze steadily. "You can be certain that no one of George Montague's intelligence would wish to claim any part of this family, but against the vagaries of health and fortune, I would suggest a little insurance. A trust fund sufficient to provide a reasonable income for life would be my recommendation, drawn up in the name of . . . let us say, Faith Henrietta Montague? It's a small enough sum to protect against the ill fortunes the future might bring. Registered at the Bank of England, it should be safe enough, and should no one ever claim it, it can always revert to the estate. What could be more fair?''

At this confirmation that the brat lived, Thomas flinched inwardly. He didn't have that kind of money and wouldn't until the old man was dead. Once the old man was dead, it would little matter if the missing heiress appeared. It would be too late for her then. But if he didn't come up with the money, this rogue was threatening to produce the little brat. She could be a fraud for all anyone knew, but the old man was desperate enough to grasp at straws. Delaying tactics might work well until he had time for a plan. Thomas returned the stranger's glare.

''Anyone claiming such a fund would have to have damned good proof.''

''I'll grant you that.'' Morgan shrugged and took up the reins. ''Tie it up nice and neat. It might take two months to work out the details. I'll have my man check with the bank then. I give you good day.'' Morgan made a pretense at tipping his hat and spurred his stallion down the street.

Not until he reached the outskirts of the city did Morgan let his temper roil and burst into rising. Damn the bloody damn arrogant Sassenachs anyway! Who the *hell* did they think they were? He had half a mind to dress Faith in silk and lace and parade her beneath their noses on his arm. He'd hire solicitors and sue the arrogant bastard for half of everything. He could tie the estate up for years until the marquess was choked into offering name and fortune to the woman he had cheated out of her rightful home.

The only flaw in that pattern was Faith. Meek, pious Faith would never claim what was not hers, nor shame her family by behaving in anything other than a ladylike manner. To fight and claw and bribe and flaunt was not her way. Morgan was glad she was not like the rest of the world, but it seemed a damned shame the meek could inherit the earth only after it was stripped bare by greedy leeches.

Perhaps it was all for the best. She didn't belong in that world any more than she belonged in his. He didn't know what world it was that she did belong to, perhaps that of the saints in heaven. Remembering her slight form leaning out of the loft, holding a smoking pistol, and later, offering passionate kisses, Morgan thought perhaps she wasn't quite ready for that world either. There was a lot more to Faith Henrietta Montague than could be seen on the surface.

That thought brought a wicked gleaming smile to his lips. Such a simple solution to so complex a problem! Why had he not thought of it before? The granddaughter of one of the premier lords of the land, the claimant to wealth beyond imagination, and the best damned cook and housekeeper he had ever known. He'd have to be a fool to let her get away, and the good Lord only knew, Morgan de Lacy was no fool.

The descendants of two great Norman families among the British nobility belonged together. She would warm his nights and ease his days, and when the time was right, they would take London by storm. Bigad, he might even be the one to shove the mighty marquess over the precipice into the hell he deserved. And with the wealth he had stolen from beneath their very noses—not to mention off their backs—Morgan could laugh up his sleeves when the Sassenachs were forced to acknowledge him. It was a joyous dream, a blessing from above. He fully anticipated enjoying every minute of it, not the least of which would be the little sprite in his bed.

Morgan had never taken the time to imagine what kind of wife he would like, and he probably never would have imagined one like Faith had he thought about it, but she would suit him admirably. Though she was small and quiet, with a stubborn streak that was something of a nuisance, she was lovely in her own way. He would have no difficulty bedding her and getting her with child. That would drive the marquess into shock of a certainty. Once they were wedded and had found their place in society, they would undoubtedly go their own ways as everyone else did, but he could always rely on Faith's discretion. She would never turn jealous shrew or threaten him with his past. In fact, he rather thought she might be content just to have his children and adorn his home. He would dress her in silks and lace and give her a lovely house to decorate as she wished. He could even imagine being content with just that for any number of years—that, and the full enjoyment of the ultimate revenge.

The trick was to persuade Faith into marriage. She was

no silly miss who would marry the first man who asked. Morgan's credentials were of the worst. What woman in her right mind would marry a highwayman?

But he had the advantage of knowing her response to his kiss. She was too innocent to know where such kisses led. Once he had taken her to his bed, her overactive conscience and religious upbringing would force her to accept his proposal. It would be the best thing for both of them.

Then it would just be a matter of scraping together enough wealth to set themselves up in society. The trust fund couldn't be relied on. He had mentioned that threat merely to twist the bastard's arm and watch him cringe. He might repeat the threat in the future. Should anything happen to him before he could carry off this scheme, Faith would need a regular source of income. He couldn't have her working taverns or sewing other people's clothes. Yes, the trust fund was a good idea, but that would be Faith's.

He might use her name and position, but he would bring his own wealth to this marriage. His robbery had earned him a steady income for some years, since the ill-fated Jacobite uprising had destroyed his hopes and his home. He had expended a goodly sum on the cottage and his horses since then, but otherwise his expenses were few. The amount he had in the funds wouldn't buy him land as yet, but with a little work he could double that amount over the summer. By fall, Faith should be with child, and he should be ready to turn London on its ear. Morgan hoped the marquess was still around when they arrived. Perhaps even Faith would enjoy seeing her father's arrogant family forced to acknowledge an Irish papist on the family tree.

Whistling softly to himself, Morgan stopped at the Raging Bull to recover Faith's clothes and upbraid Whitehead for attempting to ruin children. Leaving the innkeeper shivering in his greasy boots, he rode on to the next village, where he had left an order with a local seamstress. It was one thing to seduce Faith's love of beauty with silk, but her practicality would be persuaded better with serviceable wool.

While he was there, he ordered gowns of dimity and lawn for when the weather changed. With any luck, Faith would not realize the cotton fabrics were nearly as costly as silk. Raising his eyebrows at the price the seamstress quoted, Morgan wondered if he shouldn't be investing in a small cotton plantation. Those colonists were making an exorbitant fortune at those rates, but they were certainly better than shipping it from the Far East. He'd have to look into that sometime. In the meantime, he added a new sewing kit and a bolt of linen to his order.

Content that his purchases would put his courtship off to a good start, Morgan started on the long ride home. He might have to curtail his activities for a while to assure his little Methodist that he was a changed man. Besides, he would need the extra time to seduce her. He didn't want to do this crudely. She was a gentle girl who knew nothing of passion—yet.

Teaching Faith the delights of love would be half the pleasure. He deserved some time off in which to just enjoy himself, and so did she. He wouldn't make a household drudge of her. He would teach her what pleasure could be, show her the joy of lying in the grass and watching the stars rise, indulge in the decadence of satin sheets, perhaps buy her some furs so he could ravish her before the fire. The thought of those wide gray eyes going smoky with desire or lighting with joy stirred his ardor as much as the memory of those firm young breasts in their torn finery.

A woman of his own. Morgan liked the thought. The lands that were to have been his had first belonged to his father, then his brother, and finally to an Englishman. The women he had possessed over his checkered career had never been his. The clothes on his back had often been rags or uniforms paid for by a mercenary army. When he had finally possessed coins enough to buy his own clothes, he had made certain that they were of the finest quality. He would be a fool to do less with a wife.

And Faith was of the finest quality. Never would he have a chance like this again. Perhaps in the past he had favored buxom women with wiles to seduce him, but he wouldn't take such common trollops as wife. Clean-scented, dainty, innocent Faith would be the bride he would have chosen had he remained in Ireland and claimed his title. Even her name suited him. Faith. She would need faith to believe he could restore her to the life she deserved. And in her trust, he saw his redemption.

Seduction for the purpose of marriage could not be so wrong. His intentions were pure. She just needed to be persuaded to see that a lifetime with him would not be so bad a thing. That wouldn't be so easily done while all he claimed was a one-room hovel and a reputation as a thief. But there was more to life than the physical present. He could teach her that.

Morgan had no illusion that she would be grateful. Not at first, leastways. But after he offered marriage and she grew accustomed to the idea, Faith would see the practicality of it. Life with him couldn't be worse than the life of an overworked seamstress or tavern maid. Not in his opinion, anyway.

11

FAITH HEARD THE thundering hoofbeats of Morgan's arrival but refused to run to the window to look out. All day she had denied the hope that Morgan's journey to London tried to raise. It would be impossible to find her family in a city that large. They would not live in London. They would all be dead or have lost their money and traveled to other shores. Worst of all, they would all be alive and well and want nothing to do with her.

The list of possibilities was too long to place any hope in Morgan's inquiries. Perhaps she would let herself hope he had found her a position in a nice house, somewhere she could be safe and comfortable while she worked hard to advance herself. That was her only dream. She knew she was educated far beyond the means of any servant; but she didn't have to let anyone know that. She was too young to be considered seriously as companion or governess, so servant it would have to be. The life of poverty she had lived with her parents had certainly taught her the position of servant well enough.

She stirred the stew and checked the bread and carefully arranged the plates on the table while Morgan took his horse to the barn. She understood why his horses came first. Even if he had the most exciting news of the century for her, he would brush down his horse first. Perhaps that was one of the reasons that she trusted the highwayman. He had a sense of duty and responsibility that she had not expected to find in a thief.

But even so, it was time that she left. March was almost over and the weather was more than suitable for her to leave. He had said she was not charity, and perhaps he did need her a little bit, but she could not in all conscience continue living off the proceeds of his immoral occupation.

To be perfectly truthful with herself, she wasn't certain

that she could continue living with this man without becoming too attached to him, and that would be disastrous. One of these nights, he would not come home, and she didn't want to be here when that happened. She had lost too much as it was. To lose Morgan to a bullet or a hangman's noose would be more than she could bear.

So she prayed for a solution as she heard Morgan's boots coming up the path. She would never grow used to the sight of him as he flung open the door and entered in a rush of fresh air and masculine energy, the lace at his throat and wrist catching in the breeze, the firelight illuminating the blue-black gleam of his clubbed hair. By day's end his jaw was shadowed by his dark beard, giving his broad cheekbones a pirate's cast, but his white smile could charm the devil himself. Faith fell for it every time.

"I don't know which is more heavenly, the sight of you or the smell of bread baking." Morgan strode in, peeling off his black coat in the room's warmth. In shirtsleeves and waistcoat he seemed some demigod ill-suited to his crude surroundings.

Faith managed a faint smile as the room suddenly filled with the sight and sound of him. "I rather suspect the bread," she murmured with a hint of humor. "When did you last eat?"

Morgan grinned and flung his satchel over the chair. Then in a stride he crossed to where she set down his pot of coffee and lifted her clear of the floor to plant a swift kiss on her surprised lips.

The suddenness left Faith quite off-balance, and she was back on her feet before she had time to protest. Morgan was already crossing the room in search of his coffee mug, but she could still feel the overpowering strength of his arms and chest surrounding her, and the surprising fierceness of his lips on hers. She touched a wondering finger to her mouth before hurriedly wiping her hands on her apron and returning to the stew. He was just happy about something and meant nothing by his exuberance.

His happiness made her hopes soar despite her best efforts. She finished setting the table and tried to ignore the bulging satchel as Morgan poured his coffee. When he started unpacking it, Faith tried to don an expression of disapproval. Surely he had not gone thieving in broad daylight—but his purchases were bought with ill-gotten coins too, she reminded herself.

"If you are to work for me, you must have some service-able clothing," Morgan announced authoritatively.

Faith's hopes plummeted, but she managed an obedient nod before turning to remove the bread from the iron oven. He had not been able to locate her family and hoped to soften the blow by buying her more useless clothing. She didn't wish to dampen his jovial mood or seem ungrateful for his generosity, but the loneliness welling up inside her right now was an awful thing. She missed her parents dread-fully. It had seemed a small wish that there might be family out there somewhere that she could claim.

Morgan eyed her turned back speculatively. He had tried all day to think of some way of softening the blow, but how did one soften the knowledge that her family would prefer she had never been born? He couldn't, so he tore open the dressmaker's package and produced a soft silver wool.

"This is not very fancy, but it will keep your knees warm when you walk to the barn."

Faith had to giggle at such a description and turned to admire the gown he held out for her. As usual, it was better than any she had possessed before, and far too grand for watering animals. A smile touched her lips as she touched the soft fabric. "You spoil me, Morgan. My other gowns are quite warm enough. Now, sit, and let me fill your plate."

Doggedly Morgan ignored her offer and produced a smoky blue gown of identical make but with the addition of a touch of lace to sleeve and modesty piece. "I couldn't decide which color would look best with your eyes, so I had the seamstress make up both."

Faith stared incredulously at the gowns. "Make it up? These are never new! Oh, Morgan, that is criminal waste! You should not have. I can do very well with the needle. I made the green gown fit, didn't I? You must not be spending your coins on me. There are too many things you need here. You could have bought seed for a garden, or a cow, or new plates and cups. Why would you do such a thing?"

He could swear there were tears in her eyes, and Morgan felt the first twinge of dismay. This wasn't going to be as easy as he had thought. The silk had worked so well, he had thought to repeat the success. He should have remem-bered the perversity of her nature.

Flinging aside his plans, Morgan drew Faith into his arms and tried to comfort her. "I'll buy you a cow and seeds if that is what you wish, but do not begrudge the few coins I spend to please myself. It is not often I have a lovely woman to come home to. I would see her dressed to suit me. You are too lovely to be hidden by old sacks and other people's castoffs. I did not mean to make you unhappy."

Faith curled her fingers into the luxurious satin of Morgan's waistcoat and let the strength and comfort of his hold seep through her veins. She was so lonely, and he held her so securely, she could not resist this moment as she ought. Leave it to Morgan to paint a selfish face on his actions. Perhaps he was right. Perhaps he had done it for himself, but he could just as easily have bought his horse new tack if that were the case. But the horse wouldn't care, and she did. She wished she dared dart a quick kiss to his rough cheek, but she had not grown so bold as that.

"The gowns are too lovely for the likes of me," she whispered against his chest before separating herself from this tempting embrace. "I know I must work for a living now. Only a lady of leisure deserves such finery."

Morgan caught her arm and didn't let go. His gaze was fierce as it held hers. "I'll buy you more should these be ruined with your perennial tasks. I can't offer you much, Faith, but you'll find me generous with what I have to give. I don't wish to lose you."

Faith's heart fluttered briefly in her chest at the sincerity in his deep voice and the possessiveness in his hold. She glanced up to catch the intensity of his green gaze, then forced herself to ask, "You found nothing of my family today?"

She made it so very easy for him. Better to leave her this small hope than dash it with the bitter truth. Morgan traced the delicate line of her cheekbones with his finger. "I could find no Lord Montague, lass. Did you not bring away your parents' marriage lines, or some official document of your birth? You will need those in any case to prove your parentage." And to claim that trust fund the deuced heir was going to cough up, if he had any say in the matter. And then when that was secured, they could flaunt those papers in the face of London society, and they would have to accept Faith for what she was.

Of course. Faith's eyes lit as she broke free and smiled

up at Morgan's distressed tones. "I left my father's books and papers behind with a neighbor. All the information will be in there, I am certain." Her smile faltered a little as she realized the import of what she said. "It could take weeks to go back to Cornwall to get them. I left in such a hurry . . ."

Morgan pushed her into the chair. "Don't fret over it now. Have a bite before it all gets cold. We will plan something. Perhaps we can write to your neighbor and have her put the papers on the coach."

Faith obediently filled her plate. "She cannot read. She would have to take the letter to the vicar or squire, and they hated my father. I would not have them learn of my father's papers. He was writing a book, and that manuscript is all I have left of him."

This was a new facet of her life he did not know, and Morgan sent her a quick look. She seemed to find it perfectly acceptable to be despised by such pillars of village society as the vicar and squire. What kind of life must she have led to have such a calm outlook on things? No wonder she had adapted so well to his life as society's outcast.

"Let me ask around and see if I cannot find someone who knows the area or will be willing to go there. Could none of your Methodist friends read?"

"Wesleyans. They are called Wesleyans. I suppose if a new teacher has been sent to the area, he would be able to read, but I would not know whom to address it to. My neighbor might take a letter to a new Wesleyan teacher if there were one. Do you really think it might help if you have those papers?"

Morgan savored his mouthful of stew before answering. If nothing else, those papers would secure that trust fund should he be able to bend her uncle's arm a little more. She deserved that much, and he would see she had it. Life was too uncertain at best to forgo any opportunity. For a female on her own, "uncertain" was a very mild word for her existence. He swallowed the stew and nodded. "There may be names and places on those papers that I could use to search for your family. Write the letter, and I will find someone to send with instructions on who's to read it.

Faith drew strength from this small hope, and she threw him the grateful look he had expected earlier. "Thank you,

Morgan de Lacy. You are a good man when you wish to be.''

He snorted and returned to his food. She knew nothing about men or she would not say that. He intended to get rich off the wealth of others and use her to reclaim his place in society. By the end of this week he meant to have her beneath him in his bed. Good had nothing to do with him. ''Clever'' and ''determined'' would have been better words.

After their meal, while Faith cleaned away the food and plates, Morgan emptied his satchel on the table and carried it out to the stable. Perhaps he ought to ride tonight, after all. His plan to lure Faith into his arms had fallen flat. It was lucky for him that his strategy on the road was more successful than at home or he'd be dangling from the gallows tree by now. Why should women be more difficult to conquer than a bloody mail coach? Perhaps he was using the wrong approach, but the idea of using force on an innocent appalled him. Perhaps he had more conscience left than he suspected.

Inside, Faith dried the last fork and tucked it neatly in its place, then turned to investigate the mess Morgan had left strewn across the table. She had already discovered that he had no patience with neatness inside the house, although he always kept his barn and horses immaculate. His priorities were quite plain.

The bolt of linen brought a smile to her lips. She had a dozen uses for the cloth, and her fingers itched to begin measuring and cutting. If she only had lace, she could make Morgan a shirt unmatched by any of the tailored ones he owned. But without lace she could make more serviceable garments. Her chemises were too small and beyond repair. She could make new stomachers for her old gowns. There wouldn't be quite enough for a petticoat, but perhaps she could sew another plain shirt for Morgan. The possibilities were tantalizing.

Lifting the cloth to better size it, Faith discovered the sewing kit beneath. Not daring to believe her eyes, she set the linen aside and gently touched the tapestried case. It was much larger than the one she owned. Perhaps it was a gentleman's shaving kit or something else private that she should not touch. Morgan always shaved outdoors, and she had very carefully avoided watching this intimate function, but the straight edge he used was much larger than this case, she decided, and a man wouldn't choose tapestry. Her fingers trailed along the edge of the case to the fastening.

She really shouldn't pry. He hadn't offered it to her. But curiosity was more than she could bear. Perhaps she didn't have a family or home, but she had a love of nice things, and the delicate pattern of the tapestry held her gaze. What would it hurt to just peer inside, to satisfy her curiosity? He hadn't hidden it, after all. Surely he knew she would tidy away whatever he left on the table.

Reassured by that thought, Faith pried open the fastening. Inside, a glitter of silver made her catch her breath. The firelight caught and reflected the polished gleam of long-nosed scissors, an assortment of fine needles, and a thimble engraved with the delicate lines of a rose. The other side of the case held several spools of thread in different colors, and tears puddled behind Faith's eyelids. Never had she owned such luxury. And beyond the shadow of any doubt, she knew the impossible man meant it for her use. Morgan de Lacy had never put thread to needle in his life.

Clutching the marvelous gift, Faith lifted her head at the sound of his contented whistle in the yard. That she had disappointed him with her reaction to his generous gift of the gowns, she knew. But she had been devastated by the dashing of all her dreams, and the gowns weren't adequate compensation. But this . . . She glanced down at the gleaming silver, and her hopes soared again. With tools like these, she could do anything.

Without giving a second thought to what she did, Faith lifted her skirts and flew out of the house.

The meager warmth of the March sun had faded with evening, but the chill of the night air could not compare to the ice of the winter. Well-fed and cosseted during these months in the highwayman's home, Faith felt none of the chill now. Warm blood flowed through her veins, stirred by the spring air and an indefinable something that emanated from the man lathering down his horse in the yard.

Morgan looked up in surprise as Faith raced toward him, her skirts flying about her legs, her curls escaping the braid's confinement, her cheeks rosy, and her lips parted with some secret joy. The image lingered, printed on his brain for many days after. She was laughing, and the happiness reached her eyes for the first time since they had met. His heart turned over in his chest, and without thinking, Morgan dropped his brush and held out his arms to take her up.

She flew into them without hesitation, her arms wrapping around his neck in exuberance. "It's lovely! Why did you not tell me you bought it? May I use it? Please? I'll sew you the finest shirt you've ever owned. I promise Morgan, tell me I may use it."

Had she not held the object of her affection in her hand, Morgan would have been hard pressed to place the source of her joy. As it was, he grinned and held her welcome slenderness a little more closely than was necessary.

"I merely sought to replace your old ones, my *cailin*. 'Twas the least I could do in return for your talented fingers."

Breathless now that she found herself trapped against his hard body, Faith turned her suddenly nervous gaze to Morgan's rugged features. A shock of ebony hair fell across his high brow, the hard lines at the corners of his mouth had softened, and his eyes crinkled with mild amusement as he smiled down at her. That smile sent a sudden jolt through her chest, and she knew she had behaved with unfitting abandon. That smile told her so, but she could not move away even as she knew his head lowered with a determination she ought to avoid. Fascinated, her gaze lingered on his lips, then rose to meet Morgan's eyes, and then there was no stopping him.

Faith's lids fluttered and closed as Morgan's mouth touched hers. She tasted of him, the flavors of beef and coffee mixing with the gentle touch of his lips to prove the reality of what was happening. The warmth of his breath flowed over her and into her, and any coldness from the night air dissipated. There was only the touch of his flesh on hers, the strength of his arms around her, and the need to be closer. Faith's hands moved to tangle in his queue, absorbing the texture of Morgan's skin above his neckcloth, reveling in the coarseness of his thick hair. This couldn't be happening, but she would deny it later. Her lips parted beneath the gentle pressure of his tongue, and all was lost.

Morgan cradled her against him, simply enjoying the pleasure of Faith's lithe body bent into his, while his mouth explored the innocence of her kiss. When she surrendered so easily, his passion soared, but her gasp of surprise kept

his feet on the ground. She had never been kissed like this.
Let her lessons begin with this simplest of pleasures.

As his tongue tenderly taught her the meaning of possession, Faith clung more tightly to Morgan's shoulders. Her
whole world was spinning around her, and this man was the
axis on which it spun. Her surrender was complete, and had
he gone further, she would not have protested. In fact, relief
swept through her at this chance to give herself into another's care. She had no experience in taking care of herself.
It would be so much easier to let a man of Morgan's strength
and knowledge lead the way.

As if he sensed the direction of her emotions, Morgan
regretfully pulled back. His lips continued to caress her face,
lingering at the corners of her eyes, brushing against the
wisps of curl along her brow, giving them both time to come
to terms with the desires rapidly overtaking them.

"*Bean sídhe*," he murmured against her hair, "you take
my breath away."

Reluctantly Faith attempted to disengage herself from his
intimate position. Color rose to her cheeks at the realization
of how wildly she had abandoned herself. She couldn't meet
his eyes as she grasped at his words for reality. "Faerie
woman? I'm scarce even a woman, and certainly not a faerie."

Morgan grinned and kept a grip on her long braid so she
wouldn't go far. "You're definitely a woman, lass, or you
would not have kissed me like that. And you must have a
faerie's magic, or I would not have kissed you back. You're
dangerous to a man's sleep, my *cailin*. I'll hear your wailin'
all the night long now."

Faith noted the laughter in his eyes with suspicion. "Why
would I wail all night long? That sounds absurdly foolish to
me."

He chuckled at the pragmatic expression in those lovely
gray eyes. No romantic miss, this, but it wasn't romance he
was offering. Morgan tilted her small chin with his finger
and placed a light kiss on her nose. "I'll explain someday.
Would you like to see a bit o' town on the morrow? I'm
thinking you'll stay on the mare well enough now."

She knew to distrust his brogue. He turned it off and on
with the same charm as his elusive smile. Morgan de Lacy
was a dangerous man, in more ways than one. But the
thought of seeing something other than the four walls of the

cottage damned suspicion. She responded eagerly to the suggestion, forgetting that she meant to be cook and house-keeper and nothing more.

"Could we? London? I've always dreamed of London. Is it as large as they say?"

He might live to regret showing her the world outside his meager habitation, but Morgan could no more deprive her of this treat than he could starve his horses. Besides, he needed to get a messenger to Cornwall, and his best con-tacts were in the city.

"It is, so you'd best be up early to see it all. Write that letter to your neighbor and we'll send it off while we're there. And kiss me one more time to keep me warm until I come in."

Faith turned him an uncertain glance, but Morgan gave her little time for indecision. With a swiftness that left her gasping, he bent and took what he wanted. The heated touch of his lips was swift and searing.

Faith turned around and fled to the house the instant he released her. By the time she reached the protection of the door, her heart was pounding painfully in her chest, and it wasn't from the exertion of the run.

12

FAITH SQUIRMED NERVOUSLY under the scrutiny of the wizened old man behind the counter. She didn't like this place Morgan had brought her to. The stench of the docks crept in through every nook and cranny, and there were more than enough of those. Her gaze drifted to the bare cobweb-coated rafters, and she shivered, imagining a giant wharf rat staring back at her. The filthy windows high above the floor gave no light. Only the ancient lantern behind the clerk provided any illumination at all. Faith decided it was better that way.

The man's shrewd eyes followed her movement as she stopped behind Morgan, lifting her petticoats from the filth of the floor. She was as out-of-place in this den of iniquity as the sun on a moonless night, but she did not realize this reason for his stare. She only felt nervous and wished Morgan would hurry with his business.

From the odd assortment of items lining the shelves and walls of the warehouse, Faith greatly suspected this was where Morgan brought his ill-gotten goods to sell. That meant the old man was as much a thief as Morgan, and she shivered at the thought. She had difficulty remembering that her employer was a man with a price on his head, that he had in all probability murdered and wounded in his efforts to enrich himself. She ought to be looking for a way out, planning her escape, but instead, she moved closer to his protection.

His business completed, Morgan took Faith's arm and led her out into the spring sunshine. The unexpected warmth of this early spring promised rain later in the day, but for the moment, he was glad for it. Faith's small face turned eagerly to the sunshine as a flower does after a long night, and he breathed a small sigh of relief. He had felt her tension back there in the warehouse, but there had been no help for it if they were to get her letter read by the proper people. She didn't belong in these dark environs along the river, but in the elegance of those mansions in the West End. The thought was momentarily depressing, but Morgan banished it with a smile.

"Where would you like to begin, milady? The shops in Bond Street, perhaps? We could buy you a frilly cap and some ribbons for your hair. Or find you some of those high-heeled shoes the ladies are so fond of wearing. What is your choice?"

Faith bit her bottom lip and threw Morgan a hesitant glance. She had only wanted to see the city. She hadn't meant for him to spend money on her. If she reprimanded him for spending his stolen coin, he would be insulted and it would ruin their outing. But if he insisted on spending his money . . . Her glance grew thoughtful as she regarded his impatient expression.

"Is there a market where I might buy a few herbs? And seeds, for a garden. And if they had some new onions . . ."

Morgan stared at her as if she had gone berserk; then, shrugging his shoulders, he hoisted her back on the mare. "Let us stable these nags and then we'll walk through Covent Garden. Perhaps you'll find something a little less prosaic than onions there."

As they rode, Morgan eyed her slender back, emphasized by the fullness of the blue skirt he had bought for her. He had envisioned wining and dining his little maid, then wooing her with baubles and trinkets before tumbling her into his bed. Why did he keep thinking his Faith was anything like other women? A pretty bonnet and a silk stocking wouldn't persuade her into giddiness. But onions?

He snorted at this unromantic notion and plotted more carefully. Tumble her, he would, but he wanted her to have as few regrets afterward as he could arrange. If onions and herbs were what it took to make her feel secure, he would shower her with every leaf and vegetable in the market.

Faith's eyes were wide from staring up at the towering limestone buildings and magnificent Gothic cathedrals they passed before they reached Covent Garden. All thoughts of onions fled when the sun caught on the stained glass of St. Paul's. The towering dome drew her gaze to the heavens, and she felt as if God were looking directly on her. Staring upward, she almost missed the ragged urchin darting beneath her horse's nose, and the peddler who chased him screamed a curse as she came between him and his prey.

The mare gave a whinny of protest and threw her head nervously, nearly unsettling Faith's precarious hold, but Morgan was swiftly at her side, soothing the animal and sending the peddler on his way with a stream of invectives that singed Faith's ears. She didn't know whether to offer him gratitude for his help or scold him for his language. He was always doing this to her, leaving her bewildered and confused.

Morgan took a more protective position next to her, and she threw him an anxious look. He sat tall in the saddle, managing his massive stallion with the ease of one born to ride. He made no attempt to disguise himself, but rode the streets with his black hair neatly queued beneath his silver-trimmed cockaded hat. Instead of his black cloak, he wore a long black frock coat with the split seam in back for riding. The hilt of his sword gleamed through another slit, giving a hint of his dangerousness, but otherwise he could be a gentleman in heavy mourning. The expensive lace at his throat and wrist had been discarded for a plain cravat and just a ruffle of linen at the cuff. No one would suspect such a superior-looking gentleman of being other than what he appeared.

Faith glanced down at her own attire and sighed. The elegant blue wool fitted neatly to her slender waist, but there was little enough for the lovely satin stomacher to conceal. Her long skirts spread out like a lady's, but she had no hoops or panniers to give them grace. Her unpowdered hair was pinned as neatly as she could make it beneath her frilly cap, but she had no illusion that she appeared a lady. Restlessly she watched the other inhabitants of the city for a sight of real elegance.

Her eyes narrowed as she watched Morgan's gaze follow a woman in a puce *robe à la française*. Her powdered wig was dressed higher than fashion decreed, and her square-cut bodice went without the modesty piece that should conceal her voluptuous bosom. Firm white curves rose high and full against the clinging silk of her gown, and a gold necklace dangled between these bounteous hills to draw the eye. Faith could not tell if Morgan eyed the necklace or the beauty more covetously.

Irritated, Faith urged her mount to a faster gait, distracting Morgan from his musings. She knew very little of men, but she was quite certain her father was right on this: men would take whatever was offered them, with little or no discrimination. And she had all but offered herself to Morgan last night.

She must be ten times a fool. She was no more than cook or housekeeper to him. He called her pretty names and brought her lovely presents because he was a charmer and wished to keep her services. If she offered him more than he bargained for, she had only herself to blame. Only a fool would think the highwayman had any real interest in someone who looked as she did.

Morgan caught up with her and threw her a puzzled look, but the street was growing too noisy and crowded to carry on a conversation. Deciding they had gone far enough, he guided her toward a livery on a nearby street and helped her to dismount.

"We'll go from here by foot, lass, if you do not mind. I've no wish to be pulling you out from under a horses' hooves if the mare gets nervous." Morgan caught Faith's waist and brought her down beside him, not immediately letting her go. He felt her tension beneath his fingers, and her averted gaze made him smile. She was learning, but not fast enough. Morgan tilted her chin with his finger and brought it back around. "A smile, *cailin*, I would have a smile from you. Have I done aught that is wrong this day?"

Faith shook her head but did not meet his gaze. "You need not lead me about like a child. I can find my way if you wish to go about your own business," she answered diffidently, without the smile he requested.

"What business? Did ye think I'd spend the day robbing people at gunpoint? Lass, have a little of what your name proclaims you to be. I'll not shame you like that."

Astounded that he would think such a thing of her, Faith finally looked up to meet his fierce gaze. "I never thought such a thing. I just thought . . ." She stumbled over speaking her wayward thoughts, but his gaze demanded reply. "I thought . . . perhaps there were *men* things you wished to do. You cannot be interested in herbs and seeds."

Green eyes lit with irreverent laughter as Morgan translated her shyness correctly. A wicked smile working the corners of his mouth, he released her chin and ran his broad hand seductively over the curve of her tiny waist. " 'Tis *men* things that hold my interest, to be sure, but why would I look elsewhere than my very own faerie woman? Let us proceed to the herbs and seeds, my lady, and I'll take care of my business while you take care of yours.''

Faith studied him uncertainly, not knowing what to make of this brash statement. Deciding he was teasing her, she nodded slowly and allowed herself to be led away. Morgan's hold upon her waist was light and protective, not anything to fear. Why did she feel as if he meant a good deal more when he caressed her like that?

The stableman accepted Morgan's coins and led the horses away, struggling to hold the restive stallion in line. Morgan watched them go with the frown of a concerned father, but then he caught himself, and whistling, led Faith toward the markets. She did not yet understand her powers as a woman, and he rather preferred it that way. He had no time or patience for a woman's nagging demands or constant ploys for attention. A woman like that lightskirt he had seen down the road would never be content with the isolation and meager time and housing he could provide. She would soon find the inn and spread her legs for every man who offered her a trinket. But Faith, now . . .

Ahhh, Faith, the innocent. Morgan bent her an amused look as she eagerly scanned the market stalls. Perhaps she appeared little more than a child, but he had bedded more voluptuous beauties with less passion than Faith possessed in her little finger. It wasn't the wrapping that counted, but the contents, and Faith's delicate wrapping concealed a powder keg of explosives, he was willing to gamble. Just the thought brought a stirring to his loins, and he idled the morning away imagining how and when he would finally take her.

His thoughts were not all lustful ones, however. When Faith indicated an interest in a bunch of new onions, Morgan reached for his purse, but to his surprise, Faith stayed him. With a firm set to her jaw, she announced the greens were much too dear, and she would look elsewhere. The peddler instantly raised a protest, and the two set down to serious haggling, while Morgan listened in amazement. It was the first time that morning that he heard his shy companion's skills, but not the last.

By luncheon, Faith had flirted with a butcher to achieve the best cut of meat, carried on a learned discussion with the herbmonger and doubled her purchase for half the price, and wistfully rejected the purchase of a blue ribbon for her hair because the man counted on Morgan to pay the higher price and wouldn't believe Faith could walk away. Morgan almost fell for it, except something in the determined shake of her russet curls warned he would be in dire trouble should he undermine her pride. He bought the ribbon elsewhere for less, bringing the brilliant smile he had requested earlier.

By the time they found a respectable inn and stopped for a midday meal, they were loaded down with paper-wrapped parcels. Faith contentedly arranged them all in a straw basket Morgan purchased for the occasion, and made no complaint that all she had seen of the city was a street full of market stalls. Her smile was just as rapturous as if he had presented her with the crown jewels. More so, Morgan decided, for she wouldn't know what to do with jewels.

In a tavern full of flamboyant silks and satins—and that just the men—Faith's discreetly modest appearance succeeded in causing quite a stir. Morgan noted with satisfaction the heads that turned as she walked by on his arm, and he signaled the proprietor for a private parlor. Despite her poverty, Faith had the grace of a duchess. Men would always notice her, but she didn't seem to notice them.

There wasn't an ounce of vanity in her, Morgan observed as she willingly followed him into the privacy of the small chamber. A beautiful woman would prefer the attention she drew in the public rooms. He would be forced to share her with every man who made her head turn. But Faith . . . Faith had that indefinable something that made her a lady. She wasn't beautiful in the classical way, but men liked to look at her and imagine what they couldn't have. Only she didn't realize that, and therein lay his advantage.

Morgan ordered for both of them and turned his attention back to his lovely companion. Her cheeks were still flushed with the morning's triumphs, and her eyes sparkled with enjoyment as she gazed around the tiny parlor with its brocade settee and blackened oils on the walls. He doubted if she had ever eaten in a private parlor, and he let her take her time in absorbing what was, after all, a very unsophisticated room. He used the time wisely by studying the loveliest object to grace the room—Faith.

Her slender white throat would look well wrapped in pearls. The modesty piece of her gown hid the young firm curves beneath, but Morgan imagined removing that scrap of cloth to cherish those soft mounds in his rough hands. He knew she deserved a gentleman's uncallused hands, but the likelihood of her ever meeting the right sort of gentleman was small. He would have to make that up to her somehow, but that wasn't his most pressing concern.

He watched the color rise from her breasts to her throat and realized he was staring. With an apologetic smile, Morgan took her hand. "You're a beautiful woman, lass. What are you doing being seen with the likes of me?"

Faith blushed deeper, her eyes not quite meeting his. She had been thinking how handsome he was, how much more dashing than those feeble fops in the other room. To have those blazing eyes turned on her as if she were a princess at a ball was unsettling to a deep degree. She preferred the friendly companionship they had developed at the cottage.

"Don't waste your wicked tongue on me, Morgan de Lady." She strained for the easy give-and-take of earlier. "It's polished enough, and you'll not be turning my head."

"Aye, and you're a hard woman to win, me Faith, but I'll have you yet. Where would I be without a haggler like yourself at my side? Had I only met you sooner, I'd be a rich man this day. Say you'll never leave me, *cailin.*"

That kind of banter she had learned to expect of him, and Faith responded with a relieved smile. "I'll not leave you if you promise to show me the lions. I've never seen lions. Are they as magnificent as I have heard?"

She didn't believe a word he said, and rightly so, Morgan supposed. Nevertheless, she would be his, and tonight would not be soon enough for him. Still holding her hand, he leaned back in the chair. "They are poor, mangy beasts that have lived in squalor too long. I cannot imagine what it is the English feel when they bring a mighty creature to its knees, but I have no stomach for it. If that is the price of your fair body, I must pass with regrets. Perhaps you would compromise and do me the pleasure of attending the theater with me tonight? I cannot find you a box seat, but I shall do the best I can."

His references to her body made Faith glance up quickly with a blush, but Morgan so smoothly moved on to a topic of more interest that she found herself listening intently. The idea of actually attending a theater performance brought sparkles to her eyes.

"A real theater? One with lights and everything? Not just a puppet show?" she demanded eagerly.

"Covent Garden, on my honor." Morgan crossed himself solemnly.

"But I am not dressed!" She threw a look down at her gown. It was the loveliest thing she had ever known, but she remembered well her mother's tales of glorious silks and feathers and jewels. How could she go like this? She needed the yellow gown, but she could not have worn it on horseback.

Morgan pressed her hand reassuringly. "We will have to sit in the pit, not among the nobility, lass. You'll be more beautiful than any other around us, I promise."

He wouldn't lie in this. Faith breathed a sigh of bliss and smiled at his angularly lined features. The concern in his gaze instantly fled, to be replaced with mischievous humor. He was many men at once, but she preferred this one. There had been so little humor in her life, she could not even object when he laughed at her. The highwayman would not ride this night, and her smile broadened at the thought. To-night he would be the laughing gentleman. The thought sent delicious shivers down her spine.

Had she known the ride the highwayman planned for this night, she would have shivered in earnest. Morgan watched her eager expression with the hunger of a cat about to pounce. He would wine her and dine her and woo her, and when it was too late for anything else, he would bring her back here and they would ride together to a world of passion he would introduce to her. Then there would be no further questions of her ever leaving him, and he could go back to the business of robbing the Sassenachs blind.

More than a little pleased with his plan, Morgan didn't argue when Faith refused the ale the waiter brought. There was all of the day and night to go, and he didn't wish her ill with drink. There was time enough for everything.

After luncheon they meandered through the market and down to the Strand, where Morgan pointed out Somerset House, the Savoy Palace, the law courts, and Temple Bar. He turned back toward the markets before they strayed too close to the devil's hole of Fleet Street and its environs. The prisons and the motley denizens living in their shadows cut too close to home. They passed by innumerable coffee-houses, where gentlemen sat sipping their favorite beverages, reading their newssheets, and discussing the latest Jacobite scandal or laying wagers on the completion date for Westminster Bridge.

Faith was content to drink in the sights and sounds of the bustling streets. She stopped at a bookseller's and admired the latest edition by Goldsmith, dawdled before a display of straw hats in a milliner's window, and watched the variety of silks and satins on parade around her. She refused Morgan's offers to buy her any of these, but she could not refuse his offer of a candied apple from a street vendor or a nosegay of flowers from an urchin. She sniffed the flowers with delight and offered him the same smile he would have received had he given her diamonds and pearls.

That smile was almost his undoing. The complete innocence and joy of it made Morgan have second and third thoughts about his callous plans. Who was he to rob her of the last remnants of childhood? She deserved better than a thief with a price on his head, a man who could offer her nothing but the shelter of his home. Once, his name would have been strong protection and a reason to hold her head high, but the bloody Sassenachs had robbed the best of it and he had himself destroyed the remainder. De Lacy stood for nothing more now than a rabid Irishman determined to have his own back.

But it would mean more eventually, and she had no better offer. Morgan satisfied his conscience with that thought. No honest man would have her after she had spent the winter with him. He was only doing the right thing, albeit in the wrong way. Had he the proper time and circumstances, he would woo her and wed her and then bed her, but there wasn't time for those niceties. Too many obstacles stood in their way. No, it was much better to have this done and out of the way. Then he could be about the business of seeking their fortune. He had only her best interests in mind.

So, with Faith's best interests in mind, Morgan bought a jug of wine, a hunk of cheese, and a loaf of bread, and escorted Faith to an evening at the theater.

Romeo and Juliet offered the most promising performance.

13

TEARS POURED DOWN Faith's cheeks as the final curtain closed, and she clung to Morgan's large arm as they stumbled with the crowd out of the theater.

"Why didn't you tell me it had an unhappy ending?" She hiccuped slightly, a result of the wine she had consumed throughout the evening. Her head felt giddy, but she was perfectly sober, she knew. And angry. Plays shouldn't end like that.

Morgan glanced at her with surprise, and smiled slightly at the sight of her tearstained face. "It's Shakespeare. I thought you would be familiar with it."

Faith shook her head vehemently, loosening a few more curls to soften the sharp bones of her face. "My father didn't believe in fiction. I'm glad I never read Shakespeare, if that's what he wrote. They died! That's a terrible way to end the play. People aren't supposed to die in make-believe. They're supposed to live happily ever after. People only die in real life."

Morgan's smile was indulgent. "You've had a trifle too much wine, my faerie. The best fiction reflects real life. Shakespeare wrote humorous plays too, but his tragedies are said to be the best."

"Well, I don't want to see tragedies. I can cry easily enough over the tragedies I see around me. Don't ever take me to another, Morgan de Lacy. I'll never forgive Shakespeare for writing such a horrible play."

He chuckled at the petulant pout of her lower lip. The wine had loosened her rigid inhibitions very successfully. Here was the real Faith Montague, not the starched-up doll she tried to portray. He was glad he'd never met the straitlaced father who had transformed the magical child into a pasteboard caricature of himself. There were emotions buried deep, indeed, behind the gray walls of her eyes. Tonight he would start plumbing for them.

With that thought in mind, Morgan caught Faith's waist and swung her into the darkness of a narrow alley. She gasped with surprise, but did not pull away when he leaned over her, one hand braced against the wall behind her. "I apologize and I shall never take you to another tragedy again. Will you ever forgive me?"

He was laughing at her, Faith knew. She didn't need to see the twinkle in his eyes to verify it. But she didn't care. She looked up expectantly to the bright flash of Morgan's smile against the dark and knew he had something more pleasant in mind than the tragedy of the play. "There is nothing to forgive, Morgan," she murmured, the brashness of a moment ago suddenly fled. "I thank you very much for the evening. I have never seen anything like it, and I would not have you think me ungrateful."

"Then let us seal the evening with a kiss, my love. All good evenings should end with a kiss."

He made no move to take what he wanted, but waited politely for her acceptance. Faith felt her heart pounding against her chest and wondered that he did not see it as well as hear it. To kiss this man was as dangerous as to ride into his path on a moonless night, but she could not say no. The wine spun through her head with a mystical magic, accelerating the fire he stirred in her blood with just the proximity of his large masculine frame.

"Just one kiss." It came out more question than statement, and Faith inhaled sharply as Morgan bent toward her.

"Just one kiss." His wine-flavored breath caressed her as his lips brushed her cheek.

Then Morgan's arm tightened about her waist and Faith felt herself lifted upward, her hands coming to rest against the breadth of his hard chest. The first touch of his lips on hers sent her senses spinning wildly, and then she was lost to the sweetness of his passion, the fierceness of the need overtaking her.

One kiss. It was a lifetime of kisses, yet it was the briefest of pleasures. Their lips met and clung, then parted greedily for more. Morgan's hand moved from the wall to cup Faith's face and hold her still while his mouth plundered the treasure she willingly offered. The length and breadth of his hand covered half her face, strong enough to tear her head from her shoulders, but gentle enough to tear her heart from her breast. Tears formed in Faith's eyes at the tenderness of Morgan's passion and the gaping need his touch opened within.

Drunken laughter at the alley's mouth brought a curse to the lips that had caressed her so sweetly just a brief moment before. Faith shrank back against the wall as Morgan returned her to her feet, but his arm wrapped about her securely as he turned to face the intruders.

"Here's one, Thornton. She's a mite occupied, but perhaps she can be persuaded away. How much did you pay for her, man? I'll double your price. My friend's in the direst need, and that skirt looks suitable for what ails him."

Morgan gave the elegantly garbed dandy in his blue satin coat and lace frills a diminishing stare. One black brow raised haughtily, he straightened, keeping Faith close to his side. "You're well in your cups or I'd demand satisfaction for your insult to my wife. Stand aside, and do not try my patience further." Hand on the hilt of his sword, he stepped forward, until the light from the man's lamp boy threw his profile in full relief.

The dandy glanced hastily from the arrogant high-boned features of the weaponed gentleman to the delicate features of the obviously terrified lady; then his gaze slowly moved to the gleaming hilt of the sword loosened from its scabbard. He gulped and stepped backward.

"Begging your pardon, sir. We did not realize . . . It is a trifle irregular, you know." His cheeks flushed with irate color.

Mockery laced his words as Morgan pushed past him and his equally drunken companion, keeping Faith securely on his far side. "Not for newlyweds, I think. Come, my dear, we'd best be home before I needs must fend off your admirers."

They escaped hastily, Faith trembling beneath his firm hold, Morgan cursing at the interruption that had cost him an evening's work. How would he ever return her to the mood of moments earlier? Her innocent passion still burned on his lips, and he had yet to so much as breach the barriers of her clothing. Could he have but a few more minutes . . .

His breath caught and his loins throbbed at the possibilities that opened for him. A woman of his own, a lady. Not a trollop, but a true innocent. Morgan's fevered imagination played the scenes well in his head. She would know nothing of men; he alone would teach her. And she would cry gratefully for his release each time he came to her. The thought excited him more than the challenge of a well-rewarded theft.

He would win her. He wanted her willing eagerness. He wanted to know she had chosen him, an Irish highwayman, over all the other possibilities of her life. He would not have her say he forced her. He could, easily enough. He could take her anytime, and when she bore the consequences, force her to marriage. But this was one thing he didn't wish to steal by force. He would have her willingly given, or their marriage would be a mockery.

Excitement carried Morgan through the dark streets and back to the inn. There was time yet. The night was not over. Faith followed him trustingly, her fingers clinging to his coat sleeve as they hurried through unlit streets. The taste of her passionate kiss still lingered in his mouth. He would have more than just a taste when this night ended.

Morgan's silence caused a vague apprehension to form in Faith's chest as they hurried up the narrow steps to the room Morgan had obviously taken in advance. She knew it would be foolish to ride across the city and its desolate outskirts to their cottage at this hour of the night, but she wished desperately for the security of her private loft right now. They had shared a roof for over four months now. She should have no fear of Morgan's intentions, but something in his behavior warned that things had changed. She knew little about the behavior between men and women, but were her own feelings any rule to judge by, she was in desperate trouble.

Morgan used the candle the clerk had given him to light several more in the room's interior. Though the night was damp, no fire burned in the grate, and he efficiently set about correcting that situation. Why should she doubt him now, when he was only seeing to her care as he had done these past months? She should be grateful for his concern, not suspicious of his intentions.

When Morgan rose to stand before her, Faith resisted the inclination to step backward. In the flickering light of the candles, he seemed somehow taller and more primitive. His hair gleamed with a deep black sheen against his carved features, and the light in his eyes was almost feral as he regarded her.

"This is a clean inn. You need not fear the contents of the bed or the rooms below. Have some respect for my taste, if you will."

Faith managed a small smile at this practical statement. "I have never stayed at an inn. I will trust your judgment."

So the look on her face was for him and not the room. He should not be surprised. She might know little of men, but she was a lady and he was no longer a gentleman. The difference was there, whether she recognized it or not. It served his interests to ignore it, but Morgan couldn't help but wonder if he would pull Faith down to his level or if she could raise him to hers. Only time would tell. His resolve did not falter.

Tilting her chin upward with his finger, he placed a light kiss on Faith's parted lips. "I will have someone bring you warm water to wash while I wait below. Perhaps then we could continue what we left off when we were interrupted."

He did not give her time to refuse. Faith held her tongue as Morgan strode out, so strong and proud. How could she tell him his kisses terrified her? That they left her weak and incapable of thought?

Perhaps it was just the wine. Her head still spun dizzily, and she was grateful when the maid brought her water. She would feel better for having washed, and then perhaps she could think again. Surely the look she had seen in the highwayman's eyes could not mean what it seemed.

Below, Morgan steadfastly drank the tankard of ale that he didn't taste. He wanted to pace nervously up and down and check the room every five minutes like an expectant bridegroom, but he refused to relegate himself to that role. He'd had any number of wenches in his bed. This one was just another. Why, then, did he feel the veriest green stripling as he waited to go to her?

He hadn't felt this nervous with his first roll in the hay. That particular lass had merely meant to say a solemn farewell to him before he left the green shores of Eire. Things had gone a little out of hand, and before either knew it, her skirts were up above her head and he was between her thighs. They were warm, welcoming thighs, to be sure, but she had known what she was doing and he had known a little more when he was done. There had been many such occasions in the years since. The ladies had never been averse to his attentions. Why, then, did he feel so nervous now?

It was foolish, and he was not a fool. Tossing a coin down on the table, Morgan rose and walked unhurriedly toward the stairs. There had been time enough for Faith to undress and wash and crawl between the sheets. If she did not know what to expect next, he would teach her. It was as simple as that.

But when he opened the door on their room, he realized nothing was as simple as that with Faith. The firelight flickered across russet curls twisted neatly in a single braid on the pillow—on the hearth. Morgan sucked in his breath and grimaced as he regarded the cocoon of covers the little imp had created by the fire. From the even rise and fall of her shoulders, he judged her to be already asleep. Far be it from him to awake her if she were in such dire need of rest that she could sleep while waiting to be tumbled.

Snarling wrathfully to himself, Morgan sat and jerked off his boots.

The holiday mood disappeared with their return trip to the cottage. Faith tried to blame it on the fact that Morgan had discovered a stone in his stallion's hoof that the stableboy should have found, but in reality, his stormy mood had begun well before his visit to the stable.

Although she was uncertain of her fault, Faith felt certain she was the cause of Morgan's irascible humor. She had risen before him to stir the fire so he could get up to warmth. She had dressed in the cold and summoned a maid to bring him the coffee he preferred. But when he woke to a warm room and a steaming pot of coffee and Faith dressed and waiting obediently to return home, he had scowled as fiercely as if she had created some major transgression.

Perhaps he'd drunk too much wine. Her own head still felt fuzzy this morning. Or perhaps he had found someone to drink with in the tavern and had consumed too much gin or whatever it was men drank in those places. She had heard of a concoction of ale and eggs and herbs that eased the headache after such a night. She would prepare it when they returned home.

She sent his stormy features another anxious look. She couldn't afford to offend him. Morgan offered the best employment she had been able to find. Now that she had seen the immensity of London and the poverty that stalked the streets, she was more uncertain than ever of her ability to make her own way. Besides, Morgan had sent off the message that would bring her father's papers. She needed to be here when they arrived. Surely he wouldn't put her out before they came.

Surely he wouldn't put her out at all. Her eyes widened in fear at the thought. It was no longer cold, but her experiences at the taproom had made it quite clear that Morgan was right when he said she had no idea of what awaited her in London. She didn't know what future there was in staying in the forest, but at least it felt safe. Or Morgan made her feel safe. The idea of being on her own again was paralyzing. She didn't want to ever be alone again.

Morgan felt the brunt of the anxious glances she kept sending him, but they were almost back at the cottage before he worked off his evil temper enough to place the blame where it belonged. Faith was a delicate creature unaccustomed to the exertion and long hours of traveling to London and staying up half the night. Top that off with the wine he had given her, and it was no wonder she had fallen asleep. He shouldn't have been surprised had she passed out. Only her incredible desire to please him had kept her on her feet as long as it had.

That thought returned his assurance a little. He might have been as nervous as a bridegroom last night, but she had not known she was about to become a bride. He had nearly made a fool of himself. He was not accustomed to that feeling and hoped having a wife wouldn't make it a habit, but he remained unswerved from his course. Sooner or later, they must marry. He just needed to make Faith aware of it.

So when they reached the cottage, Morgan swung her down from the saddle with a jauntier smile than he had been able to offer earlier. When he saw the relief in those troubled gray eyes, he felt a cad, and he brushed a kiss against the sun-warmed copper of her hair. "I'm a brute, lass. Don't pay mind to my black ways. I always come around."

"I shall fix you a sweet to sweeten your humor." Thoroughly relieved, Faith answered with more bravery than was her habit. "Do you have a preference?"

"Lass, I prefer you not spoil me. I deserve a good

thrashin' and not a reward. Now, go put away your spoils of war and let me see to the animals. It's time I think of breeding the roan mare. She should be almost ready.'' If nothing else, the stallion was ready, and Morgan sympathized with the animal's plight. Perhaps at least one of them could have some relief. Perhaps he ought to visit Molly tonight.

But the slender curves standing trustingly in his arms were more provocative than Molly's full-blown charms would ever be. He hadn't so much as touched the small upthrust breasts beneath the heavy gown, nor knew the feel of Faith's flesh in his palms, but he was ready for her. She would be special; he knew it instinctively. He would bide his time a while longer.

Faith hid her blush at this casual mention of the crudities of farm life. She must get used to it, but her own feelings were too near the surface to withstand close examination. Morgan's hands were burning a hole to her waist, and her lips kept waiting for that exquisite torment she knew he could exact. She didn't know what ''breeding'' entailed, but she had enough instinct to know her feelings had some relation to the animal act. She would rather not imagine the act, if she could.

Unfortunately, by the following day she was not only imagining it but also witnessing it.

Carrying the mug of ale she had thought Morgan might be ready for after a hard morning's work, Faith stopped short before she was halfway to the paddock, stunned by the scene coming to life before her.

Morgan stood, naked to the waist, holding the halter of the roan mare she had named Annette. He was sweating as profusely as the terrified horse, and Faith knew she should turn away, but a strange fascination held her gaze fastened to the mating being performed before her.

Morgan's magnificent black stallion was raised on his hind legs, his forelegs straddling the mare in a dance older than mankind. The mare squealed and rocked and protested as Morgan held her still, but she never pulled away from the instrument of her impalement. Faith gasped and her hands rose to her heated cheeks as the stallion emitted a cry of triumph that split the spring air. The ale in the mug splashed down her apron, but she scarce noticed. Never had she seen

148 • Patricia Rice

a more primitive sight, and the burning in her cheeks seemed to take root in her belly.

Across the grassy field, Morgan's gaze came to find hers, and the burning became something much more fiery lodging in Faith's breast. She had never really seen Morgan half-dressed before. He had always kept at least a shirt over his torso; her eyes could not avert from his nakedness now. He was as magnificent as the stallion, his wide, well-muscled shoulders gleaming in the sunlight, the pattern of dark hair across his chest emphasizing his breadth before narrowing to his taut abdomen. Faith gulped as she tried not to think of where that fine line of hair led when it slid beneath the band of his breeches. She had no right thinking such thoughts, but Morgan's fierce gaze said otherwise. She could almost feel his thoughts enter hers with that look, and she felt a sudden sympathy for the mare.

With that realization, Faith fled into the house.

14

"MILORD, there's an . . . er . . . personage here to see you." The staid butler refrained from rolling his eyes in disdain, but his words had the same effect.

Edward Montague, Lord Stepney, rolled the stem of his wineglass between his thick fingers and kept his smile of satisfaction to himself. The runner could wait. He was more fascinated by the spectacle of his cousin, Thomas, ingratiating himself for a change. He really didn't care to know what was at the bottom of this change of heart, but it was amusing to watch.

"How much did you say?" he asked with bored unconcern, dismissing the butler with a nod.

The handsome Thomas, the Montague who should have been the lord if one were to judge by appearances, swung around from his position by the window. His pretty features gave away nothing of his feelings for his massive cousin, the heir to all this fortune. He merely sipped his wine and behaved as if this were a business discussion.

"Ten thousand pounds should be sufficient. Invested wisely, it ought to produce enough income to keep a body alive. The sum may seem enormous, but we have more to gain from spending it than not."

"Ten thousand pounds." Edward admired his cousin's audacity. "Had we the sum between us, we would be rich men. I doubt that the old man has given us that much in our lifetimes."

"Bahh, had he given us half so much, I'd not be here today. It's damnable folly to keep us on such short shrift." Thomas crossed to the decanter and refilled his glass. "Now he has this bee in his bonnet about finding George's lost brat, and he's likely to leave all that belongs to us to her."

"So it seems." Edward wondered where this topic would lead, but he did not stir himself to find out. Admittedly, old age and guilt had driven the marquess a little off the beam over the missing child, but Edward had his title and the entailment to look forward to, and he was not overly concerned about the loss of an additional fortune. Only the puzzle kept him interested—and Thomas's frustration. He truly did enjoy watching Thomas chafing at the bit.

Thomas glared at the corpulent figure lounging across the settee. "It does not seem to concern you that the fortune we have waited for all these years is likely to end up in Bedlam or the hands of some Methodist nobody. Do you share some secret that I don't?"

Edward lifted his massive shoulders idly and set his glass aside. "I cannot imagine what worrying about it will accomplish, no more than I can imagine where ten thousand pounds will come from or what it will do. Perhaps you should enlighten me."

"I don't know where it will come from. Perhaps we can have some of the family jewels replaced with paste. I doubt that there's ten thousand pounds in artwork in all the family holdings, but there might be a valuable oil or two here and there to supplement the jewels. Certainly no one will miss them. As for its purpose, I've tried to tell you. We need to manufacture an heiress."

"Manufacture an heiress? How droll." Edward brushed an invisible speck of dust from his cuff. Now that he knew the game, he was bored again. Thomas was so very predictable. All hustle and bustle and no brains.'Twas a pity. Like the ant, all he would have was crumbs for his work.

Thomas gave his idle cousin a look of disgust. "Have you a better idea? We can find some poor waif from the country, offer her an income for life, and pass her off to the marquess as George's daughter. Once the old man is dead, we send her packing, and her share is split between us. The old man will be happy, the girl will be happy, and we'll be rich men."

Thomas' thought processes were quite astounding sometimes. There were enough holes in that plan for someone as large as himself to fall through, as Thomas undoubtedly intended. There were some advantages to his large size, after all. Large body, small brain, the general populace believed. Why disillusion the rabble?

Smiling benevolently, Edward lifted a heavy hand in languid acquiescence. "Jewels, you say? Never gave them a thought. Might manage that. Give me a little time." He furrowed his brow as if in deep thought. "Just might manage that. Come back later and we'll see."

Looking both impatient and relieved, Thomas nodded curtly and set his empty glass aside. "I'll scout around for the right sort of girl. Send me word when you're ready."

It was all Edward could do to hide his smile as his cousin walked out one door and the runner was introduced through the next. Poor Thomas. Had he ever applied all that ambition to honest work, he'd be a wealthy fellow today. Fortunately, Edward had never been bothered by ambition himself. An inquiring mind was his downfall. Sometimes a fellow just had to know the answer to pressing questions. One never knew when the information might be useful.

As the rotund runner sidled uncertainly into Edward's lavish chamber, the heir to a marquessate permitted himself a small smile. He had already discovered the obsequious but diligent thief-taker to be a man after his own tastes. He poured a glass of wine and held it out to his visitor.

"Welcome, Watson. What is it you have for me today?"

Eyeing the wine approvingly, Watson relaxed under these more genial circumstances than he had been hitherto subjected to in this house. "Aye, and it's not more than I warned you of before, milord. It will take a bit of time to ferret the wolf from his den. He's a clever one, and they're feared of him. And there's no guarantee she's the lass you seek."

"But she's still alive after all this time?" Edward prompted.

"Oh, right enough, she is that. The man they call Black Jack nearly took the lids off several of Whitehead's patrons when they tried to have some fun with the girl. Of course, you realize she's the man's doxy by now." The runner added this with a bit of wariness. The marquess would have pitched that plaster statue at him for that remark, but it had to be said.

Edward waved his hand languidly. "It goes to be said, of course. Quite enterprising of the wench, I must say. A highwayman's doxy. How fascinating. I doubt that she's the right one, after all. No offspring of pious George would ever trade her fair body for sustenance. She's undoubtedly dead in some ditch, as you suggested earlier. But just as a matter of interest, try to trace her, Watson. And my cousin too. He's onto something, and I'd rather know what it is.''

Watson tugged his forelock and grinned. ''Right enough, guv'nor. He's known to us already. Don't mind being paid a little to do what needs to be done. You'll have my report regular.''

Edward leaned back against the pillows with an air of supreme indifference. ''That will be all, Watson. By the way, I'll have that next report in writing. It wouldn't do to have Thomas see you here again.''

Watson grimaced, but his lordship was no longer watching. Taking the hint, he bowed out.

Edward beamed benevolently at the ceiling. The possibilities were fascinating. The missing heiress, a highwayman's doxy. She could already be breeding. His father wanted an heir. What if. . . ? His grin grew even more fatuous.

The crickets were singing a lonesome melody, and somewhere a toad galumphed his love call to an unresponsive sweetheart. The birds had finally settled their differences after the day's rivalry of warbling and settled down to their newly found mates. Stirring the fudge she'd made for Morgan's sweet tooth, Faith stared out the blackened windowpanes to the night beyond.

Never had she realized the riotous sounds and scents of spring were mating rituals dating back to the beginnings of time. The earth practically throbbed with life tonight, as it had all the day. Even the newly tilled sod of the garden Morgan had dug for her burgeoned with new life. Earthworms swarmed to the surface and seedlings of every plant imaginable sprang up overnight. Everything she touched or saw or heard reminded her of the heady birth of the season. The new colt in the stable was just another symbol of that fertility.

And the restless stirrings inside her had the same source. She could attribute them to no other cause. She tried not to see Morgan in his half-naked state with her mind's eye, but the pictures became clearer instead of fading. He had never mentioned the incident. When he came back to the house that day, he had been wearing his shirt, but now that Faith was aware of the man beneath it, it didn't matter. Beneath the untied opening of the linen, she could see the curl of crisp dark hair on his chest, and her imagination led her to contemplate touching the rugged planes that they covered. The urge to do so had almost become an obsession these past days, and Morgan hadn't made it any easier.

He had not ridden out once. He was there every minute of the day and night, tweaking her hair, teasing her with his damned Irish endearments, taking her riding across the countryside. If only he would treat her as a housekeeper and ignore her, she would be fine, she was certain. But as it was, his presence was a constant reminder of the turmoil inside her.

Tonight Morgan had carried water to heat over the fire so she might bathe and wash her hair. In the past, she had always tried to wait until he was gone for the evening to perform those ablutions, but he hadn't left her side in days, and she could not endure the wait any longer. Her intentions had been to keep the highwayman from his calling, not encourage him to go back to the road again. She couldn't wish him away, but if she waited one more day, her smell would drive him off forever.

But the idea of Morgan knowing full well what she was doing in here drove Faith crazy. She draped a sheet over the window, but it wasn't enough to keep him out of her thoughts. When she stripped to her chemise, she felt as if he were right there beside her, grinning.

The shame of it was that she wanted him there. Lifting the cloth from the large basin, Faith buried her burning cheeks in it. For some reason, the wet cloth only brought back the memories of Morgan's heated kiss, and the steam seemed to curl down inside of her and smolder. She was going to hell of a certainty if her thoughts continued this way.

With practiced maneuvers she managed to soak her hair thoroughly in the basin and scrub until it hurt. Somehow, she would return to normal. She would just have to keep him from kissing her again. That's all it was, an act of nature like the birds singing in the spring.

But when she finally had to strip off her chemise to finish washing, her body told another story. Her breasts would never be large, but they were filling out nicely. Perhaps that was the reason they prickled and grew sharp points when the cloth caressed them. The stirring in her belly grew to an ache as she cleansed lower, and Faith's cheeks gained a heated flush at the thought of Morgan just outside the door. What was he doing to her that she could not even bathe in peace?

Faith hastily finished washing and grabbed clean garments. The dirty water would need to be carried out. She couldn't leave Morgan to that. She would much prefer to scurry up to the loft and hide from him for the evening, but she knew her place. The water had to go out, and she had to get dressed to do it.

Not bothering with stockings or shoes, Faith slipped her clean blue gown on, hastily tucked a white kerchief around her shoulders, and opened the door before lifting the heavy basin. As she had suspected, Morgan was not far away, but instead of facing the cottage, he was staring up at the heavens. From the way his hair lay plastered against his neck, he had gone bathing in the stream behind the barn. At the sound of the door opening, he turned and gestured at her.

"Come see, *cailin*. The heavens are raining fire this night."

She was a candidate for Bedlam to go near him. Morgan's shoulders strained at the seams of his old shirt, and Faith could tell from here that he wore no neckcloth and had not bothered to fasten the shirt ties. The old leather breeches he wore when working with the horses clung to his narrow hips and strong thighs like a soft glove, and like her, he had left off his stockings and shoes. He was as pagan as the night, and she could not resist the smiling gleam he sent her way.

As if pulled two ways by the forces of moon and tide, Faith reluctantly stepped out onto the cool grass and set down her basin. The day had been unusually warm, and some of the sun's heat lingered on the blades between her toes. Knowing she shouldn't, unable to stop, she went toward Morgan reluctantly, her gaze fastened on the insistent man-god in the clearing and not on the heavens above.

Revealing no sign that he noticed or understood her slowness, Morgan pointed to the arc of the sky where the meteor shower continued unabated. "Think you 'tis a sign of import?" he murmured as she came to stand beside him.

The fiery lights sped and disappeared across the black bowl of the heavens with incredible magic. Faith's eyes finally turned in their direction, and she gave an awe-filled gasp at the majesty of the night sky. It had never occurred to her to watch the moon and stars, even had she been allowed outside in the dark to do so. The magnificence spread before her was so inspiring that she scarcely noticed when Morgan came to stand behind her, placing his hands on her shoulders.

" 'Tis so beautiful," she whispered, watching the play of light as a star seemingly leapt from the firmament to dash through velvet darkness and disappear.

" 'Tis the only thing that keeps my faith that God exists. Perhaps he has gone elsewhere and forgotten our poor miserable world, but only a god could have created such a spectacle."

"I think it is man who has forgotten God." Faith shivered, not from cold, but from some strange sensation that Morgan's deep voice generated, or perhaps his presence. His hands tightened on her shoulders, and she leaned closer to his welcoming warmth. Against the immensity of the sky, they seemed very small, and his touch offered security.

"Perhaps so," His voice was sad as he stared upward. "I'd like to think there is a heaven up there, and that those we loved look down upon occasion to see how we fare. They deserve a heaven after their hell on earth."

The pain in his voice struck a chord in her heart, and Faith leaned closer against him, letting his hands slide down her arms to circle her waist, not knowing how else to offer comfort. She knew the anguish of death as well as anybody, but time had numbed some of the sharpness of the loss. It did not reassure her to think her father watched over her even now. She felt quite certain he would not approve. But she did not mention this to Morgan. Perhaps his family was different, and they would be glad he was alive and well and fighting the people who had stolen his home.

"There has to be a heaven." She spoke softly, uncertain how to phrase her feelings. "The sky is proof enough. Those are angels out there watching over us. If we could only lead the lives they expect, they need not cry over us anymore."

Morgan sent a surprised look to Faith's upturned gaze, but she was staring at the stars with a dreamy expression and no thought to him. He studied the lovely oval of her face, admiring the thick fringe of lashes and the sculptured lines of her nose and cheeks. A few short hairs had begun to dry and curl about her brow, and they glowed with almost a copper hue in the starlight. Morgan tried not to focus on the softness of her slightly parted lips, but he knew how they would melt beneath his own should he touch them, and his loins responded to just the image. It had been a long time since he'd had a woman, and this slip of a girl was beginning to get under his skin. Perhaps the falling stars had an import, after all. Perhaps tonight was the night.

She smelled of the jasmine-scented soap he had bought for her. He had never seen a jasmine in bloom, but it could not be more beautiful than the innocent in his arms right now. Wanting just a taste of that innocence to fill the gaping hole in his soul, Morgan turned his faerie-woman around and bent to lay his lips upon her mouth.

This time, Faith felt no surprise when Morgan's lips feathered across hers. It was as if the time had come and the curtain had risen and the characters were on the stage where they belonged. Only the touch of his kiss was needed to dim the theater lights and set the actors in motion.

Her hands went about his strong neck of their own accord. Her fingers explored the warm flesh and supple tendons there, then traveled on to the silken textures of Morgan's damp hair while his mouth tempted and persuaded and heated her lips until they did his bidding. She knew what he wanted this time, and her lips parted invitingly, welcoming the dark explorations to come.

As Morgan's tongue accepted her invitation, excitement twisted and circled deep inside Faith where she had felt the heat of strange sensations earlier. His kiss was like fuel to the fire, and she rose to greet it, firing the blaze to a roar. Morgan's arms closed around her, lifting her against him so her mouth could twist and seal more tightly to his, and the touch of his tongue ignited more awe than the falling stars overhead.

His hands began to roam as their mouths eagerly explored their new claims. The brush of strong fingers over the sides of her breasts sent new flames of excitement through Faith's veins, but when Morgan's hand moved downward to cup her buttocks and draw her closer, Faith's newfound confidence faltered.

Faith pulled away and looked up at Morgan's angular face with an expression of bewilderment and fear. The fire still breathed inside her, and she tingled in places best not thought of, but she knew more now of the danger she courted, and she was terrified of where this excitement led.

The tenderness in Morgan's green gaze reassured her, and the gentle curve of his lip as he touched a finger to her mouth sent panic back to its lidded box. This was Morgan, the only man who had come to her aid, who provided for her better than her own father. Despite his trade, she had no reason not to trust him.

"Don't be afraid, little faerie. I'll not do anything you don't want me to." The soft caress of his voice did nothing to reveal the two-edged sword of his words.

Ignorant of the way her body worked, Faith allowed herself to be led up the slight hillock in the clearing behind the cottage. Morgan spread out a saddle blanket he had picked up from the paddock fence, and he gallantly assisted her to a seat. The stars spread out far and wide above them, and it was sheer bliss to lie back and imagine reaching those high spaces. Peace exuded from those spaces, and Faith longed to know them more intimately.

Morgan pointed out the constellations he knew, trying to make her see a bear where there was only a dipper, and laughing low in his throat when she insisted all she could see were two dippers, and did they have any water?

His kiss brushed her forehead, then her nose, and it wasn't long before Faith was pulling Morgan's head down to sample the giddy wine of his lips again. It seemed so simple now, so much a part of the spring around them, that she wondered why she had ever feared it. The throbbing life of the earth beneath them seemed to rise and flow through their hands and mouths and flood through their veins like the tides to the shores. The warm breeze rippling the grass ruffled their hair, and whispered along their skin, and the day's heat rose from the ground to encompass them.

The loose kerchief over Faith's breasts fell easily before Morgan's exploring fingers. The unfocused excitement that had been growing within her now had a center as Morgan's hands cupped the swell of her breast and his fingers caressed the flesh rising above her bodice. Faith's desire grew to be as great as his for the removal of this encumbrance keeping flesh from touching flesh. Faith offered no protest other than a small cry of surprise and relief when the hooks of her bodice came undone and only the sheer chemise stood between her and the heat of Morgan's palm.

"You are so beautiful, *cailin,*" he murmured against her hair. "God made you to fit into my hand just so." Morgan filled his palm with her loosely covered breast and stroked it gently, feeling her shivers of excitement as he did so. Knowing he was arousing her as well as himself enhanced his desire. She was no whore practiced in stimulating a man's interests with feigned pleasure. His touch truly excited her, to the point of casting aside her inhibitions. Nothing had ever aroused him so much, and Morgan's gaze was heavy-lidded with desire as he looked down upon her rapturous expression. His praises were no lie.

Silhouetted against the sky, Morgan appeared more demigod than ever. His wide shoulders filled her field of vision, and Faith's fingers searched the hollows and angles of his face as he hovered over her. She didn't know what was happening, but she wasn't ready to call it to a halt yet. The knowledge that he would stop when she asked it of him was reassurance enough.

Morgan's gaze held Faith's as his strong fingers untied her chemise and pushed it aside. The night air caressed her heated flesh, and Faith felt her breasts rise to sharp points as they had earlier. She held her breath as Morgan gently touched her there, but the pleasure was an exquisite pain that swirled all the way down to her middle and made her hips rise in expectation of something she did not understand.

"Ahhh, Faith, you have the passions of a thousand women all wrapped in one. Thank God I found you before anyone else did. You're a treasure, my love, and I'm not likely to ever let you go."

His words should have terrified her, but instead, they made her soul rise in rapture. Or perhaps it was just the way his hands made her breasts swell as he teased and stroked until she was heedless of his meanings. The question in Morgan's gaze disappeared when Faith raised her hands once more to bring him down to her kiss. As their lips met, his eyes smoldered with renewed intensity.

That gesture sealed her fate. Her desire was obvious, and even when she gave a small cry of fright as his lips moved to encompass her breast, Morgan did not relent. He knew she wanted him, and that was enough for now. The morrow would be time for recriminations.

Faith writhed beneath the slow seduction of his tongue, wanting to call a halt to these terrifying sensations overwhelming her, but encouraging him with her stroking hands and fingers.

Morgan's body was large and heavy as he leaned over her, but he balanced himself so only his hips pressed close with a threatening intimacy. A heaviness in her lower regions kept Faith from moving away, and his tempting caresses filled her senses like a heady wine, defying thought. She wanted Morgan's kisses against her skin, she wanted his mouth on her breasts, and when his hand stole down to her skirts, she did not stop him.

The breeze playing over her bare leg as the heavy material slid upward gave fair warning. The spring warmth was gentle as the air lapped over her exposed calf, and Morgan's deepening kiss induced a languor that defied protest. But primeval instinct clamored insistently somewhere in the back of Faith's mind.

Her hands began to tug rather than caress Morgan's thick hair. She needed time to think, to grasp what he was doing to her, but there was no lessening of the pressure of his tongue and lips. His callused hand slid higher, bringing her skirt with it. She had donned no petticoat, and the absence of any other protection acted as a spur to the warnings in her mind, and panic raised its ugly head. Air rushed over Faith's bare thighs, and though she exploded with some need that made her arch upward to meet him when Morgan lifted himself slightly to push the skirt higher, the panic increased at this exposure.

This wasn't as it was meant to be. Something was wrong, though Morgan's touch said it was right. Faith tried to twist away from his mouth, to tell him to stop, but his tongue slid like honey between her teeth and she accepted him hungrily. He shifted his weight to run his hand over her uncovered hip and thigh, and Faith cried out with more need than anger. His heated palm slid beneath her, lifting her bare buttock toward him, and she splintered in two at the forces fighting within her.

"No, Morgan, don't," she wailed as his lips moved to lave her breasts once again, but the cry came out a whisper whipped away by the breeze.

Faith felt the day's growth of his beard chafe at her skin as Morgan peeled back her bodice completely and shoved the chemise aside to better explore the satin of her skin. As long as his attentions rested there, she felt safe, but his hand hadn't forgotten what lay below her waist, and it returned time and again to stroke and touch and lift until she was moist with need and a kind of panic that paralyzed her into remaining.

When his fingers finally touched her *there*, where she most feared him, Faith nearly jumped from her skin, but Morgan was already plying her mouth with sweet kisses and tender words.

" 'Tis so sweet and fair, ye are, my *cailin alainn*. So soft and gentle. I need you next to me, my love. Just let me feel you close to me, just for a little while. I need you, little faerie. Can you not feel it, deep inside you? We were meant to be like this. The stars say it is so."

The words were magnetic in their attraction, lulling Faith's senses as easily as his kisses. She did feel it, knew the need he spoke of. And it did feel so right, so special. When he unfastened his breeches, allowing her to slide her hands beneath his loosened shirt, she felt Morgan's intake of breath at her touch as a pleasure beyond comparison. She could touch him, and he wanted her to. It seemed an amazing power, a secret never before revealed to her. The self-contained highwayman needed her touch, and she indulged in it wantonly, the fear fading to smothered protests beneath the onslaught to her senses as strong muscles rippled beneath her fingers and heated skin scorched her palms.

While her hands rode his back, Morgan's unclothed hips somehow insinuated themselves between Faith's thighs. She felt the fierce heat of him burning her there where she was most vulnerable, but he had said just for a little while. She needed his nakedness next to hers, and she wished for all their cumbersome clothes to be gone. The play of muscles along Morgan's back as he braced himself above her did strange things to her insides, and Faith's gaze rose to his as he lifted his head from her lips to look down.

"You'll never regret this, my *cailin*. 'Tis a gift from heaven you are, and I'm not likely to forget it. Spread your legs a little wider, lass, and I'll show you what I mean."

With her gaze trustingly fastened on his and his persuasive words to warm her heart, Faith did as she was told, feeling the naturalness of his command. Just the movement heightened the excitement now centering at the juncture of her thighs, and when something warm and strong moved against her there, she rose to meet the pleasure he promised.

"Yes, lass, now." With a sigh, Morgan bent to take her lips and slide deep between her welcoming thighs.

She was small and tight and resisted him at first, and Morgan felt a sudden wash of guilt at what he was doing. But then her lips parted in an "Oh" of surprise and his tongue plunged in and her hips bucked upward and he was through the barrier and well sheathed in her passage.

Faith fought him then, terrified of the entrapment, unable to move away, pressed into the earth by his heavy weight, and suffocated by the need to escape. Her hips twisted and turned, but Morgan only sank deeper until she knew she was only worsening the situation, and a sob of despair escaped her as she fell still.

Morgan's soothing words lost all meaning as he began to move inside her. The feeling was frightening, terrifying to an extreme, bringing back the memory of the stallion covering the mare. He filled her until Faith thought she could bear no more, then withdrew, leaving her barren. He repeated the motion, and something began to stir inside her again.

Faith fought the feeling, knowing its consequence now, but Morgan's body posed atop and inside her refused to be ignored. His thrusts grew quicker, more demanding, and she found herself opening to him, easing his entrance and taking him deeper, until his cries mixed with her own.

With one final thrust he tore away what remained of her innocence. The liquid heat spilling deep into her womb and overflowing to fall to the earth below them sealed all that had lingered of childhood and launched Faith into the world as woman. Still pinned by Morgan's heavy hips, Faith felt tears creeping to the corner of her eyes as he gathered her in his arms and kissed a path along her face.

"Don't cry, little one. I'm here to take care of you. We're good for each other, don't you see?" Morgan brushed the hair back from Faith's pale face and felt his heart swell in sorrow at the tearstains down her cheek. He had done this cruel thing to her, and he would pay for it for the rest of his life, but it was a price well worth paying. She was his means to an end, and he would use her as he used every resource at hand to gain his goals, but he would risk heart and soul to see she didn't suffer in consequence.

Morgan slid off and pushed Faith's skirt down to keep her legs warm. His lips lingered on her young, sweet breasts, and his pride soared at how much he had won this night. This was a prize to be stolen and carried off just like any other, but this one he would keep. Sighing with pleasure, he moved his lips back to hers.

They were salty with tears now, but he would dry them quickly enough. She responded instantly to his kiss, craving the apology he didn't mean to offer, and Morgan deepened the contact. She was his, and tonight he would show her what that meant.

15

FAITH STIRRED SLEEPILY, but the unexpected ache between her thighs jolted her closer to wakefulness. A wonderful warmth filled her bed, and she tried to succumb to the temptation of going back to sleep. Never in her life had she been allowed to indulge in such sin as sleeping past dawn, but somehow it felt right this morning.

She rolled on her side, only to wake more fully to the fact that a man's broad bare back formed a wall between herself and the bed's edge. Shock rippled through her, bringing her to full wakefulness—and to the reason for her aching body and the furnace of heat warming the sheets.

Humiliation swept through her, a humiliation so deep and burning that she thought she would die of it. She was a fallen woman, a common trollop, a tool of the devil. She had taken a man in sin and would surely go to hell, but the far-distant future didn't worry her so much as the immediate present. How could she ever look Morgan in the eye again, knowing what they had done together?

Her hand flew to the unfastened chemise over her breasts. He had left her that, at least. It had been dark when he carried her to bed. He couldn't have seen everything. But he had touched everything.

She couldn't drive away the memory of Morgan's hands upon her, and the proximity of his nakedness now only served as a strong reminder of what else had possessed her. She might never recover from the shock of what he had done. She hadn't thought it possible. How could he. . . ?

Trying not to think of that part of Morgan that made him male, Faith concentrated on finding her way out of this trap. First she had to get out of bed. Scanning the long length of male body blocking access to the room, she had to admit that was an impossibility without actually touching him. And she couldn't touch him.

Despair engulfed her, despair and deep, abiding shame. Why escape when there was nowhere to go? She would be walking the streets soon enough, for that's what happened to women who did what she had. Why hurry from Morgan's bed to some other man's? She would never find honest employment now. The mark of shame would be upon her forever. Would he be tired of her already? Had he only kept her until he had accomplished what he did last night? Would he take her to those men in the tavern and sell her now? She had heard of such things, and with Morgan, anything seemed possible.

If only she could get away . . . Faith squirmed a little more, trying to see if there were some opening at the bottom of the bed. If she crawled from beneath the covers and over those lumps that were his feet . . .

A heavy hand caught in the tangled thickness of her hair, and Faith jumped nervously, turning terrified eyes to Morgan. He turned on his back and gazed up at her, his eyes darkened to a jungle green that sent steamy, sensuous messages. A shiver coursed down her spine as her body reacted to that look, but her hands pulled the covers protectively to her breasts.

Morgan carefully perused the tumble of titian hair over slim shoulders and young breasts and felt his body respond readily to the sight. He lifted his gaze to her delicately sculptured face and read the terror there. He knew terror well enough to call it friend. His victims were paralyzed by it, making it easier to command them without firing a shot. He wasn't certain that it was the best effect for Faith, but if it worked, it suited his purpose. He tugged, pulling her back to the mattress and him.

"No," she whispered, frantically pulling back, but there was only the wall behind her.

"Yes," Morgan said firmly, applying more pressure.

Faith resisted the tug of his hand, but the pull of his eyes was another matter entirely. He must be a demon who had possessed her and now had a hold on her soul, for she couldn't hold out long against that hungry gaze. Even as she pulled back, her legs were stretching toward him, touching the heated nakedness beneath the covers where he lay.

"It's too late to play coy, my *cailin*. Give me a kiss, and I'll let you go."

The devil lied, she knew that now. She knew as soon as

she touched him she would be lost. But she could see no other escape, and vaguely she hoped he spoke the truth. Perhaps now that he'd done that to her, he didn't need to do it again. Perhaps now that it was daylight, he would only want his breakfast.

Gingerly Faith leaned toward him, still clutching the sheet to her breast. Morgan's beard was rougher this morning, but his lips were moist and warm and welcoming. The sheet fell from her hands as Morgan pulled her down to his chest and filled her mouth with his need just as he had filled her body the night before.

Then she was sprawled half across him, only the sheet over his hips and her thin chemise between them as Morgan's hands moved possessively to reclaim what he had taken the night before. Just the touch of those knowing fingers and the heat of his mouth were sufficient to rekindle the fires that had destroyed her last night, and Faith moaned deep against his mouth as he pressed her closer.

"Shhh, my *cailin alainn*. There will be no pain this time. Let me pleasure you, as you please me." Morgan shifted to his side, returning Faith to the bed. Her gray eyes seemed wider than was possible, and her soul shone accusingly in them, but he ignored her conscience and his to place a kiss on her brow and a hand on her breast. "Kiss me, Faith, and let me show you."

She had no choice, but she offered no reluctance either as his head bent to hers and his big hand kneaded her breast. Her body was on fire for him already. How could she resist? He wore not a shred of clothing, and she was supremely aware of the masculine hardness pressing against her. Her chemise was her only protection, and that a flimsy one.

As Morgan's kiss deepened, Faith shuddered and raised her hands to his shoulders. The skin slid smooth and supple beneath her palms, and the muscles rippling below her touch reminded her of the foolishness of seeking escape. She was his for as long as he wanted her, and at the moment, she could think of nowhere else she wanted to be.

His mouth came to caress her breast, and then the chemise was sliding upward and disappearing over the side of the bed, and she was naked to his gaze. Faith felt the heat of her flesh rise between her breasts and flood upward at Morgan's unabashed stare, but his touch was gentle and reverent as he explored every curve laid bare before him. When his kisses followed where his hand led, she squirmed in protest that turned to ecstasy with each nip and touch and caress.

When his hands reached the soreness between her legs, Faith made one last effort to resist, but the invasion of his fingers put an end to that with amazing speed. At the same time embarrassment and shame swept over her, her hips rose hungrily to his touch, and her legs opened without need of his request.

At this response, Morgan returned his mouth to hers and renewed the fires there. "This is our secret, my sweet. No one will ever know how good you are but me. Don't ever tell me no, Faith, for 'twill kill us both."

He moved over her then, and she had no chance to see the maleness that matched her femininity before he slid into her, gently this time, rocking carefully against her so she felt no pain.

It was more wonderful than she remembered. All the heat and excitement that had been building between them now centered at this place where they joined, and with each movement, the pleasure doubled until Faith thought she could bear no more. Then Morgan's thrusts took new meaning, and she struggled upward to meet him, needing some release from this unbearable pressure, some release only he could provide.

Faith's movements brought a low moan from Morgan's lips, and swearing softly beneath his breath, he tried to slow his motion to meet her demands. But she was too tight and ready, and in mere seconds he had lost all thought of control in his need to bury himself as deeply as possible into her hungry warmth.

His last thrust hit that height she had been striving for, and the explosion rocked them both at the same time. Faith cried out as the hot, convulsive waves of pleasure shot through her, and it was some while later before the trembling stopped, and she realized Morgan had once more spent his seed inside her, just like the stallion and the mare.

She turned her heated cheek aside as Morgan rose on his elbows to kiss her brow. She could still feel him inside her, and the knowledge that his body was joined so intimately with hers caused no end of confusion. She knew it was wrong. She knew he had shamed her. But the pleasure he had given still warmed her all the way to the core, and she had no desire to be unburdened by his heavy weight.

"Don't turn away, Faith. Look me in the eye." Morgan caught her chin between his fingers and forced her to look up at him. Instead of fear, he read her confusion, and he smiled a little. "You please me much, little one. Don't ever be ashamed of that. That's what your body is for. Did you think you would feel pleasure if it were not?"

Faith met his gaze uncertainly. She had trusted him, and he had stolen her virtue. She shouldn't have expected more from a thief, but there was that in Morgan's voice that made her glad she had pleased him. She could read his contentment in the easing of the lines on his face and the way the little dent appeared at the corner of his mouth. He looked so much younger that way, almost her own age, and she managed a tentative smile at the thought of the highwayman as a boy.

"Aren't all pleasures sinful?" she inquired hesitantly, not daring to put more of her thoughts to words than this.

Morgan wanted her again. There was something about Faith's tender innocence that made him whole again, and he wanted to experience it over and over until the past was no more and the future was bright and welcoming. He felt himself growing hard within her, and reluctantly he withdrew before he damaged what she so trustingly gave him.

At her look of bewilderment, he pressed a kiss to her brow. "Perhaps in your religion, pleasures are sin, but not in mine. We are only doing what God has told us to do. There is just a little matter of obtaining His blessing, but that can be arranged soon enough. Now we had best get up before I am tempted to ravish you again."

Faith's gaze fell hurriedly down Morgan's rampantly masculine frame as he rose, unashamed, from their bed. At the sight of the maleness that had captured her, she blushed heatedly, but perversely, the desire he had taught her reawakened deep in her belly, and she felt no urge to follow him to the cold of the floor.

At her slowness to follow, Morgan turned and regarded her abandoned image speculatively. Russet tresses spilled across his pillows and over a slender form of perfect proportions. Small round hills curved upward from a valley so tiny that he knew he could encompass it with his hands. Instead of being narrow and boyish as expected from her size, her hips swelled to a pleasing roundness that beckoned a man's touch. Her thighs were firm and taut and narrowed to curved calves that he could easily imagine lifted above him. The thought brought perspiration to Morgan's brow as he gallantly resisted the temptation to ride there one more time.

"Up, *cailin,* or you will regret it, I assure you. You are not quite ready for a gallop yet, and I would not break you before we're started."

Something in his voice warned her to move. Grabbing the sheet, Faith scrambled from the bed, trying to hold the linen modestly around her. She needed water and privacy, but their circumstances were so changed, she didn't know how to ask for them.

Pulling on his breeches, Morgan solved her dilemma. "I'll see to the horses, little one. Take your time." He kissed her confused brow hastily, not daring to do more, and fled.

Faith was washed and dressed and preparing breakfast by the time he returned. At Morgan's entrance, she looked up and flushed slightly, then returned to what she was doing. The ease with which the color rose to her cheeks intrigued him, but it was his turn to feel uncertain now. He had never asked a woman to marry him, and she had made no comment on his earlier attempt. If he could, he would just carry her off to the priest and order the vows said, but he suspected there was the small matter of her acquiescence to be achieved first.

"I like the blue on you, lass. It makes your eyes look like the Irish skies." Words had never been a problem for him, but Faith's silences were a barrier he had yet to demolish. Morgan took the heavy pot from her hands and swung it to the table. His compliment didn't make her blush, he noticed. She just watched him a little more warily.

"Will you not speak to me, then?" he inquired briskly. Goals were never achieved by hanging back.

Faith poured his mug of coffee and handed it to him, studying his masculine features without flinching. "You're a liar and a thief, Morgan de Lacy. Will you have me speak more?"

He grinned, relieved to be on a footing that he understood. "Indeed, I would. I'd have you spew it all out rather than wondering at your thoughts. I'm a rascal and a rogue and all the other names you can think of, and some you don't know. That doesn't change what we did together, nor the fact that you wanted it as much as I.''

"I did not!" Irritated by his casualness, Faith slammed the frying pan onto the trivet. "I didn't even know what it was you were doing to me. You took advantage of me, de Lacy, and you know it.''

"I'll not deny it.'' Morgan slid onto his barrel seat and helped himself to the eggs. The hens were laying more these days, and there was even a flock of chickens cluttering one of the stalls, although he had thought the rooster well beyond his salad days. Faith had brought new life to this place, and he meant to enjoy every minute of it.

His nonchalant admission of guilt only infuriated Faith more. Hands on hips, she glared at him. "How can you sit there and look me in the face after saying that?''

He glanced up from his plate. "I don't remember looking you in the face when I said it, but I'd be happy to oblige. You have a very pretty face, *cailin*, even when it goes all red with temper.''

Her hand acted before her brain thought, and the pewter sugar bowl went flying over his arrogant black head. Morgan ducked, laughing, then rose to come around the table after her.

She made no attempt to avoid him. Her stiff little figure stood proudly beneath his gaze, her eyes smoking with a fire that should have scorched. Morgan grinned and wrapped his arms firmly around her and lifted her off her feet. The passion wouldn't be reserved entirely for their bed, then. That suited him well, better than silence, in any case. When she kicked out at him, he only crushed her closer.

"You'll be grieved at me often enough in the times to come, little one. I'm accustomed to having things my way, and I'm not used to listening to another. But I remember an old saying that makes sense to me, and I hope you'll remember it too. If we never carry our differences to bed, *cailin*, we'll never part. Now, give us a kiss and let's eat before we starve.''

Faith wanted to tear his damned arrogant green eyes out, but when his lips swept hers, all the anger went out of her and her hands clung to his neck. He was a demon straight from hell, but he was all she had, and she could not get enough of him.

Beaming as he set Faith gasping to the floor, Morgan brushed a stray strand of hair from her face and cupped her cheek gently. "I'll go to see the priest this day, and we'll make an honest woman of ye. Will that take away the wrong I've done?"

Stunned by this pronouncement, Faith could only stare at him. Marry? Is that what he asked her to do? Marry him? The idea was so far beyond her ability to imagine that she could only gape at him.

A wry quirk lifted Morgan's lips at her astonished expression. "That's not precisely the reaction a man wants to see when he asks a maid to be his wife."

Marry. Faith shook her head free of his entrapping fingers and took her seat at the table. Marriage was for life. She had never envisioned spending her life here. She had thought it just a temporary haven for the winter. Then she remained to wait for her father's papers. Always she had thought of leaving.

She glanced up quickly as Morgan took his seat across from her. He looked so sure of himself, so full of male pride and arrogance. All the choices were his. He had decided she could stay. He had decided to take her to his bed. He could decide whether or not to ride out again, endanger his neck and leave her abandoned. She had no voice in any of this. She was tired of always doing what other people told her to do. It had been a mistake last time, and it would be a mistake this time. He said they must marry, but this time she had a choice.

Keeping her smile of triumph to herself, Faith lifted her eyes to challenge his. "I'll not marry you."

16

FAITH'S REFUSAL STILL rankled as Morgan saddled up his stallion in preparation to ride. The moonless night beckoned. He had wasted weeks wooing the stubborn wench. He wasn't one to stand and argue when the fight was done. He had a life to live and goals to seek, and there was no reason she had to be a part of them.

But when he remembered the despair shadowing her deep eyes as he had announced his intention after supper, Morgan's shoulders slumped. He had taken on a responsibility, and despite Faith's lack of cooperation, he had to live up to it. There had been others he had neglected too long, until it was too late, and he remembered only too well another time when he had ridden out, only to come back to a cold hearth. He didn't want that worry on his mind while he was gone.

Tying the saddled horse to a post, Morgan strode quickly back to the house, his boots moving soundlessly in the thick grass. Beads of moisture had already formed on his cloak from the damp air as he flung open the door. The hope flaring in Faith's eyes as he entered made him feel a cad, but he had no intention of giving up his quest for a pair of long-lashed eyes.

"I may not be back by morn, but I'll not have you go to bed with anger in your heart. If it's not marriage you want, what would you have of me?"

He was the highwayman tonight, from the blinding white of his lace to the gleaming polish of his high boots. Only the eyes belonged to the Morgan she knew, the sad green that could be both warm and tender, heated and fierce. She longed to fling her arms around his neck and plead with him not to go, but she had her pride and he had his.

Faith considered his question. What would she have of him? She would have him give up his profession, but that wasn't what he asked, she knew. She could ask for dresses and jewels, and he would gladly shower her with them, but she didn't want the position of his paid whore. He had offered marriage, but that was scarcely the honor it should be from a man who might be hanging from a gallows tree by their wedding night. He had nothing to lose by marrying her, and she had little to gain beyond the name of a hunted man. What would she have? Her independence.

Throwing her head back, Faith met Morgan's gaze easily, as she had learned to do this past day. They were equals now. She owed him nothing. He had taken all that she had. There was nothing left to hide. "I'd have employment of my own," she said firmly. "I would not be put in the way of seeking the road again, should aught happen to you."

Relief and just a hint of hope rose to Morgan's eyes. She meant to stay, if he could meet her terms. They weren't easy ones, but he nodded his head slowly. "I'd not see that either, lass. I'll make arrangements. Will you be patient and wait for me until I do?"

Faith's expression softened at the gentleness of his words. He had all the power and strength on his side, but he did not use it against her. She sensed there were few men who would be so lenient, and something unexpected tugged at her heart. Denying its pull, she nodded. "I'll wait. You know I would not do otherwise."

The promise that she would be here to share his bed on his return buoyed Morgan's spirits further. Stepping forward, his cloak flapping around them, he lifted her chin and kissed her soundly. "Keep the bed warm, lass, I'll be back sooner than you know it."

And he was gone, leaving the cottage colder for his absence.

The days were long, but the nights were longer. The slightest sound sent Faith flying to the window in hopes of Morgan's return. She ought to be praying he had been captured so he could repent and save his immortal soul—and hers—but suddenly that seemed less important than his return. He was the closest thing she had to family, and the threat of his loss kept her in constant terror.

It shouldn't be like that. She shouldn't be desiring his return. She ought to be running away as fast as her feet could carry her, for she knew of a certainty what he would expect of her as soon as he returned. She blushed crimson just thinking of it, but stubbornly, she remained.

Faith tried to fathom her reasons for remaining, when all she knew and believed cried out against it, but she could not. In these last months she had become another person. Morgan had saved her body from death out on that road, but something else had died, and she no longer missed it. Whether it was youth or innocence or conscience, she could not say, but it was gone. She had killed a man, taken shelter with a thief, and lost her virtue in this strange world she had stumbled upon. But still, somehow, she felt protected, and she was not yet ready to surrender that protection.

Or perhaps it was Morgan she was not ready to surrender. Just the thought of him returned the fiery heat to her belly. He was a man unlike any she had ever known. Her father had been a gentleman, but he'd had none of Morgan's charm and vitality. The men in the villages where they had resided were crude and uncouth compared to Morgan, and the elegantly garbed aristocrats she had caught glimpses of upon occasion seemed somehow feminine in contrast. The glimpses he occasionally allowed her to see of the hurt, proud man behind the dashing facade touched her even more. The knowledge that a man like that had admired her enough to take her to his bed, and even offered to marry her, was still a little overwhelming to contemplate.

The thought that he might even now be taking his pleasure in some other woman's bed kept Faith from taking too much pride in herself. She was convenient, nothing more. Morgan was a rogue and a rascal and not to be trusted, but he had promised to find her a position. She would have room and board and employment. That was the reason she was staying.

The high cost of that security made her uneasy, but living without Morgan made her even uneasier. Perhaps he would allow her to go back to sleeping in the loft, since she would not marry him.

She soothed her conscience by sleeping in her own bed every night, although the demon in her longed to stay in Morgan's bed to await his return. He had truly planted something unholy inside her that made her ache with need for his touch, that left her restless despite her fevered exertions in the care of the horses and the cottage. She remembered too well the thrust of his hard body, and she spent too many hours at night reliving it. She drew the ladder into the loft with her just to preserve her sanity.

Coming in so late one evening that the April night had left the cottage damp and cold, Morgan swung his satchel to the floor and glanced eagerly toward his bed. His journey had been successful, but he had spent the entire time imagining his return. He had hoped to arrive early enough that his little faerie would be waiting for him, but he could not complain if she were already warming his bed. A man needed a little softness in his life, and Faith offered that and more.

He swiftly shed his outer garments and shirt and washed in the water she always left on the hearth. It was only lukewarm, but he didn't feel the chill for the fever burning in his body. He hadn't had enough of his little Methodist, and this time he would sample her gaits more thoroughly, now that she'd had time to heal from their first ride. Perhaps tonight he would teach her to gallop. His loins throbbed in eagerness at just the thought.

He wanted to see her surprise when he came to her. He found a candle and held it to the dying embers of the fire until it kindled. Wearing only his breeches, Morgan held the candle high and approached the bed, eager to see the spill of russet curls across his pillow and to admire the sleeping innocence of Faith's delicate face.

The shock at finding the bed empty was like taking a blow to the stomach. Morgan stared at it incredulously, not believing his eyes. She had promised! His thoughtful, obedient, and honest Faith had promised to wait. She had to be here.

That thought sent Morgan swinging toward the loft. Holding the candle high, he realized what he should have seen earlier—the ladder was missing.

Rather than feel pain, Morgan allowed anger to boil up in him. She was his. They both knew it. It was childish and spiteful to deny it this way. Grabbing his sword from the nail where he had hung it, he banged the metal against the frame opening to the loft and roared, "Faith Henrietta Montague, remove yourself down here now!"

The noises he had been making earlier had jarred Faith from sleep some time ago, but she had been terrified to betray her wakefulness. She had prayed he would go to bed and think no more about her, but she had known in her heart that would never happen. Morgan's outraged roar now sent her small reserves of courage quaking to her knees.

"Let's see the ladder, lass, or I'm coming up there after you!"

He was quite capable of doing that. His six-foot height put him near enough to the ceiling. It was just a matter of pulling up a chair or an athletic tug to bring him up here. Knowing defiance would never work against his rage, Faith reluctantly leaned over the opening to look down to Morgan's irate features, her braid tumbling through the opening and practically into his hands with the motion.

"Is there aught wrong?" she asked sleepily.

In the candlelight, she was beautiful. She was more than beautiful. Soft shadows played along the hollows of her delicate cheekbones, and her dark lashes made wide ribbons of color against her creamy skin. He ought to be ashamed of his rage and for waking her, but he was not.

"Get down here, lass. I didn't ride all this way tonight to sleep in an empty bed. You've had your rest. Now I need your services."

The sleep disappeared from Faith's eyes and angry tinges of color accented her cheeks. "Morgan de Lacy, that's disgusting! What do you think I am, some whore to come at your beck and call?"

"I think you're my woman and you belong in my bed! Or is your bloody Sassenach breeding too blue for the likes o' me?"

"I'm not your woman, I'm your housekeeper, and I don't belong in your bed unless I want to go there. And I don't know what a Sassenach is, but a bloody *pig* would be too good for the likes of you!"

The combination of the fury and the curse coming from the prim lips of his little Methodist jolted Morgan back to humor. He stared up at her with a growing grin and watched the blush creep across her fair skin.

"A pig is it, now? Then if you'll be my sow, I'll be your boar, and we can rut together. Now, come down from there before I come up to get you." Setting candle and sword aside, Morgan held up his hands to catch her.

"I'll not." Stubbornly Faith started to retreat.

Catching her braid, Morgan tugged. "You will, if only to warm my sheets."

That would be the best compromise he would offer, she knew. Faith didn't trust him to keep his word, but if he had to come up here after her, there wouldn't even be that much conciliation on his part. She didn't expect rape. He didn't need to rape her, and he knew it. That's why he was so damned smilingly confident down there now. All it took was his touch.

Resignedly she gave in. "Let me fetch the ladder."

"Leave the damned ladder up there. I'll not come home to find you there again. Just swing your legs down and I'll catch you."

Swing her legs down! My dear Lord, but the man was a reprobate of the worst kind. He would be able to see all the way up her chemise. Blessedly, it was too dark to see much.

Morgan saw quite enough as long slender limbs appeared in the entrance. His fingers wrapped around one enticing ankle, and his lips quirked at the muffled shriek from above. He had stayed away too long, and she had forgotten everything he'd taught her. He'd rectify that situation soon enough.

Faith eased herself down, and he caught her hips, and then she was in his arms again, where she belonged. Morgan crushed her slender body next to his and felt her arms slide over his shoulders. Now he was home. He needed this bit of fluff and fire, but never would he admit it. To acknowledge the need would be to expose his aloneness and his weakness. A man of strength needed no one. To feel otherwise would inhibit his actions. But there was no wrong in liking a little comfort. Faith was his comfort against the pains of the heart.

His bare chest pressed against Faith's breasts until she felt the crisp hairs through her thin chemise. That sensation alone was enough to light fires, but the exploration of Morgan's mouth and tongue wiped away any remaining resistance. Faith gave herself up to his demands and scarcely knew it when he laid her down upon the bed.

There was a brief instance of coldness while Morgan stopped to remove his breeches, but then he was beside her, stripping off her last shred of clothing, and she was naked in his arms and without shame.

"This is where you belong, lass. You'll get used to the idea with time. A man and a woman belong together, and you're the woman I want."

Morgan's lips closed over hers before Faith could reply, but his words had already sent a thrill of pride through her. A woman! He thought her a woman, and one worth keeping. Compliments had been few and far between in her life, and she found it hard to believe Morgan's pretty phrases, but these words had the ring of truth. She was a woman; she knew it, and he recognized it. That alone gave her a sense of accomplishment. The ardent play of his hands across her flesh only accented it.

He didn't linger with soft praises and gentle touches this time. Their need was too great. While Morgan's lips plundered, his fingers invaded, and before long Faith was rising frantically against him, nearly begging him for the act she had sworn not to repeat. She welcomed the heavy weight covering her, and with Morgan's guidance she lifted her knees and cried out her shock and pleasure at the male hardness penetrating and filling the emptiness he had created within her.

Their bodies fought briefly for the rhythm Faith was just beginning to learn before the explosion caught and overwhelmed them and carried them over the precipice. She'd never had a chance with this man. Circling Morgan's shoulders with her arms, Faith pressed a kiss to his unshaven cheek. For once, her body was content. She would struggle with her conscience on the morrow.

They slept then, and woke long after the dawn to make love again. Faith's shyness disappeared with her need to please, and Morgan's praises and loving touches aroused and inflamed until she could think of nothing else but giving him all he wanted. When he'd taken his fill, she curled up within the protection of his embrace and slept again.

Morgan caressed the slender curve of her back and wondered what would become of this arrangement he had initiated, but he was a man who had learned to live from day to day. He had not abandoned his plans to marry her and flaunt her before London society, but delayed them a little. She did not yet realize that a child could come of their coupling, but it would occur to her in time. He would be prepared when it did.

Until then, he needed to ensure that she would stay, and to that end he applied his nimble mind. There were few opportunities in these misbegotten wilds for the likes of his faerie-woman. He would need to go to London and see that all he possessed would become hers in the very likely event that anything happened to him. But she wasn't ready to accept that as a feasible solution. She wanted to make her own way, and not on her back. That was a little harder.

Gently Morgan cupped her small breast and stroked the crest with his thumb. The little nub grew to an aroused point that beckoned his lips. Even in her inexperience, Faith was more woman than he'd ever had the pleasure of knowing before. Obviously he had been fishing in the wrong waters. Would all of London's society ladies be so responsive? He thought not.

Before Faith was fully awake, Morgan eased into her again, gaining pleasure just from knowing he had an English lady beneath him, spreading her legs for him. That she was like no English lady he had ever seen did not affect his triumph. He had stolen something far more valuable than gold, and he meant to enjoy the prize for a long time to come.

Tousled and spent, Faith felt no inclination to rise from the bed when Morgan did. She watched languorously as he strode naked to stoke the fire and set his coffee on to brew. She had become someone she did not recognize but would soon learn to accept if Morgan continued treating her like this. Perhaps a life of sin had its advantages.

She watched in disappointment as he dressed to see to his horses. The place between her legs ached with Morgan's ardent attentions, and she should be satisfied, but somehow, it wasn't quite enough. Not wishing to contemplate the source of this dissatisfaction, Faith rose to start the day's chores.

Morgan rode to the Raging Bull that afternoon and cornered the proprietor in his private parlor, much to Whitehead's dismay.

"I've not touched the girl again, Jack! Honest, I ain't even seen her."

Morgan propped his booted foot on a chair and considered this unanticipated reaction. Had he terrorized the man that much? "I didn't say you had, Nate. Is there some reason I should?"

Whitehead stopped backing against the wall to study the highwayman's pleasantly arranged features. The black scowl he had expected wasn't there, and that made him nervous. "There's them that's been askin' after her, that's all."

Morgan's dark brows soared. "Who's after asking for her? And how do you know it's her they're looking for?"

Nate shrugged. "She calls herself Faith and she's got the ways of gentry. You know any other come through here that fits the description? The fellow's a runner, I'll be bound, Jack. You'd best watch your step."

A runner. That wasn't a good sign. Surely the London courts weren't interested in the disappearance of a common thief like Tucker, nor could they put Faith's name to the disappearance. Someone must be looking for the missing Montague, and if the example of her noble family he had met was any indication, they didn't mean to shower her with wealth.

Morgan didn't like it. His instincts were to keep her hidden, but he had promised Faith to find her a position, and Whitehead had the only establishment within miles. Perhaps he could hide her right beneath the nose of the runners. That audacious ploy had worked well enough for him in the past, and the runners weren't known for their perspicacity.

"The fellow's a fool, Nate, but you're not. Faith never hurt a tadpole, but there's those who would see her disappear forever. Now, I can't be looking after her all the time, but if we all watch for each other as we do, we can keep her and ourselves safe too. She's gentry, Nate, and she knows nothing of our ways. I'll not be teaching her, but she has it in her that she wants honest employment."

Nate smirked. "Since when is being your doxy not enough, Jack? There's more than enough willing to take her place if you want to be rid of her."

The scowl the innkeeper feared returned to Jack's face. "I'm keeping her, Nate, and one more remark like that will see your foul tongue on the floor. This place stinks, Nate. Even the food stinks. The vermin are the only inhabitants you'll have if you don't clean up. I've heard tell the London coach may start putting over at the Stag down the line. I know how to encourage them in that direction, if you catch my meaning."

The smirk had quickly disappeared from the innkeeper's face with Jack's first words. Now he stared at the highwayman in wordless horror. Jack didn't muddy his own yard by robbing the coach through here, but whispers of a highwayman operating from this inn would destroy the Raging Bull forever. Whitehead understood full well the threat. What he didn't know was the question.

"What are you asking, Jack? You want your fancy miss to stay here? I can't be scouring the floors for the likes of her."

Jack smiled benevolently. "You're a lucky man, Nate. I've found the perfect remedy for your filthy reputation. Her name is . . ." He hesitated and thought a moment. "Alice. Alice Henwood. She can cook and clean and keep books better than you've ever known. She'll only work mornings, and she's shy and doesn't like to be seen by strangers, but she'll have this place looking like a posh London hotel before you know it."

Nate understood. Gulping, he considered the alternatives and found there weren't any. He could hide the chit and have the place cleaned as the lazy slut Molly never did, or he could have a highwayman posted at his front door, ruining his business. Nate wasn't particularly intelligent, but even he understood the advantages of doing Jack's bidding.

He nodded. "Been thinking of hiring a new girl. I'll give 'er a try. Just mornings, you say?"

"When there's the least number here," Jack agreed, "after the first coach leaves and before the next." He shoved his hands in his pockets with satisfaction at a job well done.

And so Alice Henwood was created and employed.

17

FAITH TASTED THE fruit tart, ordered a little sugar to be added to the cream when served, then, leaving the steaming kitchen, started up the back stairs to the bedchambers.

The unusual late-June heat had built up to uncomfortable proportions even here, and the stifling air struck her with a wave of dizziness. Faith gripped the stair rail until she felt she couldn't balance any longer, then sat down abruptly on the landing to steady her swaying head.

Mrs. Whitehead would have changed the linens by now, but Faith doubted Molly had carried the dirty laundry out to the buckets of wash being prepared in the yard. It had taken Faith nearly two entire months to persuade the inn-keeper to take on the expense of hiring village girls to come in and do the extensive laundry at least twice a week. Only because Faith's other suggestions had attracted the kind of clientele willing to pay higher rates did Whitehead finally acquiesce to this expense. She had to make it successful or he would go back to his usual slovenly ways.

But the dizziness lingered and she feared to stand up. To Faith's annoyance, Molly took this moment to pull her bulky body up the stairs. Her bloated features took on a sardonic cast at finding Miss Aristocrat sitting down on the job. "Not feelin' the heat, are ye?" she gloated, noting the pale color of Faith's cheeks. "Maybe somethin' else's caught ye. I'm just waitin' to see what Miss Hoity-Toity looks like when she's all swelled up with Black Jack's brat. Then mayhap you'll know what it's like."

Molly had become more impossible than usual since her pregnancy had become obvious, and Faith ignored her taunts. "Mr. Whitehead said you could work as long as you felt up to it, Molly. But if the heat's bothering you, I'll take care of the laundry while you lie down awhile. Jack's gone to London and I don't expect him back soon."

Instead of looking relieved, Molly's expression darkened. "Just because they hired a new girl for the taproom don't mean you can lord it over me, you slut. You ain't no better than me any day, and when my baby's father gets back from sea, he'll make an honest woman of me, and that's more than you can say."

Faith gave up. Molly's bile spewed nastier every day. It was doubtful if she even knew the father of her child, and even if she did, it was even more doubtful if he intended to return. Ever since her tips had started falling off in the taproom and she'd found fewer men willing to dally with her because of her size and condition, Molly had grown more spiteful and nastier. Faith had tried being nice, tried speaking up for herself, and had even once threatened the maid with a frying pan. Trial and error had taught her that ignoring the nastiness was the best solution.

When Molly received no response, she stomped off in a huff, leaving Faith blessedly alone. The dizziness had passed, but Molly's bile had left its mark. Until this day, Faith had never questioned the origins of babies. They were simply a fact of life, like leaves on trees and snow in winter. But Molly's obvious pregnancy and the knowledge of her trade clicked together at last, and other pieces began to fall in place.

Faith had never thought of loose women like Molly getting pregnant. They didn't have husbands, so they shouldn't have babies. But that logic failed when carried a little further. Animals didn't marry, but they had babies. The fact that Morgan had announced last night that Annette was in foal now took on new significance. Annette had been the mare Faith had witnessed Morgan's stallion covering just days before Morgan first took her to his bed.

Faith's cheeks began to burn as the sums began to add up. The barn was swarming with new kittens. The first crop of chickens were fast becoming hens and roosters and there was another flock of fuzzy yellow balls in the stall. One foal already frolicked in the paddock, and another was on its way. The baby growing inside Molly was plain to see, and there could only be one way she could come by it—the same way the animals came by theirs. The same way Faith and Morgan shared every night.

It wouldn't do to think about it. She knew very little of babies. Her mother had never allowed her to attend a birthing. She had held a few infants upon occasion, but they had been alien creatures of little interest. Faith couldn't imagine what one did with one, but she supposed she would find out when Molly had hers. That would be soon enough. She didn't want to think about one of her own. Hers and Morgan's.

Rising from the stairs, Faith stopped to hold a hand to her flat abdomen. It couldn't be possible.

But as she trudged up the stairs to haul down the laundry, she knew it could. Morgan was as virile as any stallion. It was just a matter of time. How did one know when a baby started? The whole premise sounded vaguely improbable.

Morgan carefully checked the valuable documents in his coat pocket. The trunk with George Montague's papers had arrived with perfect timing. While Faith pored and cooed over musty tomes on religion and a spider-scrawled sheaf of vellum, he had carefully sorted out the ones that counted. He had it all in writing now, in legally witnessed formal documents suitable for any court of British law. One George Henry Montague, second son to Henry, Marquess of Mountjoy, wed to Leticia Carlisle, only daughter of the Earl of Carlisle, parents of one Faith Henrietta Montague. Holy Mary, Mother of Jesus, but a marquess and an earl!

She was a scion of British society, the *crème de la crème*. And she was working as cook and housekeeper in one of England's less savory wayside inns. And sleeping with a highwayman. Morgan's glee would have been greater had she been anyone but Faith. As it was, he was having a hard time reconciling the downfall of two great Sassenach houses with his need to protect his innocent faerie.

Still, he would do it. Morgan watched in satisfaction as his man of business entered the coffeehouse and looked around. His plans were made. He had only to see them out.

The man spotted him and strode forward, hat in hand. He looked perfectly respectable in this meeting place of gentlemen, just as Morgan did. To all outer appearances, they were two gentlemen engaged in a spot of business— nothing tawdry like trade, but perchance a real-estate exchange or fund investment. Morgan smiled at the image as Miles Golden took the seat across from him. Wouldn't their fellow coffee drinkers be stunned to know they dined in the company of an Irish papist highwayman and the son of a Jewish bastard?

Miles frowned at his client's smile. "I think someone was trying to follow me."

"You lost them, I trust?" The news didn't surprise Morgan so much as cause him to give his enemies a little more respect. He hadn't thought the Sassenach rogue to be so clever.

"I hope so. I know these alleys as well as anyone. The money's there. I've brought a list of instructions on how your ward is to claim it." Miles no more believed the wench was Morgan's "ward" than he believed the sun rose in the west, but the term sufficed to keep relations pleasant.

Morgan hadn't thought it would be quite so easy. He had hoped to return to Montague House for a little more arm-twisting. But for Faith's sake, he was happy he had secured some form of safety for her. He handed the sheaf of documents to Golden.

"Here's all the proof that should be necessary. You're holding the girl's life there, Miles. See that you take care of it."

Miles scanned the documents, raised his eyebrows, and neatly tucked each one in a different pocket. "I'll have copies made, witnesses confirm the originals, and register them. Then I'll return them to you. These are more than adequate to meet their demands. Unfortunately, if they've hired someone at the bank to follow any claimant to the trust, she'll be in jeopardy the instant she comes to claim it."

Miles was clever. He had already surmised the circumstances. Morgan nodded in agreement. "You'll have to act as go-between, Golden. Once Faith's authenticity is established, it might be necessary to transfer the entire trust elsewhere. I'll give her your name, and not the bank's. Should anything happen to me, she'll be in your hands. I trust you have adequate protection and someone you can rely on in the event of your unanticipated demise."

Miles grimaced, an expression that came naturally to his long, bony face. "If you weren't such a damned good client, I'd tell you to go to hell. But to answer your question, I'm protected, and I have eight brothers, four uncles, and a squadron of cousins who can step into my shoes at any time. She'll be safe."

"You'll own London by the turn of the century." Morgan grinned. "Do you intend to enjoy yourself before you're eighty?"

Stiffly the solicitor rose. "Indeed I do. She's eighteen, with hair as gold as her father's pockets. I have none of the aristocracy's prejudice against trade."

Morgan leaned back in his chair and held out his hand. "Neither have I, my friend. We'll meet over dinner when we're rich and living in St. James's. We can compare our respective choices then."

Miles took his hand firmly. "You'd best marry her, then," he answered in farewell.

Sipping his coffee, Morgan watched the solicitor weave his way through the tables. Marriage sounded good to him, but he was growing more and more uncertain of its advantages for Faith. The granddaughter of an earl and a marquess. It was preposterous. How could the bloody thick-headed Sassenachs produce a brilliant gem like his little Methodist? It didn't bear thinking on.

Out of curiosity, on his way home Morgan took a detour to the Montague mansion. Staying out of sight in an alley between two houses, he watched a sedan chair arrive and waited to see the occupant. Were he at all familiar with family crests and livery, he might identify the house from the servants' garb, but he was not. So he watched with curiosity as an elderly lady was helped from the chair by one of her footmen. She was so tiny as to be almost doll-like in size, but her back was as stiff and straight as any martinet's. A frilled cap covered her hair and lapped over her cheeks, hiding what little he could see of her face, but it wasn't the face he noticed. It was her carriage, the posture, the grace, and above all, the daintiness. By the time the woman was taken into the Montague home, Morgan had no doubt that he'd just seen Faith's grandmother.

Somehow, he had never pictured a grandmother in his scheme to destroy the Sassenachs. All he knew of the Montague family was the scheming, devious bastard who had tried to deny Faith's existence. It had been easy envisioning rubbing the heir's face in the mud, or the faces of any of the other self-righteous criminals who had left Faith to starve. But a grandmother?

Thoughtfully Morgan reared his stallion in the other direction. He had a healthy respect for women. Would a grandmother leave her grandchild to starve?

It sat uneasy on his mind all the way home.

Faith coaxed the colt to the fence with a baby carrot from her garden. The treat was barely more than a nibble, but the young animal took it eagerly, allowing her to pet him for just a second before he gamboled off after a butterfly.

She watched the patient mare as she chewed at the thick turf, undisturbed, even when the colt came skidding up to grab a teat for a drink. Faith winced and covered her own small breast as she recognized the similarity between herself and the mare. The sight of the foal contentedly nursing at his mother's side stirred odd feelings in her own breasts.

She glanced toward Annette in the far paddock, but did not know what signs to look for to identify her quickening. The stallion had quite a harem, and a right to strut. Would Morgan be the same? How many bastards had he sired in his lifetime?

She had no right to think such thoughts. He had offered marriage, and she had refused. He had found her a paying position, and she had continued to share his bed. She wasn't certain she could have left had she tried, but she had never tried.

Wondering at the changes that had taken her from starving innocent to highwayman's bedmate, Faith entered the cottage to start the evening meal. The changes weren't all emotional or mental, but physical as well. She had become a woman in Morgan's hands, a woman who needed a man to share her pleasures.

As she tied a clean apron around her neck, Faith glanced down at her swelling breasts. They were still growing, and they felt a bit sore at times now. She had thought she would never have a figure to entice a man, but it seemed it took a man to develop a figure. She had curves now that she had never possessed before, and she felt slightly awkward in the newness of it.

As she reached for the kettle, the dizziness struck again. It wasn't so severe this time, and she managed to remain standing until the spell passed, but it left an uneasiness behind. The cottage was warm, but not so heat-bound as the inn. Fresh air entered the open door and window, and she hadn't lit the fire yet.

Was she sickening for something? Remembering her mother's illness, Faith clasped her hands in silent prayer.

Six months ago she had been prepared to die. Today she had a whole future before her. She didn't want to die.

Chasing away these morbid thoughts, Faith set the kettle on and started the fire. But as she chopped new onions and carrots and crushed the fresh young leaves of herbs, she had plenty of time to let her mind wander over other physical changes that might give some clue to her illness.

She had never been regular. She had stopped her monthly flux before. But counting back, it had been March when she'd had her last bleeding. There had been none in April or May, and June was almost over.

But Morgan had first taken her to his bed in early April, and that seemed the most natural explanation for the flux to stop. It would be much too embarrassing for a woman to tell a man she couldn't share his bed because of her monthly woman's time. So it only seemed natural that it would go away while she shared her bed with a man. There could be nothing in that to cause her illness.

Perhaps she was just imagining things. She wasn't accustomed to heat, and she had been working hard. She just needed a bit of a rest. She would put a simple stew on to cook with the beef she had bought this day from the inn, then she would read some more of her father's manuscript. She would feel better then.

She had the stew simmering and was just about to take out the bread dough and knead it when she heard the sound of a horse in the yard. Hurriedly Faith wiped her hands and untied her apron, patting her hair to see if all was in place. There was scarce time to smooth her skirts before Morgan threw open the door and strode across the floor.

Faith squealed as he swept her off her feet and buried his lips against the uncovered skin at her throat. She clung to his thick hair and bent her head back to allow him better access as the thrill of his touch coursed through her.

But when Morgan's mouth strayed lower and his fingers began working the laces of her bodice, Faith gave his hair a tug and she tried to wriggle away. "What do you think you're doing, Morgan de Lacy? 'Tis broad daylight. Now, put me down."

"I'm a starving man, my dear. I just wanted a taste to tide me over. Can I not have just a taste?"

He wasn't waiting for her permission. Already he had her laces untied. The chemise tie was next, and then Faith felt the tug of his lips at her breast, and there was no further fighting him. The sensations he had taught her were swelling up inside, begging for release, and her cry of pleasure only urged him on.

" 'Tis shameless, Morgan," she whispered in one final weak protest as his kisses grew bolder.

"Have I never taken you in day, then?" Morgan murmured from the perfumed softness between her lovely uptilted breasts. "Then it is time we corrected that error. Undress me, my *cailin*, and let us show the sun a thing or two."

Undress him. The thought was even more shameless than seeing each other in daylight, but the need to touch him, to feel him close, was even greater than shame. The lace of his jabot untied easily. His shirt fell open to reveal the dark crisp hairs of his chest, and as Morgan eased her feet to the floor, Faith daringly placed her kisses at the V of his neckline.

But that wasn't enough. She wanted to touch *all* of him. Such thoughts had only been a mist of sensation during their nights together. Morgan always came to their bed unclothed, and she was given little chance to explore while he drove her to new, frantic heights of desire. What he offered now was different, but she wasn't certain how to pursue it.

Morgan was already unhooking her bodice and pulling it off her shoulders without separating it from the skirt. His big hands were amazingly swift and nimble, and they stroked and teased until she forgot all the day's concerns and concentrated on only one thing: the man in front of her.

In the June warmth he had doffed coat and waistcoat long ago. He stood there now in wide-sleeved shirt, breeches, and boots, defying her to bring them closer. The long tails of the shirt were tucked into the tight waist of his breeches, and there would be no removing the one without unfastening the other. Beneath Morgan's amused gaze, Faith bit her bottom lip and twisted her fingers into the fastenings of his breeches.

When they were released, she tugged at his shirt until she could, at last, run her hands up his bare chest. Morgan gave a gasp of pleasure as she tweaked his nipples as he did hers, and then his kiss was moist and hot against her mouth again.

Faith felt her skirt and petticoat fall loose from her waist; then strong hands pushed them to the floor until she stood there in only her stockings and chemise. The air felt warm and good against her bare skin, and Morgan's fingers caressed and stroked until she ached for what was to come.

" 'Tis not fair, I cannot reach to take yours off," she murmured, pushing his shirt upward so she could explore more fully the firm planes of his chest. "You have all the advantages."

Morgan's eyes crinkled at the corners as he swept the shirt off and contemplated this fey spirit who had entered his life. Her breasts were fuller and pulled the cloth of her chemise taut now, but she was still no bigger than a minute. And she spoke of fairness in this arena of the sexes. He grinned as she kept her wide-eyed gaze on his face and not the expanse of flesh he uncovered as he obligingly dropped his shirt to the floor.

"Fair, is it, now? Is it equal you would be? Undress me, lass, and I will show you equality."

Faith knew Morgan's charm to be dangerous to a fatal degree, but the challenge was thrown and she must accept it. She glanced down at his knee-high boots and frowned. His clothing posed too many obstacles.

Noting the direction of her gaze, Morgan bent a kiss to her plump breasts beneath the open chemise, then sat down on the chair and held up his leg. "Off with the boots, wench."

She had seen him do it innumerable times, but it still did not appear easy. Straddling the leg he held out, Faith began to tug—leaving Morgan to admire at leisure the delicate swell of flesh above the fine linen gaping enticingly to reveal the pink rosebuds at their crest. His gaze thoroughly absorbed the curve of tiny waist to the roundness of hips and buttocks meant to fit a man's pleasure and the long length of neatly formed legs meant to cradle him. She did not need to powder and paint and flaunt and strut to arouse his desires. She was his desire, and he grew impatient to seek his satisfaction.

The boot slid loose and Morgan helped her with the other one, not without catching Faith by surprise and riding her briefly on his knee, rubbing her woman's place until her eyes smoked in pleasure and desire as strong as his own. Then he stood, and she was faced with the feat of rolling his breeches down over his narrow hips.

"It's all right to touch me, my sweet. I'll not break. Well

you should know that by now," Morgan chuckled as she hesitated.

Faith's cheeks colored briefly, but she needed what he hid beneath that cloth to satisfy the itch he had aroused. Setting her jaw in determination, she rolled the cloth down over lean hips, releasing the hardened length of his maleness that had been confined by the civilization of his breeches.

She tried not to stare, but she never saw him in daylight. He was so magnificent, so marvelously made, that she could scarce keep her eyes away. Wide chest and shoulders, lean flanks, narrow hips, and flat belly, all tightly muscled and shaped to move with careless grace, as he did now.

"Now, my Faith, I'll show you equality." Morgan slid the chemise off her shoulders and to the ground, until they were both naked in the puddle of sunlight from the window. Then he lifted her in his arms and carried her to the bed, but instead of laying her down on it, he sat down and left her in his lap.

Faith stared at him in disbelief. They were full naked, with his manhood jutting awkwardly between them, and he was sitting down as if to table. Spread wide by his thighs, her legs dangled awkwardly over his, and the ache in her belly began to swell with demands she could scarcely suppress.

"Equality, Faith." Morgan pulled the pins from her hair until it tumbled down between them. Then he sought her mouth with his lips and her breasts with his hands until she was moaning with the need she kept barely under control.

When she felt him hot and heavy against her belly, Faith finally understood what he meant for her to do. It seemed impossible. He was much too large, almost fearsome in the light of day. How could he enter her? But she had spent nearly three months in his bed and knew the length of him filled her with remarkable ease. But how could she . . . ?

Morgan lifted her slightly, and then he was there, right where she needed him, and it was but a moment's work to guide him inside, to take him more fully than she ever remembered. She found her place and moved cautiously at first, then with increasing vigor as Morgan responded wildly to her movement, and she learned the joy of giving him pleasure as well as finding her own.

She could do it. She could drive him to the same wanton abandonment as he drove her, and the joy she received of this knowledge was equal to or greater than the explosion of their mutual release.

He needed her. They truly were equals. And for the first time, Faith realized, she was in love.

18

FAITH WASN'T PARTICULARLY happy with her new discovery. As she watched Morgan don his breeches to tend to his horses, he suddenly seemed a masculine stranger who had taken her to his bed and held her captive with his charms, with no intention of letting her go until he tired of her. Then she would be left to find her own way in this cold world, her heart broken and her virtue stolen.

She knew she was being unfair, but a part of that feeling had some basis in fact. Morgan used his charm to hold her, knowing it was to his benefit to keep her around, but she possessed no charm with which to hold him captive in return. He came and went as he willed, plying his terrible trade without a thought to her. He had made her love him, tied her to him more surely than with rope and chain, but nothing held him bound.

The miserable feeling of unrequited love burned in Faith's belly as she watched Morgan over their meal later that evening. He had washed, and his black hair still gleamed with moisture, slicked back from his strong features and held with a strip of leather. The firelight caught an occasional shadow on his cheek and illuminated it, but it was his eyes that dominated her vision.

She tried to ease the ache by introducing a topic that had played in her mind ever since Toby had spoken of it one day at the inn. "Do you think the colonists live much differently than this?"

Morgan shrugged. "We don't have red Indians, leastways."

Faith pursued the subject. "Toby said his brother lives in a town over there. It isn't all Indians. They have inns and stores, just like here."

"I suppose they must." Morgan eyed her quizzically. It

was unlike her to introduce such a topic. "What is your interest in the colonists?"

Faith squirmed slightly beneath his piercing stare. He could look right through her sometimes and know her every thought. It was an uncomfortable feeling. "Toby's brother just bought a lot of land. He says anyone can make a living over there. He wants Toby to join him."

"Toby is a young fool and will probably be better off over there. How do you know so much about Toby's brother?"

Faith ducked her head to hide the heat in her cheeks. She didn't want Morgan to know the direction of her thoughts just yet. "Toby can't read and he brings me his brother's letters to read for him."

There was that. Morgan gazed at her thoughtfully. He kept forgetting she was educated far beyond the limited horizons of this life he led. How much longer could he keep her like this before the world beckoned?

"And is Toby going to join his brother?" he asked casually.

Faith shook her head. "He doesn't want to be a farmer, he says, but I think he's afraid of the journey alone."

"As I said, Toby's a young fool."

He seemed prepared to dismiss the topic, and Faith hastily fumbled for the words to keep it open. "You once said a man needed land to be gentry. Land is cheap over there. You could probably buy a whole farm with the price of this place here."

Morgan's black brow quirked upward as he finally fathomed the direction of her thoughts. " 'Tis not a dirt farmer I am, lass, nor a farmer's wife you'll be. You belong in satins and lace in a great terrace house in St. James's, with servants at your beck and call. You'll have that one day, lass."

Gray eyes grew stormy as Faith regarded Morgan's placid expression across the table. "On a highwayman's take? I'm more likely to see your dead body hanging from a noose than I am to see inside the great houses of London. I do not know who's the greater fool here, Toby for not grabbing the chance when it's offered, or you for being too blind to see it!"

He had not realized how much she had thought on this. Dismayed by this unexpected turn of events, Morgan waited for the flood of her anger to pass before replying. He wasn't certain how to reply. Here he had been concentrating all his efforts on returning them to the society where they belonged, and she had been planning a future on the other side of the world.

"Lass, you worry over naught." Morgan rose to come around the table and place his hands on her shoulders. "I've seen that you're provided for, whatever might happen to me. There's a man in London, Miles Golden, who looks after my business. I'll leave you his direction. I don't think you'll be needin' it. I need only ride a little longer, and I'll have all that I need to set us up royally. We'll have that house in London, lass, see if we don't."

On a highwayman's ill-gotten coins, with the threat of his death ever present. It was not a future she placed any reliance on, and Faith shook off his hands and rose to clear the table. "You may live as a king if you wish, but I don't feel like a queen. I don't need satins and lace. I am willing to work for my wages. I just need a roof over my head and food in my stomach." And you by my side—but she couldn't say that. Her heart longed to say it, to talk of babies and homes and her need for his love, but it would be madness even to think it.

"You deserve better than that, Faith." Morgan caught her by the waist and pressed a kiss against her hair, but she shook him off irritably. His passionate Faith never turned aside his kisses. He watched her in puzzlement and tried again. "I mean to see you have it, little one, as my wife or not, as you will."

His wife. He still offered marriage. She ought seriously to consider it. But he would always be a highwayman and she could not be a highwayman's wife. She simply could not. Someday she would have to leave. Someday, when she was strong enough.

Faith slammed the kettle on the hook and kept her back to him. "I'll not marry a thief," she declared firmly.

Pain shot through Morgan with the swiftness of a bullet. Refusing to acknowledge the rightness of her words, refusing to acknowledge his reaction to them, he stalked toward the door. "Fine, then. Be a thief's doxy. I'll find some fine lady to walk the aisle when the time comes. Money always talks."

He slammed out of the house, and Faith bent over, holding her stomach against the pain crippling her. She hadn't wanted to fight. She hadn't wanted to make him angry. But she could not bear the thought of him hanging from a gallows or lying in the dust of the road with a bullet through his heart. The pain of it wouldn't go away. Why had no one warned her that love hurt so bad?

She was already in bed when Morgan finally came in out of the dark and undressed. It had taken time to work through her rejection, to understand he might never call her his, but he was a practical man. He hadn't needed her before; he could live without her as he had lived without everyone else these long years. But he wasn't quite willing to give it all up just yet.

He slid into bed beside her, curving his hand around Faith's breast and kissing the nape of her neck. He could tell by her breathing that she was awake, and he pressed his advantage further, pulling her back against him until he lay wrapped around her. "I'd not have you go to bed angry, lass. How can I make it up to you?"

By getting rid of the highwayman, Faith replied silently, as she did a thousand times a day, but she knew better than to say it aloud. Her love was too new, too fragile, to challenge it. She only knew she needed Morgan by her side, whatever the price. She caressed his hand where it lay over her belly and wished for the stars.

Understanding her gesture, Morgan gladly obliged. In this, they were together. Their needs were mutual, not just for the demands of passion, but in the craving for affection that came of it. He could take her as he wanted, but when all was said and done, she owned a piece of him as surely as he did her. This that was between them would never be denied.

And when they had sought their release and Faith was sleeping peacefully in his arms, Morgan ran his hand possessively down her swelling breasts and rounded abdomen and prayed as he had never prayed in these last ten years. He wanted more than revenge for the lives torn from him. He wanted a family again. Closing his eyes, Morgan tried to see the future, but only flashes of the past came back to knot his fists and increase the tension he had just released in Faith's sweet, unknowing body.

He should have ridden with Bonnie Prince Charlie when he took Scotland. Then his bones could be bleaching on Culloden Moor with all the others, and there would not be this hatred burning in his soul, condemning him to hell. But he had been scarce a lad of twenty and fiercely eager to free his own lands from the German fist of the Hanovers. He had offered—and been accepted—to organize a battalion of Irish to join the prince when he came to free Ireland, as he surely would, or so they had thought in those days. So Morgan had gone home for the first time in years.

And the last. Morgan clenched his eyes shut and tried to drive out the pictures of the crumbling ruin of his home and the three unmarked graves, but the ghosts of his father and his father before him rose up to demand justice, and he could not deny them. The de Lacys had owned that land since the invasion of the Normans. There had always been a Lord de Lacy to walk those emerald fields. And he was the last of them. If he could not win the lands back, he must die trying.

He tried to say a Hail Mary for the inhabitants of those cold graves, but he could not. He could only remember his little sister's dark curls and imagine the emaciated face they must have framed when she died, a face like those of the starving children he had found when he returned to the village that day.

A tear slid down his cheek, and Morgan turned to curl protectively around Faith and rest his hand on her abdomen. It had all happened too quickly, he had been told. There hadn't been time to write. In truth, they had not known how to write or where to send such a missive. His family had died bearing the secret of his whereabouts, protecting lands they no longer owned.

It had taken no more than a quick visit to find the meaning for the gaping holes in the de Lacy castle and the origins of the sparkling new Palladian residence rising on the meadows where his horses used to romp. The lands were no longer his. The new owner meant to dismantle the "dismal" castle to build his own very British idea of a home. The men of the village whispered the tale late at night over their beers, how the de Lacy that was had been struck down in the night and left to freeze in the road. Morgan could well imagine the whiskey that must have been consumed before his father would lie senseless in the road. There could have been foul play, but none knew of it. Yet the very next night, when the lord's younger son, Sean, recklessly agreed to a secret Mass for his father's soul, the redcoats knew of it and were waiting for him. They hanged him from the rafters over his father's coffin.

Morgan had flinched and turned away and tried to hide the sobs of anguish and hatred threatening to erupt as he heard this tale of his father's and brother's deaths, but the final story hadn't been told. When they spoke of his fair young sister thrown from her home when the land was confiscated, left to starve and die among the villagers, the then-twenty-year-old Morgan had broken down and cried.

As he would now if he did not learn to control his thoughts. Caressing Faith's warm satin skin, Morgan forced his mind to the present, and the future represented by the slight swelling covered by his hand. He had tried to time his absences for those times of the month when she could not take him, but he was not fool enough to think he was so deadly accurate as to always miss them. How long had it been? How soon would she guess?

And then, would she marry him?

Edward, Lord Stepney, removed his bulky body from the hackney with a curse. He would crown the deuced thief-taker for forcing him out like this. Why couldn't anyone do a job as told? Bigad, he was beginning to sound like his father now. But the fact that he had to come to these unenlightened corners of the city to meet a bloody runner did not ease his choler.

Watson hurried forward to lead his noble visitor into the privacy of the darkened tavern. The place stank of smoking lanterns and stale ale, and Edward turned up his nose in disgust.

"You had best have good reason for this, Watson. My patience is wearing thin."

The runner settled him in a booth with a glass of port and hastened onto the bench across from him. He was not a man of letters, and written reports would do only when there was no news to report. This time, he needed a man's face across from him to speak to. "Remember I told you your cousin hocked those jewels you got him and took the proceeds to a bank?"

Edward nodded irritably.

"Well, I told the judge I was on the trail of Black Jack, and he gave me a piece of paper to the bank so I could post a bloke there to keep an eye on whoever came to claim that money.''

''Very clever.'' Edward sat back, relaxing. He'd known the thief-taker's ambitions. He hadn't realized they would go so far as to actually lie to the only honest judge in the kingdom. Well, perhaps it wasn't quite a lie, but close enough.

Encouraged, Watson continued. ''A legal fellow came to check on it, but the blunderer let him get away. So I took over the watch myself. The next day, a boy shows up with this bundle or papers, and the clerk signals me right quick. They gabble awhile, and the boy goes away empty-handed, but I follow him. He takes me straight back to the money-lenders' quarter, but he don't report to nobody. He just idles away the rest of the day as if he ain't got a care in the world.''

A frown crept between Edward's eyes, but he folded his hands placidly over his walking stick. ''And the papers?''

The runner took a deep breath. ''The clerk says them papers prove ir-re-triev-ably that their owner is the missing heiress.''

Edward stared at a space somewhere over the thief-taker's head as he worked this piece of information through several elaborate thought processes. The papers did not necessarily mean Faith Montague was alive. They did not even mean she had been found. They could mean Thomas was double-crossing him, but Edward already knew about *that*. The game was to stay one step ahead of his cousin until the plan was revealed and opportunity availed. It was growing to be a deuced boring game, but it occasionally had its moments.

A smile playing about the corners of his mouth, Edward returned his gaze to his informant. ''Well, then, it seems to me our next step is to catch Black Jack.''

The runner's eyes widened, but they soon gleamed with approval. That wouldn't have been his choice of action for locating a missing heiress, but the gentry had strange ways, and the idea had merit. They had no connection between the highwayman and the bank account or Thomas, but there was still that reporting of the girl at the inn—the girl that Black Jack defended. It was worth a chance. If nothing else, they would remove one more criminal from the road.

The pain in the small of her back had kept her awake most of the night, that and Morgan's absence. Faith looked with distaste at the breakfast she had fixed and rose from the table to see to the horses. She had come a long way since that starving child of last November who longed for just a bite of egg.

She didn't like it when Morgan was gone for days like this. He could be in some filthy cell somewhere awaiting trial and she might never know it until too late. He could be dead, and she would have no way of knowing, except that she thought she ought to feel it. A world without Morgan would suddenly seem hollow. It was empty enough just knowing he wouldn't be riding into the yard any minute now. She needed him near, just his physical presence if nothing else. She needed that security right now, while everything else was in turmoil.

She was going to have to talk to Molly about babies. Faith didn't relish the thought, but she desperately needed information. It was mid-July and her monthly flow still hadn't started, just occasional spots that never came to anything. And she felt terrible, more terrible than that dizzying day at the end of June. How could Molly keep working if she ached as badly as this?

Faith made an involuntary gesture toward her stomach as another pain cramped her middle. She'd never had cramps before. Perhaps there was something deathly wrong with her. Where would she find a physician with Morgan gone? Would she dare tell a physician what she had done? Mortification at the idea seeped through her, but the feeling that something was terribly wrong took a stronger hold.

She could scarcely lift the pails to water the horses. Morgan had warned her not to let them out of their stalls while he was gone, but the temptation was great to let them into the paddock to forage for themselves. Surely by evening she would feel better.

But by noon she was lying in bed groaning with a pain that had no beginning and no end, and as she arched her back in agony, terror erased all thought of anything else.

Having stopped in London to exchange his ill-gotten goods for cash and to leave the proceeds with Miles, Morgan cantered along the dusty road to home with a whistle on his lips. Miles had verified that the trust fund was established and ready to be transferred at his word, and Morgan's investments in the funds were doing exceedingly well. The future seemed promising, if only he could get one Faith Henrietta Montague to agree.

She still hadn't mentioned the baby to him. He couldn't be positive himself without questioning her, and Faith's shyness made questioning difficult. Still and all, it was time they faced a few facts. He couldn't have her slaving at Whitehead's inn if she was carrying his child. That situation would need to be rectified immediately.

He still needed a few more large hauls before he would have enough to think about that house in town. London property came high. The new terrace houses seemed the best investment, but perhaps he could rent for just a while. He needed to get Faith out of this forest and back to civilization. He had been selfish in keeping her here this long.

But he needed Faith's cooperation. He couldn't take her anywhere until she bore his name. He didn't know how dangerous her family was, and he needed to find out before London knew of her existence. He could protect her much easier once they were married.

Deciding there was no reason to delay the inevitable, Morgan turned the stallion toward Whitehead's inn. Faith would be there at this time of day. Whitehead would just have to do without her for a while.

When Morgan arrived at the Raging Bull, it was on a scene of utter chaos. Molly's curses carried in a shrill stream from above. Whitehead's angry replies thundered down the stairs with his heavy steps. His wife's voice rose in wails of despair as smoke curled from the back kitchen, and the excited chatter of the cook wove in between the cacophony in some form of syncopated rhythm.

The innkeeper glared at Morgan's towering form as if he were somehow the instigator of this confusion. Cursing, he threw down his filthy towel. "Where the hell is she? I pay that wench good wages to keep this place in order. And the day I need her most, she doesn't show."

Morgan tried not to make too much of this declaration, but his instinct for danger made his flesh crawl, and he edged toward the door he had just entered. "Faith's not here?"

Whitehead stared at him in incredulity. "Does it look like she's here? Her and her fancy ways . . . Now nobody can do nothing . . ." His eyes narrowed shrewdly as Morgan started for the door. "She up and leave you too?"

But he got no answer. Morgan was already racing for his stallion. Faith would never leave her employer without notice. Something was wrong.

He could feel it stronger all the way home. He never feared for himself, but this fear emanated from outside of him. He didn't know the how or why of it, but he knew Faith's fear, and he raced the tired stallion as he never would have done had not hell been at his heels.

Flinging the reins over a fencepost, Morgan dived for the ground and hit it running, practically flying through the door as he heard the panicked groans inside.

The light from the window and the open door was sufficient to give Morgan the scare of his life, in a life that was riddled with horrors.

Faith lay twisted on the bedcovers, her face pale and drawn with pain as soft whimpers occasionally escaped her lips. Beneath her, the bright splash of red grew, soaking her silver gown and the sheets and growing before Morgan's horrified eyes.

He had spent half a score of years living on his own, learning the atrocity of war, watching men die in rivers of blood, binding the wounds of those who lived. He knew how to kill. He knew how to survive. He didn't know how to save Faith and his child. His ignorance brought a moan to his lips and a prayer to God as he fell on his knees beside her.

She was scarcely conscious of his presence when he knelt beside her. He had to do something, but he was afraid to move her and afraid not to. He couldn't leave her, but he didn't know how to handle this alone.

Sweat breaking out on his brow, Morgan discarded his coat and murmured soothing noises as he tested her forehead for fever. He couldn't find one, but he was burning all over himself, and chilled cold as ice inside, so he was a poor judge. Faith's eyelashes flickered briefly at his touch, and her hand pushed restlessly at her ruined skirts. Morgan took this as a sign and began unfastening the intricacies of her clothing that would free her from the heat and blood.

His fingers fumbled and knotted laces and he finally pulled out his knife and began cutting her free. The fine fabric shredded beneath his strength, giving him some satisfaction, some sense of accomplishment. He wanted to close his eyes at the sight revealed, but Faith shivered and cried, and he drew on the resources that made him cold and calm on the battlefield. Action, not emotion, was required. His faerie needed him, and he wouldn't let her down.

By the time Morgan stripped Faith and the bed and removed the bloody remains to the yard, he knew the worst was over. He rummaged until he found the strips of cloth she had used to bind herself during the winter and packed them as neatly as he could to stem the slight but steady flow. Then he found her a clean chemise and awkwardly managed to slide it over her head and arms so she could rest decently.

Faith seemed in some state between consciousness and unconsciousness as Morgan worked. She lifted her arm when ordered, but closed her eyes again when he had the garment adjusted. Her hands roved restlessly, catching at his, picking at the sheets, straying to her belly. Pain occasionally puckered her brow, but the terror had subsided, and she no longer made those sounds that made Morgan shake in his boots.

He pulled the covers around her, and a frail hand reached to hold his. He knelt beside her, stroking her brow, wishing he could find the words that usually came so easily to his tongue.

"Was it . . . ?" She licked her dry lips. ". . . a baby?"

This last was said so soft that Morgan could barely hear her. His broad hand crushed her fingers, and he suddenly realized his face was wet. He hadn't cried in years. It had to be sweat. It was bloody damn hot in here. He wiped the salty beads from his cheeks and tried to speak.

"There'll be others someday, my *cailin alainn*. We'll have beautiful babies together." He choked on the words, holding back the lump in his throat that threatened to become more. "This one just wasn't ready to be born. He's better off in heaven, lass. We'll see him by and by," he whispered in anguish, praying for the truth of the words.

Morgan could see the tears roll in great drops from beneath the dark fringe of Faith's lashes, and he finally choked on the sob and turned his head away. Now that there was no further action he could take, guilt welled up in him, and he struggled to keep it in check. He had no right to feel guilty. She had given herself freely. The outcome would have been the same had they married or not. But he couldn't deal with her anguish. The last thing in the world he wanted to do was hurt his generous little faerie-woman. But he had hurt her far beyond his ability to repair. He had not been there when she needed him, as he had not been there for the others. The ugly truth of that invaded his soul, blackening and shriveling what remained of it.

19

FAITH WOKE TO Morgan's lean silhouette bent over a pot at the fire, tasting whatever vile brew fouled the air. She watched him move as she would watch the shadows on the wall. He did not seem quite real somehow. His white shirt picked up the gleams of firelight, but the rest of him blended in with the darkness like some insubstantial ghost. She could not relate this shadow to the man who had taken her to his bed and got her with his child.

The hollowness inside her held new meaning. Her hand went to her flat abdomen, and she felt the ache inside where their child had grown. Their child. It seemed very strange to think of it that way after all these months of not knowing. She and Morgan had created a child.

And lost it. The coldness crept up on her, making her long for Morgan's comforting arms. But he would not want her now. Not after what he had seen.

The loneliness that lived inside her grew like an evil thing, and Faith clenched her eyes closed and turned away.

Morgan poured some of the meat broth into a cup and let it sit to cool a while. Meat broth had been more valuable than gold after a battle. Surely the same principle applied here. Faith had lost more blood than he had ever seen a body lose and still survive. Or it seemed that way.

He had buried the clothes and the meager remains of what should have been his child. The sight would haunt him for the rest of his life. He had done that to her, planted his seed, made her belly grow round with the living being created from his loins. And he had left her to suffer the agony of its loss alone.

The guilt wouldn't leave him. He could tell himself he wasn't responsible for Sean's death. His brother had been the one unable to leave the outlawed priests alone. It hadn't been Morgan's fault that he was still in France when the redcoats uncovered the Mass and arrested Sean and hanged him along with the priests. Perhaps he should have come home sooner, but it wouldn't have changed the outcome.

The guilt was there a little stronger for the others. His father had always been a heavy drinker. No one had told Morgan it had grown worse in his absence, but he should have known. He should have gone home instead of nourishing hatred like a viper in his bosom, leaving his father to drink himself to death.

And had he gone home, he would have saved Aislin from starving in the hedgerows. Clenching his fists, Morgan bowed his head and tried desperately to drive away the memories. It had been too late, too late for anyone or anything by the time he had returned to Ireland. They had all been gone. There was nothing left but the moldering castle on the hill, and that no longer belonged to him.

He had nothing and no one and had lived like this these last few years. Why hadn't he left well enough alone? He knew why, and the guilt seeped through Morgan once again as he raised his head and looked toward the bed. He had seen Aislin in Faith's fair face. He had seen a second chance, and he had taken it. And he had destroyed still another life.

Morgan's hold was gentle as he lifted Faith's shoulders to help her drink the mug of broth. The taste was bitter, but the heat curled down inside of her, and Faith drank it because Morgan held her. He made none of the reassuring promises of earlier, and his silence gnawed at her, but she was too tired to contemplate the meaning of his unusual taciturnity. She just needed his presence for now, so she wouldn't feel so alone.

When Faith finally slept, Morgan made up a pallet on the floor for himself and sprawled out on it, hands behind head as he stared at the ceiling. If he let her, the woman in his bed would rip the one purpose in his life out from under him. He had spent ten long years despising the Sassenach bastards and devising ways to get back at them. He had finally almost succeeded in one step toward that goal. Did he give it all up and settle for the life of a dirt-grubbing farmer for Faith's sake?

He wrestled with the problem throughout the night, but there could only be one conclusion. Faith deserved better than the life of a poor farmer's wife, and he could not surrender his goals without a fight. He didn't know what would become of them, but he would wait to see Faith well before deciding. Beyond that, he would not plan.

"Add a little salt, Morgan, and not so much water."

Morgan turned from the fire to observe the pale creature in his bed. "Who's cooking this, me or you?" He lifted a quizzical eyebrow, hiding the hope bouncing around crazily in his chest at these first words in days.

"Me, if you would just help me up from here. I cannot lie about forever." Faith struggled restlessly with the covers, pushing herself to a sitting position.

Morgan waved a wooden spoon at her. "One foot out of that bed and I'll paddle you, young lady. You have to recover your strength. Besides, I'm enjoying learning how to cook."

That was a blatant lie and Faith sent him a fond smile as she closed her eyes and leaned back against the pillow. In a little while she would try to rise again.

Morgan entered the cottage carrying a stack of wood and stopped short. "What the devil do ye think ye're doin'!"

Faith looked up guiltily from where she stirred a touch of sugar into the beans boiling over the fire. She had pulled the sheet over her shoulders for a robe, and her feet were bare, but the July warmth and the fire kept her from feeling any draft. She offered an uncertain smile. "I thought to help, Morgan. You cannot do everything."

"I did everything before ye came, and I've not grown old since then. Now, get back to that bed!"

Faith returned obediently, but his words ignited the fears that stayed with her night and day now. Morgan no longer needed her. He had not returned to their bed since she had lost the baby well over a week ago. He had coddled her, fed her, looked after her most intimate functions as she once had for him, but there he had drawn some invisible line. He no longer kissed or caressed her or held her in his arms. He no longer spoke of his horses or his dreams or even his desires. There were no sweet phrases, no endearments, no charming smiles to send gooseflesh up her arms. She ached just to see that gleam she knew so well in his eye, but it didn't come. Now it seemed he did not even need her to cook and clean.

He no longer wanted or needed her. Faith could understand that. If she looked half so miserable as she felt, she must seem a hag. She knew she had lost weight and her breasts had shrunk and her hair hung in dull knots about her shoulders. Morgan could never want her now, but did that mean she would have to leave when she got better?

She didn't think she could do it. She had lost her father and mother and now her baby. If she lost Morgan too, life would not be worth living any longer. He didn't need to love her. She would be content just to have him near, but that was a fool's paradise. The first time she realized he had been with another woman, she would die just as surely as if he had put her out. And if he didn't want her anymore, he would find another woman. Morgan wasn't meant to be a monk.

That meant she had to leave. So each day Faith pushed the barriers Morgan set for her a little further. She insisted on sitting at the table to eat. Then she insisted on sitting up awhile longer, helping him to wash and dry the dishes. Then she demanded a bath and refused his assistance. It was hard, like learning to walk all over again, but she couldn't be the docile, obedient child any longer. If she had to make her way in this world alone, she had to learn to make her wants known. If Morgan didn't want her anymore, he had no right to tell her what to do. She couldn't fear losing what she never had.

Morgan noticed the change in her and wondered at it. His docile Faith had suddenly developed a stubborn streak a mile wide. Her refusal to take care of herself angered him, but he couldn't chain her to the bed. She looked like hell, with huge shadows beneath her eyes and her fair skin so translucent sometimes he swore he could see right through it. For once, his lust was quiescent. His concern for her overrode his body's needs, although the unexpected sight of a breast bared for washing or an ankle exposed by a lifted chemise stirred banked embers. Still, he knew she was not ready for him, nor would be for some time, and he was willing to wait. But if she didn't take care of herself, she would never be ready.

Why in hell did she pick now to decide to be as stubborn as any mule? She deliberately ignored his orders, refused to heed his warnings, and generally defied good sense by rising from bed before she ought, doing more than she was able. Morgan wanted to shake her until her teeth rattled, but he knew if he touched her, it wouldn't be to punish her. He wanted to hold her with relief and cry out his thanks to God and promise never to let it happen again.

But it could. God knew, it could. If he took her to bed, eventually she would come with child again. It hadn't taken long last time; there was no reason it should the next time. And there was that chance that the same thing might happen again, and this time he might not be so lucky as to have another chance. Faith was small and delicate. She worked too hard. She needed to be protected, not exposed to hardship. She needed to lie between satin sheets, dining on the best foods, lifting nothing heavier than a good book. There should be the best physicians at her beck and call, maids to watch over her, footmen to run for help. He could give her none of that. Yet.

Toby arrived one day, his thin face drawn and anxious as he found Morgan outside examining the mare in foal. His glance drifted briefly toward the house, but he trotted over to the paddock and tugged his forelock as Morgan rose to greet him.

"What brings ye here, lad? Did I not tell Whitehead clear enough that Faith won't be returnin'?"

"How is she? Is she better?" Toby couldn't hide his eagerness for firsthand information. The other patrons of the inn knew little of the maid "Alice," who cleaned and cooked and disappeared well before they arrived. But having been introduced to her once, Toby hadn't forgotten, and since then she had shown herself to be the kind of friend he'd never had. He didn't know the cause of her illness, but he hoped for her speedy return.

"She's well enough to drive me out of me own home, as ye can see," Morgan admitted, glancing toward the window in hopes of some glimpse of Faith. "Is there aught I can do for ye, lad?" Failing to see Faith, Morgan returned a quizzical look to his visitor.

Toby shifted from foot to foot. "Well, there's one thing. There's been a bloke askin' after Faith, not by her other name, but as 'Faith.' He looks a thief-taker to me, and he seems to have an interest in you too."

"And what do they say about us in reply?" Morgan unsnapped the mare's bridle and sent her back into the paddock, then reached for his shirt. Instead of donning it, he began wiping himself down. The August warmth had raised a sheen of perspiration across his skin, and he dried himself off as Toby spoke.

"Don't none of 'em know Faith by name, so they answer honestly enough. Never heard of her, they say. The man can't describe her but to say she's gentry, and they laugh at that."

Morgan kept his relief to himself. Nodding, he encouraged Toby to go on. "And myself?"

Toby grinned. "Everyone has a different tale. 'Tis enough to drive the man mad. One says ye were caught in last winter's storm and froze. Another said as you were hanged somewhere up north. Another said a bullet pierced your bloody heart, and none too soon. They'll have ye drawn and quartered if the bloke asks much more."

Morgan threw his shirt over his shoulder and started for the cottage. "Buy the house a round for me, Toby, lad, and come in and have a sip before ye go. It's good to have friends like yourself."

Faith looked up with a smile from where she was drawing mugs of ale, obviously awaiting their entrance. Her smile faltered slightly at the sight of Morgan's broad tanned shoulders and bare chest, but she handed him his drink and turned to their visitor. "It's good to see you, Toby. Have you heard any more from your brother?"

Toby nodded nervously, then threw a look to Morgan, who had taken the chair and sat with legs sprawled away from the fire. Morgan's gaze never left the two of them, and Toby answered politely, "There's come a letter. I'll not be botherin' ye with it now."

"Nonsense. Let me have it. It's too hot to make much of a meal, and I have bread and cheese if you'd have a bite to eat. Mor . . . ." Remembering herself, Faith hastily inserted the name Morgan was known by to the rest of the world: "Jack, would you care for a bite to eat now? There's a green-apple tart I baked last night for your sweet."

Morgan watched the two young people together, and deciding there was no more to the relationship—at least on Faith's part—than Faith had declared, he nodded genially. "Sit down and read the lad his letter. I can slice bread and cheese as well as you."

Toby openly gaped as the tall highwayman removed himself from the chair, offered it to Faith, then ambled to the cupboard to produce their meal. His broad shoulders rip-

pling with the muscles of a horseman, his bare chest darkened by the black hairs Toby longed to sport, his lean back
gleaming with the bronze of hours in the sun, Morgan was
every inch the masculine image Toby wished to emulate.
But never in his young life had he ever imagined a man
waiting on a woman.

His eyes widened as Jack set out the bread and cheese
and rummaged for knives and poured a cup of tea for Faith.
Jealously he watched the smile Faith gave him and the exchange of looks that followed, and realized if that were the
reward for such services, he would get down on his hands
and knees to perform them. Enlightened by this discovery,
Toby missed most of the first part of his brother's letter.

Faith seemed thoroughly absorbed in his brother's words,
and even Jack listened with half an ear. Toby tried to concentrate, but he'd heard it all before and it had little meaning to him. The banknote in his pocket had been the only
concrete information he understood.

Faith looked up excitedly as she finished the letter. "Will
you go, Toby? Did he send enough? It's such an opportunity!"

Jack seemed to have more interest in locating the apple
tart, and Toby shrugged off Faith's raptures. "It's a fair
amount, but I don't see nothin' in my goin'. He's gettin'
married; says so right there. He won't be needin' my company. Those letters just been an excuse to go visit the
schoolmaster and court his daughter. Now that he's got what
he wanted, I won't hear more of it."

Faith looked disappointed as she continued to read and
reread the lines that had come all the way from the colonies.
"He sent money, Toby. Surely he must mean it. And here
he says he's building a house and needs to hire help with
the farm. That means he could use you, but he doesn't want
to say it."

"I'm doin' all right for myself here," Toby replied de-
fensively. "I'm puttin' a little aside like Jack said, and
someday I'll own me a little place like this."

Morgan slapped a dish before the youngster. "More
likely, someday you'll be hanging from a tree and the bank
will have your pennies. Don't be a fool, lad. You've got
family. Join them while you can."

Toby looked surprised, but wisely held his tongue. Faith's

eyes reflected surprise too as they followed Morgan across the room and back, but she merely tasted her tart and smiled at Morgan as he returned with his own dish.

Later that night, after Toby had gone and she had prepared for bed, Faith waited for Morgan's footsteps in the darkness. She lay in his bed every night, hoping he would join her, wondering if she ought to return to her pallet in the loft, but Morgan never said a word. Tonight she had other thoughts on her mind, and she was eager to have them said.

When the door opened and closed and the room filled with the scent of soap from his washing, Faith waited patiently until she knew he was rolling out his pallet before speaking. "Morgan?"

He had hoped she would be asleep. The tired circles were beginning to leave her eyes, but she still fell asleep with exhaustion each night. That was the only thing that eased this distance he must keep between them. Pillow talk would decimate his control, but Morgan couldn't stay away from that soft voice in his bed.

He sat on the edge and took the delicate hand resting on the counterpane. "You're supposed to be asleep, *cailin.*"

Faith let the luxury of Morgan's strong hand seep through her. It felt good to have him close. She had forgotten what it felt like when he leaned over her. How could one man be so exciting, yet at the same time feel so secure? Her fingers curled inside of his as she fumbled for words.

"You told Toby to go to the colonies. Would not that advice be good for yourself too?"

Morgan sighed and stroked her palm with his finger. "The lad does not have the experience I do. Ye need not fret over me lass. There's almost enough now to take you to the city, where you belong. I'd thought to buy a piece of land in the country for my horses, but I can stable them in town for now. When you're well enough, I'll go to London for a few days and see what can be done."

She wanted to hope. She wanted to believe he meant to give up the road. But she was innocent no longer. Had he meant that, he would have said so. Closing her eyes, she clung to his hand. "I don't need the city, Morgan."

"You don't know the city, *cailin.*"

Kissing her cheek, Morgan rose and returned to his pallet. His soul was damned for hell anyway. Would it matter if he took his little piece of heaven while here on earth?

God wasn't likely to answer that question anytime soon. Wrapping himself in the old blanket, Morgan eased into sleep.

20

"HOW DO I LOOK?"

Thomas watched with jaded eye as Sarah twirled around the plainly furnished room. He had made her his mistress for her buxom good looks, but somehow they did not quite fit in this new role. The modest, high-necked gray stuff bodice she wore still seemed to fill to overflowing, and the heavy skirt did not disguise the provocative sway of full round hips. He wanted to lay her down on the carpet right then and there and throw her skirts over her head. That wasn't the kind of reaction one expected a meek Methodist virgin to provoke.

"Wear a cap down around your ears and bind your chest," he suggested coldly.

The woman gave him a heavy-lidded, pouting look that did not diminish the issue. When his handsome lips turned down in a disapproving snarl, she flashed him a smile. "Do we have a problem, darling?" she purred. "Do you wish to solve it now? Or shall I practice being your little cousin awhile longer?"

"You'd better take this seriously," Thomas warned. "If we fail, I'm out a vast amount of wealth, and I shall be forced to find a rich wife."

She snuggled onto his lap and threw her arms around his shoulders. "Don't you think it would be much more believable if you told your uncle that we were married? Then he could start looking forward to that heir and he wouldn't mind at all when you look at me like that." She nibbled at his ear and squirmed deliberately against his rising lust.

Thomas shoved her from him and stood up to pace the room. "If it's marriage you want, then you'd better behave. You must play the part of mewling Methodist, not wanton hussy. Now, give me the story you'll tell the old man."

Giving a sigh of exasperation, she stood and put her hands

behind her back, her downcast eyes studying the floor. "I went to stay with my old nanny. I was scared, and she took me in for the winter. I don't know London and didn't know how to find my parents' families. Then Nanny got sick, and I stayed with her until you found me. When Nanny died, you helped me bury her, then brought me back here. But I don't know any of you. How do I know you are who you say you are? I want to see Mr. Wesley."

Thomas gave a grim smile at this last innovation. "Very good. Challenge the old bastard before he can challenge you. I like that. You'll have him eating out of your hand. That might almost do the trick."

She threw her head back up and braced her hands on her hips, completely undoing the image of a moment ago. "Shall we try it, then? I'm tired of these dreary quarters. I'd like to see the life of the rotten rich for a change."

Thomas reached for the large handkerchief covering her voluptuous bosom. "When the time's right, my little dove, when the time's right. I have to pry those papers loose from the bank first. That bastard may cost me a fortune, but those papers will do the trick. He sold out cheaply compared to what we'll soon have in our hands." The cloth fell from her shoulders as Thomas dipped his hand beneath the gown's neckline to pinch her tight nipple while his other hand brought her hips to rub the place where he needed her most. "Spread your legs awhile longer, Sarah, it will be a long, cold night once we reach Montague House."

At the sounds of giggling and murmurs from inside the rented room, the boy scrubbing the mud off his boots on the landing gave a snort of disgust. Stealing a fortune was one thing, but having to put up with a female's wiles to do it was quite another. Just imagining the wet, nasty kiss that must be going on behind that door, he wiped his dirty sleeve across his mouth and jumped up from his post. The gentleman would pay well for this piece of information, he'd be bound. That thought returned the smile to his lips, and he ran down the stairs, whistling contentedly.

Watson took the report from his informant at the Raging Bull to the judge. Henry Fielding operated his court out of his own home on Bow Street, and the thief-taker found the gentleman sitting before a summer fire, wrapped in a muffler, and nursing a hot mug of grog. Watson held back a groan at the stifling heat and waited patiently for the judge to acknowledge him. His admiration for the man's honesty mixed with his frustration at his insistence that his runners stay within the bounds of the law. Things would be a good deal simpler if the judge would simply let them take certain matters into their own hands.

Fielding looked up from the report to the portly runner waiting hat in hand for his permission to commit an unlawful act. The judge's chronic ill health never undermined his determination to turn the streets from jungle to civilization. Watson was dabbling well beyond his command, however, and he shook his head dolefully.

"This is out of my jurisdiction, Watson, and you know it. If this highwayman is committing crimes here in London, I might have some influence, but as far as you are aware, he's never strayed closer than the forest. Have you any proof that he's kidnapped this girl?"

"He has to have. He's the last person she's been seen with. They can't have both disappeared into thin air. The inhabitants of the Raging Bull are thieves and rogues and covering for one of their own. A man answering to Black Jack's description stopped Lord Anson's carriage just last June. I know damned good and well—excuse me, sir—I know he's alive. And I'm willing to wager the poor girl's still with him. Just imagine a poor wench come from good family having to live like that, sir. It fair bleeds the heart. And Black Jack's had more crimes to his name than any can count. There's something havey-cavey going on here, and I'd like to find it."

Fielding scratched beneath his wig and waggled his quill pen thoughtfully. "Nothing came of your bank endeavor?"

Watson grimaced. "He's clever. I'll give him that. The bank has acknowledged his claim, but he got away before we could find him. There's some dispute over the papers, still. There's no doubt that they belong to the girl, but they're only copies. The bank wants to hold them and the fund. I reckon Montague has some influence over that. But there's been legal papers filed to have the fund moved elsewhere and the papers returned to their owner. I don't know nothin' about that part of it. I guess I could go down to Temple Bar and try to trace those papers."

The runner's obvious reluctance to go near the legal system raised an amused look from the judge and he nodded knowingly. "I'll look into that for you. If this Montague chit is being held for ransom, I want to know it. And you're telling me this Black Jack is the most likely perpetrator. If he hasn't committed a crime since June, but hasn't collected the ransom either, he must be getting a trifle hungry. Do you think he can be tempted out of hiding?"

Watson looked relieved at Fielding's quickness. "Yes, sir, I do believe so, sir. A word or two in the right place, and he's bound to hear it. There's no promise that another rogue or two might not make the same attempt, but I reckon Black Jack can be told from all the others. They say he has a gentleman's ways, though he looks like something straight from hell."

The judge nodded. "It's still out of my jurisdiction. Find his fence and catch him there, and he's ours."

That was no easy task, but Watson had a few ideas along that route too. After exchanging a few final words, he bowed out with his hopes buoyed. No highwayman could resist a fortune in jewels, and jewels were so easy to trace. Edward Montague had a head on his shoulders; that much was for certain.

As Morgan carried in the last bucket of water to place over the fire, he threw a glance to Faith's blanket-clad figure standing beside the bed and felt his body groan in a protest of denial. Her heavy hair fell in a wicked waterfall of russet curls over her bare shoulders and down breasts concealed by the rough wool. Small bare feet peeped out from beneath the concealing blanket, and a well-turned ankle revealed itself with just the slightest movement. He didn't need more than that to remind him of what lay beneath all that confounded wool. It had been well over six weeks since he had enjoyed the pleasures she kept hidden, and he didn't think he could last much longer.

Thinking of another time when she had come from bathing straight into his arms, Morgan felt the sweat break out on his brow. He didn't know if she was well enough now to take him, but his vow to keep her safe restrained his lust. He would have her installed somewhere with servants around her before he put her through that hell again. It was time he thought about London.

"If you have all you need, *cailin,* I'll be going down the road a ways for a while. Will you be all right here alone?"

Faith looked at him in surprise. She had wondered at his staying home this long. Now he asked her permission just to go down the road? Did this mean he had truly turned over a new leaf and meant to become a law-abiding citizen? If so, he had said naught to her about it.

She offered a tentative smile. "I'll not be needing you to wash my back, if that's what you ask. Do you think you could ask Mr. Whitehead if I might go back to my duties soon?"

"You'll not be going back there. I have other plans, but you'll have to wait. There's plenty for you to do here, and we don't need the few coins the bastard pays you."

The small bundle of coins she kept wrapped in a handkerchief had become a bone of contention these last days. She had wanted to pay Morgan for some new shoes and a bit of cloth to replace the chemise that had been ruined. His refusal had been so adamant that it had left her shaken, but not shaken enough to accept his offer to buy the articles for her. Every time they turned around, they seemed to be stumbling over some new obstacle in their odd relationship. It had been easier when she had been his mistress.

Faith held back her anger now. Morgan had done too much for her to snap at him for his hardheadedness, and he had been the soul of gentleness in her care these last weeks. She owed him much, and she raised a daring hand to his shirt sleeve. "Don't let's start on that, Morgan. Go have your ale and say hello to Toby for me. Tell him again he's a fool for staying."

The temptation to take Faith in his arms, throw away the blanket, and make sweet love to her for the rest of the night was great, and Morgan gritted his teeth in resistance. Moving away from her tempting hand, he nodded curtly. "I'll leave you in peace, then. I'll bring home a meat pie so you needn't cook."

Faith watched him go with aching heart. He no longer wanted her, that much was obvious. What were his plans, then? Did he mean to ransom her now? Surely he knew better than that, even if he had found her family. And she couldn't imagine Morgan selling her into the trade, as she heard was often done when a man tired of his mistress. He had been too kind, too generous, and the loss of the baby had torn his heart as much as hers, she could tell. Perhaps he had found her a better position in a private house, but he was reluctant to let her go. That would explain much.

Giving up on second-guessing Morgan, Faith dropped the blanket and dipped her hair in the warm water in the basin. If ever she were rich, the first thing she would buy was a tub like she had heard of for bathing the whole body. A maid to wet her hair and rinse it would be lovely too. But Morgan's dreams weren't hers. She would never be rich, even through hard work, but someday perhaps she would be comfortable. How much did a tub cost?

Morgan rode to the Bull and took some solace in the all-male company. The new tavern maid wasn't as saucy as Molly, although he'd heard her favors could be bought just as easily. He eyed her lissome figure from afar but kept his attention on the conversation around him. Faith would hear of it if he strayed, and he wasn't seriously tempted. The maid didn't look overly clean, and he had grown discriminating in his old age.

Toby's vivid description of some jewels to be had for the taking flew by his ear, but the lad's mention of the Montague name swung Morgan's head around. He frowned fiercely and grabbed the lad by the collar. "Repeat that, but without the glory, boy. What jewels and what Montague?"

Toby looked surprised, but he obliged. "A fortune in emeralds, they say. The heir to the Montague fortune is to be betrothed, and they're his gift to his future bride. The fools think they're going to smuggle them right beneath our noses, but every thief in London knows about them by now."

The damned arrogant, presumptuous Sassenach thought to marry and continue the line, did he? Morgan sat back in his seat and let his thoughts wander while he absorbed the details Toby spouted for all to hear. The man had more money than was good for him, and he would deny Faith both family and fortune to keep it all for himself. That was typical Sassenach behavior, the kind of behavior that caused them to take all of Ireland for themselves and leave the other ninety-five percent of the population to starve. It was no comfort to know that they treated their own the same. The only comfort was in knowing that with Faith, he possessed the wedge to pry into that noble five percent. A bitter smile edged Morgan's lips as his plans began to form themselves.

The Lord had provided this opportunity. It was the same

as saying, "Here, my son. Take this wealth that belongs to your bride and make her happy with it." Perhaps it was sacrilege to put words in the mouth of the Lord, but Morgan was content with it. This was the chance he needed. Just this one haul, and he could set Faith up in a terrace house in London, lavish her with gowns and servants, and persuade her to be his bride. He didn't know which he wanted more: Faith in his bed or the shock on Montague's face when he arrived with Faith on his arm.

But first, the emeralds. With a shrug of his broad shoulders, Morgan shoved himself from the table. "I don't know about you lads, but the job looks a setup to me. If all the thieves in London know if it, someone has told them. And the one who's told them has to come from the house itself. I wager the jewels are already gone, and someone wants us to take the blame. Give Molly my regards if you see her. I'm off now."

He strode out, leaving a disappointed Toby behind. From up the stairs, Morgan caught the wail of a babe, and he hesitated for just a moment. He'd heard Molly had popped hers. It wouldn't do to have Faith find out. The reminder would be too cruel. Just the sound of the babe's cries twisted his own heart. He would give Faith a babe of her own to love in a little while. It was just a matter of time now.

Faith watched in trepidation as Morgan donned his frilled shirt and black coat and polished his boots to a gleam. She had prayed he had changed his ways, but she should have known better. Unable to watch without trying somehow to stop him, she squared her shoulders and approached as he rose from the chair.

"Morgan."

He turned as she came nearer than she had in weeks, resting her hand against his waistcoat and looking up at him with those bewitching eyes. He said nothing.

Faith hid her grimace at his silence. A silent Morgan was dangerous, but she had nothing to lose for trying. She slid her hand beneath the embroidered waistcoat to the fine lawn of the shirt beneath. "I don't want you to go to London tonight, Morgan. Stay with me?"

Her voice and fingers made it plain that this was no ordinary request. Morgan felt her palm like a burning torch against his chest, and the tilt of those full lips beckoned with just a suggestion of a pout. Faith had never come to him like this, not even when he had taken her to his bed nightly. His hand ached to reach for her, to bring her close, to feel her softness against him just for a moment. She offered the balm to heal his soul, but just a single moment would be enough to sway him from his purpose.

But a few minutes would never be enough. He wanted a lifetime. Morgan caught her chin and pressed a swift kiss to her lips. "Don't, *cailin,* or we'll both regret it. I'll be back. Tempt me then."

He caught his cloak and swung out of the house. The crash of something breakable followed him out, but Morgan didn't turn back. His Faith was alive and well, and he grinned at the night. Soon he would make her a princess.

He had verified the story with his sources. He had checked for a trap. He hadn't believed even the Montagues could be such fools as to carry a fortune in jewels by carriage without outriders. He was right. But it was easy enough to buy off the guards and have them far behind when the carriage reached the darkest turn in the road. The driver and footman were armed, but Black Jack hadn't earned his reputation by shooting innocent victims. He waited in the shadows of the trees, the well-trained stallion standing motionless as he wrapped the satin cloak to hide the gleam of his shirt. As the rumble of the approaching coach came closer, his grin flashed white against the night, and with an idle tug he raised the thin wire across the road. One for his faerie, he murmured as the coach came racing down the highway.

The driver screamed as the wire caught him full across the chest and he tumbled forward, loosing the reins. The guard at his side lost the blunderbuss he was carrying as the wire caught his arm and wrist. He grabbed for the weapon as he started falling, but the flash of silver and the wicked laugh from atop a great black beast bearing down on him made him flinch from his goal.

And then it was too late, the reins appropriated by the laughing highwayman, weapons gone, and the coach halted and vulnerable for whatever depredations awaited.

Cloak blowing in the breeze, the highwayman ordered his victim from the carriage. He hid his surprise behind his mask as a bulky figure garbed in gentleman's clothes and wig awkwardly lowered himself from the vehicle. He had hoped for the dark-haired devil, but this broad giant made an interesting spectacle. Black Jack grinned as the man seemed to study him closely. "You aren't afraid like the others. Are you waiting for some showmanship to convince you to release that pouch you're carrying?"

The giant shrugged carelessly. "My life is worth more than gold. Have it your way if you will, but do not think you'll get away with it. I'll have you behind bars before day is done. I give you this warning in all fairness."

The highwayman laughed, a deep laugh that echoed on the darkness and quivered off the nerves of the huddling servants standing near. "A fair Sassenach, by all that's holy! I thank you for your warning, and if it's not entertainment you want, hand over the pouch and I'll be disturbin' you no more."

The pouch was released and disappeared into the highwayman's enveloping cloak. Before anyone could raise an alarm or move in any way, the black horse and rider reared and swung into the woods, blending into the surrounding nighttime like a wisp of smoke. Only the parting scream of the stallion from a distance gave away the fact that they had been robbed by more than a phantom.

21

FAITH PACED THE cottage floor, rubbing her arms and occasionally glancing toward the open window. This nervousness was just a reaction to Morgan's unaccustomed absence, nothing more. She had grown used to his rising before her, lighting the fire, carrying in the water. He had been underfoot constantly these past weeks. It felt very strange not to look up and see those green eyes watching her, that dent beside his mouth forming as he laughed at some of her ways.

He had been quieter than usual since she lost the child, and his laughter didn't come as easily. She rather missed the laughing, charming rogue, but this other Morgan had stolen what remained of her heart. She wanted to comfort him when the dark shadow passed over his face. She wanted to fling herself into his arms and weep on his shoulder and let him find the comfort they both needed. She wanted to hear his moan of pleasure again. She wanted to hear him laugh with joy. She wanted him.

Faith slapped her hands against her arms and strode determinedly outside to see to the horses. She loved him, with all her heart and soul, she loved him. But he thought only of his bloody revenge and the wealth he would accumulate by robbing the rich. She knew that and accepted it. Why romanticize what could never be? Morgan was an unhappy man despite his laughing charm. She wasn't the cause or the cure for his unhappiness. She was beginning to believe only the gallows would end his memory of the past. But she couldn't leave him.

If these past weeks had taught her nothing else, they had taught her that much. She was well and had been for some time, but still he didn't come to her bed. And still she stayed. The possibility that he had finally given up his profession had raised her hopes, but now that he rode again, she still lingered. To live without Morgan had become as

impossible to imagine as living without breathing. Their
lives had become so interwoven that it was impossible to
separate warp from weft. She had to be there to see that he
returned. He had to return to see that she was still here. He
might wish her gone, but he needed her to fill his emptiness.
She might wish he was other than he was, but she needed
him to be the family she no longer had. They could grow
to hate each other this way, but neither would know how to
part.

But now that he had returned to his profession, Faith could
see no reason why she shouldn't return to hers. That thought
struck blindly as she watched the foal romping in the paddock
with his mother. She wasn't confined to these yards by fences
and stalls. Morgan could be gone for days. He hadn't obeyed
her wishes when he left. Why should she obey his?

Taking a deep breath of determination, Faith finished her
tasks and went to pin up her hair. She would see if Whitehead would take her back. There might come a time when
she needed to earn honest coins. She refused to think that
the time might already have come.

Faith glanced around the inn's lobby and read the signs
of disrepair with distaste. Whitehead had not hired help in
her place; that much was obvious. When he hurried out at
her call, she merely nodded and asked for her apron. He
looked terrified, and she didn't need to ask why. Morgan
had been here, but he would soon learn that she had a life
of her own. Perhaps that would shake him up a little. She
had been the obedient little girl for too long. It was time
she grew up.

The proprietor dubiously allowed Faith to return to her
old tasks. The first day, he kept a nervous eye on the doorway, expecting Morgan to show up at any minute, breathing
fire and waving his blade. But when Faith left alone at her
appointed hour, he breathed a little easier and welcomed
her return on the following day. There weren't enough hands
for all the tasks in this place, and the hands he had weren't
as efficient as the hands of the little maid they called Alice.

After that first day, however, Faith had doubts about returning. The cries of Molly's infant had wrung her heart the
first time she heard him. She had avoided the third-floor
attic where Molly slept, but when the cries continued and
she knew Molly to be flirting with the butcher in the kitchen,

Faith had climbed the stairs to rescue the little fellow. Her heart had crumbled into a million pieces at the sight of him.

He was so tiny and helpless, so perfect in every way. Faith changed his wet cloth and wrapped him in the blanket beside the bed and lifted him from the box where he slept. He quieted instantly, and his big brown eyes tried to focus on her as if to ask who she was and what she was doing there. Faith smiled, and his mouth made a funny little grimace that tore her heart from her chest. She hugged him, and he made a contented little babble. Tears flooded her eyes, and an emptiness yawned deep and wide somewhere in her center, big enough to swallow her whole.

It wouldn't do. She couldn't become attached to Molly's babe. Faith carried the infant downstairs to hand to his mother for feeding. Then she returned to sweeping briskly in the upstairs chambers. She wasn't married. It wasn't proper to have babies without a home and father and security. God had told her that when he took away Morgan's child. He had done it for a reason. Even Morgan knew that. That was why he hadn't come to her bed anymore. She had received her warning and now she had best learn to obey it. An innocent child deserved the best a parent could offer. She and Morgan had nothing to offer as they were. She had best stop thinking about it.

But it was impossible to stop thinking of the child they had lost when she listened to Molly's babe crying and fretting or laughing and cooing. The sounds ate at Faith during the day, as their absence destroyed her at night.

Or perhaps it was just Morgan's absence that decimated her nerves. She couldn't believe he would leave her alone this long. She knew now that London was only a few hours away. She also knew that London was just a euphemism he used when he meant to ride out, but she didn't think Morgan would go far just yet. Not this soon. He would worry about her. She knew he would. He wouldn't have spent all these weeks with her if he didn't care a little.

The emptiness of the cottage brought tears to Faith's eyes every time she returned to it. If it weren't for the horses, she'd be tempted to stay at the inn. At least there she could stay busy, and the only time she had to think was when the infant cried. Molly let the babe cry more than was good for it, and Faith had taken to listening for him, going to him when his cries broke into heartbroken sobs. At least then she could hold a warm, living human being in her empty arms. And the babe seemed to appreciate it, even if she couldn't feed him.

The nights were growing chillier, and the bed seemed colder than it had all last winter. Why didn't Morgan return?

Faith's stomach twisted as she imagined him striding through the door as she lay in bed. She could hear his boots drop and feel his heavy weight as he descended to the mattress. She refused to think further. They couldn't do that again. She knew now that it caused babies, and they couldn't have babies. She tossed restlessly as she struggled with the conflict. She needed Morgan in her bed. She wanted his baby. She couldn't have either. It was wicked to think of it while they weren't married. He hadn't asked her to marry him again. He didn't want her anymore.

Her thoughts were like nightmares chasing around inside her head. She couldn't get rid of them. Why didn't he return?

When Toby rode in a panic to the inn door one afternoon as she was leaving, Faith felt the nightmare solidify. She heard his words in a daze that didn't allow words, just feelings. Feelings flooded her, feelings of terror, of loss, of loneliness, of protest and rebellion. This couldn't be happening, not again. They couldn't take him away. Not Morgan. He was too vital, too alive. He didn't deserve this fate.

Images replaced feelings: images of Morgan riding his stallion, his black hair blowing back from his face, streaming in the breeze as he laughed and reared the horse upward; images of Morgan lighting the fire and turning to her with open arms and need in the shadows of his eyes; images of Morgan holding a newborn foal, cooing words of love while the blood still dripped from his bare hands; images of Morgan with his heart in his eyes as he stripped away the sheets carrying his child.

Faith broke down then, the sobs ripping from her soul as Toby's arms closed around her. She couldn't seem to stop. The tears that had never come since the day she lost the child now welled up in her and spilled out in a waterfall that had no end. Not Morgan. She couldn't lose Morgan. Morgan was her soul. He was what she could never be. They couldn't take away his freedom, for it would mean his life. Caged eagles never lived.

* * *

Not at all certain how it had come about, Toby found himself standing beside Faith on the doorstep of a narrow house in the moneylenders' section of London later that evening. Beside him, Faith's pinched pale face turned expectantly to the door upon which they knocked. Her fragile dimity was the worse for wear after her hours at the inn and their mad ride, but her face rivaled an angel's, and he gulped and looked nervously to their surroundings. Whoever this Miles Golden was that she had brought him to, he had best have the power of God. Naught other could save Morgan now.

A small girl answered the door, and a large man looked at Faith and Toby suspiciously as he stood in the room behind the girl. But at the mention of Miles Golden, he ushered them in and left them standing in a front room. A moment later a lanky man in sober frock coat and clubbed hair came down the stairs, looked them over briefly, and led them into a book-lined study inundated with papers and strewn books with their pages dog-eared and lying open all about.

As he cleared off a chair, Miles studied the exhausted, tearstained face of the young girl, then watched the tight, set features of her companion, coming to instant conclusions without their having said a word. The lad had bitten off more than he could chew and was about to destroy his already shabby hat by twisting it in his fingers as he kept glancing anxiously to the girl and around the room. He was out of his orbit here, terrified by what the books represented, unused to the room's confinement, but determined to look after his delicate companion.

The girl was a fascinating enigma, and Miles deliberately dallied over his straightening to watch her. She was distraught, hovering on some emotional precipice that he feared she might leap over at any moment. Her hands were callused and rough, as if she were accustomed to hard work, but the delicate angles of high-boned cheeks and huge eyes and soft, unblemished skin were not the features of the working class. There was intelligence as well as miles of pain in those eyes as they followed him about. She swept her dusty skirts with a lady's grace as she took the seat he offered, and she folded her hands primly in her lap as she waited for him to find a seat. The fact that the hysteria lingering in her eyes did not escape in tears and voluble complaints impressed him, and Miles finally spoke.

"What can I do for you?"

Toby looked to Faith, who raised her chin and tried to keep her words calm. "Morgan said I was to come to you if there were any trouble."

As their story spilled out, Miles felt a frisson of fear with the recognition of the girl's identity. Faith. The missing heiress. Accepting the inevitable, Miles studied her carefully, finding the truth of his knowledge in the girl's dainty bones and graceful movements. At the very best, Morgan could hope to be transported for theft, he knew. Should his part in Faith's disappearance be revealed, he would hang of a certainty.

Morgan's will left his entire fortune in the hands of this slender girl. Did she know that? Many another woman would simply have waited for fate to remove the obstacle to such wealth. Somehow, Miles didn't think that observation applied to this one.

"Please, Mr. Golden, I must see Morgan. I've got to get him out. He doesn't belong in prison. Whatever he did, he'll never do it again, I promise. Can you not help me? I can't see him die. He has no family to defend him but me. His family was destroyed by injustice. Don't let the same happen to him."

Her pleas were very effective. They could be very effective in other places. Combined with the money at her disposal . . . Miles didn't wish to get her hopes up. He sat back in his chair and regarded her dispassionately. "There is nothing that can be done tonight. In the morning I will try to locate Mr. de Lacy and discover his status. Leave word here as to where you will be staying and I will come to you as soon as I have some information. You'll do him no good by wandering the streets at this hour or wrecking your health. Take her out of here, Mr. O'Reilly, and see that she gets some rest."

Miles stood in harsh dismissal and watched them go with a small twist of his heart. Toby tucked his arm around Faith's slumping shoulders and nearly carried her from the room. That child no more belonged in this environment than a man belonged on the moon. Morgan must be mad to keep her hidden away. He would give the villain a piece of his mind as soon as he sought him out in the morning.

He didn't tell the young pair that he already knew of Morgan's incarceration. What good would it do to tell them that one of the most powerful men in London had charged the highwayman with stealing his family jewels and demanded the death penalty? Morgan had known what he was doing and accepted his fate.

Miles was quite certain Morgan's mistress wasn't so obliging.

22

MILES GOLDEN ARRIVED at the inn where Toby and Faith stayed the next afternoon. Taking one look at Faith's white, stiff face, he gave Toby a sympathetic look and held out his arm. "I have found him, my lady. I will take you there because I promised, but I will warn you, Morgan doesn't wish to see you. He is quite likely to dismiss me on the spot should he discover I have brought you with me."

Faith set her small chin with determination. "Is he well?"

"As well as can be expected." Miles watched her carefully, feeding her bits of information rather than the whole, waiting for her reaction. "The runner who took him stripped him of all his coins, so he had nothing to pay the garnish when they threw him in the common cell. He rather objected to being divested of his fine coat, so he is a little worse for wear, but well."

Faith faltered slightly as she took his arm. "Garnish?"

"The fee the prisoners extort when a newcomer is introduced to their midst. Newgate is not one of our finer class of prisons." Miles didn't lead her out the door he had left open. "I will understand if you prefer to stay here and let me deal with this problem, my lady. There is no need to subject yourself to the abysmal denizens of that hellhole."

The gray eyes that had seemed so cold and distant a moment before suddenly flashed with icicles. "I wish to see Morgan. You will not scare me away, Mr. Golden."

Miles exchanged a look with Toby, who shrugged his thin shoulders. He returned his gaze to Faith's obstinate expression. "I can promise nothing. I have paid to see him in a private cell rather than the common room, but if he knows you are with me, he may refuse to let the warder unlock the cell. I have told him you are here, and he is not happy about it."

"Well, I am not happy about Morgan being where he is,

either. Let us go, Mr. Golden.'' Impatiently Faith started toward the door without him.

Not caring what the men around her thought, Faith followed them out to the dismal street. Toby had taken a room near Temple Bar in a semirespectable section near the law courts and prisons. But in the gray gloom of the day she could see the mass of humanity crowding the street was not of the finest. Lawyers in worn black coats threaded their way among sailors still drunk from the night before. Gentlemen with frayed cuffs and without their fine wigs mixed with common trollops and rogues in stocking caps and clothing that hadn't seen a wash in many a year. She didn't know whether to be dismayed or relieved when Mr. Golden indicated she was to ride in the sedan chair waiting at the door.

She threw him an astonished look. ''The expense is not necessary, sir. I can walk as well as you.''

Miles looked grim. ''You will ride, and you will pull the curtains. I am not de Lacy. I cannot rescue you if a few thugs decide you would look well among their possessions. We must go through an area that is not accustomed to seeing ladies such as yourself.''

She didn't have time to argue. Lifting her skirts, Faith climbed into the chair and allowed the curtains to be pulled down around her.

When the chair slowed shortly later, Faith pushed aside the hangings. The cold stone walls of Newgate rose up on either side and in front of them. There was no way to ignore the cries echoing through open windows. Some sounded quite mad, others were more like laments unleashed by the sight of the sedan chair and the possibility of wealth that it represented. Faith shivered as the chair was returned to the street, and she didn't meet Miles Golden's eyes as she stepped out. The shrieks and cries raised bumps across her flesh, and she had all she could do to keep from shaking as she took his arm.

She caught the flash of a golden guinea as they met a guard and were hastened down darkened corridors. Everything in here was paid for at a high price, and she tried not to imagine what was happening to the small store of coins Miles held for Morgan. They were stolen coins. It seemed only appropriate that they be taken by more thieves. At least they served the purpose of providing Morgan with what small comforts could be found.

Faith tried to ignore the filth of the walls and floors. She could smell the stench of the old straw used for bedding and the open latrines for the prisoners and knew vermin and rodents must live in profusion in such conditions. She should have brought bucket and broom, but she doubted the men would have appreciated trying to get such objects past the guards.

The warden stopped before a narrow door and inserted the key. No sound came from within, and Faith held her breath. Morgan didn't want her here. She hadn't seen him in days. They had not been lovers in weeks. Would he hate her for coming against his wishes? It didn't matter. He could hate her as much as he liked, as long as he was alive to hate her. There had to be something they could do to get him out.

The men stepped back to let Faith through first. Morgan was sprawled along a bench, hands behind his head as he leaned against the hard wall. Miles had evidently brought him clean shirt and breeches, but nothing could be done to disguise the blackened bruise along his jaw or the thick scab above his eye. He turned a questioning gaze to the door, and jerked involuntarily at seeing Faith standing there.

The chains on his wrists gave an ominous rattle, and he flinched, but he was on his feet in a minute, his big fists clenching against the iron bands as he looked beyond Faith to Miles and Toby. Taut muscles strained across his angular cheekbones, and there was nothing sultry about the green of his eyes today. They smoldered as they fastened on the two men easing into the tiny cell behind Faith.

"Get her the hell out of here! By all the saints, Miles, I'll see you beaten within an inch of your life for this. Get her out of here. Quit wasting my coins on these wretches and find her a decent place to live. I gave you instructions yesterday. What in hell do you mean by bringing her here?"

He was deliberately ignoring her. A frown puckered the bridge above her nose, and Faith stepped forward, touching her hand to Morgan's linen-covered chest, disregarding the symbols of his incarceration. She could feel the curls of hair beneath his linen cushioning her touch, and she wished to wrap her fingers in them and feel the heat of his sun-browned torso. His swift intake of breath was the only sign he gave that he knew her presence.

"I'll not go away like a bad dream, Morgan de Lacy. I'm not an object that can be moved about at your convenience. I am here. You had best yell at me and not the men who sought to protect me."

Morgan closed his eyes and prayed for strength. Perhaps if he closed his eyes long enough, she would disappear. The tantalizing scent of jasmine wafted up to him, reminding him of all that he had given up. He clenched his fists tighter at his sides, resisting the thought. He had gambled and lost. She should not be punished for his failure. He had lost his piece of heaven. He wouldn't take her down to hell with him.

"For the love of Mary, lass, leave. There is naught ye can do. I would wish you to think of me as we were, not like this. Remember the stars, Faith, not this. Now, let Miles take you away. He will help you. I promised to take care of you, and I'll not fail you in that. Go now, if you have any feelings for me at all."

His voice was strained, and Faith heard the emotion behind it. Tears filled her eyes, for Morgan was not given to public displays of emotion. He worked hard to keep a face of laughter and charm turned to the world. Only she had touched the other Morgan, the Morgan who cried over his lost babe, the Morgan who looked at the heavens and prayed for his lost family. And it was that Morgan she saw there, and the others would see, should she remain.

She turned to Miles and Toby and motioned them out. They went gladly, though she knew they stood just outside with the warden and the key. It was better that they could not see.

"You would have to be a blind man not to know how I feel, Morgan. And a blind man you are, but I cannot help that now. What I want to know is what I must do to get you out of here. I do not know your Miles Golden or if he would help. That is why I had to talk to you. Tell me whom to go to, what to do. I'll not leave until I have your word you'll help me in this."

Morgan opened his eyes to find Faith still standing there alone. He wanted to crush her to him, but he didn't dare touch her. He had to drive her away, but he needed her softness too much. He had spent long nights dreaming of her here, beside him, in his arms. When by some miracle she appeared, he could not for the life of him drive her away.

"*Bean sídhe*," he muttered, reaching to touch her hair, remembering the chains when they clanked, and drawing away. "There is nothing even a witch could do for me now. Do not drive yourself to madness trying."

At these soft words, Faith shuddered in mixed relief and horror. Morgan was recognizing her, but still denying her. She stepped closer, forcing him to take her in his arms or fall back to the bench. When his arms with their harsh bindings finally closed around her, she leaned against his broad chest and sighed. "You are such a fool, Morgan de Lacy. I'll go mad if I do nothing. Hold me, and tell me what to do."

Morgan held her, but he called to the others standing outside. "Miles, come in here and get this silly woman."

Faith beat her hand ineffectively against Morgan's chest as he held her imprisoned. She could feel his heart pounding against her ear, feel the blood pumping through his veins as his arms cuddled her against his length, knew the pressure against her belly for what it was. He wanted her, and he would send her away.

She stayed where she was when the door opened, refusing to move when Morgan's arms fell to his side. She wrapped her fingers in his shirt and glared up at his square jaw. "This banshee isn't wailing, Morgan. You'll not die. I'll not let you. You're going to live whether you want to or not. You can cooperate or not, as you wish. But I'll spend every penny you ever earned to get you out of here with or without your wishes."

A glimmer of amusement flickered in Morgan's eyes for a moment and was gone. He looked to Miles. "You see why I had to keep her hidden, Golden? The world isn't ready for her yet. She still believes in God and truth and justice. Explain things to her, will you? Then do what I told you earlier."

"I did that long ago, Morgan," Miles replied angrily, "when I thought you might be just a little prejudiced in keeping her to yourself. Would you like the report now? Do you want to hear about her grandfather, who wrote off his second son as if he didn't exist, ignored the pleas of wife and mother-in-law when her mother died, refused to answer his son's letters or acknowledge his only granddaughter's existence? Or perhaps you would prefer to hear about the Montague heir. You met him the other night, I believe. Pleasant chap, wasn't he? Do you want to hear the report on him? Or on the cousin, the one you described to me? He's not the heir, you know, but he fancies himself that. Do you want to hear about Faith's cousin, Morgan? Then you can tell me which one of the charming chaps you'd like me to send her to.''

Morgan gripped Faith's shoulders and set her back, then glared at Miles. ''There's a grandmother. Send her to her grandmother.''

''Certainly.'' Miles shrugged and held out his arm to Faith. ''Let us go, my lady. Your grandmother is no bigger than you are and not so fearsome. She hasn't been able to stop your grandfather from anything yet, but there's always a first time. Perhaps she can protect you from the scoundrels who set up this plan to have Morgan taken. I'm sure she will try.''

This bombardment of information left Faith too shaken to think for herself. Grandfather? Cousin? Did Miles know her family, then? She threw a stunned look to Morgan, only to meet a similar reaction there. He grabbed her arm and held her, glaring at Miles as if he would decapitate him on the spot had he possessed a sword.

''You damned Jewish bastard! Did you have to say these things in front of her? Bigad, man, if you weren't the only man I could trust . . .''

Miles lowered his arm and returned Morgan's glare. ''My father was the bastard, not I. And were you not such a thick-headed Irishman, I'd call you out for the insult, but I'll consider the source this time. You've paid me well to take care of your little maid, and I'll carry out my task to the best of my ability. If that means shaking you out of your self-pity to see what's right before your nose, then I'll do it. Wake up, de Lacy, and listen to the girl.''

Golden was shorter and two stone lighter than Morgan, his lanky frame fit only for lifting the books he pored over each day, but his fists were knotted in anger as if for use against his stubborn client. Faith clung to Morgan's side, but she stared at the solicitor with a growing smile of appreciation.

Feeling Faith's trusting weight pressed against his ribs,

Morgan ran his hand up and down her arm and shook his head as if to clear it. Long ago he had accepted his fate. He had known what would happen should he ever be careless enough to get caught. He hadn't thought himself careless this time. He couldn't have known anyone would deliberately set a trap for him. Had he taken the precaution to look carefully at the stones in the pouch, he might have guessed the truth, but he had been in too much of a hurry to return to Faith. That was carelessness enough, and he was prepared to pay for his mistake. But they weren't going to let him. He stared at his company in bewilderment, then glanced down to Faith's open gaze, and was lost.

"I wanted to take care of you, lass," he whispered, as if in explanation.

"I know, but can I not take care of you just a little too? I don't like being helpless, Morgan. Being helpless is the worst feeling in the world. Let me help, please." Tears glimmered in her eyes as she watched him, praying there would be something, anything, that she could do.

Remembering only too well the helplessness he felt when she lost the babe, Morgan felt her words pierce his soul. There would be no denying her this, though he knew the quest was futile and doomed only to hurt her worse. Perhaps the pain would ease quicker if she thought she had tried.

"Lass, if I knew what to tell you, I would, but I see no way of getting out. I know no one in this city who will help, and your family would only gladly see me hang. I suppose your John Wesley would be happy to pray for my immortal soul, but I'd rather not have religious palavering until I am gone, thank you. Speak for me in your prayers, and go with Miles, Faith. There's naught else I can tell you."

Faith turned an inquiring look to the young solicitor, who nodded silently. He had a plan, then. Since he said nothing, she assumed it was one that would not gain Morgan's approval. Biting her lip, she looked uncertainly to the immovable man at her side. He was watching her, not the lawyer. She offered a weak smile and stood on her toes to press a kiss to his rough cheek. "You will let me visit you again?"

Morgan's expression was bleak as he looked into the fresh face of her innocence. " 'Tis no place for you here, *cailin*. If you must plot and plan, let Miles be your messenger. I'm trusting him with your life, and that means more to me than my own."

"Then think what you would do were our places exchanged." With this tart reply, Faith stepped from his hold. She wanted his kiss, needed his reassurance, but she would not beg. She faced him as the equal she had declared herself to be and wished with all her soul that things could be otherwise. She would never know another man like Morgan. She could not lose him without a fight. She watched the green of his eyes gleam briefly as they slowly swept her from head to foot, his gaze lingering briefly on her breasts beneath the thin bodice and kerchief, sweeping downward to her slender waist, burning her in other parts as the memories flared between them. She was on fire by the time his gaze returned to her face, and she knew he could see her desire by the look in his eyes.

"You would do better to keep me leashed, lass, but 'tis your choice if you wish me otherwise. I'm not a man to gratefully take his hat and walk away."

"I didn't think you were." Feeling slightly breathless at the force she sensed behind his words, Faith returned to Miles and Toby and signaled her readiness to leave. She felt as if Morgan had fully unclothed her right before their eyes, and even if they didn't understand the meaning of his words, she knew his intent. Should she ever gain Morgan's freedom, she would be in his bed again, and subject to his pleasure or displeasure at whatever she did to free him.

She would do well to take his words to heart.

23

"YOU'VE DONE WHAT?"

Thomas' horrified tones brought a smile to Edward's lips, a smile he quickly hid behind his glass of wine. Sipping unconcernedly, he regarded Thomas' impatient pacing with amusement. Having garnered the reaction he wished, he set the glass aside and flipped over another card on the game of patience before him. "I've caught the highwayman. It should be only a matter of time before his doxy shows up. We'll discover once and for all if we have our missing heiress."

Thomas turned abruptly toward the window and away from the sight of his complacent, well-fed cousin. It infuriated him every time he looked at that fat dumb animal and thought "but for the grace of God go I." To hell with God. Had his uncle not been born the elder of his father by a mere few minutes, it would be he sitting there in that rich velvet chair, unhurriedly awaiting the inheritance of title and vast amounts of wealth. As it was, he had no expectations at all, or none that he did not make for himself.

Thinking of the actress waiting in rooms not more than a few streets from here, Thomas glanced at his reflection in the window. Why in hell had Edward agreed with his plan to set up an actress as their lost relation if he meant to keep on searching for the real one? Stupid pig, he probably hadn't thought at all. Edward just liked playing childish games, and this was another to him. He hadn't even thought out the consequences.

"And what will you do with her once you find her?" Thomas asked idly.

His tone didn't fool Edward. The tension in the shoulders beneath his cousin's buckram-padded coat revealed the importance of this question. Edward laconically debated several replies, gauging the variety of reactions he could expect.

It struck him that this conversation was very much like fishing, an amiable sport he meant to try someday. He flipped another card.

"One can only wonder. Shall I marry her, do you think?" Edward didn't even glance upward as he made this improper suggestion threatening the borders of consanguinity. Thomas was too dull-witted to see beyond himself.

Thomas winced as his own idea was spoken aloud. He gave the window another glare before turning a bored expression back to the room. "And bring a highwayman's bastard up as the next marquess? How droll you are, Cuz."

Edward shrugged disinterestedly. "Well, then, perhaps you shall marry her. But you must share the wealth with which you will undoubtedly be rewarded, for it is I who found her, after all."

Over his dead body, Thomas muttered inwardly, reaching for the decanter. Or better yet, over Edward's dead body.

Contemplating that pleasantry, Thomas smiled again. He could marry or dispose of the missing heiress, it made no matter. One way or another, he would have his hands on her wealth. Then he would have all the time in the world to accomplish the rest of his goals.

Giving the fat earl's bent head an almost benevolent look, Thomas sipped his wine. Being a marquess should be a very pleasant thing indeed.

"The man who nabbed Morgan is a runner, but he is also in the employ of your uncle, Lord Stepney."

Faith gripped her fingers together and stared at her plate as Miles explained what little he had been able to find out about Morgan's arrest. The family she had hoped to find only a little less than a year ago now made her stomach roil and churn, and she could barely stand to hear another word. Miles couldn't explain why they would hunt and badger Morgan while making little or no attempt to find herself. He couldn't even swear that Morgan had been the target of their trap, but Miles wasn't a believer in coincidence, and although Faith believed the Lord moved in mysterious ways, this wasn't the Lord's work. Her uncle had counted on being robbed, and planned for Morgan to be followed. That was not the normal method of catching a highwayman.

"Perhaps, if I were to go to him and plead Morgan's case,

he would drop the charges,'' Faith suggested timidly, terrified of the idea but willing to try anything.

Miles reached across the table to pick up her neglected fork and hand it to her. "Haven't you heard a word I said? Your uncle is a dangerously clever man. Your cousin is merely dangerous. I know little or nothing of the marquess other than he has a heart of stone. Are these the kind of people you wish to plead with? Don't you think they might possibly be hoping you will do just that? I cannot imagine how they might have made the connection between you and Morgan, but it seems very reasonable to believe they have.'' Miles hadn't mentioned the bank account to Faith, but it was only one more piece of the puzzle. Her family knew of the connection, no doubt. Those papers at the bank verified her existence. He had been very careful to keep Morgan's name away from that account, but the connection was there somehow.

When Faith halfheartedly lifted a forkful of food toward her lips, Miles tried to explain his intentions. "Morgan wishes to keep you protected. Your family has not yet acted in your behalf, and it seems reasonable to assume that they will not. It also seems reasonable to assume that they believe there is some connection between you and Morgan. I believe if we can convince them that you are not who they believe you are and that Morgan has nothing to do with any member of the family, we can divert them from your trail. With any luck, they will lose interest in Morgan after that. It will be much easier to pry him out of prison if there are no wealthy Montagues breathing down the judge's back.''

The food in her mouth was dry as dust, but Faith obediently swallowed it. "I do not understand how my family's intentions can make a difference to a judge. Morgan is in all probability guilty. Even I cannot deny that. Shouldn't we just be planning some way to help him escape?''

Toby's eyes lit briefly at this suggestion, but Miles frowned formidably. "He would have to live in hiding for the rest of his life if he escaped, and that's not what Morgan wants. Leave the British system of justice to me. It might be costly, but I can arrange things, if only the Montagues are out of the picture.''

No, that wasn't what Morgan wanted, but Faith thought it might be very good for him. With a warrant hanging over his head, he might be more easily persuaded to leave this country for another, but that was her dream and not Morgan's. She had no right to force her dream on him when there were other alternatives.

"I'll admit, I do not understand, but if you can arrange things, what do I need to do to help?"

Miles wondered how to broach the subject that would save Morgan and shackle this innocent to a notorious reprobate for life. Or if he should. There were ways and ways. Shaking his head at the thought of denying his client for a woman he scarcely knew, Miles launched into his argument. "There is a way you can help, but it is asking a great deal of you. Morgan has never explained his relationship with you, and I hesitate to ask without knowing your place in his life."

Faith looked up and caught his eye at that. Trying not to flush, she answered directly, "I daresay whatever you are imagining is close enough to the truth. I cannot speak for Morgan, but he saved my life and I would do anything for him. Does that answer your question?"

Miles nodded, noting Toby's uneasy squirming. Morgan had said the lad could be trusted, and there was nothing for it now but to speak before him, but the passions of the heart were not easy to deal with logically. He prayed Toby's passions did not betray them.

"Would you have any objection to marrying Morgan?" Miles watched the shock appear and disappear quickly in her eyes. The question was an old one, then, and only shocking in his presenting it. Good.

Faith fought the battle within herself only briefly. Morgan was a thief and she had told him she would never marry a thief. He could change. He would have to after this, if only he could be brought out of it alive. After what they had done together, marriage was the only possible solution. She didn't know if Morgan would appreciate that now, but that wasn't the question. Slowly she nodded her head.

"I would hear that said more firmly, Miss Montague. What I have in mind may be easily annulled in the future, but circumstances are not always as we would have them. Once the ceremony is performed, you will be legally bound. Think hard on what that means."

Remembering Morgan's hungry eyes on her and the threat that lingered between them, Faith knew what Miles was asking. A wife became her husband's property. She understood that much. Morgan had not taken her to his bed in weeks, but she knew now that was not from lack of desire but out of fear of a child. He had no wish to give up his occupation for her, nor share her bed if it meant keeping him bound to the cottage. That was not a basis on which to build an everlasting marriage. He would be angry at her interference, and in his anger, he was capable of anything.

Yet in her heart there was no other choice. Raising her head, Faith met Miles's eyes defiantly. "I will marry him. How will that help?"

Miles took another sip of his drink before giving her the rest of his suggestion. "By giving you a new identity. I mean for you to marry him under the name you are known by outside of here. I want it on record that you are one Alice Henwood of Epping Forest. With Morgan married to such an obscure personage, your family will no longer have to worry that he conspires with a Faith Henrietta Montague."

Before Faith could reply to this outrageous declaration, Toby shoved back his chair. "Now, wait a minute!" He glared from Faith to the man of books whom he distrusted instinctively. "Jack . . . Morgan ought to marry her right enough, but all legallike. Faith's a lady; she deserves that much."

Faith covered Toby's hand reassuringly, but it was Miles who replied. "The legality of what I have in mind has never been tested in court. On the face of it, they will be legally wed. If they wish, they can have another ceremony later with their real names. My main concern is that it be done immediately and made known so that the pressure will ease before Morgan comes to trial."

Faith frowned in puzzlement. "But there is not time for banns, and how can we be wedded if Morgan is in prison? I thought there were all sorts of complications in getting married. How can what you suggest be legal?"

Miles smiled. "The law is a fascinating field, Miss Montague, one that criminals and rascals delight in twisting to their own use whenever profitable. Parliament has been trying to shove legal, proper marriages down the throats of the English citizenry for these last fifty years, but they have not yet succeeded. All they have succeeded in requiring is a license and that the ceremony be registered. The church demands banns and so forth, but the church has no jurisdiction over everyone. That's where the loophole begins. I will find someone who will not only marry you but also do it without asking for your documents or caring what name you use, and, for a sum, will date the certificate to any time I request. As I said, the legality of such a marriage has never been tested, but they are performed by the hundreds every day.''

Faith could tell by Miles's expression that this would not be the kind of marriage she had in mind. It would be a piece of paper that could be produced in court, and no more. He had even admitted that such a marriage might be easily annulled. She had never thought of committing herself for life to a highwayman, but to do it under the auspices of some unsavory minister in the shadows of a prison did not hold out hope of happiness. But if that was what was required to free Morgan, she had little choice. He could have left her to die that winter's night, and he hadn't. She could do no less for him.

''If that is what it takes to see Morgan out of that dreadful place, I will agree.'' She said the words quite firmly, although her insides quaked as the impact of them slowly seeped through her. Whatever the legality of the ceremony, she was committing herself for life. Her beliefs would allow no other choice.

''Are you certain? I will hold you under no misapprehension, Miss Montague. The ceremony could very well be valid and lasting. Even should you decide to return to your powerful family, they may not be able to break it. You might wish to consider this awhile longer.''

Toby seemed ready to urge her to do so, but Faith stayed his tongue with her quiet reply. ''I am trusting you will make it as valid as can be, Mr. Golden. And I was under the impression that haste was of importance. How soon can it be done?''

Miles set his chair back down on all four feet and stood up. ''Be ready first thing in the morning, Miss Montague. I have yet to talk to Morgan of this, but sometimes it is easier to confront him with the inevitable, wouldn't you agree?''

Faith bent her lips in a weak imitation of a smile. ''I agree.'' Morgan would be furious. They both knew it. He would be climbing the walls and bending bars and forcing his escape more certainly than Jack Shepard ever did should he learn of their plans. Jack Shepard ended up on the gallows. It was better that Morgan receive no warning.

Morgan stared at them in astonishment when the little conclave poured into his narrow cell the next day. He rose reluctantly from his bench, shoving his shirt back into his breeches and brushing his hair back from his face as he studied their faces, acutely aware of the humiliating chains on his wrists. The man wearing a priest's robe and carrying a little black book was like no priest he had ever seen. His double-chinned jaw still sported yesterday's beard and his filthy full-bottomed wig hadn't seen soap in many a day. The man's black smock and white collar bore the stains of half the food that had gone to fill his stout stomach.

Morgan scarcely spared Miles a second glance, but turned directly to Faith. She looked pale and nervous, but someone had given her a small bouquet of Michaelmas daisies and she had exchanged her frilly cap for a delicate lace mantua that framed her enormous eyes and tiny chin and fell loosely over the gown that had been more modestly covered with a kerchief yesterday. His glance told him that a sweep of his hand would strip away the fragile lace and leave her throat and shoulders and half her bosom exposed to his gaze, and that of everyone around him. Morgan frowned fiercely at that thought and threw his suspicious glance toward Toby.

Toby had slicked his frizzy red hair back into a queue and borrowed a frock coat to cover his dirty leather jerkin. He also sported a gentleman's neckcloth, although it was arranged in an odd knot that showed his inexperience with such niceties. Morgan would have laughed had not the expression in Toby's eyes been such that he had serious cause for concern. The lad who had once followed him about like an adoring puppy now met his gaze with nervousness and a definite defiance that did not bode well.

Morgan finally turned back to Miles, who had been whispering instructions to the disreputable priest. Or vicar. Or whatever in hell he was. Morgan had a very good suspicion of what he was from the little book. That was no Bible. Characters like that were an everyday occurrence in the street below, although they operated more frequently in the vicinity of Fleet Prison. For a coin or two, they would marry anyone who came along, no questions asked. He had heard it said that they didn't always require the compliance of both parties. All it required was a license and the names of both parties in that little black "register." That thought tightened Morgan's lips to a grim line.

"Miles, I don't know what the hell you think you're perpetrating, but I'll not be having Faith in the same room with the likes of that one. I told you to keep her away from here. Do I need to persuade the weapon from our gallant warden to show you what I mean?"

Faith turned to catch the fat guard's face blanch a shade whiter as he hastily stepped from the cell and slammed the door closed. That would teach the man to let his curiosity get the better of him, but it would not ease Morgan's temper. She turned a questioning glance back to her husband-to-be.

Miles straightened, and brushing off his jacket, confronted his irate client. "We'll be gone shortly. Even my friend here requires both parties for this ceremony. Once we get it over, we'll be on our way, and she needn't come back here again. Just a few words and we'll be done. Are you ready?"

Despite her nervousness, Faith felt her lips twitch as the lanky solicitor easily threw his much larger client off-balance with these words. Miles Golden had a knack for managing people. Perhaps there was some hope, after all. Some of that hope rose to her eyes as they met Morgan's.

It was that look in her eyes that did him in more certainly than any word of the lawyer's. Morgan resisted it, but he knew his weakness. Should Faith be allowed to have her say, he would be lost. Furiously he turned back to Miles. "Out," he demanded firmly. Raising his voice, he yelled to the guard just beyond the door, "Get them out of here, you dolt, or I'll carve my initials in your bloody heart!"

The threat sounded very real, and there was a gulp and the scrape of a key on the other side of the door. Miles quickly waved another golden guinea in the opening doorway. The coin disappeared and the door closed again.

"You bloody damn fool! That's my money you're wasting! You're dismissed, Golden. I want you to turn over all my papers to Toby here. Toby, go find another man to handle my business. Find two men. I don't trust any of them. If there's anything left after this rascal is done, perhaps you'd better find three men. Then there might be something left for the lass when I am gone."

"There will be nothing left for me when you are gone,"

Faith intervened quietly, stepping forward until she could nearly touch the lace of Morgan's jabot. Undoubtedly Miles had seen to that symbol of gentility. She would not see the solicitor so maligned. "Look at me, Morgan, and tell me you would deny me what you have offered and should have given long ago."

Morgan was afraid of no man, and never turned down a challenge, but he was seriously tempted to turn down this one. She did not belong here. She did not belong in his life. He had proved that time and again. Marrying her now was too late. He could never give her what he had intended before. He was not a blind man or a stupid one. The only way Miles could get him out of here was with quantities of money. The only way he could ever dream of keeping Faith was by giving up the means to earn that money back again. He would never have the wealth and life he wished to offer her. She deserved better.

"I take back my offer, *cailin*. It was a cruel one. It may not seem so now, but you will be better for my absence. If that cad Miles"—Morgan threw the disgraced solicitor an angry glance—"leaves you enough, you can go to the colonies with Toby as you wanted. Your family will never look for you there, and you can make a new life. We are even now, little one. You don't need to do this for my sake."

Faith stared up into his angry expression until she found the pain behind the shadows of Morgan's eyes. He was being deliberately cruel, and he was very good at it. Had he railed and shouted, she could have defied him easily. These calm, cajoling words were harder to fight, for they almost seemed reasonable. She could almost feel the men around her nodding in agreement. Without giving thought to what she did, she knotted her fist and punched Morgan swiftly in the solid, flat expanse of his abdomen.

Morgan scarcely gave an "oof" of breath at the blow, but his eyes lit with an unholy gleam. "You'll pay for that, brat."

"And you'll pay for my virtue, Black Jack. Give the man your vows. I would hear them said properly."

When Morgan raised his head with that terrible glow in his eyes, Miles had second and third thoughts about this contest. When the chained highwayman clasped the delicate lady by the arm and dragged her to his side, the solicitor almost called the whole thing off.

But when the lady removed the mantle covering her hair to reveal the shimmering copper waves hanging down her back and raised her chin in defiance of Morgan's harsh hold, Miles held his words and signaled the self-described clergyman to start the service.

Somehow, he had the feeling the Irishman had finally met his match.

24

FAITH SCARCELY HEARD or understood the clergyman's thick accents as he rumbled off the words to the Church of England's marriage ceremony. Her whole being seemed centered in that hard hand circling her upper arm, crushing the skin until she knew she would be sorely bruised. Morgan had never treated her with anything but tenderness before, but she had never tried him this severely, either. She didn't know where she had found the courage. She wished she could find it again.

She felt Morgan's jerk as the clergyman uttered the name Alice Henwood. She didn't want to see what was in his eyes as they burned through her while she made the response. Let him think what he would. Miles would explain it in all due time. She just wanted that piece of paper that would disown her family's claim and free him from their scrutiny.

Morgan's voice rumbled in reply, and she realized Miles had not given Morgan's full name either. She would be Mrs. James O'Neill on the marriage records. It was all a lie. There was nothing here that made a real marriage. It was just a piece of paper. She didn't know whether to be sad or glad over that knowledge.

There had been so much between them that was good and honest and right. How had it come to this? She could remember the night of the falling stars as if it were yesterday, but looking back on it from this viewpoint, she knew Morgan had seduced her as surely as he had held his mare for the stallion's use. That he had offered to marry her afterward was even more suspicious. She didn't want to think about that. She wanted to think about the times he had loved her, the times he had held her and touched her and poured sweet words of praise into her ear. He had used her, but in their own ways so had her father and every other man she had ever known. They had taught her the words to say that pleased themselves, taught her the ways to think that most reflected their beliefs. Morgan had done none of that. He had merely taken what she offered. For that, she had no one to blame but herself.

As she had no one to blame but herself in this. They had both had their choices. If the truth be told, Morgan had slightly less choice than she. He could go to the hangman's noose, or he could marry her and hope Miles could work the proper magic to see him free. She wasn't even certain he had that much choice. From something Miles had said, she gathered the marriage could be registered even without Morgan's consent. If he knew that, he would hate her of a certainty.

The final sonorous words of the ceremony brought Faith back to the moment. Her heart did a backhanded flip and fell flat as Morgan's grip loosened at the same time as the words "I now pronounce you man and wife" quivered in the close air. Then both Morgan's hands were on her arms and she was being drawn up against him, her mantua falling to the floor and her flowers crushing flat between them as his mouth swooped down to take the possession she had just granted with her vows.

Morgan's kiss was hot and fierce and knowing, and Faith trembled as she realized they had an audience for this performance. Whether the marriage was a mockery or not, all knew the intimacy of their relationship was real. Morgan's arms clasped her more firmly, and the heated thrust of his tongue bent her backward in his embrace, forcing her to cling to his shoulders. She tried to deny the excitement of this closeness, but she had denied his touch too long. Heat rushed over her, and her struggles died as quickly as they were born. Even the rattle of chains and the flames of hell couldn't keep her from him.

Sensing her surrender, Morgan swiftly returned his new wife to her feet and dared the gazes of their witnesses. Miles put his fist to his mouth and coughed politely, Toby looked pale and angry but held his thoughts, and the clergyman merely scribbled in his book. It was Faith's eyes Morgan had to meet, and he turned his challenge to her.

She seemed stricken, almost terrified, but he knew the fast beat of her heart as well as his own. His mouth hardening into a bitter smile, Morgan turned back to glare at the intruders.

"Out, the lot of you. A man's entitled to some time with his wife after they're wedded."

It was Miles's turn to look stricken. He turned a hasty glance to Faith as if he would protest, but she looked resigned to her fate. She must have known what Morgan's demands would be before she ever came, but she might not know the consequences of those demands. The lawyer coughed uncertainly and offered in warning, "If the marriage is consummated, there is less chance of annulment afterward. I can plead the irregularity of the license, but—"

Morgan released Faith and caught Miles by the shoulder, shoving him toward the door with all the force his chained wrists would allow. "It's too late to think of these things now, you bastard. Go play your slimy games elsewhere. You've got what you wanted, now leave me to mine."

Miles straightened himself and pounded on the door, but Toby dug in his heels and glared at his hero. "This ain't no place for a lady, Jack. You can have her once you get out. Let me take her home now."

For once, the lad spoke sense, but it was too late. Ruthlessly Morgan pointed toward the door. "Out, O'Reilly. You can stand outside the door and listen for her cries if you wish, or you can come back later, whatever you prefer, but she's mine now, and there are matters between her and me that need no interference from outside. Leave before I have to throw you out."

Faith couldn't answer the question in Toby's eyes as the door opened and Miles grabbed his arm to drag him away. The clergyman ambled out without a qualm, and the guard stared in lascivious fascination at her while he waited for Miles and Toby to depart. Noting Faith paling before the stare, Toby caught the guard's coat and jerked him into the corridor. With a considering look, Miles turned one more time to face his furious client, then he too left them alone.

The door clanged shut, and Faith turned bravely to face her furious husband. Morgan's sharply angular features revealed no trace of his anger, but there was no hint of humor in his eyes or in the twist of his lips. She was not to see the laughing gentleman on this, their wedding day, but she very much suspected she was seeing the ruthless highwayman. Her heart quivered, but she held her ground.

Hazel eyes darkening to a jungle brown, Morgan let his gaze slowly devour his newly acquired bride. She had worn her rich russet curls down about her shoulders to please him, and he savored the contrast between their vivid color and the pale cream of her bare throat and bosom. Without the protection of kerchief or mantua, her breasts curved sweetly above the gown's square bodice, and he felt his loins constrict at just the sight. She was his, to do with as he willed. Someday his son might suckle there, and the thought filled Morgan with an overwhelming desire to live. Desire was followed by despair.

Faith knew the instant her fate was decided. The shadows of the past filled Morgan's eyes, and she could almost imagine all those lost generations of de Lacys crowding his soul as he reached for her. There would be no going back now. She would be his wife in all senses of the word.

"Mrs. O'Neill," Morgan murmured mockingly as he pulled her forward, brushing his lips against her hair. "Isn't that grand, now? Come here, Mrs. O'Neill, and comfort your husband."

The coldness of their surroundings had seeped into her bones, but Morgan's touch had the heat of a fire. Perhaps he held the fires of hell in his hands, but it was too late to flee now. Uncertainly Faith stepped into his arms, seeking the shelter of his warmth, fearing the ice in his eyes. His arms closed around her, drawing her closer, surrounding her, but the hold was as much a prison as an embrace. She leaned her head against his shoulder and felt his kisses fall upon her hair and brow, but they weren't the same. She stiffened as his chains beat against her back, but his arms didn't loose their hold.

When she struggled slightly against him, Morgan held her tighter. "Oh, no, Mrs. O'Neill." He lifted her from the floor until Faith could only grab his neck and hold on. "This is what you requested, and I'll not deny your request. Should I hang at Tyburn next execution day, I'll have some hope that another de Lacy will take my place. I'll have you bear my son, Mrs. O'Neill. Is that too much for a husband to ask his wife?"

There was something terrible in his voice that made Faith quake with fear, but at the same time, Morgan's words unlodged the need inside her. Her eyes flew to his and held there, even as she felt him lift her to the hard bench that would serve as their marriage bed. His child. Morgan's child. The cold began to dissipate, and shyly she pressed a kiss to his hard cheek.

She felt the muscle beneath Morgan's skin tighten and his fingers dig into her side, and then he was laying her down against the bench and kneeling over her, his face a frozen mask as he stared down at her, his chains forming a barrier on either side of her head.

"Don't," he warned. "Don't let me ruin your life as I have all the others. Run from me just as fast as you can, Mrs. O'Neill."

He frightened her, just as he meant to do, but Faith refused to let him see it. As the cold, hard wood pressed against her back, she reached to caress his stern jaw, and a smile flickered across her lips. "When I'm good and ready, Mr. O'Neill," she murmured as mockingly as he had earlier. "Give me your son, then, and I'll think about it."

Relief washed over him, relief, and a hint of sorrow. She was strong now, stronger than she had ever been. She would need that strength in the days to come, but Morgan missed the proud innocence he had stolen from her. Yet this new Faith was an exciting enigma, one he wished to know better—were he given the chance. His hand came between them, unfastening the hooks of the bodice he had bought for her. She was warm and soft beneath his touch. That was all he needed to think about now.

Faith gasped and arched against his hand when at last he touched her. It had been so long. . . . She cried out softly as Morgan's fingers caressed her there, teasing her to aching peaks, stirring the long-neglected needs and desires that had brought them together from the first. His mouth followed his fingers, giving her no time for thought, wasting no time on tenderness. His rapacious hunger aroused her more swiftly than lingering kisses, and though she regretted his haste as he raised her skirts, she met his needs with a speed that startled both of them.

Thinking only that this might be the last chance he had to have her, that at any minute someone would arrive to deprive him of what he might be denied into eternity, Morgan made haste to claim what he had never expected to be given. He had planted his seed inside her once before; he could do so again. He had yet one more chance to bring another de Lacy into the world. He owed his ancestors that much. They would be proud of his choice of brides.

Morgan's entry was swift and searing, and only his mouth covering hers stopped Faith's cry. He filled her, possessed her, carried her along on some mad journey whose destination only he knew. She was forced to follow, rising to meet his needs whether she willed or not, taking him in and giving him full rein until she thought she would burst from the need of him, until she ached and her body clamored for more, until his lunges sundered her in two and she was no more herself but part of him, part of the man gasping and crying and flooding her with new life.

They lay together briefly then, the moisture on their faces mixing so none could say what belonged to whom. Morgan's heavy weight pressed Faith into the bench, his hips narrow and strong where they lay joined, until she moved to ease the pain, and he slid away, not taking her with him. Then there was only the cold emptiness between them again, and Faith looked up to scan his face.

Morgan's black brows had formed a line across the bridge of his aquiline nose, and the green of his eyes was muddied and murky beneath their thick lashes. The set of his mouth made her quail inside, and she wished despairingly for some sight of that familiar dent that accompanied his smile. He could at least give her a smile, but he did not.

"Don't come back, Faith." The words were cold and without hope. "I'll not have any more sins upon my head than I already bear. If you have any sense at all, you will leave here and never look back. You've given me all you can. Don't burden me with any more debts I cannot repay."

Those were not the words she wished to hear, and Faith's despair deepened with the bleakness of them. She felt empty and used, and she brushed hastily at her skirts to cover her legs. Morgan stopped her. Leaning on one arm, he gently ran his fingers down her thighs, his gaze drinking in the life and loveliness of her warm skin, the texture and firmness that had held him so briefly. When his hand reached the juncture of her thighs, he raised his gaze to hers.

"If by some luck a child comes of this, I would have him know his proper name, *cailin*. Will you teach him of me?"

Pain grabbed and twisted at her, and Faith hastily sat up, pulling her skirts primly down about her ankles as she turned away from him. She didn't want to hear these things. He would live. Miles had promised.

"Teach him yourself, de Lacy. I'll be waiting for you when you come out."

She rose from the narrow bench, and fastening his breeches, Morgan did the same. He didn't like the sound of the coldness in her usually soft voice, but he had asked for it. If the truth be told, he had brought it about on purpose. The road to hell would be a lonely one, but this was one life he would not take with him. He didn't touch her as she fumbled with her laces and rearranged her clothing. She looked tousled and sleepy and altogether too provocative for him to resist long.

Watching as those lovely young breasts disappeared beneath chemise and bodice, Morgan fought between the twin needs to protect her and to keep her. He didn't think they were one and the same. She didn't need him anymore. In fact, she would be much better off without him. He could resign himself to his fate if he could believe that wholly. But the very human desire to keep her and hold her and watch her bear his children lurked in his heart. He could have had all that, had things been different.

But he had thrown all that away when he had gambled on fate and lost. Morgan picked up her lacy mantua and handed it to her. "You owe me nothing now, Faith. You have done all you possibly can. You are free to go as you please. Miles will help you. Let me remember you with a smile in your eyes. Look at me, Faith, and give me just one smile."

Startled at the farewell in his voice, Faith looked, and instead of a smile, tears flooded her eyes. The tenderness was back as he looked on her, and there was even a hint of a dent by his mouth when he raised his hand to stroke her hair. This was the man she loved, and the tears spilled as she tried to go to him.

Morgan caught her wrists and didn't let her come closer. "No, my *cailin alainn*. Go with God. There is a life for you out there. Live it better than I have."

Faith wanted to cry out a protest, but tears choked her throat and she couldn't say a word. She shook her arms free and turned away to hide her tears, and before she could gain control of herself, Morgan was pounding on the door and the key was scraping in the lock. She tried to turn back to him, wanting his arms around her again, needing his kiss, but his hand was at her back, shoving her through the open-

ing, and the door slammed between them before she could
do more than throw him one last despairing glance.

"I'm afraid, m'lord, we have a problem."

Dressed impeccably in the height of fashion, his cravat
neatly folded in a pristine waterfall, his brocade waistcoat
adorned with the requisite braid and watch fob, his silk coat
billowing out in stiff lengths as he took a seat, Lord Stepney
curbed his impatience. "In what way, Fielding?"

The older man rested against the chair back near the blazing fire and regarded his visitor with mild curiosity. "Your
highwayman married his tavern wench yesterday."

A flicker of annoyance appeared on the large lord's face,
then quickly disappeared. "That is only to be expected, I
suppose. My niece has a very religious background. She
would wish to arrange for some modicum of respectability
from the situation, I suppose. When the highwayman
swings, as I'm sure you can arrange, she will be a widow."

Watson made a coughing sound in his throat, and the
barrister yielded the floor to the eager runner.

Watson stepped forward, scarcely disguising his triumph.
"I told you as it was no use to look for the tavern wench.
She gave her name as Alice Henwood, all right and tight, just
like I said. And accordin' to my snitches, she punched the
bloody bastard until he agreed to the vows."

Edward momentarily entertained a feeling of defeat as he
turned his gaze to the heavily shrouded windows of the
judge's small study. Try as he might, he could not feature
the meek Methodist niece that had been described to him
as a tavern wench who beat highwaymen. And she would
certainly never agree to an illegal marriage by some miscreant in a prison cell, let alone use a name as preposterous
as Alice Henwood. He had lost this gamble, but there were
more to be had if he played his cards right.

Stiffening his shoulders, Stepney returned his gaze to the
two men waiting for him. "To hell with the damned highwayman, then. Let us trace the claimant to the bank account. On second thought, perhaps we ought to let the
highwayman walk and follow him too. He has to be the one
who arranged that bank account. Perhaps she will show up
if we follow him closely enough."

Fielding began to shake his head in disapproval. "He's a
notorious thief, m'lord. And it is a perfectly respectable

firm of solicitors who has taken over the matter of the bank account. You must face the fact that your niece has no wish to be identified.''

"Fie on you, sir!" Stepney rose and crushed his three-cornered hat over his new clubbed wig. "I'll admit no such thing, nor will I admit failure. I *will* find her. Come along, Watson, we have some matters to discuss.''

The judge shook his head as the pair strode out. The earl was a stubborn man. He hadn't thought him to be a fool. Well, a missing heiress was of little concern to him. Let the wealthy take care of their own. He had more important tasks to see to in his self-appointed goal of clearing the streets of crime.

He just hoped Watson wouldn't step too far out of bounds in seeing that thief released.

25

THE STRAIN WAS showing on Faith's fair face, but she spoke calmly of the food and the lumpiness of her bed and even managed a smile at Toby's jest about thin walls and thumps in the night. Or perhaps she smiled more at the flush that infused his face as he realized what he had said. Miles didn't think it mattered. He was in a fair way of being enchanted himself by this dainty faerie, and because of that, he felt her fears more deeply.

"We should look about for better rooms," Miles inserted into a lull in the conversation, if conversation it could be called. Whenever silence fell, someone said something to fill it. None of them wished to speak of what was uppermost in their minds.

"Are there any closer?" Faith didn't say closer to what, but they all knew. The towering gray walls loomed in all their minds.

"No," Toby announced emphatically. "You'll not rest any better in the hellhole that surrounds the prison."

Miles nodded agreement. "I was thinking in terms of rooms in a respectable house somewhere a little farther from here, where you might walk the street without fear."

Aghast, Faith stared at him, forgetting her food. "Will it take that long? Surely it cannot. He will die in there. There is no heat or air or sun. No one could survive for long. You said you would get him out."

Miles drank deeply of the ale he never drank until he had become involved with Morgan and his lady. Then, wiping his mouth on his napkin, he tried to pry her loose from her grip on fantasy. "Even should he be released tomorrow, you should be thinking of finding a respectable place to stay. Morgan has told me to begin looking for one."

Panic began to fill Faith's eyes. "Why? The cottage is fine with me. The horses have been left alone too long. I must see to them. Annette is in foal, you know. Perhaps I should just go back there to wait.''

Miles glanced to Toby, who gripped the table so hard his knuckles whitened. The young highwayman cleared his throat. ''Morgan said I was to sell them. I can't leave you here alone to go fetch them unless you're stayin' somewhere respectable.''

Faith pushed away from the table and rose from her chair, pacing the sagging wooden floor of the private room they had taken. She twisted her handkerchief between her hands and saw nothing of her surroundings as she paced back and forth. ''Sell them? He can't sell them. How will he live? Not all of them?'' She turned with a flare of hope.

Toby had his instructions on that matter too, but there was no use in telling Faith. ''The fair starts today. I can get a good price. Will you go with Mr. Golden and find a decent place to stay?''

Panic had a firm grip on her now. Faith's gaze swung from one man to the other, and the cloth in her hands knotted into a ball. ''What does he mean to do? Tell me, Miles. What is Morgan going to do?''

She had never called him Miles before. The attorney shrugged nervously and stood up. ''I assume he is going to find you a decent place to live now that you're married. Now, sit back down here and finish eating. It will do you no good to make yourself ill. I know of some very respectable rooms that won't cost much. I hate to mention this, but you're being followed. I think it best if I move you out of here to somewhere you can't be easily found.''

That made some kind of crooked sense. Faith sat where indicated but didn't lift her spoon. ''You said my family would forget me and look elsewhere if they thought me someone else.''

''I said your uncle is very clever and, presumably, very dangerous. He doesn't give up easily. If I must, I will go to him and ask his intentions, but not knowing, I would rather wait until things are desperate indeed before I reveal any connection between you and me and Morgan.''

Faith nodded and stared at her plate. ''If you think it best, I will go where you say. When will Morgan come up for trial?''

She no sooner laid to rest one problem than she poured another one on them. The two men sighed and twitched and gave their food a look of despair. It would be well cold before their stomachs saw any of it.

"I've asked to have it postponed for a few days. That will give your family time to get bored with the proceedings and give me time to settle a few matters. I've paid a week's rent on the cell. We may as well get our money's worth."

"Rent? You must pay rent? To keep him in prison?" Faith stared at him, astonished. No wonder Morgan was feeling so surly. All his ill-gotten gains were spilling rapidly into the pockets of thieves worse than he. Did that mean he had to sell his horses just for his upkeep?

"There is a charge for admitting a prisoner, a deposit to be paid in advance to be given a decent room—"

"Decent! They call that decent? My word, what can the others be if that filth is called decent?"

Miles explained patiently. "Much, much worse. You do not want to hear of such things over your meal. He is clean and dry. That has a high price in Newgate. Decent meals have a high price in Newgate. For more, I could have furniture installed, but we'll trust we can get him out before that is necessary. There will still be fees to have him discharged once the trial is ended. The wardens don't miss a chance to line their pockets. It is their only way of making money."

"They aren't paid? How can that be? Surely the king or the city or someone must pay them for their services." Faith picked irritably at her food. None of this made any sense. The city was filled with lunatics. She just wanted to get Morgan and get out of here. And never come back.

"On the contrary, they had to pay to obtain their positions. The king and the city are perennially bankrupt. Selling positions is a nice source of income. In return, they allow the wardens to charge fees for their services. It has a certain warped sense of justice. Why should innocent people be made to pay to support criminals? Let the criminals pay for their own support. But as you can see, the prisoners are at the wardens' complete mercy, and a man would have to be a fool to let such easy victims get away before he extorted the last shilling from their pockets. It will be more difficult to pry Morgan from the hands of his wardens than from the auspices of the court."

Faith looked a little frightened at the thought, but she couldn't believe Morgan would allow those grubby little men to bleed him dry. He would know what to do. She had to be practical and plan for when he got out. She finished chewing the tough piece of gristle they called roast lamb in this place and arranged her next question carefully.

"What will happen when he goes to court?" She didn't want to say: how are you going to prove he's not guilty? In this lunatic world, it didn't seem to matter much whether you were guilty. They robbed you blind whether you were or not, then dared you to get away. She was beginning to see that it might be very difficult not to turn to a life of crime once you were in the hands of this strange system of justice. How else would some of the poor wretches pay for their prison expenses?

"The judge will call for witnesses. If I'm successful, there won't be any. If I'm not, it becomes a little more tricky. Don't worry about it for now. It does no good to worry."

Faith could see that Miles was worried. He didn't hide his feelings very well. Rather than harass him, Faith turned questioning eyes to Toby. "What happens to highwaymen when they're caught, Toby?"

Toby had removed his stifling neckcloth and coat. He tugged now at his leather jerkin as he contemplated the question. He wasn't any good at words like Morgan was. Only the truth came to mind, and it was out before he could stop it. "They hang them if they can."

She had known that. But the qualifying "if they can" intrigued her. "Is there some possibility that they can't?"

Miles made an irritated rumble in his throat and answered gruffly. "Judges can be bought. Prisoners can plead clergy; although it's meaningless these days, it gives the court something to chew on. If they've never been before the court before, they might be branded. Or they can be transported. It's just a matter of who pays what to whom. You're not to think on it. We'll buy Morgan off."

"Branded?" Horrified, Faith raised her head to stare at Miles. Just the image of burning flesh, Morgan's burning flesh, made her gorge rise. "Branded?" she repeated.

"I told you not to think on it." Miles slammed his fork down and took another deep drink of his ale. He choked, then recovered himself as he realized Faith wasn't going to let him off so easily. He met her horrified look with a calm he didn't feel. "It's better than hanging. It's probably better than being transported and sold into servitude for fourteen years. Now, let's change the subject.''

Silence fell as everyone's thoughts turned to Morgan's proud character being submitted to the humiliation of being publicly branded and scarred for life or forced to work at degrading labor for the better part of his years. Hanging almost seemed preferable.

Faith couldn't bear to think of it. She scrambled desperately for a different topic, something to distract them from these horrifying images. Her mind sought the peace and security of their cottage in the forest, and there she found her one and only treasure. She played with it for a while, steadying her nerves by forming new ideas and questions, until the silence around her became unbearable and she released the toy to ease their anxiety.

''What do you know of publishing books, Miles?'' She asked the question calmly as she forked a leathery carrot and brought it to her mouth.

Both men stared at her as if she had taken leave of her senses, but finding her calmer than themselves, they relaxed, and Miles studied the question. ''I don't know much, but it is easy enough to find out. One of my mother's brothers has a printing press and prints pamphlets. He'll know whom to talk to. Are you planning on writing a book?''

Faith smiled slightly at the idea. ''I think not, but my father did. The copy is not perfectly clear, and he never had time to go back and correct it, but he was a very good writer, almost as good as he was at speaking. Do you think anyone might be interested in seeing it?''

This was a beautiful topic. Miles took a deep breath of relief, and even Toby looked less green. The poor lad had taken on a formidable task. It would do him good to get away to the roads where he belonged for a while. Miles could handle the lady while she was being reasonable like this.

''I don't see why not. Would you have it printed under your father's name or a pseudonym?''

Faith hadn't considered that question. She tilted her head and gave it some thought. ''I would like to see his name on it, if I could. The world shouldn't be allowed to ignore his existence. Yes, I think I would very much like to see his name in print, with a dedication to my mother.''

What she was suggesting was very dangerous to her

health, but Miles could see it made her happier to think of it. He gave her a smile of approval. "Then once we get you settled into your new rooms, and Toby goes back to fetch the horses, he can also fetch your father's papers. You can go through and edit any errors you find and copy those pages in need of it in a fair hand while I look for someone who might be interested in publishing it."

Faith offered a faint smile in return, and their conversation carried on in choppy fits and starts until it was time to leave. As Miles guided her out into the streets, she threw one last look in the direction of the tower block of Newgate, then turned her back and walked away. When next she saw Morgan, he would be a free man.

"I thought Edward said he had found the girl." Lady Carlisle winced at the almost querulous tone of her words. The nightmares were back, and she couldn't seem to escape them. The lack of sleep had stretched her nerves to a thin elastic that might rupture at any moment. Wrapping her frail hands around the knob of her walking stick, she held her back straight as she sat before the fire, watching the marquess stride restlessly about the brilliant carpet.

"It wasn't the right chit. Edward should have known better than to believe any harebrained notion of that runner's. Imagine believing George's daughter would live in sin with a highwayman! I hate to say it, Lettice, but that son of mine has mush between his ears."

Lady Carlisle sniffed disdainfully. "And your brains have always been in a different location, Harry. After siring two sons, you wasted yourself on actresses and lightskirts instead of producing more legitimate heirs. I feel no sorrow for you. George was a good boy. A trifle loose in the beam on some subjects, perhaps, but we cannot all be practical. You should never have thrown him out, Harry. I place the sole responsibility for my granddaughter's loss on your shoulders."

Mountjoy growled and glared at the fire. "Don't call me the only guilty party, Lettice. Your infernal husband—and to hell with the dead—was as eager to disown him as I. Methodists! Whoever heard of such puling, miserable—"

Lady Carlisle rapped the floor with her stick. "I will not hear another word of it, Harry! My granddaughter can be a heathen Oriental for all I care. I want her returned to me, and I want her now." Her voice broke, and she struggled briefly for the regal composure that had held her together all these years. "She's alone, Harry. I know what it means to be alone. You *must* find her. I cannot bear to think . . . What if this highwayman . . . ?" She couldn't bring herself to say the words. They came too close to her worst nightmares.

The marquess stiffened as her fears met his. "We'll find her, Lettice. And if that damned highwayman has touched a hair on her head, I'll see him hanged. That's a promise."

That was a promise he would have no difficulty keeping, since he had no confidence at all that the highwayman knew aught of his granddaughter. Edward was being led around like a pig with a ring in his nose by that wretched runner. To hell with the highwayman. No, the Methodists were where the search should begin. Wesley hadn't produced any satisfactory results yet, but at least he was a gentleman. That was more than could be said of that damned lying runner who had got their hopes up once too often.

Talking himself into the confidence that he was doing all that could be done, the marquess took his chair and poured himself some brandy. Let Edward chase after phantoms in the night. He had better things to do.

Faith was still making promises to herself two days later when she tied the hood of her mantle and started down the stairs to the first floor and the street. Any day now, Morgan would be a free man. Any day now, they could step out into the world as man and wife. Today she would meet with Miles and he would tell her Morgan was ready to leave that dreadful place.

In the last two days, Toby had brought not only her father's papers but also changes of clothing, and Miles had insisted that she buy the small necessities to make her a lady in the eyes of her neighbors. He didn't know she had chosen the hooded mantle not because it was stylish, but because it hid her face. She felt as if there were a thousand things written in her face that no proper lady would ever know. She felt safer somehow hidden behind its protection, from herself as well as the rest of the world.

Arriving at their appointed meeting place, Faith shook back her hood and unfastened her mantle in the warmth of the inn's fire. A streak of sun from a dirty window caught briefly in the red glint of her hair before she turned away, but it was enough to make Miles catch his breath. Faith had always seemed rather plain and small to him, her beauty coming from within more than without, but he suddenly had a glimpse of what had caught and held Morgan's eye. It was as if the sun had turned on some inner glow, and she had come to life before him. Her smile, when it came, was almost devastating.

"You have news for me?" she asked eagerly.

It wasn't the news she most wanted to hear, but Faith was intelligent enough to know that. Miles held out a chair for her, and after she was seated, waited for the servant to take their order and leave before speaking.

"Only to tell you that Morgan is scheduled to come before the court tomorrow. The docket is a long one. I cannot give you the time. Some days, it is long into the night. Do not get your hopes up too far."

Faith twisted her fingers together and obediently forced her hopes into abeyance, but she couldn't help the sudden leap of happiness in her heart. She had waited in misery for so long, she should be allowed just a ray of hope. She turned large gray eyes to the man who had assured her Morgan would be freed. "Have you arranged everything as you said? There will be no complications?"

Miles laid his hands upon the table and gave her a stern look. "Do not look at me as if I am God. I am only human. I have arranged everything that I know how. I have seen to it that the fence who was arrested with him got off easily and is now out of the country, so he cannot testify against Morgan. The only other witness is the runner who followed Morgan. He is the most dangerous part of the plan, for he not only witnessed Morgan selling the jewels but also saw the actual robbery. Since he is in your uncle's employ, he is not easily bought. I have made other arrangements to keep him away from the trial tomorrow. If they fail, I have one of the best barristers in the business to stand up for Morgan in court. I make no promises. Without a witness, there is no case, but I cannot know if your uncle is still interested or to what lengths he is prepared to go."

Faith nodded in understanding, hiding her fears as well as her hopes. The servant came in and brought their hot chocolate and buns, and she waited for the man to leave again before she asked the next question. "And if all goes wrong and he is found guilty?"

Miles flattened his tricorne against the table as he lifted his cup. "We will bribe him out of Newgate and you will have to run for a ship. He won't be safe here any longer, but the long arm of the law has not yet reached the colonies to any great effect. Morgan didn't hire me because of my simple mind."

Faith smiled faintly. "I have observed that. You seem an honest man, Mr. Golden. I do not know how you know so much about these nefarious duties."

Miles shrugged. "I was brought up in the streets of London, Mrs. O'Neill. I was fortunate enough to have a large and caring family, but others were not. I learned from what I had and from those who had not. And I never turned up my nose at any man because of his profession or breeding. One in my position cannot."

He did not say one of his religion could not, but it was understood. Centuries of their presence had not made Jews any more English to the English eye than Gypsies. Faith did not know his whole story and probably never would, but there were undoubtedly many similarities to Morgan's. Her own paled in comparison. "Morgan is fortunate to have you for friend. I hope he has not strained the relationship too far in this."

Miles allowed himself a small grin. "He pays me well to test the boundaries of our friendship. I have never asked of his family, but only a true nobleman can afford to be as generous as he. And I am not talking just of money. There are those who are willing to take my coins and my services but will not sit at the same table with me. Perhaps Morgan is a right royal bastard at times, excuse my language, but he has character. I'll take that against all the noble names you can produce."

Just to be able to talk of Morgan eased Faith's pain. Sheltered as she had been, there had been no one to speak of him, no one who could confirm her opinions or call her fool if she were. It was good to have her loyalty to Morgan justified by someone else. There were times when she was so uncertain of herself that she wondered if she were not being taken for three times a fool for loving Morgan. She smiled gratefully at this confirmation of some small part of her feelings.

"From what I understand, my family's noble names mean little in the way of true nobility. I am glad my parents taught me to place small reliance on such things. I hope when this is over that you will still call me friend too."

Miles ignored the sudden cloud that seemed to cover the sun. From what he understood of Morgan's curt commands, she would be needing a friend when this was over.

With a feeling of dread, he touched his hand to hers where it rested on her cup. "I hope when this is over, you won't turn me aside."

26

THE WEIGHT OF a hundred pounds of chains on his wrists and ankles was heavier on Morgan's pride than his strength. He kept his gaze turned straight ahead without looking at the equally weighted wretches to either side of him. Some were practically bent double beneath the iron. Others coughed constantly with the hacking croup that spoke of near-death. But besides those whose imprisonment had left them weak and ailing, there were those who were quite familiar with their surroundings and joked and capered and gambled and pressed their attentions on the various and assorted females in this chilly holding place. All waited for judgments on their crimes, and most were certainly heading for the gallows or transportation. There were few crimes that allowed for anything else.

They had already been here for hours, and the stench was becoming unbearable. Morgan had learned to stand his own in any kind of company, but he had always before had the freedom to leave when he pleased. Being trapped in these unhealthy environs with these dregs of humanity dragged his pride a little lower in the mud. The guilt that had eaten at him for so long found an outlet as he saw himself in these craven creatures.

Morgan tried to concentrate on the court proceedings below, but it was like watching a Punchinello show and he could not concentrate on the elaborate arguments and voluble tirades and outbreaks of angry cries and wails. Every so often, as another victim was branded, the courtroom grew quiet to savor the screams of pain, but these only served to tighten the knot around the meager breakfast Morgan had taken.

He had already scanned the crowd in search of anyone he knew, and felt some measure of relief that she was not here. He had feared Faith would overcome Miles's objections and insist on waiting throughout the day for his turn to come, and he had known he would say anything to get her out of here. Not having that problem to worry about, he sought others, just to keep his mind from his surroundings.

Miles was here somewhere, but Morgan wasn't interested in facing him either. The humiliation of being caught was great enough. To be subjected to this circus was beneath a man's dignity. If they wished to hang him, Morgan wished they would just get it over with and be done. He had known this day would come, but now that it was here, he wondered if he should have done things a little differently. He wasn't quite ready yet to leave this world.

Morgan squared his shoulders and clenched his teeth as another poor soul was put to the brand. His main regret was that he had not accomplished what he set out to do, he told himself. He had allowed the bloody Sassenachs to win. The anger of that thought kept him strong. If he could just get out of here, he would have his revenge. The world would know the de Lacys had not died in vain.

The image of Faith's trusting face floated before his mind's eye, but Morgan deliberately ignored it. There was one sin he would not carry on his soul should he fail. Faith would be taken care of. Perhaps he should not have forced himself on her that last time. It might be better if she could have that farce of a marriage easily annulled without the fear of a child coming of their brief affair. But he could not regret the thought of a child being left behind should he go to the gallows.

She had his name, or part of it. She would survive. She would survive much better without him. That fact was as plain as the nose on his face, and he had a very distinctive nose. If she stayed with him, he would only pull her down into the gutter. He had caused her all the pain that he intended to cause. It was better to cut her off now while she was strong and ready for it. If he left her now, he could look back on Faith as being the one good thing he had done in his life. He had given her life, taught her to be strong, and extorted the money from her family that she should have had from the first. He was rather proud of that accomplishment. No, he wouldn't think of Faith with regret. She was good and whole and he would tarnish her no more.

A cynical smile crossed Morgan's lips as he watched the approach of a stout man in feathered hat and gold braid. He knew who the man was; his brief time in gaol had taught him that. The fact that the man had set his beady eyes on Morgan did not bode well for the future, but he could always kill the bloody rogue if he didn't like what he said. It might pay to hear what the man had to say. If rumor held fact, the feathered macaroni had his hands on the biggest crime network in the history of London. What interest could he find in a lone Irish highwayman?

He was not to hear immediately. James O'Neill was summoned to the bench, and the guard jerked Morgan's chains, shoving him toward the stairs. His time had come.

"There 'e is, that one talking to the bloke in the feathery 'at. Fine figure of a man, must 'ave paid well to keep that fancy shirt on his back. Look at 'im! Mean as any they come, I'd say. Want me to fetch 'im for ye?"

Edward grimaced in distaste at the sidewalk urchin. "Scarcely. Where's your employer? Why isn't Watson here? And why in bloody hell is that bastard out on the street? Shouldn't he be in chains?"

The grimy boy shrugged his skinny shoulders. "Don't keep up with Watson. Now, the bloke on the rattlin' lay, he's out on the street 'cause some fancy man got 'im off. I wouldn't mind workin' for the likes o' 'im. Bejesus iffen 'e don't seem fine. There's coins there, mind you. And if 'es's paired up with the thief-taker general, then there's accountin' for the coin."

Edward let this idle blather pass on by, not caring to decipher the cant. The highwayman was out on the street and not in chains, and Watson was nowhere to be seen. His choler rose to detrimental proportions, but there was one chance left. Pulling a coin from his purse, he held it out to the ragged urchin. "Here, boy. There's more where this came from if you follow the highwayman and report back to me. Find out where he stays, whom he meets with. Do you understand?"

The boy's eyes grew round at the sight of the coin. The task was much easier than the nob imagined. Everyone knew where the general went. And the highwayman was walking off in his company now. He bobbed his head, grabbed the coin, and took off at a run. The general wouldn't care if he sat under the table while they talked.

* * *

Miles Golden waited in a fury for his client to come out of the meeting with the biggest piece of scum to walk the face of London. When Morgan finally appeared, cordially shaking hands with the oily scoundrel, Miles had half a mind to walk off and leave him there. But there was the matter of a certain lady waiting patiently in lonely rooms for the cad's arrival, and for her sake the attorney lingered.

"What in bloody hell do you think you're doing?" Miles spat out as Morgan found him and sauntered over. "The general has his hand in every scam and shady undertaking in the city. They say he trains children to steal from the time they're old enough to walk. And any who dare try to escape his hold end up on the gallows. I get you out of Newgate to let you fall into the hands of scum like that?"

Morgan began striding toward a well-lighted tavern spilling drunken laughter and riotous music onto the street. "It is more a matter of the other way around, if the truth be told, but you needn't concern yourself. I owe you a tidy sum for whatever you did to buy off that runner. Reckon my accounts, and I'll see you in the morning."

Cold fury got the better of him, and Miles grabbed Morgan's coat sleeve and jerked him around. "Aren't you forgetting something?"

Morgan raised a black eyebrow. "Am I?"

Now Miles understood how Faith had felt when she punched the bastard in the stomach. The urge was great, but he had learned patience the hard way, and he exerted it now. "You have a wife waiting to hear how you fared. If you do not appear, she will think you on the way to the gallows. And if I am not mistaken, you do not know where to find her. Shouldn't you let me take you there first?"

Morgan shook his arm free, and his gaze was fierce as it focused on his attorney. "For her own good, let's leave it that way, shall we? Let her think me dead, if you wish. I'd advise her to leave the city, if I were you. She has a curiosity about the colonies that you might encourage. You haven't touched her money in my affair, have you?"

The week of tension finally erupted. Not a large man or a strong one, Miles seldom engaged in fisticuffs, but words were inadequate to express his rage. His awkward swing had only the advantage of surprise. His fist connected sharply with Morgan's jaw, but the highwayman merely staggered backward.

"You may have your accounts in the morning, de Lacy, and then you can go to hell." Miles turned around and stalked away, leaving the Irishman to stare after him, hand to jaw.

Faith nearly cried when the footsteps finally sounded on the stairs below. She rushed to the tiny mirror to check her hair, straightened her kerchief, and glanced around the room to be certain all was in order. The two tiny rooms were scarcely large enough to hold Morgan, but they were clean and fresh, and they would be here only a little while. She tried not to look at the newly made bed. It was small, but adequate for their means. She put her hands over the blush that rose to her cheeks. She was a wife now. It was unseemly to blush.

She nearly danced to the door, throwing it open before the footsteps reached the landing. That Miles came first surprised her, but she gave him a smile and looked eagerly over his shoulder for some sign of Morgan. The candle in her visitor's hand revealed only shadows, empty shadows. Faith died a little inside as she turned her gaze slowly back to the solicitor.

Miles gestured for her to go back into the room, and he followed with halting step. The room was illuminated by a lantern and a branch of candles, and he rubbed his sore knuckles as he absorbed the small signs of welcome she had prepared. A bouquet of marguerites brightened the table under the window. Morgan's clean clothing lay pressed and ready on a chair. A few pieces of coal burned in the grate to chase away the damp. His gaze wandered back to the woman who had prepared all this, and he could tell she had made no exception for herself. Her hair gleamed with brushing, her kerchief and gown were spotless and arranged just a little more provocatively than was her custom. The smile that had been on her lips just a moment ago still strained to remain in place. His heart ached in despair of ever explaining Morgan's absence.

"Where is he?" Faith whispered, trying to tell herself that all was well, that there was just some delay.

"He's not coming." Miles's voice was flat as he circled the room, locating a small decanter of wine and helping himself without asking. Perhaps he ought to tell her Morgan was dead, but he could not lie.

''Not coming?'' She sounded weak and foolish even to herself, but she could think of no other words.

''He has some idea it would be better if you didn't see him again.'' That sounded almost reasonable. She probably was better off without the scoundrel, but one didn't tell a new bride that. Mayhap Morgan was even doing the right thing, but Miles didn't feel encumbered to be the one to tell her. Morgan should be the one saying the words to break her heart.

''Not see him again?'' She was beginning to sound like a parrot. Faith shook herself and tried again. ''He is free? He's not in that terrible place anymore? What happened?''

Miles took a drink and stared at the coals. ''The witness did not appear, and the judge let him go. All the fees have been paid, and he is free. The last I saw of him, he was heading for a tavern.''

There didn't seem to be much to say to that. Faith had known he had another life and that London was part of it. Morgan might very well have a mistress here, or other women of some sort. He had never promised to be faithful. He had not wanted their marriage. It had simply been an expedient solution to a difficult problem. He owed her nothing. Why had she thought that they had something special? He had never said the words. He had just used her because she was convenient, and offered to marry her to keep her happy. With Morgan she couldn't expect anything more. So why had she? Why did she feel as if she were dead or dying and that the sun would never rise again? He had done only what she should have expected, if she had any sense at all.

''I see.'' Faith picked up another wineglass and held it out. Miles filled it for her, and she sipped at the rich liquid as she tried to pull together all the shattered fragments that were her illusions. Morgan wasn't coming. She couldn't seem to see beyond that.

''Morgan wished me to look after you. He said something about your wishing to go to the colonies. I can arrange that, or if you prefer, I can make some arrangement to meet with your family and sound out their intentions. Perhaps they are only interested in finding you for your safety's sake.''

Faith acted as if she hadn't heard him. ''Did you know my father was shot? Miners can't afford guns. I shouldn't think the squire or vicar or any of the shopkeepers would have been there at dawn. Who do you think would want to shoot my father? He was harmless. He never hurt anyone.''

Miles felt his stomach wrench. Had she taken leave of her senses? Cautiously he set her glass aside and took her hands. ''That was a long time ago, Faith. We have to think about now. I hate to leave you alone like this. Shall I call your landlady?''

Faith smiled wanly and pulled free before wandering away. ''You have done what I asked of you. You may go home now with an easy conscience. Have you seen Toby? Will he come again?''

''I'm not going anywhere until I know what you plan. My conscience will never rest easy by leaving you here alone. I want to begin making arrangements immediately to see you to safety. Perhaps you would like to live in a village somewhere instead of London. I can have someone look about for a suitable house and arrange for your quarterly interest to be sent to you. I'll see to having your marriage annulled. I'm not certain of its legality in any case. You can look about and find some suitable young man. It would be better if you went about in society, but if you fear your family . . .''

Faith wasn't really listening. Her thoughts were already outside of London, in a small cottage in a forest where she had known some of the happiest days of her life. A poor life it must have been for those to be her happiest days, but she had been content like that. More than content. Morgan had filled her with life and love and laughter. She hadn't known life could be like that.

''If you can find Toby, I'd like to go home. I suppose the mare has been sold. Is it possible to hire a horse? Or I suppose I could walk. The days aren't very chilly yet.''

He wasn't going to get any sense out of her tonight. Miles drained his glass. ''I'll send Toby to you as soon as he appears. Get some sleep, and I'll be back in the morning. Perhaps Morgan will have come to his senses by then. I'll have Mrs. Thwaite send Mary up here.''

Faith scarcely noticed when he left. If Mary arrived, she didn't notice that either. She went into the bedroom and closed the door. She lay down on the bed she had meant to share with Morgan for the rest of their lives. And she stared at the ceiling until her eyes couldn't stay open any longer.

Then she slept like one of the dead until Toby pounded on the door the next morning.

She ignored Toby's arguments. Nothing anyone suggested felt right. She needed to go back to the cottage, back to the place where she and Morgan had been happy. He *had* been happy, she knew it. He couldn't find her here in London. If he changed his mind, he would look for her at the cottage. There was simply no other choice.

Faith came out of her daze long enough to give Toby a look of surprise at the mare he held for her when they came down to the street. Morgan's mare. Her lifted eyebrows spoke what her words did not.

Toby shrugged with embarrassment. "I didn't sell her. Morgan didn't ask. She's a lovely thing. It seemed a shame to let some big brute buy and ruin her."

Faith ran her hand over Dolly's high, arched neck and mane, and the Arabian blew a soft breath and nuzzled her gently. Not everything was black, then. There was always hope. With tears in her eyes, Faith accepted Toby's assistance and gained the animal's back. If she could only hold on to this one small part of Morgan, perhaps someday she would hold the rest. The notion of ever holding Morgan in her arms again brought new tears, and she took the reins and hurriedly started down the road. She would go mad to think like that.

She would have to take one day at a time. Staring at the teeming multitude of people swarming the streets of London, Faith wondered where in all this huge city Morgan was, but she refused to wonder why he had done this to her. She understood what no one had said. Morgan had gone back to a life of theft. He wouldn't give up his revenge for her.

27

"I'M SORRY, MY LADY. I have done everything within my power to find her, but every trace has disappeared. Even the runner I relied upon to help me in my search has failed me. The highwayman has not even led me to his wife, and certainly not to anyone who might be George's daughter." Edward didn't mention the bank account that he and Thomas had set up to entice either the highwayman or the heiress to appear. The money was gone, spirited away by tribes of lawyers and legal paperwork. He still had a solicitor following the paper trail, but he already knew where the bank's copies of the heiress's papers had gone. Or had a strong suspicion.

Lady Carlisle held up her fragile chin and tapped her fingers on her walking stick as she gazed in the direction of the draped windows. "I thank you for your efforts, Edward. I'm not quite certain how this highwayman became involved in your tale, but I'm certain you meant well. I think your father might be right. We should begin in Cornwall and trace her from there."

In his high-backed chair in the corner, the marquess gave a grunt and rubbed at his foot. "Wesley has been worse than useless. None of his pious followers admit to having seen a hair of the girl. We'd best start facing up to the facts, Lettice. She's gone. Wherever or however, she's disappeared, and we're not likely to find her after all this time."

The lady paled beneath her papery skin, but she continued clinging to her walking stick. "I won't give up, Harry. She's all I have left to live for. I will find her, if I must go to Cornwall myself."

For once, father and son exchanged mutual looks of agreement. The marquess was the one to step forward and offer his hand to the lady. "Lettice, you look tired. Why don't you go home and get some rest? You know we will let you know as soon as we have some news.''

Looking down her nose, Lady Carlisle disdained his hand. "I am not an idiot, Harry. If someone has murdered my granddaughter, I want to know. Just tell me the truth, and perhaps someday I can get a little sleep.''

A commotion on the stairs outside the parlor drew their attention. A moment later, a servant threw open the double doors and made a deep obeisance. "Master Thomas Montague and Lady Faith Henrietta Montague, milords, milady.''

Lady Carlisle gasped and held her hand to her breast as the roguish Thomas entered with a demure young woman in dove-gray gown and modest bonnet. Edward glared thunderously, and abruptly turned his back on the newcomers. But it was the old marquess's approval they sought, and Mountjoy's sharp gaze softened to one of relief as the girl made a dutiful and graceful curtsy.

"Welcome home, granddaughter. It is good to see you at last.''

Thomas stole a triumphant look at his cousin's back, then smoothly accepted the congratulations and eager questions that followed. Edward's smoldering anger went unnoticed by all but its object. Thomas smugly tucked his newfound cousin's arm through his and relished the feeling of the shoe being on the other foot for a change. Things were starting to change around here.

"Word is, he's in high circles now, rubbing elbows with the Quality. I don't know his lay, but it's payin' well if he can keep up with the likes of them. You needn't worry 'bout Jack, Faith. He's a right one." Toby tried to reassure her as he quaffed his ale and watched her polish the high table in the taproom. It was early afternoon and there was none about but themselves.

Faith didn't even attempt to smile. She turned from the table to the row of pewter mugs. "That's nice, Toby. And what are you doing these days?''

Toby watched her busy hands with something akin to despair. Faith wasn't Faith anymore, but some scullery maid named Alice. Before long, she would begin blending in with Whitehead's dingy woodwork. He didn't know how to change things, but putting a bullet in Jack's back probably wouldn't help.

"I'm just round and about. With winter coming, maybe I ought to take up my brother's offer and go to Virginia if it's as warm there as he says. Want to go with me?" Toby had been trying for weeks to get up the courage to ask this. Jack's fancy man of business had urged it, and even offered to pay him to persuade Faith, but it wasn't the money that made him ask.

Faith didn't answer. She stared at the mugs as she polished them to a high gleam. It was somehow reassuring to know that she had some control over objects, that she could make them gleam and shine and visibly bring life back to these dismal surroundings. She was proud of her accomplishment, but Toby's words wandered around in the back of her mind.

It was early November, almost a year since she had met Morgan. It seemed a lifetime, and then again, it didn't seem long enough. Going home to face the empty cottage each night had become an ordeal she found more and more difficult to face. At first she had done so eagerly, hoping against hope to find Morgan there waiting for her. After more than two months, it was becoming obvious even to her that he didn't plan to return. With the weather turning bad, she had taken to saddling and riding Dolly to the inn every day. It would be a simple enough matter to leave the mare in the stable and take one of the upstairs rooms for herself and not go back at all. When the weather got a little colder, perhaps that was what she would do.

The front door creaked and the sound echoed in the empty corridor outside the taproom. Whitehead had gone into the village and his wife was in the kitchen with the cook and the new tavern maid. Molly had left for London soon after she sold her babe to a couple who couldn't have children. That left only Faith and Toby to man the front rooms, and Faith didn't deal with customers if she could avoid it.

Toby frowned and nodded toward the room where the kegs were kept. "Go on in there. I'll see what they want and call Mrs. Whitehead for you."

Faith hesitated, then did as told. She had learned caution these last months, and she suspected there might be extra reason for caution now. She stepped into the storage room and listened as the stranger or strangers spoke to Toby.

"Where's Whitehead?" The voice spoke with authority, although the accent held a definite cockney note to it.

"To town. If you're needin' a room, I'll fetch his missus."

"Just give me an ale. You live in these parts?"

Faith smiled at the wary tone Toby adopted immediately. She had heard that tone often enough in these rooms. The men that frequented the Raging Bull had reason to avoid questions, and they did so adroitly. Unlike their London brethren, they were not given to selling information to the law. The last one who had tried that had mysteriously disappeared, never to be heard from again.

"For a piece," Toby answered evasively, drawing the requested drink.

"You remember a gentry mort who worked here a while back? What was her name?"

Faith felt the bottom drop out of her stomach, and the unusual coldness of Toby's reply was indicative of his nervousness. "You must be thinkin' of somewhere else. Ain't no gentry in these parts, and no one ever mistook Molly for gentry."

"Molly? No, that ain't the name. Alice, she was. I remember now. Alice. Went to London with Black Jack, if I remember rightly. Pretty thing, wasn't she?"

Standing in the darkness of the closet, Faith nearly succumbed to a wave of dizziness. Why should anyone be looking for her? And under that name? It couldn't be her family. Why would the law be looking for Alice Henwood? There was only one reason Faith could think of, and the long-ago memory of a black night and a gunshot and a fallen man came back to haunt her. She had blacked the memory out, refusing to think of it, and Morgan had spoken of it no more, but it couldn't go away entirely. Never would it go away entirely. She had killed a man, and the law had finally come for her. She held her hand to her spinning head and sat down abruptly.

Toby sent the man on his way, but when Faith didn't immediately reappear, he went around the bar to find her. She was sitting on a keg, holding her head, looking as if she had just been struck by a wheel iron. He crouched down beside her and took her hand. "Faith? He's gone. Everything's all right."

The wide gray eyes that looked back at him held ghosts.

Faith's hand fell to her lap and cradled her abdomen as if she were about to be ill. Fear began to curl at Toby's insides, but her first words were calm and sane.

"Jack isn't coming back, is he?"

Toby wished he dared take her hand, but he merely clenched his fingers into his palms. "Not likely, lass. He's doin' the best thing for you. Them that he's with would use you in turn if he let them. It's not a life for the likes of you."

And it wasn't the life for a child. Faith clenched her teeth and held her chin up to keep the tears from falling. God had punished her once for living in sin, and He had punished Morgan for his life of crime. She had learned her lesson. She didn't know if she was married in God's eyes now, but she had done as well as she could. She had a name and a piece of paper that gave this child she was carrying a father. Morgan had done his job well. Had he gone to the gallows, there would still be a part of him to live on. He might go to the gallows yet if he insisted on this sinful life. She would never let his son know of it. His son would know only of the proud man who had lost his home and died earning it back. He would have the father that Morgan could have been.

"How often do ships go to Virginia, Toby?"

Toby stared at her in mixed relief and dismay. The voyage terrified him, but for Faith he would sail the seven seas. He rose and pulled her up with him. "I'll find out, then, lass. You go home and wait for me."

Miles Golden had given Toby a bank draft in Faith's name, and coins enough to pay their passage, but Faith wouldn't touch them. Carrying her small horde of hard-earned money and riding Morgan's mare, she insisted on paying her own way. It was bad enough that she rode a horse purchased with stolen money and wore gowns from the same source. She would start out in the New World with only honest wages. She would have no part of Morgan's ill-gotten coins, not even to ease his conscience if that were their source.

Toby held his tongue and shook his head after they arrived in Portsmouth and Faith argued the ship's captain into taking the mare in exchange for their passage. Having no knowledge of the cost of the journey, Toby couldn't decide if the deal were a fair one or not, but the tears in Faith's eyes as she said her farewells to the horse were enough to make a man weep.

He had reason enough for second thoughts in all the weeks that followed.

Faith groaned and turned green as the ship hit another swell. Even the fact that Toby had just arrived to tell her that land had been sighted wasn't sufficient to ease the churning of her insides. The brazier Toby had bought before sailing wasn't sufficient to heat the cold and damp from the tiny cabin, and the weevily bread and watered soup that had been much of their fare this past week made her ill just to think of. Huddled in her blanket, Faith turned and retched over the chamber pot and wished Toby and the rest of the world to hell.

Perhaps God hadn't thought her sufficiently punished. Perhaps she should not have taken the mare or the gowns, but left the cottage as she had arrived. As another wave of illness swept over her, Faith knew that to be impossible. She wasn't the same as she had arrived—a child grew within her, Morgan's child—and she would never be that person again. She had to give the child what few advantages she could take. To lose it would be to lose herself. She couldn't bear another loss.

The error had been in leaving in December. The winter seas had been miserable. She hadn't seen the deck since they set sail. The dank cabin and the noisome stenches of the close air only added to her misery. She was being punished of a certainty, but only for her stupidity.

As the nausea subsided, Faith sat back in her bunk and pushed her hair from her face. Toby stood in uncertainty just inside the door, his hands in his pockets and his face a pale red as his gaze drifted to the visible mound of Faith's stomach. They had not spoken of this growing symbol of Morgan's possession, but it was time that silence ended.

"Do not look so, Toby. I'll not die of it. Once we are onshore, I'll be fine. Women have babies all the time. You would do better to speak to the captain and find out where we should stay when we arrive. I'd not be left in a flea-infested hole while I look for work and you hunt your brother."

Toby grew a little redder, but he ran his hand through his hair and spoke with some degree of authority. "I already talked with the captain. Williamsburg is some few miles inland. We'll need to hire a cart. He says it's one of the biggest cities in the colonies and there's lots of places to stay as long as the House isn't in session. It being February, it might be, but he gave me the names of one or two places to try. We'll be fine, don't you worry." He bit his lip anxiously, then offered, "Maybe you should try to eat a bite again? Seems like the babe ought to be fed more regular."

Perhaps the babe ought, but Faith couldn't face the thought of food again. She shook her head. "If you can persuade some hot water from the cook, there's a little of our tea left. I'll share a cup with you."

Perhaps she would take a bit of toast with the tea. Toby nodded and strode off, leaving Faith to stare at the hated four walls again.

Her mind wandered back to the cottage, the place where she had found peace if for only so brief a while. In those days while Toby had sought shipping, she had polished and cleaned and straightened. The shirt she had started for Morgan, she finished and laid upon his trunk. She was quite proud of her workmanship. The lace had looked every bit as professional as a tailor's. If Morgan ever came back, he would have a decent shirt in exchange for the gowns he had given her. It wasn't much, but she had little to work with. The cottage was in better shape than when she had arrived, but she doubted that Morgan would notice such a thing.

She tried not to think of the aching, lonely nights she had spent there since she returned from London. If she didn't think about Morgan, didn't think about how it felt to be held in his arms, how she loved watching him rise and stretch in the mornings, the way she felt when she watched the muscles ripple across his back and chest, she could almost forget the ache of emptiness in her center. But if she didn't think about Morgan, her mind was an echoing chasm with nothing to fill it.

She had left him a note. It had been a foolish thing to do, but at the last minute she could not leave without saying farewell. The note hadn't said much, just a few senseless words of gratitude and a reassurance that she was gone and wouldn't bother him anymore, but tears had poured down her face as she wrote it. She didn't want him to know she had cried, and she almost tore it up and threw it in the fireplace, but the fire had died and Toby was waiting and she had left it with the last fading flowers she had found in the garden. She should never have signed it as she had, though. It would make him feel bad, and she hadn't wanted to make him feel bad. But there had been no other honest way to sign it. Perhaps he wouldn't mind knowing that she had left without bitterness.

Perhaps she ought to be bitter, but she wasn't. Toby and Miles didn't understand that she had never expected anything from Morgan and that he had never given her reason to believe she deserved anything. They were partners, nothing more. When neither of them could benefit from the partnership, he had dissolved it. He had been quite right to do so. She had told him she could not marry a thief. She had, but it had been in hopes that he would give up his life of crime. Morgan understood that. Morgan understood her better than anyone else ever had. She just wished that understanding and love could be the same thing.

But they weren't, so there was no use in crying over it anymore. She had cried until there were no longer any tears left to shed. Somehow, she would make a new life here, and their child would grow up believing in God and living the life of respectability that Morgan had lost with his home. Morgan would want that.

By the time the ship docked, Faith was ready to say farewell to the past. She wrapped herself in the mantle she had bought in London, pulled the hood up to hide the tracks of tears, and waited on deck while Toby found a cart and loaded their few trunks. The sky was overcast and the wind strong, but it wasn't a bitterly cold wind. There was even some green in the weeds along the shore. The birds crying overhead gave her the feeling of impending spring, and Faith allowed a small smile to tilt her lips. It had been spring when Morgan first took her to his bed. It would be spring when his child arrived. She touched her hand to the swelling hidden beneath her cloak and felt the butterfly movements that told her all was well. She didn't intend to lose this one.

The cart driver grudgingly took them to the inn that the captain had recommended instead of the one that he was paid best to deliver them to. When the proprietor apologized to say he was full, the driver muttered "I told you so" and set out for his usual accommodation. Toby insisted that they try the next place on the captain's list, and the man gave him a surly look.

"They be closed. Needham died last month and his widow's selling the place. You got any more suggestions before I take you where you belong?"

Disliking the man's insolence and intrigued by the idea of an inn for sale, Faith spoke up for the first time since they had set out. "Take us to Needham's or set us down, please. I would speak to the widow."

Toby looked at her in surprise, but the determination in her voice sounded much better than the emptiness that had been there before. Besides, she was as pale as a ghost and leaned on him for support while they rode. They needed an inn immediately, and he wouldn't trust this character to find them a respectable one.

The building the driver brought them to was on the outskirts of town, out of the way of the main thoroughfare. It was small, but solidly built of brick, with shutters to pull against the cold and rain. The place looked deserted, but Faith ordered the trunks brought down and dismissed the driver. She was too tired to go farther. Somehow, they would persuade the widow to let them in. She liked the looks of this tiny inn.

Toby tried the door and found it open, but the chambers echoed empty when they stepped inside. A loud "Halloa!" brought the sound of scurrying feet from above, and a white apron over a black wool skirt appeared on the stairway. Soon a woman with neatly dressed white hair nearly covered by a full mobcap came into sight, her gaze straining anxiously through wire-rimmed glasses. "Who is there?"

Finding the young couple and their trunks in the front hall, she wrung her hands together and glared at them suspiciously. The young woman appeared ready to sink to the floor as she held on to her husband's arm, and the young man watched her so anxiously that Mrs. Needham couldn't help feeling her heart go out to them in sympathy. "The inn's closed; I'm sorry. I have no help. Would the lady care to take a seat while you go to look for better accommodations, sir?"

Toby looked resigned as he handed Faith into a wooden chair set beside the door. "I'd be grateful, ma'am, if you could offer a cup of tea or suchlike. She's not been well and the journey's been a long one."

Faith untied her hood and let it fall back to her shoulders. Her cheeks were pale against the unruly russet curls, but she managed a faint smile. "I apologize for intruding, Mrs. . . . Needham?"

The innkeeper looked vaguely perplexed. The young man's accents were the uncultured ones of the London back streets, with a hint of brogue that was reflected in his coloring and dress. But the lady, now . . . She bobbed a curtsy of respect. "Bess Needham, at your service, my lady. Let your young man be about his business while we share a cup of tea. You look all tuckered out. Do you have family here?"

Faith gestured to her awkward companion. "Mr. O'Reilly has family here. He has generously offered to see me settled. I am Alice O'Neill. It is good to meet you, Mrs. Needham."

By the time Toby returned from his explorations, Faith had the landlady's life story and list of woes without revealing a hint of theirs. Bess Needham had been in service with a duke until she married and come away to the colonies. She knew Quality when she saw them, and she knew rascals when they crossed her path. She sent Toby a shrewd look when he reappeared in the private parlor where they were taking tea.

"Sit down and have a sip of tea, Mr. O'Reilly. I've been telling Mrs. O'Neill that she may stay here while she looks about for a place of her own. A lady in her delicate condition shouldn't be wandering about in this weather. I'll take good care of her. You needn't worry about her anymore."

At this effective dismissal, Toby shot Faith a worried look. She had discarded her mantle, and the warmth of the fire and the tea had returned some of the color to her cheeks. The sparkle had never returned to her eyes, but she seemed content for the moment. She gave him a small smile and touched his callused hand.

"I am trying to persuade Mrs. Needham that she needs to keep the inn open. You will always be welcome, Toby, but I don't want you to feel responsible for looking after me. Your brother will be thrilled to see you, and I will be happy to have you here. So you will have two homes while you look for one of your own."

The look of distress on the lad's face softened the landlady's generous heart. Perhaps he wasn't too great a rascal. After all, he had looked after the young lady well enough. Bess poured him a cup of tea and handed him a large plate of molasses bread. "We won't send you out this night. In the morning you can begin to make inquiries. If your brother doesn't have need of you, perhaps you could help us out here. If the taproom is reopened, we'll need a man about the place.''

Toby looked in astonishment from Faith's serene expression to the smiling landlady. In less than an hour, Faith had found home and employment for both of them, and convinced an elderly widow to take on the insurmountable task of running an inn and tavern without the help of a man's strength.

He should have known that anyone who could have Black Jack O'Neill waiting on her hand and foot was capable of moving mountains.

28

THE COLD March night kept his hosts from opening the doors at the end of the ballroom, but Morgan threw a longing look in that direction. The heat of a thousand candles and hundreds of overdressed bodies pressed around him, and the stink of their unwashed skin perfumed with acrid scents made his head ache. His gorge rose at the sight of the pomaded and powdered hair of the woman dancing on his arm. He was certain she had not washed that creation since he had seen her the week before. It made his own scalp itch to think of it.

And as usual, such thoughts turned his memories to Faith. She had always smelled clean and fresh. Her hair had gleamed with health and not pomade. She had worn only the lightest of fragrances, scents so subtle he could never be certain if they were of perfume or her own skin. She had been an enchantment that Morgan had never experienced before and obviously never would again. He didn't know why he had ever thought that she belonged in these crowded ballrooms, breathing the same air as these polluted souls. Perhaps somewhere in this mob there were characters as pure as Faith's, but he wasn't destined to meet them. He gazed into the face of the painted beauty on his arm and gave her the smile she expected. She simpered, and Morgan had all he could do to keep from shoving her aside and striding out of the room.

Tonight he would take her to her chambers and give her what she wanted, and in the morning he would tell the general just how to enter the rooms and where her jewels were kept. She was a whore and another man's wife and she deserved to be robbed of what she had gained by selling her body, but Morgan couldn't for the life of him remember why he had determined this would even his score with the Sassenachs. He must have been mad. If he continued as he was, he would be as wretched as they, but he saw no other course open for him.

A footman came to stand at the top of the steps to announce still another contingent of guests to this already overcrowded room. Morgan scarcely paid attention to their arrival, but the music stopped as their names were called, and the sound brought him to attention.

"The Marquess of Mountjoy, Earl Stepney, Lady Lettice Carlisle, Miss Faith Henrietta Montague, and Mr. Thomas Montague." The intonations rang out clearly, leaving Morgan to gape openly at the new arrivals, his heart pounding erratically as he searched the arriving throng.

It took only a moment's work to know that Faith wasn't among the elegant people descending the stairway, despite the servant's introduction. Sharp disappointment pierced him, easing only briefly when Morgan discovered the delicate woman clinging to an older gentleman's arm, but it was clear even from across the room that she was elderly. Disappointment once more wrapped him in cold embrace, but Morgan tried to ignore it, turning his cynical gaze on the frail woman. Thin, wrinkled arms reached from beneath a swathe of black lace covering regal shoulders and proudly held head. This, then, was the woman he had seen so long ago entering Montague House.

Morgan's gaze drifted to the only other female in the group, and he froze. His black glare should have scorched the impostor even from this distance, but she was too caught up in her charade to notice one man in a room of elegant gentlemen. He watched as she smiled at the rogue at her side, whom Morgan identified immediately as the man who had offered him ten thousand pounds to keep Faith away. He was beginning to understand the stakes that were being played here, and his jaw clenched in fury.

The woman was no more the image of Faith Henrietta Montague than Morgan was God. By the saints, he would have her crucified for even attempting this charade. Were they blind? This impostor was a whore, pure and simple. Her painted face sparkled with expensive diamond dust and wore the patches of fashion to accent features that were crude in comparison to Faith's delicacy. Her bountiful bosom was held up by a tight corset that hid the sag of more years than Faith's nineteen. The gold crepe gown she wore rode so low that she was in danger of falling out of it with every movement. Did the fools think his little Methodist would ever display herself so? They had to be mad, all of them.

Morgan turned his gaze to the last member of the party, Edward Montague, Earl Stepney. It had been dark the night he had robbed the man's coach, but he wouldn't forget his form easily. The earl was a massive man, but Morgan wasn't fooled by his size. He moved with the agility of an athlete, not the cumbersome gait of unhealthy lard. The man was definitely dangerous and should be avoided at all costs.

But Morgan couldn't let this masquerade go unmarked. His blood boiled at the thought. What did they hope to accomplish by passing off that London molly as Faith? Morgan's gaze returned thoughtfully to the older woman and gentleman being greeted by their host. Brushing off the irate woman trying to cling to his arm, Morgan eased himself in the direction of the stairway, all thought of the evening's adventure lost as he contemplated this new development. The marquess had two living heirs and had written off his younger son without a qualm. Obviously, whoever was perpetrating this fraud did not seek to impress the marquess with an impostor. Morgan's gaze focused on Lady Lettice Carlisle. There was no doubting Faith's heritage if one just looked upon this fragile woman with her proud bearing. The grief in her eyes could tell stories, and Morgan smelled their victim now.

He bided his time, watching the fools introduce their "newly discovered" relative. The painted "Faith" hung on to Thomas' arm, making her place in this charade apparent. Morgan sneered to himself. Let the young fool have her. It would serve him right. He felt no sympathy for the Montague saddled with a strumpet. But for Faith's sake, he would know if the Lady Carlisle might be interested in her real granddaughter.

It was remarkably easy to place himself at her side, and Morgan was amazed at himself when it was done. He simply cut the lady off from her usual cronies by placing himself between them, and backed her into a nook behind a statue where she couldn't be seen from the room. If Edward Montague saw them, there would be a price to pay, but Morgan counted on the crowd and the element of surprise to hide him.

Lady Carlisle caught sight of Morgan's harsh features and

her glance back to the stairway indicated she realized she had become separated from the others, but her attempt at escape was halted by Morgan's casual words.

"Are you party to that strumpet's charade or do you really have some interest in your granddaughter?"

Lettice's head jerked upward to observe more closely the elegantly garbed young gentleman who blocked her path. The burning fire of his eyes caught her aback, but his words held her in place. "I don't know what you're talking about, sir. She is my granddaughter. She has the papers to prove it."

The green eyes grew cynical. "And you always believe what you read? Did she show you the originals?" He read the doubt clearly in her eyes. She was no fool, but she had pride and wouldn't give in easily.

"No, of course not, but after all she's been through . . ." She hesitated as the young man's sneer became evident.

"Your granddaughter has been through hell, my lady, but she still has her parents' marriage papers and her own birth records. She is very much like you, you know." Morgan surprised himself with these words. He had only meant to stir doubt, to force her to question more closely, but the urge to talk to this slender woman was too strong to ignore. She reminded him so much of Faith. . . . He'd had a sister and mother once. They'd given him more than he had ever deserved. His instincts were to protect Faith's only female relative.

The lady's eyes lit with eagerness. "You know her? You have seen her? Where? Please, you have to tell me where. Is she well? She is still alive, isn't she? Please, whoever you are, tell me the truth."

Now he was in over his head. This woman couldn't look after herself and certainly couldn't protect Faith, but Morgan couldn't ignore her pleas either. He, too, wished he knew where Faith was. All he could offer the lady was old news, and he did that hesitantly. "The last I saw of your granddaughter, my lady, she was alive and well. I cannot tell you more than that. I know of a man who might know more, but for Faith's protection, I would not give away his name. I suspect there are those who would see her harmed." Morgan threw a glance in the direction of Thomas and his brazen mistress.

Lady Carlisle followed his glance. "Yes, I see. It is difficult, but not impossible. I must find her, sir. Can you not help me?''

Morgan made a bow and began to ease himself away. ''I will mention your request to the man I spoke about. I can do nothing more. Good evening, my lady.'' He turned and strode away as quickly as he could, losing himself in the crowd.

He had been mad to confront her. With any luck, Faith had successfully made her escape from this decadent society. What on earth had possessed him to reveal what he had refrained from telling anyone for so long? Why didn't he go ahead and tell the woman he was Faith's husband while he was at it?

He shouldn't have thought about that. The pain behind Morgan's eyes grew tighter, and he aimed for the doors to the outside, completely forgetting his assignment for the evening. He had to get away from here. Thinking about Faith in the same room with these people was a sacrilege.

Her husband. He was her husband, and he had allowed her to get away. There were good reasons for that, but Morgan had long since forgotten them. The hole where she had been in his life gaped and hurt worse than an amputated limb. It worked much better if he didn't think about it. He had spent months not thinking about what he had done. Why had he chosen to bring it all to a head tonight?

The fresh March air hit him like a cold bath. Morgan sent for his mount and waited, drinking in the breeze like a starving man. The stench of a thousand chimneys ruined the effect, and when he had his horse under him, he turned it toward the open roads of the country. He had need of real air, of the wind in his face and the stars in the sky. To hell with the city. Tonight he would ride the roads again.

The crawling scum of the streets cursed as Morgan raced by. As he neared the heath on the outskirts of the city, two thieves on the hookpole-lay tried to bring him from his horse, but the stallion was too quick and Morgan's sword caught one by the arm and sent him groaning into the ditch. It was dangerous to ride these roads alone at night, but he couldn't stay in the city one second longer than necessary.

As the countryside flew up around him, Morgan eased the stallion's pace. He had been thinking about going back to raising horses. He would never earn his fortune that way, but the dissolute life he led now left little for savings. There was scant satisfaction in bleeding the Sassenachs dry vicariously. His cut was high and his risk was low, and at the same time, he mingled with the society he had hoped to gain at Faith's side, but none of this made him happy. Being introduced to the upper echelons as a friend of the general's irked his sense of pride. Under any other circumstances he wouldn't be caught dead with the man. He must be mad to fall into the thief-taker's web. It was time he got out.

The horses were his first love. He still had the earnings from the sale of the mares. They had brought good prices. He could start a new line. Perhaps he would go back and look at the cottage again. He might make something of it for a while. It was not the kind of place gentlemen would go to purchase their expensive mounts, but he needed to find and breed the mares first. That would take a little time. He would think about selling them later.

The thought of the cottage eased Morgan's mind a little. It had only been a roof over his head until Faith came, but his memory of it now was strong and good. He needed some of that goodness tonight. Perhaps a little bit of Faith would rub off on him and lead him in the right direction. He knew what Faith would say, knew what she would want him to do. But the idea of giving up all his goals did not sit well with him. The Sassenachs had taken his bloody damn life, for Christ's sake. How could he let them get away with it without a fight?

A man had to fight for what was his. But as Morgan reached the cottage and swung down from his horse, he was assailed by doubts as to what was his. This was his. He had earned this piece of land with his years in the armies of others. No one could take it away from him. But did he have any right to anything else at all? The lands in Ireland had been his father's. Maeve had been his, but he had avenged her theft more than once. They'd taken his family, but how could he bring the dead back? He could have taken one of theirs, had taken one of theirs, but he would still never see his family again. Fighting wouldn't return them.

Dawn began to break over a bank of clouds in the east as Morgan opened the cottage door. The mustiness assailed him, and he knew with sinking heart that Faith had long been gone from these walls. Somewhere in the back of his mind he had imagined her here, waiting for him, keeping the hearth fire burning. That was a fool's thought.

The meager light of daybreak illuminated the emptiness. Dust coated the tall bed they had shared. She had left the pallet covered with a single sheet to protect from dirt, and there was still a faint odor of rosemary coming from the linen. He smiled, remembering her earnestness in telling him the uses of the various plants she had grown in their garden. He had paid little attention at the time, but he remembered the scent now. Rosemary kept the insects away. The gleam of white on his trunk caught his eye, and Morgan crossed the room to gently touch the lovingly sewn shirt Faith had left behind. He read her gratitude in the gesture, or perhaps her despair, and it made him feel more the filthy bastard.

Straightening his shoulders and shoving that thought away, Morgan turned and faced the table that Faith had polished so carefully once a week. The surface was coated with dust, and a vase of brittle flowers waited where it had been left, the beauty and life long since dried and gone, as what had once been now was gone. Morgan's heart twisted in remembrance of other such touches of the home he had left behind. He remembered Faith's blithe fingers picking the flowers and lovingly arranging them, as she had so carefully brightened and arranged those small portions of his life she had touched. He knew of a certainty that she had left this bouquet to welcome him. But he had never come. The emptiness of that lost bouquet tore at what remained of his heart.

He wondered when she had gone, how long she had waited before leaving, or if she had even come back here at all. Those flowers could have been picked while he was in Newgate and she was here dying inside, wondering what had become of him. She had never accused him of heartlessness, never held him back with possessive words or gazes, but Morgan knew he had hurt her, and hurt her badly. His Faith wouldn't have given herself had she not felt something for him.

Morgan sneered at the sentimentality of his thoughts. Faith had human needs just as everyone else did. She wasn't a saint. He had merely played upon her natural desires. Why should he place any more emphasis on the matter than that? By now she had probably found some quiet religious man who could offer her home and family, and she was quite contentedly sleeping in his bed.

He didn't want to think about that either. He wanted to

remember Faith as purely his. He needed that tonight. Or this morning. The dawn was growing brighter, sending golden rays across the dust-covered floor, catching on the polished kettle and plate on the shelves. Creeping across the table, the light illuminated a scrap of paper held down by the vase, and Morgan felt an odd catch in his throat as he crossed the room to examine it.

The words were hers, a piece of the past stealing back to seize him. He recognized the style immediately. Who else would apologize for saving his life while sacrificing her own? The guilt inside hardened and crystallized as Morgan read Faith's careful farewells. He had done it again, destroyed another tender life. The bloody Sassenachs held nothing in comparison to his single-handed destruction of the best thing ever to come into his life. Someone should just hold a gun to his head and put him out of his misery.

It was her final words that delivered the fatal blow. "Thank you for restoring my life, Morgan. I will carry you always in my heart. Love, Faith."

Love. Faith. The letter crumpled in his fingers as tears swam to his eyes. Love. Faith. God, but he'd been a fool.

Anguish ripping at his entrails, Morgan strode out of the cottage he had once called home, carrying nothing with him but a hand-sewn shirt and a crumpled bit of paper.

"Come here, my love. I've got an awful itch and I need you to scratch it."

Since she was lying naked in his bed with her fingers placed suggestively between her thighs, Thomas well understood the nature of her itch, but he wasn't in the mood just yet. She was getting too damned demanding. He liked the challenge of the chase, but Sarah made it too easy. He scowled at the scarlet velvet of her gown sprawled wantonly at the foot of his bed.

"Deuce take it, Sarah, you shouldn't be coming here like this. You're a pious Methodist, remember?"

The woman in his bed pouted and sat up, pulling her long legs beneath her. "Well, marry me, and that problem will be solved. I can't hide the bun in my oven much longer, you know. That old harridan has eyes like a hawk."

There was the crux of it. Thomas kicked the washstand. He had to marry her as long as she was parading as Faith, or the marquess would have his head. Or something a little more personal. His loins shriveled at just the thought. But marrying Sarah now was pointless. He'd already soaked every guinea out of the old man he was ever going to get, and the old lady was getting deuced suspicious. There wouldn't be much more forthcoming from that direction unless she had a sudden apoplexy and died. He wasn't even certain her granddaughter would be provided for in that alternative, either. Not unless he proved beyond a shadow of a doubt that Sarah was the real Faith Montague. They'd have to leave her the money, then.

Thomas played with the thought awhile. There were any number of paths he could take. After all, he couldn't be certain the real Faith was alive. The man he had sent to the Raging Bull couldn't even locate Alice Henwood. Like Faith, she had disappeared off the face of the earth. Deuced suspicious, but not impossible. The kind of lowlife inhabiting that den of iniquity would soon make mincemeat of any gently bred female hapless enough to fall into their hands. No doubt Faith and her counterpart, Alice, were long since raped and dead of disease, or used and forgotten in one of London's brothels. He would be doing everyone a favor to prove Sarah was the true Faith.

The damned highwayman was the sticking point. He'd seen the rogue in a gambling hell just the other night, parading as a gentleman. De Lacy, he called himself. De Lacy, hell. A damned Irishman, and a highwayman to boot. But the rogue knew what the real Faith looked like, he'd wager his last ha'penny on that. And he might even know where to find her original papers.

The threads were getting much thicker now that he neared his goal. He would have to be cautious not to get caught in one. Turning and finding his mistress gazing in a mirror and worrying at a blemish, Thomas began to unbutton his breeches. Women were easily disposable. He'd not worry about the wench just yet.

But wouldn't it be amazingly fortunate if the highwayman should take it into his head to rob and murder Earl Stepney, the man who had turned him over to the law?

"Mrs. O'Neill! Will you come here and tell this rascal we won't pay a ha'penny more for this watered-down rum than we paid last week? He don't seem to be hearing me."

Faith looked up from her books to find the sturdy frame

of Acton Amory in the doorway. He was not an overtall man, but there was strength in his solid shoulders and broad chest, and he served very well as their bartender. Unfortunately, he could neither read nor write, and the merchants took advantage of him when they could. But he was clever, and he knew the price of things in his head. She nodded at his request and picked up her ledger.

Amory instantly reached to help her up. Gratefully she took his arm. Although the babe was not large, he drew on her strength, and she felt awkward and ungainly when she moved about. She found her balance and released Amory's arm, but he continued to frown upon her with concern.

"You ought to be resting, Mrs. O'Neill. You're not big enough to carry such a burden. My wife was a large, healthy woman, but carrying a babe worked on her, it did."

Amory's wife had died of fever, not childbirth, but he never failed to mention his concerns. Faith offered him a faint smile and set out to find the rum merchant. She didn't need to hear about Amory's fears. He meant well, but he had been left with a small daughter to rear and he was searching for someone to take his wife's place. She hadn't a mind to be that woman.

After dealing with the merchant, Faith stopped to talk with the cook, agreed on the market list, and went in search of Mrs. Needham. The widow had taken on the responsibility of dealing with the housekeeping staff, such as it was. Bess had a granddaughter who worked hard when there were no men about to flirt with, and an indentured servant who did as little as she could get away with. Faith had some sympathy with that attitude and thought it might be preferable to hire someone for wages rather than buy a person's life, but the inn belonged to Mrs. Needham and she couldn't change her ways.

Bess Needham took one look at her new manager's weary face, grabbed her arm, and steered Faith toward her bedroom. "That's enough. You're to lie down now and not get up until morning. Mary will bring you your dinner. I don't know where I'd be without you, and I mean to take care of you."

"You'd probably be a wealthy woman sitting in luxury with servants at your beck and call," Faith responded wryly. "I'll sit down for a bit, but I need to see that the new tavern maid doesn't turn out like the last one. I persuaded you to keep this place open. I'll not let it become overrun with the types she attracted.''

Bess helped Faith to a chair and then stood with hands on hips, glaring at her. ''You only persuaded me to do what I wanted to do in the first place but just didn't have the courage on my own. There's no reason I can't tame a saucy maid as well as you. Acton is about to chew my ear off for letting you downstairs in the evening, and he's quite right. You no more belong in that taproom than I belong in a duke's ballroom. You earn your keep. There's no need for you to risk the babe for naught.''

Faith murmured words of assent, but by the time the April darkness fell, she was nimbly maneuvering the stairs to greet their regular guests and check that the cook did not leave the lamb on the fire too long. It still surprised her that their customers treated her with respect and even a certain amount of shyness in some cases. Of course, she had to take into account that Needham Inn attracted a much better class of customer than the Raging Bull, but she didn't think men usually treated women who worked in taverns with respect. This new country had odd ways, but she appreciated this one.

She shouldn't be appearing in public now that her skirts couldn't hide her pregnancy, and Faith did her best to stay behind her desk in the room off the front lobby, but she had begun to make friends here, and they didn't hesitate to search her out. Toby was the worst of the lot. He haunted the place on a regular basis, bringing his brother and his new wife, introducing their neighbors, and proudly showing off his newfound respectability. Faith had to laugh when Mary always seemed to appear whenever Toby was about, or his gaze constantly swept the inn in search of her if she did not appear. Faith had no illusion that she was the only reason Toby came into town.

Tonight the young solicitor who had taken permanent rooms hovered in the doorway, telling her of the latest activities in the Assembly, nervously working up the courage to ask her to dine with him. He was a nice young man with a great deal of intelligence. Faith was certain he would go far someday, but she had no words to tell him that her world was closed, that all she wanted right now was to stay busy and care for Morgan's child. She had no thought beyond the babe.

Except to occasionally wonder where Morgan was now. She had sent a letter to Miles giving her new direction but imploring that he not reveal it to anyone. She merely wished to be kept informed of what was happening in London, she had told herself at the time. The fact that Miles's letters never mentioned Morgan brought home the truth. She continued to read each one eagerly in hopes of some grain of information.

But it had been well over half a year since she had last seen Morgan, and she was learning to resign herself to his loss. It wasn't as if he had ever really been hers in the first place. She would never know another man like him, would probably never marry because of that, but he had given her a child to make her days brighter. When she felt the familiar longing build inside her, she could always imagine the future when a young Morgan would romp at her feet, and the blackness receded for a while.

Faith placed her hand in the small of her back where an ache had begun to build earlier in the day. Perhaps she was working too hard. It wouldn't do to harm the child. She would go up early and get some rest.

Waving a hand to some new arrivals, Faith began to take the steps to her room. The simple task of lifting her foot to the next step brought a pain across her middle, and she halted, grabbing her abdomen as the contraction increased rather than passing on.

As a flood of hot liquid burst down her legs, someone screamed, but Faith was no longer conscious of anything but the pain as she crumpled toward the floor.

29

ALL EYES FOCUSED on the tiny woman sitting straight and stiff on the bow-legged damask chair near the fire. Behind her stood an incongruous sight in rough-woven, ill-fitted coat and a wig that looked as if it had been made for another. The men lounging in various positions around the room glared at the burly intruder, but in respect for the elderly woman, they held their tongues.

"Thomas, I believe it is time you had the banns declared. If you wish to pass that woman off as my granddaughter, I will not have her bearing a bastard. If Harry will not, I suppose I could settle a sum on you so you will not starve, but do not expect more than that. I do not believe for a minute that she is my granddaughter."

Thomas jerked, then relaxed into his usual sprawl against the mantel. "I'm sorry if she does not live up to your expectations, Lady Carlisle, but there is no doubt as to who she is. We were only waiting for an appropriate time to announce our intentions. If you wish to provide Faith a dowry, we will gladly accept your gracious gift, but Uncle Harry has already offered a generous allowance. You need not burden yourself."

The sneer was evident in his voice, but Lady Carlisle ignored it. She had always found Thomas Montague to be beneath her dignity. She had never favored any of the Montagues, and her daughter had been a fool to fall in love with one, but at least she had fallen in love with an intelligent, respectable one. She turned her gaze to the marquess.

"He is your brother's son, and as such, deserves some share of the family fortune, but that is your concern and not mine. My concern is that after all this time you have not found my granddaughter, and I have taken it upon myself to do what should have been done long ago."

Mountjoy moved uncomfortably in the large chair by the

window, trying not to disturb the leg propped against a stool. Gout had taken its toll these last months, and he cursed the inactivity that kept him tied to the house. "You're getting senile, Lettice. The girl's got all the papers to prove who she is. She even looks a bit like myself in my younger years. That rogue behind you is only after your pockets. He certainly robbed enough out of mine."

Watson drew himself up with an indignant sniff, but the lady ignored him and continued, "Did you never question what became of the original papers? You know as well as I that those papers are copies. Did you never try to trace that woman's activity before she came here? Watson has given me a report that should open your eyes. If you wish to invite a lightskirt into the family bosom, far be it from me to stop you, but I'll not give up until I know my real granddaughter is safe."

The heavy man lounging across the love seat lifted his wineglass in toast to the old woman. "Very good, my lady. But did Watson here tell you how he was bought off and so let the thief who may have abducted our dear relative go free after all my efforts to catch him? I would not rely too heavily on his honesty."

Watson could not hold his tongue another minute. "I tried to explain to you, milord . . . I was coshed over the head and tied up and kept hidden until it was all over. I could have found the rogue for you the minute I was free, but you told me to bugger off." The shocked silence that followed this *faux pas* made him stutter and pull at his crumpled stock. "He was right here under your noses until just a few weeks ago, but there warn't no sign of the lady."

"That is in the past. Look at this." Lady Carlisle picked up the book lying in her lap. Watson took it and passed it to the marquess. All attention turned to the gout-ridden man as he opened the flyleaf and turned gray.

"George? Are you trying to tell me George wrote this?" He looked at the Roman numerals across the bottom of the page and counted them mentally to be certain he read them correctly. "This has just come out. Are you saying George is still alive?"

Lady Carlisle looked impatient. "Of course not. Read the dedication. Watson has already talked to the publisher. It seems the man who brought in this manuscript is a relative of the same man who hired the barrister who saw Edward's thief free. I do not like coincidences, Harry. I want those men questioned. They know where my granddaughter is, I am sure of it."

The marquess looked up in astonishment as his massive son suddenly loomed over him to remove the book from his hands. Edward never stirred himself for anybody, but he was scanning the book rapidly now.

"Plague take it," he muttered as he read the dedication once more. "Devilish little witch, wait until I get my hands on her."

Thomas stirred uneasily from his post. "What is it? A forgery?"

Edward shoved the book into his hands. "If you know how to read, see for yourself. I must be getting as dull-witted as you. You might as well marry your whore. She's carrying the only heir you'll ever know. The woman who wrote this isn't going to fall for your schemes."

Edward moved his heavy frame toward the door and waved impatiently at the runner. "Come along, then, let's find this plaguey Jew you ranted on about."

Lady Carlisle watched Watson and the earl leave; with a look of smug satisfaction she turned to Harry as soon as Thomas hurried out after them. "Well, my lord, what do you think of your granddaughter now?"

Mountjoy ran his hand up beneath his wig and regarded the book that had been returned to his lap as if it were a particularly obnoxious specimen of vermin. "A damned Methodist, is what I think. Matyred for his cause, my foot and eye! George was shot because he talked too much, I wager. Wanted to shoot him often enough myself."

Lady Carlisle replied gently, "But his daughter loved him. Surely you must see that. She loved him and she still grieves for him. And if she is clever enough to see that book published and escape all the men you have placed on her trail, she just might be right about George's death. Perhaps, just perhaps, it was not accidental. And if the woman who calls herself Faith is not really our granddaughter, who do you think was the one foisting her off on us?"

In that moment Mountjoy felt old. He stared at the spacious salon that had known the company of the wealthy and the noble of several nations. He had led a proud life, increased his fortunes, made his name a commonplace at the tables of the powerful. He couldn't do that without making a few mistakes along the way. The thought of his two incredibly unalike sons made him sober. He wasn't even certain they were both his sons. He rather figured Edward, as the elder, would be. His wife had been young and innocent when Edward was born. But George . . . Well, George resembled several ascetic politicians that his wife had favored in later years. There was every chance that he hadn't been of Montague blood. Perhaps that was why he had driven the boy off.

But George had borne the Montague name, as did his daughter. And perhaps—if Edward were any example—it was better that the bloodline had been diverted. A son who could write a book and a granddaughter who could outwit men were not to be overlooked easily. He muttered and looked at the book in his lap again.

"You win, Lettice, although how in hell I'll protect the girl, I cannot fathom."

Lady Carlisle smiled knowingly. "I rather think if you find a man who currently goes by the name of Morgan de Lacy, you'll have the solution to that particular problem."

The name meant nothing to him, but the marquess filed it away for future reference. The challenge of finding a granddaughter who had hidden from him for a year and a half while producing a book gave life new meaning. Mayhap she was worth the fortune he had threatened to bestow upon her.

"But with the Assembly still in session, the inn is full to overflowing! I cannot let you do all the work. I am quite well, really I am. You will make me feel as if I'm not needed if you don't let me do more."

Bess Needham snorted inelegantly. "We are full to overflowing because you made this a respectable house with meals they come for miles around to enjoy. You have made neat columns of these bundles of receipts and invoices that look like so much gibberish to me. We have made a profit because you pay attention to the prices the merchants would make me pay. And you think you're not needed? You just take care of that precious little boy there and I'll tell you when you're not needed."

Faith wiped the bottom of the "precious little boy" and wrapped him in dry cloths. He wiggled his tiny feet impatiently at her, and she had to smile. With that head full of black hair, he could resemble no one but Morgan, and his restless energy only proved the fact. She had been told infants slept all the time, but George Morgan O'Neill had let her know in no fine terms that he wasn't about to be kept in a cradle all day. Big bright eyes stared back at her expectantly as she lifted him to her shoulder.

"Well, I can at least come down and see that the maids are keeping the silverware clean and the tables polished. Do give me a chance to show off my son a little, Bess."

Bess smiled and nodded knowingly. "He's a fine one. His papa would be mighty proud of him. A handsome man he must have been, just to look at all that wavy hair. You bring him down to say hello, then get yourself back up here. You gave us a terrible scare and I'm not ready to repeat it again anytime soon."

The hours of birthing were hazy in Faith's mind, but she was aware that there had been some concern for her life. They shouldn't have worried, though. She would never have left Morgan's child alone to face the world. Still, it had given her reason to wonder if she shouldn't let Miles know about the child. Should anything, God forbid, happen to her, she wouldn't want little George to be left with nothing or no one. Morgan would have to know about him, then.

As she came downstairs, cuddling the babe in her arms, a cheer went up in the taproom just off the hall. She raised her eyebrows in question, then, spying Toby and friends at a table just inside the door watching her, she smiled shyly.

"You're embarrassing me," she admonished as she came forward to greet them. "It's not as if I've returned from the dead."

"Give 'im over, lass. Let's see what Black Jack has produced." When Faith seemed reluctant to hand over her bundle, Toby grinned. "I'm used to handling the little baggages now, since I'm an uncle. I won't break 'im, I promise."

Acton ambled over to join the idlers admiring the babe, and when the young attorney arrived, he too added his compliments. The son of one of the burgesses, who had taken to dropping by frequently, proposed a toast, and soon there was a crowd of young men drinking to the newborn and to the young widow, who blushed and smiled and didn't know where to turn under their attentions.

She was almost grateful when little George made his complaints known. As the men laughingly cheered the lustiness of his cries, she bundled him back into her arms and curtsied prettily, leaving them with smiles as she hastened from the room. She felt her ears burning as she started for the kitchens outside. If she had learned nothing else, she had learned the colonies were full of young men looking for a wife. Were she vain, their attentions would turn her head. As it was, she was more embarrassed than not by her popularity with the opposite sex.

The May sun felt delightful on her cheeks as she stepped into the garden behind the inn. Faith halted and turned her face up to the sky and soaked in the healing rays. There had never been days quite like this in England, but she remembered spring warmth and scents and the blood coursing through her veins as Morgan took her in his arms, and her heart pounded a little faster with the memory. Surely the memory could not be wrong. She had felt so right in his arms, their bodies clinging together as their lips met, with the birds singing around their heads and the earth warm and fragrant beneath their feet. She would never know such days again. They were God-given days. They had to be. She would treasure them always.

Refusing to cry when she had so many reasons to be happy, Faith swung around in a circle amidst the evergreen hedges and circular beds of herbs and flowers, her skirts billowing around her, her son gurgling contentedly in her arms. Now that winter was gone, she would be happy. She knew she would.

"Hang on the reins, man! Hold her down!"

Morgan clung tightly to his stallion's bridle as he shouted at the young boy trying to manage the frantic mare. Both horses had weathered the ocean voyage in reasonably good health, but not without making their protests known. Now that they felt solid ground beneath their feet, they were ready to make their escape. He patted and soothed the restive stallion while the lad he had hired tried to calm the smaller of the two mounts.

Finding the mare had been a piece of luck. Miles had refused to give out any information about Faith's destination, but Morgan knew his little Methodist well. Discovering Toby had disappeared at the same time as Faith, he knew at once where to begin searching. There were only so many ports where they could have found shipping to the colonies. It had taken every cent Morgan had made these last months to bribe open the records of the London shipping offices. When he had found no entry resembling Faith and Toby, Morgan had started next in Portsmouth. He would have searched every port in England until he found them, but it was in Portsmouth that he had found the mare.

A bit of persuasion had found the owner, a ship's captain just in port. A night of drinking had pried loose the memory of the young couple traveling to Virginia. He had even remembered Williamsburg as their destination, because he had recommended several inns there to the red-haired young man. Morgan had signed on the first ship for Virginia the next morning.

Now here he was, but he had no time to admire this new country he found himself in. He had grown up in Ireland, spent his army years on the Continent, and wasted these last years in England. New countries held no power to enthrall. His only interest lay in locating Faith. His fixation with the past had destroyed any chance of a future, but he wanted to be certain Faith was well and happy before he made his own plans. He didn't dare think beyond that.

Keeping the animals in line served to keep Morgan's hands and mind busy as his trunk was loaded into a cart and they began their journey inland to Williamsburg. The voyage had given him over two months in which to quietly go mad. He had envisioned everything from Faith being forced into the streets to make her living, to seeing her married to some rabid preacher who would make life hell for her. He had tried to keep himself occupied with the horses, but there was only so much he could do for them. He had watched the ship's crew, haunted the captain, learned as much as he could of navigation and sailing, but he couldn't stay on deck twenty-four hours a day. Somewhere in every night he had to stop to sleep, and that was when Faith came to him.

After a while he had begun to accept her presence. There had been several attractive women on board, bound to the colonies to try their luck where they had heard there was an overabundance of men to be had. They had practiced their wiles on him, but Morgan had found himself singularly uninterested in their charms. He found himself preferring his lonely bed, where Faith came to him in his dreams.

It was a fair way to madness, but then, Morgan was quite

certain he suffered from some lunacy to be here in the first place. All the coins he had saved these last years had disappeared with Newgate and the life he had been leading. The sale of the cottage had brought him a respectable sum, but part of that had been used on buying the mare and paying for his passage. He was the next best thing to a pauper, and he had no reason to believe he was any closer to Faith than before.

But after abandoning his goals of revenge, Morgan had no other purpose in mind. The vague ideas of owning land, raising horses, and having a family were too impossible to conceive without the one woman he needed to make them come true. And she was so far beyond his reach that he had occasion to wonder at his temerity in seeking her out. Still, here he was, searching for an elusive will-o'-the-wisp who had every right to despise him. It made about as much sense as anything else he had ever done.

When Morgan arrived in Williamsburg to find every inn and tavern stacked to the rafters, he accepted it as one more punishment that he deserved. Finding a liveryman who appreciated fine horseflesh and agreed to set some of the nags into a paddock in order to stable Morgan's thoroughbreds, he left his trunks and horses and set out on foot to explore the town Faith had taken for her own. He hoped.

The main thoroughfare of the town almost put an end to his hopes. The street was wider than any Morgan had ever seen, and it was packed from end to end with expensive coaches-and-four, and even coaches-and-six. Elegantly coiffed ladies in luxurious silks and powdered hair to rival any woman in London rode behind liveried servants in scarlet and gold or buff and navy or any of a number of other uniforms representing dozens of wealthy houses. Gentlemen clad in sober black mingled on the green with wealthy planters garbed in the finest silks and laces. Such a profusion of wealth all in one place instantly brought to mind his days of riding the high toby, and Morgan mentally counted the proceeds should he take to the road again.

A man obviously wouldn't starve in this place. The streets seemed remarkably clean of the ragged urchins and maimed beggars that congregated in every major city he had ever known. It was impossible to imagine a place where everyone had enough to eat, and Morgan knew if he looked hard enough, there had to be the poor and hungry here, but he was beginning to think it would only be the lame and the mad who went without in these streets of gold.

The May sun sent him searching for shade, and he found it in a pleasant tavern fronting on Duke of Gloucester Street. He ordered rum and listened to the frock-coated gentlemen around him expound vociferously on the day's happenings in the Assembly. It seemed every man in here had an interest in the government, not just an idle, blasé interest, but an adamant, aggressive opinion on every topic to come before the Assembly. Morgan found that intriguing, but it brought him no closer to finding Faith.

But the polished pewter and neatly swept floors of the tavern gave him another idea. How many inns and taverns could there be in a colonial town? He had to find a place to stay. That gave him excuse enough to stop and question at every one. Knowing the way his little Methodist's mind worked, she would have hunted for work in the places she knew best.

Someone, somewhere, would be able to tell him of a delicate female with a lady's ways applying for position of tavern maid.

30

"I CAN'T. I simply can't. There isn't time. . . . ''

The young gallant in satin waistcoat with lace at throat and wrist made a dramatic gesture in the air to dispel these protests, then bowed deeply and held out his arm. "We will make time, Mistress O'Neill. The day is made for the out-of-doors, and I have a brand-new carriage I wish to display in style. How better than with the most beautiful woman in all of Williamsburg by my side?"

Faith's lips quirked with amusement. Randolph Blair had become a regular at Needham Inn since his father had taken a seat in the House. He was only a few years older than she but he had led a sheltered, pampered life that had left him gay and carefree, and not exceedingly wise or mature. Still, he had a lively sense of humor, a quick wit, and he treated her as if she were a princess to be admired from afar. Such treatment was exceedingly hard to resist, and she gave up her attempt now.

"I'm scarcely attired for elegance, Mr. Blair. You will have to give me a few moments to don something a little more appropriate for showing off a new carriage."

Randolph grinned, a sloping grin that spread across his narrow face and illuminated his blue eyes. "I will take one mug of your fine ale while I wait. Then the day is mine."

Faith shook her neatly capped curls. "Not quite, sir. You forget my demanding son. One hour I give, no more."

"Two, and you will be forgiven."

"We'll see." Faith escaped before he could persuade her into more with his beguiling ways. Never in his spoiled life had Randolph Blair been denied anything, and he had learned too well all the ways to turn women to his thinking. She wouldn't fall into that trap, but he did make it difficult to say no, particularly on a lovely spring day such as this one.

She came down a while later wearing the yellow silk that Morgan had given her the previous summer. The style still served here in the colonies, and she was extremely proud of being able to sport such an elegant confection. A stiff petticoat and white satin underskirt with rows of lace billowed the gown into a stylish bell, and the matching lace at the elbow-length sleeves and in the curve of the bodice declared her a lady of leisure. She had thought the gown slightly ridiculous until she had noted those of the ladies in the shops and streets. As Randolph's eyes widened in appreciation, Faith knew she had successfully made the transition from servant to lady. The thought made her smile to herself as she took the young man's arm.

"I trust I won't clash with your new carriage," she said wryly as he guided her toward the street.

"I would run the thing into the river should that be so," he declared brashly as he handed her into the waiting curricle.

Faith looked at the new vehicle with surprise, gazing upward to the sky, where there should be a roof, and to the sides, where she could easily see the dusty street below instead of a proper window. The whole thing looked extremely rackety to her, and she turned to her companion as he proudly took up the reins. Only then did she realize that there was no driver, and that he meant to leave his groom behind.

"Whatever on earth is this thing, Mr. Blair? I fear I shall be dashed to the street at any minute."

"It's a curricle. Don't you like it? Wait until you feel it run when I let the horses have their heads. It's like flying. Hold on to your curls."

His attention was entirely on his horses and the spectacle they were making as they pulled out into the road, without the least bit of concern for Faith's fears. With one hand she grabbed the scrap of lace holding her hair in place, and with the other she grabbed the side of the curricle as Randolph sent the horses into a swift canter, barely missing a narrow coach turning down this side street.

"Mr. Blair, you will walk this carriage or I shall never ride with you again." Faith spoke loudly enough that he could hear over the sound of the wheels hitting every rut in the road.

Randolph turned her a cheery grin and slowed the horses.

"A sedate walk to please the lady for now. After we have showed the town our paces, we will try her out in the country, shall we?"

"No, sir, we shall not." Faith breathed easier as the carriage slowed and turned onto the wide thoroughfare of the Duke of Gloucester. Releasing the side of the vehicle, she primly folded her hands in her lap. Refusing to respond to the young man's cajoling smile, she gazed raptly around her, admiring the sights from this vantage point.

She was thoroughly delighted with this town she had adopted. The streets lay in well-planned parallels lined with neat cottages, imposing houses, and well-kept businesses. With the new Capitol rising splendidly on one end, the impressive college at the other end, and the Governor's Palace just off to the center, it suited her sense of orderliness. All the yards had formal gardens that grew the most marvelous fruit, along with herbs for the kitchen and flowers for beauty. She would think she had found heaven had not one important piece been missing.

Just as that thought flitted through her mind, Faith saw a massive black stallion ride out of a side street. The horse would have caught her attention at any time, but the sight of the tall, immaculately turned-out rider in black frock coat managing the great beast with the ease of a natural horseman made her breath catch. The curricle rolled by before she could turn and catch his face beneath the jauntily cocked hat, but that brief sight was enough to jar loose a flood of emotions she had long since locked away.

It couldn't be him. That would be impossible. Miles Golden would never have revealed her hiding place. It had to be someone who rode like him. There must be other experienced horsemen in this world. She had no reason to believe that the one man in the world she needed to make her happiness complete was riding down this same street behind her. The thought was almost frightening. The intensity of the emotions just the idea stirred nearly broke the calm that she had worked so hard to restore. It had taken months to wipe away the tears, piece together her heart, stow away the longings that had haunted her every passing minute. Just the glimpse of someone reminding her of Morgan couldn't destroy all she had worked so hard to accomplish. Choking back the sob lurking in her throat, Faith stiffly checked the pins in her cap and turned her attention back to the young man merrily greeting friends and neighbors.

Behind her, Morgan had no doubt of the identity of the woman riding in the expensively useless vehicle beside a young fop. Of all the things he had imagined in these last months, finding Faith in the lap of luxury had not been one of them. Miles had told him she had never drawn on the bank draft he had given her. Morgan had assumed her pride would force her to work for a living. But seeing her now in silks and laces in the company of a young macaroni who could very well have made her his mistress roused a black temper Morgan had not let loose in years.

There was the chance that she had married. The legality of the marriage might be questionable, but Miles had said she had never given him word one way or another as to nullifying that fraudulent piece of paper that bound them. Perhaps in her own unworldly way Faith had assumed the marriage was null and void. He would give her credit for that much. He would make no assumptions until he knew the truth, but it was awfully easy to assume that a man like that would make her his mistress, not his wife.

Morgan wanted to strangle the arrogant bastard in the carriage ahead, who hailed all and sundry as if to show off his newest possessions. Faith seemed to be known by most of them, and few cut her publicly. From what Morgan had seen, the colonists were an amiable lot when it came to class differences. Perhaps they even greeted lightskirts. But he thought it more likely that they knew Faith and liked her. A blade twisted in his heart as he realized Faith could very possibly have found the home here that he had never offered her.

It wasn't difficult to follow the curricle. It paraded through the center of town, drawing comments, turning heads, setting tongues to clacking wherever they passed. Morgan smiled grimly to himself as he overheard some of the comments. If she had married the young rascal, Faith had fallen into the next-best thing to the nobility that she had come from. He was certainly in no position to offer her what this wealthy young lordling had.

He didn't like the idea of giving her up, but as he watched those lovely russet curls dip and bob ahead of him, Morgan knew he couldn't take her away from the kind of luxury that young man had at his command. What had he to offer in comparison? Two horses and a meager bankbook. Had simmering anger and anguished fascination not led him on, he would have turned around and given up any fool idea of wooing her back.

But he had to know that the bastard was treating her right, so Morgan followed the carriage's progress through town, around the construction at the rebuilt Capitol, and out into the open country. There the curricle began to pick up speed, and he set his horse into a fast canter to keep up.

He watched Faith grab her hair and clutch the side of the curricle. He caught sight of her pale face as the light vehicle took a turn too quickly. And when he heard her voice rise in furious tones, Morgan kicked his stallion into a gallop, pulled his sword, and set out to stop the expensive carriage in the same manner as he had once done on the roads to London.

Faith gave a small scream as the black beast bore down on them, his furious rider brandishing a sword and hurling curses. Randolph urged his team to greater lengths, but the highwayman kept easy pace. A pistol came into view, and Faith grabbed Randolph's arm to halt him before a shot could terrify the horses into bolting. She didn't even have to look to know this was the same man she had seen earlier. The huge pistol and the imposing blackness of man and beast terrified her too much to register the features beneath the hat.

But when Randolph finally brought the weary team to a halt and the horseman caught up beside them, Faith turned her head and felt her heart lodge in her throat at the sight of the familiar harsh face and green eyes muddied with anger. "Morgan," she whispered, forgetting to hide his name, and the flare of fire in his eyes made her cover her lips with surprise.

He was more handsome than she remembered, his black hair curling out from beneath the cocked hat and caught tightly in a bow at the base of his neck. The lacy jabot tied loosely at his throat looked vaguely familiar, and with shock Faith realized it was the shirt she had sewn and left for him those many months ago. She raised her eyes to his once more, and felt the breath squeeze from her lungs.

Morgan made a polite bow and doffed his hat. "Excuse me, but I thought there might be some distress. The lady appeared somewhat frightened."

Randolph looked from Faith's pale, frozen expression to the stranger's blazing glare and back. "Is he known to you?"

What should she reply? He's my husband. She didn't know that for a fact. She had assumed Morgan would have the marriage annulled. But why, then, was he here? Uncertainly she replied, "He's an old friend, from England. If you would, please, let us turn around and go home."

Randolph's usual sunny face turned hard. "Perhaps you should introduce us, my dear." He noted with pleasure that the stranger's features grew more livid with the endearment.

"Yes, yes, of course," Faith stumbled awkwardly, not knowing what Morgan was calling himself, not knowing if she should say "O'Neill" and raise a thousand other questions.

Morgan handled the matter himself. "Morgan de Lacy, at your service. If I have disturbed your idyll, I will apologize and be on my way."

One glance at his face said he lied through his teeth, but there was nothing to be done but play along. Faith gestured toward her companion. "Randolph Blair, Mr. de Lacy. We were just going home. Would you care to join us?"

Home. They were just going home. Morgan fought against the pain twisting in his gut and straightened in his saddle. "Happy to meet you, Mr. Blair. If you wouldn't mind, I have news from England that your lady might wish to hear." He lifted a questioning eyebrow.

Grudgingly Randolph lifted the reins to turn the horses about. "If the lady commands." He turned a quizzical look to Faith.

She nodded shortly, and they were on their way. She couldn't believe Morgan was here. It was as if she had stepped from the streets into a dream, or a nightmare. Morgan. Here. How could that be? Why would he do this? Her thoughts traveled ahead to the infant awaiting her return, and fear coursed through her veins. What would Morgan say when he learned of the child? She should never have kept his son from him. She had written to Miles after George was born, but there wouldn't have been time for Morgan to have received the news if he were here now. He didn't know, and she didn't know how to tell him.

She tried not to look at the tall figure riding along beside the carriage. She tried not to think at all. If she let her mind wander to Morgan's wide shoulders, she would see them bare and broad and looming over her as she lay under him. If she watched his hands, she would remember how they had taken away the bloody blankets carrying their unborn child. If she listened to his voice, she would remember the soothing words of comfort he had offered as she wept on his shoulder, or the laughter as he taught her to ride, or the pride as he displayed the mare's new foal. She shivered beneath the heat of the midday sun and felt all her newfound composure crumbling into the dust below.

They were a silent trio as they returned to the inn. Morgan cocked his brow in surprise at their destination. He had scarcely begun his search of all the numerous inns, and he certainly had not come to this one tucked away behind some shady trees on a side road. Had there not been a sign out front, he would have assumed the brick facade to be part of a particularly pleasant house belonging to the young couple. The fact that it was an inn enhanced his suspicions.

He handed his horse to a boy who came running eagerly up, and stepped to the side of the curricle before the young man could climb down and come around. Faith reluctantly took his hand, and for the first time in nearly a year, Morgan felt the touch of her warm fingers again. His hands closed around them, holding her captive as she climbed down and came to stand by his side.

"I could call another time if I am intruding," he murmured for her ears alone. He liked the idea of having her so close again, the fresh fragrance of her hair in the hot sun stimulating his senses and her delicate beauty tempting his gaze. He had no desire whatsoever to leave her here, but he could see she was flustered and embarrassed, and he had no wish to torment her. If she had become this man's mistress, she wouldn't wish him to know. Now that he knew where she could be found, he could afford to be generous.

Faith nearly cried with relief at this gentle reprieve. "If you wouldn't mind . . . I don't know what to say. I didn't expect . . ."

He put an end to her halting phrases by bowing over her hand and bringing it to his lips for a gentle kiss. "Give me a time. I'm at your command."

Randolph watched the elegant stranger with suspicion as he bowed over Faith's hand and the two whispered together, but when the man turned aside and took up his horse's reins, there was nothing he could do or say. Their outing had not come to the end he had planned, and he resented the way Faith watched the stranger ride off. He did not smile as she turned to take his arm and go inside.

Faith scarcely noticed her companion's surly attitude. Her thoughts were spinning and she could force them to no pattern or direction. As they entered, Bess ran up with a problem that needed to be solved immediately, and a wail from above warned it was nearly time for George's feeding. With a faint smile she made as gracious a farewell as she could manage, leaving Randolph to drown his sorrows in another cup of ale.

Upstairs, Faith unfastened her bodice and brought her son to her breast. As she stared down at the head of curly black hair, she knew she could not keep news of his son from Morgan. He had to know. But the complications that arose from the knowledge were deep and disturbing.

She could not live as she had before she came here. She had been dependent on Morgan then and had accepted his choice of pursuits because she had no alternative. But God had seen fit to give her independence and an opportunity to make an honest life, and she could not give them up simply because she loved Morgan more than common sense should allow.

Even if Morgan had become an honest man, she wasn't certain that it would make a difference. She didn't wish to return to England. She liked it here. She felt safe here. There weren't any Wesleyans that she knew of, although George Whitefield had visited here a few years ago, but the need for Methodism wasn't as prevalent here as in England. She could be quite satisfied with the Church of England services and give to the poor on her own. Overall, she was happier here than she had been anywhere, with one exception.

Faith sighed and leaned back against the chair and tried to let her love flow into the child at her breast instead of churning restlessly with thoughts of Morgan. Morgan had made her happy, undoubtedly, but at the same time, he had made her miserable. She would be wiser to give up all thought of him, if such a thing were possible. She couldn't be his mistress anymore, and she wouldn't be the wife of a thief. There was an end to it.

Why, then, did her thoughts keep floating ahead to their next meeting?

31

"STOP WORRYING, LETTICE. What do you think can possibly happen to the chit now that we know where she is?"

"Think we know," Lady Carlisle responded nervously, fingering the pearls at her throat. "The letters Watson found could have been forgeries. We could be chasing halfway around the world for naught."

"You mean Edward can. Damned good way to get him out from under foot, if you ask me," the marquess responded dryly, easing his aching foot to a more comfortable position. "He'll find her, if only to wring that highwayman's neck. I must say, his temper surprised me when he heard that bit of news. How does it feel to talk to a highwayman, Lettice?"

"He seemed a perfectly amiable gentleman to me, although a trifle intense, I suppose. Do you really think he followed dear Faith, or is it just some ruse to draw us out?"

The marquess sighed, then grimaced after swallowing the medicinal waters the quack had condemned him to. "How the hell would I know? What I wonder at is young Thomas rampaging off after being newly wed. It's not as if I threatened to throw him out for his deceit. I even offered to give him a place in the country where his bride could have the babe without gossips counting on their fingers. And still the ungrateful pup goes haring off without a by-your-leave. P'raps I should have kept Edward here awhile longer to look for his cousin."

The fingers working at the pearls moved even more restlessly. "I never liked young Thomas, I confess, Harry. He's handsome enough, and well-spoken, I suppose, but he has a nasty habit of sneering when he thinks one isn't looking. 'Tis a pity his father died at such an early age. You've not given him the attention he needed, I fear."

"I've not done a lot of things I should have, Lettice. I

must be growing old to admit such a thing to you. But I'm trying to make up for it now. After Edward, Thomas is the next heir to the title. It's time I took him in hand, I suppose. If only I knew where to find him.''

Lady Carlisle shifted from the window to watch the sun play about the marquess's still-handsome eyes. The years of dissipation had left their mark, but his eyes were clear now, and worried. As well they should be.

"I'm sorry to tell you this, Harry, but Watson says Thomas took ship with Edward. I do think you had better give serious consideration to the contents of your will.''

Speaking cultured French to the French wife of the owner of White's Tavern, Morgan managed to sweet-talk his way into a room. He discovered an added benefit when he was introduced to the general populace as a nobleman in disguise by the voluble and rather creative Frenchwoman. Morgan unexpectedly found himself sharing his evening meal with a table of planters and representatives to the Assembly, speaking to them authoritatively on the status of various navigation acts in Parliament.

From listening in on conversations of the society he had been keeping and talking to the ship's captain on the voyage, Morgan knew more than enough to hold his own and managed to convey the difficulty these colonists must face in turning Parliament to their way of thinking. They were overjoyed to have someone who would listen to their complaints, and the night grew long in their company.

The company and the conversation helped to ease the pain, but not enough to keep Morgan from seeking Needham Inn long after the others had gone to their beds. Faith had refused to see him until the next day, but just knowing she was close by eased the pain somewhat. Morgan took a table by the fire and gazed around at the homely tavern to learn more of this place she apparently called home.

One of the council members Morgan had just met wandered over to share a tankard. The man introduced the bartender, who was more than willing to credit the excellence of their meals to the new manager. The talk of food lured the young lawyer who kept his rooms at the inn, and soon Morgan found himself listening to some of the town's most eligible men singing Faith's praises. The praises of those accomplishments he knew she possessed—but had not prized enough to keep—struck like arrows in his heart, but Morgan took his punishment with silent grace.

It was only when he questioned the absence of this paragon of virtue that Morgan was slapped with the final blow. Dazedly he listened to these strangers speak of his son and of his wife's talents as a mother, and felt his insides crack and crumble until there was little left of him to stand up when he could take no more.

Morgan staggered as if drunk, though he could hold more than thrice the amount he had taken this night. Someone offered to accompany him back to White's, and he found himself responding negatively in French. It had been a long time since he had spoken this language he had learned at a priest's knee in the hedgerows and polished in the armies on the Continent. He didn't know why he employed it now. He only knew his foundations had been kicked out from under him, and he was struggling for solid ground.

He didn't want to go back to White's. He wanted to see his son. His son. His and Faith's. Damnation, but what a fool he'd been. One selfish roll in the hay and he had made it impossible for her to do anything else or be anyone else but his wife. She had half the bachelors in town panting at her feet, but she could take none of the advantages they offered because he had selfishly made annulment of their farcical marriage impossible if she wished to give their son a name.

It never even occurred to Morgan to doubt that the child was his. He had heard enough to realize the child had come early, and even then, with great difficulty. His Faith would never have betrayed him while he was in Newgate, and he knew from the signs she had left throughout the cottage that she had not betrayed him afterward. Her parents had chosen her name well. He could place all his faith in her. 'Twas a pity she could not do the same in him.

Morgan wandered like a lost soul around the outside of the inn, scanning windows, trying to determine which one might be Faith's. There was light in one of the upper rooms, and he watched it without much hope, just for a reason to linger. He needed to talk with her. Just to hear her voice again might soothe some of the raw places in his soul. If only he could just see her . . . His hand gripped the rough bark of a tree so tightly the pain brought tears to his eyes, or he blamed it on the pain.

The shadow that appeared against the curtained light above was small and slender, and when the feminine silhouette lifted a tiny bundle, Morgan felt his insides constrict with the first glimmer of hope. It had to be her. No one or nothing else could fit the scene that was unfolding. He could almost imagine the faint cries of an infant coming through the window. Faith would keep the panes closed to prevent night drafts even on this warmest of nights when others left theirs open. It had to be Faith.

Fate had held out a helping hand, and Morgan wasn't one to refuse an opportunity. Counting windows, he placed the room's location firmly in his mind. Then he stalked back to the darkness of the kitchen yard, pried open the latch on the back door, and slipped noiselessly up the back stairs. There was no reason to allow all of Williamsburg to know that Faith had midnight callers. He could offer her that much protection.

He didn't know what he was going to do when he got to her room, but the task of finding it was sufficient to keep his mind occupied for the nonce. Reaching the attic floor, he counted doors. The one with the light coming out from beneath it corresponded exactly with the window count. He had found her.

Knocking was out of the question. Holding his breath, Morgan turned the latch and let himself in.

He came to a halt in the doorway, the scene before him robbing him of the ability to move forward. Russet curls tumbling in abandonment down a fragile gown of lawn and lace, Faith sat propped among her pillows, holding a tiny black head to her breast. She glanced up in surprise as the door opened, but at sight of the intruder, she merely smiled softly and turned her attention back to the infant, as if giving him permission to admire what they had wrought together.

Morgan entered and shut the door. His pulse raced as it once had when he rode the highways, but for an entirely different reason now. The tableau of mother and child was foreign to him, and he felt an outsider looking in. The challenge lay in making himself welcome where he was neither wanted nor needed, for he could not imagine being anywhere else but here ever again.

This was home. Perhaps he had had more ale than he thought, but the feeling wouldn't dissipate. His home in

Ireland had been torn apart by misery and hate. He'd never known anything akin to home since then, other than the brief months with Faith. He had never known he'd wanted a home or had any need for one, but the ache opened within him now. He wanted a home, and he wanted his son and wife to live in it.

It was a foolish fancy and one that would pass with time, but Morgan gave in to it for a while. He lowered himself to the edge of the narrow bed and watched helplessly as his son fed hungrily at the breast that he had loved and caressed just the summer before. He had lived alone for the better part of his life. He had never needed anyone. But the desire to need and be needed grew up in him as he watched what he could so easily have been denied.

"He is greedy," Morgan whispered, more to be certain this was real than from the need to be heard.

Faith looked up with a smile. "He is much like his father," she agreed.

Morgan heard the admonishment and grinned, suddenly feeling the weight lifting off his chest. This was Faith. He could say anything to her. "I suppose he is an arrogant bastard, then. You will teach him better manners."

"Not a bastard," she said softly, averting her eyes to the small black head. Morgan's proximity was unsettling. She could feel the heat of his gaze as he stared at her bared breast, but she made no move to cover herself. He had seen all of her there was to see, and she was rather proud of her accomplishment. There had been some fear that she was too small to feed her own child, but she had proved them wrong.

As the babe sighed and squirmed and drifted off to sleep, Morgan reached to caress a silken black curl at his nape. "Would you let me hold him?"

Faith was uncertain as to his reasons for being here, and she ought to thoroughly distrust his intentions, but she had spent a year of her life learning to love and trust this man, and she had no reservations now. Wrapping the blankets firmly around the child, supporting his head gently so as not to disturb his slumber, Faith lifted him into Morgan's large palms.

Picking up one of the cloths on the bedside table, she folded it and put it over Morgan's shoulder as he stared in wonderment at his firstborn. "Put him over your shoulder and rub his back gently. He gets bubbles in his stomach from eating so quickly.''

The sight of the large man lifting his tiny son to his shoulder was totally incongruous, but he did it with the gentleness that Faith knew Morgan possessed. She had feared him at first, with his large size and frightening pistols and rough ways, but she had learned to see beyond the outer man, to the man who loved life and craved the innocent. It was to this inner man that she offered her life and love. 'Twas a pity that the outer man could not be dispensed with.

"He's so damned tiny, I fear I'm going to break him." Morgan awkwardly adjusted the frail bundle to his shoulder and gingerly attempted rubbing the small back with two large fingers. The infant hiccuped and settled down as if he belonged there. The warm, moist scent of milk drifted up from him, and Morgan felt the tears pool in his eyes.

"Oh, he's quite strong. He can even lift his head a little, and Bess says he is long for his age. He'll be as big as you one of these days." Without the protection of the babe, Faith felt suddenly shy, and she fumbled at the fastenings of her gown to cover herself again.

Morgan didn't dare loose his hold on the infant to catch her hands to stop her as he would like. He only watched hungrily as she covered the purity of her skin to hide herself from him. He had no right to demand more. He should be content that she allowed him the company of his child. He didn't deserve that much after what he had done.

"What have you named him?" Morgan felt the babe give a soft belch, and he looked down in surprise as small fingers curled in his coat and a sleepy head turned to breathe milky perfume on his neck.

Faith laughed softly at his reaction, then nervously laced her fingers as she replied, "George Morgan O'Neill. I did not know what to do about the 'de Lacy.' The marriage papers . . .''

Morgan looked up sharply. "I'll have Miles correct the marriage papers. O'Neill is my mother's name, and it is a fine one, but I would have him bear the de Lacy name too.''

Faith nodded uncertainly. Now that the first surprise was over, she feared to question further. Were the marriage papers legitimate? Had he had them annulled? Was she still married? Little had she known how confusing this would be that day she had said her vows in a cell in Newgate.

Carefully she asked, "Why are you here?"

The time had come to talk, but Morgan was strangely reluctant to do so. He lifted his son from his shoulder and cradled him in the crook of his arm so he could admire the tiny, perfectly formed fingers and toes. "Because I had nowhere else to go. Will you find it difficult to accept my presence in the same town?"

Faith looked startled but shook her head. "Had I thought you would come with me, I would have asked you. I thought you meant to stay in London."

"Perhaps I will again another day. I had need to see how you fared, and that cursed Miles wouldn't tell me a thing. I will have his head for not telling me of the child."

"He didn't know of him until recently." Growing nervous, Faith took the sleeping infant from Morgan's hands and rose to place him in the cradle. "It would be better if we discussed this another time. It is late, and Bess will wonder if my light is still on when she goes by."

She wore only a thin nightshift, and Morgan could trace the silhouette of her slender body in the lamplight. Childbirth had enhanced rather than detracted from her figure. She possessed womanly curves that made him ache from just looking. Just a touch of that softness . . .

He rose abruptly and strode to the door, hat in hand. "We'll need to talk. Surely you must see that. When may I see you again?"

Faith clasped her hands in front of her and met his gaze with trepidation. He practically filled her tiny room. Indeed, his head was bent to keep from bumping the rafters. This was no place for a man like Morgan. He needed open spaces and room to expand his enormous energies in. He would tire of this place quickly. She felt sadness creep around her heart as she answered him. "It is difficult to say. I stay very busy. Could I send you word?"

Morgan nodded curtly. "I stay at White's. I am using my own name now, but I'll not mention the 'O'Neill.' I will not harm you if I can prevent it."

Faith breathed a little easier. She knew he would not intentionally harm her, but Morgan had a temper and a strong will. If he had chosen to make himself known, he could have wreaked havoc with her simple life. She was grateful that he had chosen to be reasonable. "I know you would not harm me, Morgan, but it has been a long time, and I'm still . . .'' She hesitated over an appropriate word.

"You needn't spell it out, little one. I play the part of bastard well, and you're well rid of me, but there is the small matter of the child. We will have to work something out.''

"Yes, of course.'' Dully she watched as Morgan nodded farewell and walked out. He had come for the child, then, and not for herself. She should be relieved, but tears flowed freely down her face as she heard him walk away. He had not even asked to stay, or made any motion to touch her. Whatever had been between them had died. She should have known that all along, but in some small part of her heart she had clung to her fantasies.

She would be a long time recovering from the blow.

She heard the praises of the "Frenchman" the first thing next day as the young lawyer dug hungrily into his breakfast. It took a moment before Faith realized he spoke of Morgan. As Acton carried in a load of flour, he overheard their conversation and added his curiosity to the reason for the noble stranger's presence in Williamsburg. Faith stared at him in disbelief and turned away as they began to speculate on the man's background.

Morgan could turn the heads of every woman and sharpen the wits of every man in town did he but put his mind to it. Even as a stranger, his was a dangerous presence. There was something mysterious and aloof about him that caught people's interest, and he only served to stimulate it more when he spoke. Morgan had a silver tongue. She had forgotten that. Damn his unreasonable pride, he could be anything he wanted to be. Why did he choose to be a thief?

It was not her problem. Or perhaps it was. She wouldn't have little George learn his father had been hanged for thievery. If Morgan intended to claim his son, he would have to change his ways. That was all there was to it. She didn't know how she would force him to it, but she would. For her own sake, she had never tried, but for her son she would run Morgan out of town on a rail. Just see if she didn't.

With that determination made, Faith went about her tasks with a new fervor. She would send for Morgan and tell him in no uncertain terms that he had to turn to honest trade if he were to stay here. That should send him scurrying back where he belonged. That would be the best thing for everyone concerned. He couldn't linger here without ruining her reputation. And since he had no interest in her any longer, he could do nothing but cause harm by dangling after George. Perhaps it was cruel to ask him to give up his son, but he had been cruel in sending her away. She had paid the price; now he must pay his.

She didn't know where these ugly thoughts had come from. They were entirely new to her, but Faith clung to them throughout the morning. Morgan would have to leave town. That was all there was to it. He had destroyed her life once; she wouldn't allow him to do it again.

After the noon meal was served and George was fed and sleeping quietly, Faith sent word to White's that she would be available for a few hours. She didn't expect Morgan to reply immediately. She had already been told that he had been invited to speak in the House on certain matters currently before Parliament and that he had breakfasted with the Speaker. Morgan was a rogue through and through, portraying himself as a gentleman to these trusting people. But at one time he had been a gentleman, if his words could be believed. And perhaps the London society he had been keeping these last months had given him some insight into the laws governing these colonies. She ought to give him benefit of the doubt, but at the moment she was feeling ill-disposed toward such leniency.

When Morgan appeared within the half-hour, he caught Faith by surprise. She was working diligently over the prior day's receipts in her office, and the shadow of his presence made her look up. He was dressed to the inch in a gentleman's fashion this day. Holding his braid-trimmed cocked hat beneath his arm, he wore his black locks unpowdered, but the jade green of his frock coat and the striped silk of his embroidered waistcoat decimated all hint of the highwayman. Without being told, she knew he had done this for her. Yesterday, for himself, he had worn black as usual.

Faith stood and nervously looked down at her plain brown gown and simple nerkerchief. "I hope you did not wish to go somewhere fashionable. I thought you only wished a word with me."

"I do, and you know you would be lovely in my eyes were you wearing nothing." Morgan grinned and held out his arm. "But I would prefer a little privacy. This place seems overfull of your admirers. Should we come to, say, a little disagreement, I fear I would find a knife at my neck and a gun at my back."

Remembering one or two of their "disagreements," Faith had to agree with Morgan's assessment of the situation. And they were almost certainly going to come to a disagreement when she gave him his ultimatum. She nodded and took his arm. She would have this over once and for all. She did not fear Morgan's temper, but he had reason to fear hers.

Morgan gave the russet head at his shoulder a quick look at this compliance. He felt a stirring of unease but crushed it. Faith was reasonable. She could not object to his seeing his own son. He merely wished an outing to see how far he had fallen into disfavor. And he hoped to raise himself slightly in her eyes by the surprise he had waiting for her.

Faith gasped in recognition as she stepped outside the inn to find not only Morgan's stallion but also the little Arabian mare she had sold to buy her passage. "Dolly!" she cried, running to pet the mare's nose and stroke the lovely proud neck. She turned inquiring eyes to Morgan as he came up behind her.

"Dolly? That is a ridiculous name for an animal with such illustrious ancestry. You could at least call her Elizabeth or Anne."

Faith made a face at his mockery. "How did you find her? And why did you bring her here? I thought you wished to sell all your horses. That's what you told Toby."

Morgan had difficulty in keeping his hands to himself as he searched Faith's suddenly serious expression. It would be so much easier to talk to her if she were resting in his arms, exchanging kisses between words. He had a sudden premonition of the trap awaiting him, and he wanted to be able to rely on the most successful method of wooing her to his side. But he was determined to do this properly, with reasonableness and logic instead of force and bribery, or seduction.

"That's another topic open for discussion. When I find that redheaded scoundrel, I shall thrash him within an inch of his life, but I prefer more pleasant topics for today's outing. Let us at least leave town peaceably."

Faith caught her breath as Morgan grasped her by the waist and threw her into the saddle. She had forgotten how firm and strong his hold could be. As she adjusted her leg around the sidesaddle, she covertly watched Morgan mount the stallion. She really ought to be more afraid of him. Perhaps he was more lean than large, but she knew all too well the muscles rippling beneath the dandy's coat and lace. When he easily brought the restive stallion under control, she caught her breath at the grace of his movements. She was out of her mind to think she would ever get the better of him.

And she had agreed to a few hours alone with this man? She would be lucky to walk away unscathed. She ought to call a halt to this prime fallacy right now, while she still could.

Instead, Faith patted the head of the lovely mare, gazed longingly after Morgan's broad shoulders, and set her mount into a trot after him.

32

THE AFTERNOON HEAT rose around them as they paced the horses sedately down a country lane occasionally shaded with old elms and oaks. Faith regretted wearing the heavy broadcloth gown and eased her nerkerchief open discreetly to allow more air to bathe her throat. With his incredible sense of timing, Morgan turned to catch her at it, and the light flaring in his eyes and the upward tilt of his lips sent a sharp thrill to her middle.

"Let us not go too far," she reminded him sharply. "I must be back when George awakes."

Her tone didn't wipe the lilting grin from Morgan's lips. "Whatever milady requests. You know the area better than I. Will the owner of this fine property object if we rest in the shade of yon grove?"

"I cannot see why he should, since he has obviously chosen to let the land lie fallow. We won't be disturbing anything."

That was the starchy, prim Faith he remembered from long ago. She had donned her armor for battle. Morgan gave her a shrewd look and led the horses off the road to the shady protection of the trees. A brook babbled across round pebbles and beneath the wands of a willow tree, and thick tufts of grass provided an excellent seat to escape the sun. Morgan climbed down and removed the blanket he had brought along for just such an occasion. Then he turned to assist Faith in dismounting.

Faith eyed the blanket with distrust as he spread it across the glade. She had reason to remember a blanket in another time and place, beneath the stars on a spring night. She refused to be seduced as easily as that child.

She walked to the brook's edge and bent to pick up a stone or two to skip across the water. "You wished to talk?"

Morgan came up behind her and caught her by the shoulders. "I do. Just talk, Faith. Come sit down beside me."

"I am fine here." She shrugged off his encroaching hands. "Where would you like to begin?"

"By seeing your eyes. Faith, look at me. I do not mean you harm, I promise. Do you have any idea how difficult it is for me to be this close without touching? At least give me the pleasure of your face."

Faith turned questioningly to find Morgan with his fists now clenched at his side, his dark brows pulled together in an expression of pain. Surprised, she took a step backward to face him. "I did not think you wished to see me again. I am trying to make this easy for you."

Morgan took a deep breath and pointed to the blanket. "Sit. It will be much easier if one of us is sitting still."

Faith had to smile at that. His restless pacing was much a part of her memory of him. Spreading her coarse skirts, she took a place in the center of the blanket and waited expectantly. Morgan nodded a curt approval and found a tree trunk to lean against. He had thrown his hat to the blanket, but the dappled shade served to conceal much of his features as he stared down at her, arms crossed over his chest.

"I sent you away for your own safety, Faith. And for your own good. I will be the first to admit that you are better off without me. I need only to look at how well you fare now to justify what I did. Were it not for me, you could have your choice of husbands and live in the company of good people, with all the wealth and comfort that you deserve."

"I think we are past the stage of counting what we owe to each other," Faith replied softly. "There were choices I could have made all along. You always gave me that. It was I who decided we must marry, and I did so with every intention of its being permanent. I do not blame you in any way for that."

"And it was I who forced you into consummating the marriage, thus ensuring that you could not escape, particularly now that a child has come of it. That was not a fair way to thank you for saving my unworthy neck. Don't let me off so easily, Faith. I took advantage of your goodness, and now you are suffering for it. That was not what I intended. Why did you not take the bank draft Miles offered you? That was your money, from your family. It belonged to you, free and clear.''

Faith folded her hands in her lap and tried not to look at him. Miles had tried to explain that to her, but she had been unwilling to listen. She knew Morgan had somehow forced her family to pay that sum, but she had no wish to be purchased by anyone. Or to buy off anyone's guilt. She shook her head slowly. ''The money is meaningless. Perhaps it will someday ensure that your son has a proper education. I do not need it for myself.''

Morgan clenched his hands and stood away from the tree, staring down at her. ''Do you have some desire to make a martyr of yourself? Look at me, Faith, and tell me you don't wish to have pretty dresses, a home of your own, and all the little things you've never had. The income from that money would buy you all that. You wouldn't have to work for others. You could hire nursemaids for our son and go out and about a little. Why give up all that for some stupid sense of pride?''

Faith glared up at him. ''Will you quit towering over me like some vengeful bird of prey? And don't tell me about pride. I have no lock on the world's sum of pride. Who is it that has destroyed his life and nearly had himself hanged for pride? I have learned to humble myself to survive. What I will not do is turn my back on what is right anymore. Taking that money is not right. It is not mine to take. I lost our first child, Morgan, because I had turned my head away from God. I'll not ever do that again.''

Hearing the tears and anguish in her voice, Morgan dropped to his knees in front of her and caught her shoulders, forcing her to look at him. Those huge eyes he had reason to remember so well swam in tears, and the pain shot through him. The loss of that child still stayed with her, then. He had thought perhaps the new one had replaced those painful memories, but he could see he had not. That memory would always be between them. He touched the thickness of her hair gently.

''I don't think God could be so cruel as to punish you in that way. If I believed that, I would have quit believing in Him long ago. I cannot believe I or my family did anything to deserve what happened to us. People did that to us, not God. If anyone was responsible for your losing the child, it was myself for not taking better care of you. Lay the blame on my shoulders, Faith, not yours or God's. You are all that is good and right. I am the one who has taken the road to damnation. I made that choice long ago. I would not have you tainted by it."

Faith found the handkerchief and wiped her eyes, trying to ignore the heat of Morgan's touch. It was quite impossible, but she forced herself to be rational. "Then do not taint your son with it either, Morgan. I came here to protect him. Let me do so."

Morgan released her shoulders and fell back on his heels. That was the blow he had been expecting. She asked that he give up his son, but he could not do it. He shook his head dazedly. "Do not ask more than I can offer, Faith. He is my son. I have some right to see him grow. He is all the family I may ever have."

She felt his pain as she would her own, but she could not let it get the better of her. She had a cause worth fighting for, whatever the cost. Clenching her own hands, she met his gaze. "Then don't destroy him, Morgan. Would you have him hear his father branded a thief? Would you have him live in the shadow of his father's corpse hanging from a gallows? By all that is good and holy, Morgan, leave us be!"

She may as well have lifted those fists to his jaw. Morgan fell back beneath the blow of her words, watching her with a kind of desperation. It wasn't just George he wanted. She was his family. She was his home. And she was sending him away from her. As he had done to her. Clasping his hand over his eyes, Morgan steadied himself, then rose and walked to the brook, keeping his back to her.

"Is there nothing I can do to change your mind? I know what I did was cruel, but at the time, I thought it necessary. I have no more to offer you now than I did then. I am a man without family, lands, or name. But I know more now than I did then. I know I cannot continue to fight a losing battle. I cannot even remember why I thought it necessary. I stand to lose too much by it. My home and my family in Ireland are gone, and I can never win them back. What has been done to my people and my lands is wrong, but I cannot right it with more wrongs. I can only hurt myself and all around me, as I have done before. You and our son are all that I know that has any meaning anymore. Don't take away all my hopes, Faith."

She wasn't certain she could believe what she was hearing. Cautiously she watched his silhouette against the background of trees and brook and dappled sunlight. Morgan could never hold himself other than proudly, but there was a hint of his torment in the stiffness of his shoulders that held his hands in balled fists at his side. She twined her fingers together in silent prayer.

"Were it myself, I would not take anything from you, Morgan. But you must see that I must protect George. Would you have him know his father to be a thief?"

Morgan drew a deep breath and turned around to face her. "No, I would not. If I turn king's evidence on the thieves in London and clear my name, would you allow me to stay?"

She saw the shadows in his eyes, the clenching of his jaw as he fought some inner battle, but with this, she could not help him. It was his decision alone to make but she allowed a small measure of hope to enter her heart. She rose from the blanket and stepped toward him, hand held out. "I do not know the laws, Morgan. I only wish to keep our son free from any taint. If you can promise me that, I will not deny you his company."

Morgan grasped Faith's hand and pulled her toward him, his need for her beyond all sense and logic. She didn't resist for long, and shortly he found her in his arms again, her slight figure clasped firmly against him. He could feel the beating of her heart, knew the softness of her breasts pressed against him, drank in the richness of her intoxicating scent. He pressed a kiss to her hair and stroked her back the way he used to do.

"I'd promise you the sun and the moon and the stars were they mine to give. But I will not offer you lies this time, my *cailin*. I will promise only what is in me to give. I promise to do nothing to harm you or our son or the name you carry. And I shall do whatever is necessary to clear my past so you need not fear it ever coming to haunt you. I have had time enough to settle the ghosts of my father and his father before him. I can give the past up in exchange for a future. Faith, if you can ever forgive me, you will give me hope for that future. Doesn't your religion have a prayer for lost souls? You're the answer to that prayer for me. Tell me what else you need to be happy, my *cailin*, and I will gladly spend a lifetime seeing that you have anything you desire."

Faith rested her cheek against the warmth of Morgan's coat and let the magic of his hands and the silver of his words take away the pain. She heard the agony behind his lilting speech, knew the price the words cost him. If he promised to do this, he would keep his promise at whatever cost—that she knew—even if it meant giving up his revenge. She feared the cost, but she allowed hope a place in her heart.

"To know you will be safe makes me happy, Morgan. What else could I ask for? Do you have any idea how many nights I have spent wondering where you were, or if you were still in this world? It's a terrible feeling. I wish that you would not ever put me through it again."

Morgan caught her chin and turned her face up to meet his gaze. The liquid gray of Faith's eyes melted his insides, and he could not resist asking a little more. Her small body was so pliant and perfect in his arms, he would be a fool not to at least try. "I read the note you left, Faith. How much of it did you mean? Can you really forgive me for what I have done? Will you give me a chance to start anew?"

She loved the way the green of his eyes turned to the gold and brown of the jungle when he looked at her like that. She loved the way his black hair curled at his temple and the base of his neck where it came loose from the ribbon. She loved the strong brown column of his throat, the way his broad hands caressed her spine, the feel of his long length pressed against her. She loved everything about this man, including his sins and crimes. Perhaps that made her a sinner too, but she could not help herself. Bravely she touched the carved curve of his jaw.

"I meant every word of it, Morgan. Did you think I would be here with you now if I did not? I am your wife, Morgan. I took those vows before God, even if it were not a man of God who asked them of me. I never wanted or intended to be anything else but your wife."

Incredulous, Morgan caught Faith's shoulders and pushed her back so they were not touching. "You do not have to say that because of those ridiculous vows we said before that charlatan. I will not stand between you and happiness. You have a future here that I could never offer you. Dammit, *cailin,* I am trying to be noble, to show how much I love you by setting you free. You have a whole court of suitors back there more suitable than I. I'll admit, I'll wish to tear whomever you choose limb from limb, but I brought the pain upon myself and I'll not have you suffer for it. Don't be a fool, lass. You owe me nothing. Take what I offer while I'm still strong enough to offer it.''

These weren't at all the soothing phrases of love Morgan used to murmur when he took her to his bed. These were swords of steel tempered by fire and honed to hurt or protect, depending on which way they turned. Faith stared at him in amazement, read the anguish and the truth in the rigid set of his features, and felt a small ripple of hope and joy begin to spread throughout her middle.

''You are a fool, Morgan de Lacy,'' she said softly. She continued a little more fiercely, ''Must I hit you over the head with your own weapons to make you see the light? You are a rogue and a scoundrel. You deserve hanging for what you have done. Would it be of any use, I'd punch you again. But you are *my* rogue and scoundrel, and I'll have none other. Do you think one of those men back there could take your place? Do not let me feed your enormous arrogance any more than is necessary. You can declare our marriage null and void. You can go elsewhere to seek a wife if that is what you wish. But upon my soul, Morgan de Lacy, do not go ordering me to do the same! I am married. I need no other husband. The one I have is trouble enough.''

A grin began to spread across Morgan's face as he regarded the ferocity in Faith's glare after this little speech. ''And it be trouble he is, that one,'' he agreed mockingly. ''You would be wise to give him up. If he loved you at all, he'd leave you be. But he can't. Selfish bastard that he is, all he can think of is the sweetness of your lips and how long it has been since he kissed them. He's no fool, I think. He'll not be looking elsewhere for what he has right here.''

Faith caught her breath at the hint of brogue and the fire in his eyes. She didn't know what she had done. She was quite certain it wasn't what she had set out to do. But when Morgan pulled her forward again, wrapping her in his arms, it felt right, and she wouldn't surrender her place for all the gold in the world.

The touch of his lips brought remembered fire, intensified by months of longing. Faith slid her hands about Morgan's neck, clinging to the strength of his shoulders as the fire licked along her mouth and tongue and began to spread with the gales of a whirlwind. She felt Morgan stiffen, begin to pull away as the realization of what was happening hit him, but it was too late by far. The fire whipped around them, lashing them together, and instead of pulling away, he lowered her to the blanket.

His hands roved as their mouths sought the place where they had left off, filling the months of absence with an urgency that neither could deny. Faith felt the fastening of her bodice give way, and she arched joyously into the bare palm of Morgan's hand as he slid it beneath the layers of cloth. His caress was gentle, learning the fullness of her new curves, and she gave a shattered cry when he finally lowered his head to kiss her breast. The knowledge that they had created a son to suckle there surged through them, bonding them more firmly than ever, and when Morgan lifted his head to look down on her, Faith nearly cried with the tenderness of that look.

Morgan's mouth returned to hers while his hand kneaded the softness of her flesh, exulting in the pleasure he had so long denied himself. When Faith's fingers feverishly worked at the ties of his shirt and the fastenings of his waistcoat, Morgan felt an explosion of joy. Never had she come to him with such eagerness. The touch of her fingers drove hot shards of desire through him, and he was beyond helping either of them from the madness that consumed them.

This wasn't what he had intended when he brought her out here, but nothing less than death could stop him now. When Faith's fingers found the buttons to his breeches, Morgan moaned against her throat, buried his kisses in her softness, and pulled her skirts up to bring her closer.

Hot breezes blew across their naked skin as clothing tumbled about them in jumbled piles. Faith cried out in welcome as Morgan's probing fingers explored her flesh, and she rose urgently against him. It had been so long . . . too long. She couldn't wait. Daringly she reached out to stroke the maleness of him, urging him on.

"By all the saints, *cailin!*" Morgan gasped. "I'm fair ready to burst with need. Touch me like that, and I'll not wait to pleasure you." He grasped her hand firmly, returning it to his chest as he gazed down into eyes slumberous with desire. Just that look made his loins leap, and he bent to kiss her swollen lips one more time.

"Please, Morgan," she begged against his mouth. The breeze caressing her thighs was not enough. She needed to know the heat of him again, the hard male strength that she had missed and needed and not known how to name for so long. She could feel him close, and shamelessly she arched upward to encourage him.

Morgan eagerly obliged. With one swift stroke he joined them, and Faith's thrust brought him home. The need was too great, too strong, and he plunged swiftly, surely, bringing her to the peaks and nearly undoing himself in the process. When he felt her cry of pleasure and pain and release, he hurriedly withdrew, spilling his seed down her side.

Faith wrapped her arms around Morgan's shuddering shoulders, her body aching with the emptiness he had left in her despite the pleasure she had experienced. "Why did you do that?" she whispered against his skin, pushing back the shirt he had not quite removed.

Morgan nuzzled her ear, drinking in the sensuous scent of her skin before pushing himself up on his hands to look down on her. "It's something I should have done long ago, had I loved you as I ought. There will be time enough for making babies later. I'd not wear you out, lass."

"I'm nursing, you need not worry about such," Faith remonstrated, although his words sent a thrill of hope through her. She ought to be thoroughly ashamed of what they had done, but she was not. Morgan rose above her like some great animal, the dark V of hair on his chest pointing in the direction of where they had joined. She was shameless, but she couldn't help tracing the line of those soft curls.

A smile flickered across Morgan's face as he realized where her interest lay, and he felt his body stirring in response. But now was neither the time nor the place to continue this dalliance, not until he had assured their future. Sliding to one side, he gently pushed at her skirts to hide temptation. "Tell me you have never seen women with a string of children not more than a year apart. Then tell me they didn't nurse their brats. I watched my mother swell with child year after year, only to lose them one after another. I think we've proved your fertility and my virility well enough for now. I want you, lass, but I mean to keep you for a long, long time. For that I'll have to learn temperance."

Faith fumbled at her bodice while Morgan drew on his breeches. His words sung a lilting tune in her heart, and she watched him surreptitiously from beneath lowered lashes. Their argument had beaten all around the subject, but he had never quite said the words she wanted to hear. She ought to be content that he had admitted he needed her and meant to settle down and stay with her. But she had so much more she wanted to share with him.

"What are we to do, then?" she asked boldly.

Morgan fastened the last button and bent to press a kiss to her reddened cheek. "Get married."

"Married?" Just like that. Married. Faith stared at him in bewilderment. "We *are* married."

"In a church. With a proper man of the cloth. In front of witnesses. I would have the whole world know you're mine beyond any shadow of a doubt."

"A church?" Staggered, Faith tried to grapple with what he was saying. "I don't believe there is a Catholic church, Morgan. I can accept the Anglican services, but can you?"

Morgan grasped her shoulders and gave her a happy kiss. "If you say you can find God in the good Church of England, then I'll take your word for it. He is not likely to accept me back in the fold so easily, no matter which church the vows are said in. I mean only to impress mortals."

"Morgan!" Faith escaped his hold and stood up to brush out her skirts. "Don't be sacrilegious. Besides, how can we marry in front of all the town as if we were never married before? I'll not have George called a bastard."

Morgan rose and caught her waist and turned her chin so she had to face him. He was grinning wildly with a happiness that seemed ready to split his skin and leap heavenward. Trivial matters were of no concern to him, but he could see he had to soothe Faith's ruffled feathers. "Dear heart, we have our marriage papers to prove he is no bastard. We can adopt him legally under my rightful name. We can hire Miles and a dozen lawyers to make everything as proper as you can desire. We can pretend I am your second husband. It matters not to me. I just want the whole damned town to know you're mine." Suddenly gripped by an unreasonable fear, he asked, "You *will* marry me?"

She knew she would, but she stood there uncertainly, watching the pattern of emotions flitting across his eyes. "Are you certain, Morgan? I could not bear it if you left me again. Or if you found another woman. If you are doing this just for George . . ."

Morgan pulled her into his arms and buried his face against her hair. "Never again, my love. I'll never let you go again. I may give you reasons for regret. I'm not a patient man, nor always a rational one, but you can always trust in my love. If that can be enough for you . . .''

Faith breathed a sigh of joy and reached up to pull his head down to meet her lips. ''I love you, Morgan. All I ask in return is that you love me too. Will you do that?''

As his dark head lowered to meet her fair one, he whispered against her lips, ''I crossed an ocean for you, lass. I'm after thinkin' this love business is a terrible crimp in a man's style. But if it's words you need to hear, there'll be no end to them. I love you, Faith, my *cailin alainn*, my wicked *bean sídhe*. I'll love you till the moon turns blue, till the sun rises in the west, till God accepts me into eternity. Say you'll love me too.''

Instead, she giggled and found another use for her highwayman's silver tongue.

In the harbor, not many miles away, a ship from England found dock.

33

"WE CAN HAVE the banns declared this Sunday. That should give your Mrs. Needham time enough to find someone to take your place."

Morgan helped Faith from her horse outside the inn. The afternoon was drawing late and he knew she worried about George, but he had to confirm their decision before either of them thought better of it. Already he was thinking he was robbing her of the future she deserved, but the idea of his Faith in another man's arms quelled that notion successfully. Just seeing the bumbling lad's foolish notion of a carriage parked outside the inn brought that thought to mind.

Faith caught Morgan's arms to steady herself and stared at him as if he had lost his senses. "Take my place? I'll not be giving up my place. We needs must live on something, and I'm quite happy here."

The inn door opened as someone stepped out, and they had to enter the lobby when the door was held open for them. Neither noticed the curious stares they attracted as the tall "French" stranger possessively grasped the arm of the delicate woman who managed the inn and both glared at each other.

"By all the saints, Faith, you can't expect me to let you keep working around all your suitors after we're married! I'm not a pauper yet. I'll find us a place to stay and you can stay home and take care of George."

Faith jerked her arm loose from his grip and hurried to the stairs. She could hear her son's hungry cries already. She turned at the steps to glare down at Morgan. "We have a perfectly good place to stay here. We can pay rent and take a larger suite."

As she hurried up the stairs, Morgan grasped the banister and shouted after her, "By all that is holy, Faith O'Neill, you'll do as I say when the day comes!"

Echoing faintly, but very distinctly, from the second-floor landing came the words, "Go to hell, Morgan de Lacy!"

Grinning, knowing her spirit to be unharmed, Morgan turned to discover their audience. Astounded faces all around stared at him accusingly, but he rose to the occasion in grand style. With a gesture to the taproom, he declared, "We're to be married, gentlemen. Drinks are on me!"

From the doorway came a single raucous cheer, and before any other could raise a voice in protest, Morgan turned to greet the newcomer. As he found a familiar red head waiting defiantly, his grin disappeared, and he rapidly elbowed his way through the onlookers to grasp the intruder's collar firmly. "I have a bone to pick with you, Tobias, my lad." Then, shoving him into Faith's office and out of sight, Morgan swung the door closed behind them.

Toby grinned. "The blithering idiot returns, by Jove! It's about time."

With a growl, Morgan slammed the smaller man to the wall. "I ought to have your neck for taking her away from me. Give me one good reason why I shouldn't."

Toby shrugged as best he could under the circumstances. "She would have come without me if I hadn't."

Morgan felt the truth of that, and reluctantly he lowered the lad to the ground. "Damn your dirty hide, you could have at least told me."

Toby shook himself free and straightened his collar. "Could I, now? And how would I be doin' that? Those vaunted circles are not for the likes of me."

"Oh, shut up." Morgan clasped him on the back and shoved him toward the door. "Come have a drink with the rest of us. She's agreed to have the banns said and do it proper this time, that's all that matters now."

Toby beamed from ear to ear as they fell out into the lobby to see Faith's suitors still lingering curiously. Flinging caution to the winds, he pounded Morgan's back and swung his hand in introduction. "Gentlemen, meet Black Jack O'Neill, Faith's late husband!"

Rage and astonishment leapt to fill the room. Fortunately, Faith was safely ensconced in her attic room, contentedly feeding her son while the inn below exploded into turmoil.

"I don't know why in hell you had to follow me. I can take care of the bitch without your help. This is none of your affair in any case.'' Thomas Montague strode angrily across the crude dock and down to the barren expanse of land and cheap shacks that was their first sight of the colonies.

"I just thought I'd make things easier for you, dear cousin. 'Tis a pity I'm a mite heavy to throw overboard. That storm would have made quite an effective excuse.'' Edward Montague carried his large form agilely down the platform and looked about with more interest than he had displayed in months. The heat was quite oppressive, but he merely mopped his brow as he looked about for some form of transportation. Surely this was not the much-trumpeted capital of Virginia. There had to be civilization somewhere.

"That was an accident, I tell you. You caught me by surprise. I didn't invite you to come along.''

"As her closest of kin, it is my right to see to my niece's safety. That jackanapes thief-taker cannot be trusted any more than you, dear cousin. He could have sold the information to half of London.''

"Safety, my foot and eye! You want her out of the way as much as I do. The old man has his spoon half in the wall and is twanging it for all it is worth.''

"It's of no matter to you any longer. He settled all he intends on you when you married your doxy. That was a damn-fool thing to do, Thomas. Did you really think he'd believe that overblown strumpet was George's daughter?'' Edward waited languidly for a cart and driver ambling down the road to approach them. The colonial hayseed driver appeared more asleep than awake, but the conveyance looked strong enough to carry his weight. With irritation he swung his cane and tried to ignore his cousin's furious pacing.

"You had better ideas? You let the conniving highwayman get away. You didn't know about the book. You didn't even find the right damned lawyer. If it weren't for Lettice, we'd still be searching for her.''

"We *are* still searching for her, lumpkin.'' Bored with this two-month-long tirade, Edward signaled the driver. "It should be interesting to see which of us finds her first.''

From the safety of his hiding place above, a lean figure listened to this perpetual bickering with increasing irritation. More than once he'd been tempted to shove them both overboard, but that wasn't what he'd been paid to do. He wasn't even certain he was being paid to be here, but there were times when a man had to use his own initiative. Watching carefully, he saw the Montagues rumble away before advancing to the deck and signaling the captain.

As if by magic, two excellent horses appeared from behind one of the shacks, and the lean man and the captain were galloping up the dusty road at an entirely different angle from the cart and its noble passengers.

"You shouldn't be in here. 'Tis not seemly," Faith admonished as Morgan settled himself more comfortably on her narrow bed. His long masculine frame filled the meager mattress, but his shoulder provided an effective pillow as she leaned back and gently adjusted the infant at her breast.

With his arm about her shoulder, Morgan confidently ran his fingers across Faith's smooth cheek, then did the same to his son's. The infant scarcely moved from his hungry quest, and Morgan grinned at such concentration. "We're married. None can object."

Faith closed her eyes and tried to drink in all those things she had missed for so long. The hard muscles of his chest and arm held her securely, and the masculine musk of his skin aroused her senses. But it was the seductive undercurrent of Morgan's voice that sent gooseflesh down her arms. She shivered deliciously and waited for his fingers to wander farther.

"I'll have Toby's head for embarrassing me like that. What must people think?"

Morgan idly pried one pin loose from her hair, then began on another. "Does it matter? We are married and have the papers to prove it, though I would not show them as they are. We'll make it all right and proper in the church, and the good people of Williamsburg can just think ours is a romantic tale of a lost lover returning from the dead. You are so young, and I am so wicked, they will be willing to believe whatever you tell them."

Faith giggled. "You really shouldn't have got them all drunk. Poor Randolph won't be allowed out of the house for a fortnight after they carried him home and left him in his carriage without his clothes. That wasn't your idea, by any chance, was it?"

Morgan stared idly at the ceiling. "And why would you be thinkin' that, lass? I'm just a man celebrating his wedding day. We really are going to have to find a place with a higher roof. I'm like to remove the top of my head if we remain here for long.''

Faith gave him an accusing stare. ''You are a wicked, wicked man, Morgan de Lacy. That boy never did anything to you. And Acton was only trying to protect me. Why did you have to play the part of chevalier and try to skewer him to the wall? He near had apoplexy.''

''You do have big ears, my dear. Or is it friend Toby with the big mouth?'' Morgan smiled gently down on her. He could afford to forgive the world tonight, for he was the one in here with his fair Faith, and not any of the others. ''And what else is a 'damned Frenchie' supposed to do when challenged to a duel?''

''Acton did that?'' Faith gave him an astonished look, then, seeing the amusement in his eyes, realized there was in all possibility a lot more to the story than she would ever hear. ''You speak French very well. I never heard you speak it before.''

''Ahhh, *chère amie, ma petite,* how would you know what I wished to do to you if I said it in French?'' he whispered insinuatingly against her ear.

Faith adjusted her son to one arm and ran her free hand down Morgan's breeches-encased thigh. Slanting him a roguish look, she answered in perfect French, ''I might figure it out.''

Morgan grinned and began nipping at her ear while his unhampered hand hooked in the cloth of Faith's night shift. ''An educated wife is a marvelous thing to have. Can you not tell that gluttonish son of mine to hurry?''

Eyes dancing, Faith leaned back to face him. ''I thought we were to resist temptation.''

''Temptation, yes. Lust, no. Do you have any idea how long I've been without you? Did I not tell you about these marvelous devices the canny Dutch sell? Before the evening's over, you will be a ravished woman, my dear. You may as well surrender yourself now.''

He put the truth to his words as soon as Faith laid the babe to rest. Her shift was down about her feet before she returned to bed, and Morgan's own clothes fell by the wayside as he joined her there. There was scarcely room for two to lie side by side, but that was no difficulty in the coming hours. By dawn Faith's fair skin proudly wore the abrasions of Morgan's beard in the most intimate of places, and the Dutch devices had been well tried and tested. They lay momentarily sated in each other's arms as dawn broke through the curtains and their son again sleepily stirred.

"Your son doth wake, milady," Morgan murmured against her ear.

"He's your son. Fetch him, then," Faith countered sleepily, tucking her head closer into his shoulder and wrapping her leg about the warmth of his hard thigh.

"Wench," he muttered, unhurriedly extricating himself as George's cries became a little more pronounced.

"Dastard," Faith muttered a little while later when he presented her with the soggy and malodorous bundle of their son.

"Is it too late to disclaim him?" Morgan inquired warily as he watched her strip the babe to the skin and scour him with the lukewarm water in the pitcher.

Faith sent him a fleeting grin and returned to her task to the tune of George's wails of outrage. "Much too late, milord. Mrs. Needham has already proclaimed you are much alike. Who else do you know has such a full head of black curls?"

Proudly naked, Morgan stood beside the bed, running his hand through the maligned hair tangled at his neck as he looked down on them. "I never looked like that," he objected.

Faith gave their son a sweeping look, transferred the inspection to her husband as if to compare their physiques, then announced grandly, "Want to wager on that?"

Morgan fell across the bed and grabbed her. Laughing, they tussled among the covers with their son between them, their joy too new to allow worry to tarnish it.

Sometime later Morgan emerged from the inn with a happy whistle on his lips and his hat cocked rakishly over his brow. Despite Toby's revelation to the town that they were already married, Morgan fully intended to have the deed done properly in a church, with their real names. His only thought of the moment was to find a clergyman to perform the service. He knew there were problems ahead, not the least of them Faith's desire to remain in service and his lack of income, but he was confident of his own abilities. He would find a way to make it work. With Faith to gain, he could not imagine it being otherwise.

DEVIL'S LADY • 341

The sight of two familiar figures breaking into a run at his appearance caused Morgan to step backward in surprise. Then they were grabbing his arm and shoving him into a nearby tavern and all hell was breaking loose over his head as their words hit him with the rapidity of artillery fire. Thinking of the woman he had left with hair down, singing quietly to their infant child, Morgan groaned and sank to a nearby bench beneath the onslaught.

34

"STOP IT, both of you!" Morgan roared, raising his hand for silence. The hope and happiness of moments before lay in shattered pieces in the sawdust of the floor, but he still had rage to hold him upright. "Enough!"

He glared at the lawyer he had thought he had left behind in London. "What are you doing here, Golden?"

The lean young man returned his glare. "Saving your neck and protecting Faith, if I can. Any more fool questions?"

Morgan turned a black glare to Toby. "And how do you come to be in his company? Do the two of you conspire against me?"

"And how do you suppose I would be doin' that? Would you have me tell my brother of my lowlife friends so he could write for me? I was on the road home when I met him. The Montagues are right behind. Did I mention it was their henchmen who sent Faith fleeing here in the first place? We've got to get her away right now. What are we doing sitting here?"

Glaring at them from beneath black brows pulled together in a straight line, Morgan crossed his arms and made it apparent he was firmly entrenched. "I'm not running. Miles, tell me, did you give them Faith's direction?"

Disgusted, Miles signaled for the waitress and ordered ale all around. The thought of that revolting beverage at this hour churned his stomach, but he needed something stronger than tea, provided that was even to be had in this foreign land. "Do you think I would be here if I had? It was that damn runner. He tracked down my office and had it ransacked. When I found Faith's letters gone, I knew who was responsible. I went straight to her grandmother as you told me to do, but the runner had already sold the information to those scoundrels. Lady Carlisle found out what ship they sailed, and I followed. I didn't know how else to warn you.''

Morgan quaffed his ale without tasting it. As they talked, he kept his eye on the wide window to the street. It was nearly noon and the street was crowded, but he didn't think he could miss the massive battleship and the slippery shark that were the Montagues should they appear. "I apologize," he said gruffly. "You caught me at the wrong moment. Does Lady Carlisle have any idea what they intend to do?''

Not entirely mollified, Miles gave his friend and client a disgruntled look. "Hang you, I should imagine. There's evidence enough, I daresay. What they intend for Faith is anybody's guess. Her cousin has just married the strumpet he was passing off as Faith. The marquess settled a sum on them, but I imagine it's not enough, considering the debts he has accumulated. Faith stands to inherit half of the marquess's estate and all of Lady Carlisle's. The heir might object to the loss of half his funds, but he never hoped to inherit the Carlisle fortune. And as far as I can determine, Thomas only hoped to inherit a portion of the Montague money, and the marquess has already informed him he's received that and will receive no more. So I cannot fathom what they hope to gain by coming here. Unless Edward has some hope of marrying Faith and bringing all the inheritance to him.''

"In which case, he will certainly have to hang me.'' Morgan set down his empty tankard and strode to the window, scanning the street. "I think it's time I faced those two fine fellows. I'll not have Faith and our son constantly shadowed by the buzzards, and if they stand to inherit a fortune, it would be best to remove all obstacles in the way.''

The tone of Morgan's voice caused his listeners to look grim, but mention of the child brought Miles's head up. "Son? Faith carried your child?''

Morgan sent him a tired grin. "She did. She's with him now. A whopping big lad with a head full of black hair. When all this is done, you stand to be a wealthy man, Miles. I'll leave you trustee of his estate.''

That did it. Miles shoved back his chair and rose. "If you have some mad scheme of killing our noble guests and getting yourself hanged just so Faith and the child can inherit,

I'll refuse the commission. I don't want any part of it, Morgan de Lacy.''

Morgan shrugged fatalistically and turned back to the window. "Have it your way. Why don't you say hello to Faith before you go?''

Astounded by the turn of conversation, Toby looked from one man to another. Then, realizing both men had taken a position and neither made any move to find a middle ground, he stood up and came between them. "There's got to be another way. This isn't the forest, Jack. You have friends here. So does Faith. They can protect you. Let me go get them and explain what's happening. There's those who've had enough of the bloody British nobility and would give money for a chance to come to blows with them. We can drive them back across the sea.''

Morgan lifted a skeptical eyebrow. "I've been in town a week, Toby. I think you put too much faith in a few shared beers.''

Miles moved his narrow shoulders nervously beneath his heavy coat. "If there's a chance it will work . . . You don't know for certain yet that they even mean harm. Faith's grandmother has offered a reward for her return. They might simply be after that.''

Morgan's eyebrow quirked even higher, but he didn't turn away. "I have every intention of talking to them first. I just meant to warn you that I didn't expect the conversation to be beneficial. You gentlemen may do as you please. I, for one, intend to remove Faith and my son from the premises. I give you good day.''

He walked off without looking back. If the Montagues had Faith's direction, they would find her a lot more quickly than he had been able to do. Somehow, he would have to get her out of the inn without explaining why. That task seemed nigh onto impossible. Not until he nearly bumped into the kindly Mrs. Needham did a glimmer of a possibility occur. Morgan took the lady's arm and pulled her aside after entering the tavern.

"Could I ask you to do me a tremendous favor?''

Mrs. Needham smiled up at the handsome gentleman the lovely Mrs. O'Neill claimed as husband. The number of names was somewhat confusing and she wasn't at all certain what to call him, but she nodded pleasantly. "I'll see what I can do, sir. Faith has been a godsend to me, you know.''

Morgan gave her a pleased look. "I want to surprise Faith, but I need to get her away from here a little while so I can prepare it. Since we'll be needing a place to live, I thought I could send her out to look at available houses, if there are any. Would you be able to help us?"

"Of course! Do you wish to buy or just rent while you look around for land? There's the lovely little house just around the corner . . . the Johnstons return to their plantation after the Assembly is over. They would be delighted to let it to you until the fall session."

"Perfect. Could you send word to the Johnstons, then send someone with Faith to look at it? I expect to meet someone here shortly, and dare not leave myself."

"Of course." She gave him an anxious glance. "Will this mean that I need to look for a new manager?"

Morgan tried to keep a patient expression on his face as he met her gaze. "That will be up to Faith, but I suggest you begin looking, madam. I don't think she has told you exactly who she is, but you're likely to find out soon enough, though I'm not the one to tell you. I just want to prepare you."

Bess nodded knowingly. "That's as I thought. She's Quality. I knew it the first time I set eyes on her. You're quite right. I'll begin looking immediately. You just take care of your business, and I'll see that she's sent on her way."

Morgan let out a breath of relief as soon as the woman bustled off. Faith was going to kill him, if he didn't get himself killed first. Remembering those sweet eyes watching him trustfully, Morgan turned the tide of his temper on himself. He had to be the worst bastard in the history of the world, but he would do his best to make it up to her. And if it meant getting himself killed in the process . . . well, he'd known all along that was the end he would come to. She would be better off without him.

And their son would have more than he could ever offer. Hanging on to that thought, Morgan found a chair close to the door and sat down to await the arrival of their noble guests.

Upstairs, Faith laughed when Bess suggested that she go around to see the house on the corner. She knew which one Bess meant. She had admired it every time she passed. It was one of the few brick houses in town, with a shell window over the door and neat shutters inside. The walled gardens surrounded a compact kitchen and outbuildings, and fruit trees shaded the far end of the property. Such a house was well beyond their means, but she smiled happily at the thought of it.

"I am certain Morgan means well, Bess, but I really don't think it would be sensible. He will want to look for land for his horses and he will be gone much of the time. I know him well. It would be far better if I stay here. Perhaps we should consider what rooms you could best spare during the summer months when the crowds are lightest. We'll pay you a fair rent."

Bess shook her neatly starched cap. "Captain Morgan . . . He *is* a captain, isn't he? He has that military bearing about him. As I was saying, Captain Morgan was quite insistent that you go see it. I've already sent word around to tell the Johnstons to expect you. It would be most impolite not to go. Besides, it will do no harm to look. Perhaps it will be more reasonable than you expect."

Faith could tell that Morgan was right, that Bess had indeed created a wonderful romance out of their relationship, assigning titles and probably a marvelous story to why they must struggle to make a life in the New World. She sighed, and nodded reluctantly. "I will just look. That is all. I have too many things to do to take much time away."

"Don't be foolish! It's a lovely day. Take all the time you like. Take little George and show him off. He's such a beautiful child. Here, let me help you."

Faith found herself wrapped and bustled off with George in her arms before she quite knew that she was going. A boy waited at the rear door to lead her to the house through the carriage alley, which Faith found puzzling but wasn't given time to question. The idea of living in such grandeur seemed slightly ludicrous, but she certainly wouldn't mind seeing the inside of one of those houses she had admired but had never hoped to enter. The grandest house she could remember being in was the vicar's cottage in one of the towns they had lived in for a while. It had been dark and rather gloomy, but the spacious rooms with upholstered furniture and carpets and draperies had made an impression. She wondered if this house would possess such elegance.

* * *

Morgan watched in disgust as Toby arrived with his brother and some of his friends. While the Assembly was in session, most of the gentlemen in town would be otherwise occupied at this hour, but it was obvious that Faith's followers didn't include just the gentry. As word spread, the tavern began to fill with ruffians and merchants and a few young gallants eager for a fight. Morgan never went out without his sword and pistol, but few of the others had more than rusty shotguns for weapons. This wasn't a lynch crowd. This was a brawl waiting to happen.

Miles arrived in the company of a lanky stranger with a decided family resemblance. Morgan nearly choked on his drink at the notion of Golden's multitudinous family extending to these shores, but as he was introduced, the notion was confirmed. He grinned and shook his head and gestured for them to join him.

"You're out of your waters here, gentlemen. I don't think litigation is going to solve this little problem, but I don't mind the company."

Miles looked around at the crowd congregating in the taproom. "I don't think it's company you need. Where's Faith?"

"She's out looking at houses. Where's our foe?"

Miles raised a questioning brow but answered plainly enough, "Cursing the lack of accommodations and throwing their weight around at Raleigh Tavern. I think a quiet word or two would remove them permanently if the tempers over there were any indication."

Morgan grinned. "Charming family I married into, don't you agree? Do you think I ought to bring my friends here and go greet them?"

"I wouldn't waste the effort, were I you. Unless they wish to be stranded here, they have to get their business done and be back to the ship within some reasonable amount of time. The captain isn't averse to leaving them behind, however."

Morgan sobered. "He might need to be persuaded to take Faith with him when he sails. This is no life for her, when she can have all the wealth her grandmother offers."

Miles grunted, then groaned at being presented with another tankard of ale. Sardonically he replied, lifting the hated drink, "I'll be certain to encourage her in that. Why would she want to stay here with gallows bait like yourself?"

Morgan sent him a furious look, but the inn door opened, and he quickly switched his attention there. It surprised him to see Thomas Montague alone, but he had no objection to taking them one at a time. He watched, waiting to see what would happen next.

Mrs. Needham hurried in at the sound of someone beating at the front desk. Morgan watched as she frowned and shook her head. Catching sight of him in the taproom, she suddenly beamed and indicated his direction. The tall, darkly handsome man turned and gazed at the taproom with apparent disinterest, but Morgan could tell by the set of his shoulders in their elegant silk coat that he was tense. In response, Morgan relaxed into his chair and lifted his tankard in greeting.

The man scowled but came forward. He wore a neatly powdered and clubbed wig and swayed as he walked on his high heels across the rough plank floor. Morgan grinned even wider. Without bothering to rise, he indicated the chair across from him. "Did you come to offer me more money?" he questioned mockingly as the stranger looked disparagingly at his table companions.

"You didn't earn the last lot." Thomas looked down his nose as he addressed the two solicitors. "If you will excuse us, we have some private business to discuss."

Golden shrugged and lifted his cup. "By all means." He didn't move a muscle.

Morgan watched the man fume, calculating his best offense. He knew how to threaten a man out of his jewels. He knew how to wield a sword. He knew how to aim a pistol at a man's heart and pull the trigger without a qualm. But none of these tactics seemed especially suitable to this time and place. Besides, he had promised Faith that he would do nothing to sully their son's name. That did limit the field excessively. How did one go about conquering an enemy by wit alone?

"What we have to say can be said before my friends, Montague. Either take a seat or be gone. I can assure you that you won't get to Faith without going through me."

With a savage look, Thomas jerked out the chair and sat down. "I am not in the custom of sitting with your sort."

"Ahhh, sitting down with thieves and all that. Well, to be honest, these gentlemen aren't accustomed to sitting down with your sort either. Miles, wouldn't you prefer an honest thief to a dastardly scoundrel?''

Miles shrugged and gestured for his tankard to be refilled. Getting drunk seemed to be the best thing to do under the circumstances. ''I don't much care where the money comes from, but generally speaking, it's a waste of time to sit down with a bankrupt.''

Thomas spluttered at this audacity, but Morgan merely folded his arms across his chest. ''Now we see where we all stand, Montague. What can we do for you?''

''I have a warrant for your arrest, O'Neill. You're not the only one who knows people in high places. I can have what passes for the local constabulary to lock you in chains and send you back to London for trial, where you will almost certainly be hanged this time, or we can make more satisfactory arrangements.''

Morgan smiled lazily. ''Take me away, if you will. It is a trifle tedious to have to make that journey again so soon, but the weather should be fairer. I cannot imagine what more satisfactory arrangement could be made.'' Just by the billowing smoke of the long pipes being drawn behind him and the sudden lull in the conversation, Morgan knew that all attention was focused on their table. He would rather they not be overheard, but it seemed the entire town would know his life soon enough. He waited fatalistically for the charges to be named.

Thomas shoved aside the mug placed in front of him and glared at the obnoxious highwayman. ''And where will your doxy be while you're waiting in chains? Have you given that any thought?''

Those were fighting words, and Morgan was ready for any excuse to vent his anger on this encroaching Sassenach. Frowning, he placed his hands on the table and raised his six-foot frame until it towered over the scoundrel. ''I suggest you rephrase your question, sir.''

The low murmurs in the room grew silent. Suddenly aware of his surroundings, Thomas backtracked, gesturing impotently. ''Don't be ridiculous. What would you have me call her, then?''

''My wife! Your cousin! You will speak politely of her or I'll slit your throat while you're sitting here.''

''Sit down, man!'' Thomas sent a nervous gaze to the ominously silent crowd. ''So, you married her. Fine, then.

That doesn't change matters any. You're going to hang, regardless. You can make this easier on both of us and hand her over or you can do it the hard way and I'll have her anyway. It makes no difference to me. All I mean to do is take her back to the lonely old lady who wishes to know her last living kinfolk. She'll be smothered in riches. What objections can you have to that?"

Morgan sat and smirked. "You. I've decided I very much object to you. When you're six feet under, Faith can go visit her granny. How does that sound?"

"Why you damned insolent . . ."

A deep, languid voice broke the surrounding silence. "I wouldn't speak that way to the earl if I were you, Thomas. He might take objection."

35

WERE IT POSSIBLE, the silence grew more profound at these words. The newcomer drew most of the attention, if only for his massive size. A few speculative gazes, however, swung to Morgan. An earl. Eyes narrowed thoughtfully. How many poses did the man have?

To everyone's surprise, Morgan rose at the approach of the large gentleman garbed in immaculate linen and expensively embroidered gold coat. His wig had obviously been made to fit, and there wasn't a lock out of place. Tight stockings neatly tied at his breeches knee didn't dare to sag, and despite the man's size, he moved across the uneven floor with easy grace. Morgan easily matched him in height, but his trim, muscular frame was dwarfed by his noble visitor.

"This is an occasion, Lord Stepney. To what do I owe this stunning courtesy?" Morgan's mockery was light and aimed at himself as well as Edward Montague. He waited for the man to sit before taking his own chair.

Edward kept his chair well back from the table and balanced his meaty hands on the head of his walking stick as he gravely considered the company. "I wish to see my niece. Where is she?"

"Unavailable." Equally poised, Morgan nodded to the tavern maid to take Edward's order. She made a fumbled curtsy and darted away as soon as Edward made it clear that he wished to have the town's best canary wine.

Edward grimaced as he watched her progress. "Extraordinary. And this is where you dare allow a Montague to be seen?"

"This is where your father allows a Montague to be seen. This, and worse." Morgan eyed his adversary with caution. This was the man who had put him behind bars. To all appearances, he was an idle fop, but appearances could easily be deceiving.

Disliking being ignored, Thomas intervened with a sneer. "It is as I told you, Edward. She is naught but a common whore—"

A sword flashed to his throat before the cane came crashing down across the table in front of him. Morgan gave Edward Montague a grin at his quickness and lowered his blade. "Why haven't you slit his throat by now?"

Edward shrugged laconically and accepted the glass of wine brought before him. He inspected the glass carefully before sipping. "He is family, not that he has much care for such niceties. I really must insist on seeing my niece, you know."

"I really don't think you deserve to, you know." Morgan mocked the man's superior tone. "She has been nigh on twenty years on this planet without your caring to meet her. From what I can see, she is better off leaving it that way."

Edward gave their surroundings another languid survey and gave a sniff of disgust. "Surely you jest. I will admit, until we received word of George's death, I had no idea of her existence, but that cannot be sufficient reason to continue to allow her to live in such circumstances. I had rather thought you a better man than that."

Outraged, Thomas glared at him. "Have you lost your wits? Have you forgotten whom you are talking to? He's a damned—"

This time, it was the cane alone that smacked down threateningly near Thomas' knuckles. The ale in front of him sloshed and splattered the table. Edward didn't raise a muscle to frown, he simply leaned back in his chair. "You are speaking of the Earl de Lacy, am I not correct?" He nodded affably to Morgan.

This time, Morgan lost his insouciance and glowered. "The would-be Earl de Lacy, my lord. A man cannot lord over lands he does not possess."

Edward beamed approvingly. "That can be corrected. Now, where is my niece?"

The crowd behind them was growing restless. They had come for a bit of action, but this bandying of words, while admittedly interesting, was not precisely what they were in the mood for. A chair scraped, and a low mutter began to rise.

Morgan knew his advantage already lost. Montague had won another round. But so far, he could not see what the man had won. He sent a quick glance to Miles, who merely lifted his shoulders in equal puzzlement. Together the two Montagues might make a difficult enemy to conquer, but apart they accomplished nothing. Thomas sat and fumed, while Edward benevolently sipped his wine.

They had reached stalemate. The slamming of a door and the sound of a cheery voice from somewhere farther inside the building brought every man to immediate attention, however. Toby was first to his feet and on the way to the door, but he was too late.

Faith blithely floated into the room to greet their usual noon crowd and came to an instant standstill at the sight of the stiff, uneasy men bunched together over their tables. Her gaze immediately swept to Morgan, and she stiffened at the sight of the strangers with him.

"My word, the bitch has a whelp!" Thomas rose triumphantly to confront the source of all his troubles.

Before he could take two steps, his coat was caught from behind. He was jerked around, and before he could see the blow coming, a fist plowed into his jaw, making a resounding crack. He went flying backward across the wooden floor, his wig coming askew and his satin coat ripping on the rough planks. A few of the onlookers casually moved aside to allow him room to sprawl.

Edward gave his relative's unconscious form a brief glance as Morgan rubbed his bruised fist gingerly. "Very effective. I broke a perfectly good walking stick over his pate the last time he asked for that. Thank you for saving me the trouble." Carefully he raised himself from the chair and turned to greet the woman staring with arrested fascination at the form sprawled across the floor.

Bareheaded, wearing her thick curls caught in a ribbon at her nape, Faith looked no older than a schoolgirl. Her diminutive size added to the illusion. But after the first impression, it became obvious that she possessed more poise and grace than any schoolgirl would know. The sprigged-muslin bodice fitted neatly to rounded curves and emphasized a slender neck and white shoulders. A lacy apron encompassed a waist of such tiny proportions that a man's hand longed to linger to test it. But the wide-eyed infant in her arms reminded every man there that she was already taken.

Faith glanced up to her tall husband as Morgan caught her waist and tried to draw her away from the taproom. He was frowning fiercely, but she knew the frown wasn't for herself. Although he was wearing dark blue and not black today, he still appeared every inch the frightening highwayman. She touched the linen jabot at his throat and turned a questioning gaze to the massive man standing in the taproom, watching them with much interest.

"What is this all about, Morgan?" She had seen barroom brawls before. The man sprawled across the floor had no interest to her. But the action that had caused Morgan to send him there caused certain speculation.

Morgan desperately wished to take Faith and his son in his arms and carry them out of here, out of sight of all the greedy eyes and hovering buzzards, but with a feeling of regret he realized he could no longer keep her to himself. He had kept her safe for as long as he was able. Or selfishly kept her out of reach of her family. He didn't know which it was, but it had come to an end. With a gesture of resignation he indicated the massive man waiting for an introduction.

"Faith, your uncle and your cousin have arrived." At her startled jerk, he led her toward the table. "Edward, Lord Stepney, my wife, Faith Henrietta de Lacy." With a grimace of distaste Morgan indicated the man on the floor. "And that, my dear, is your cousin Thomas."

Faith glanced briefly at the man on the floor, then up to her towering uncle. Keen eyes studied with thoroughness, and she bridled slightly at the stare. "My lord," she answered stiffly, making only the briefest sketch of a curtsy. Then she glanced to the other figures at the table and broke into a delighted grin. "Miles! What are you doing here? Why didn't you tell me?"

Miles had risen with the others. Now he made a brief bow and came over to stare at the infant in her arms with interest. He poked the tiny hands curled around the blanket, and smiled when they grasped his finger. "Looks just like his father. What a pity."

Faith laughed, and her uncle watched this little scene with continued interest and almost a look of longing. Morgan registered that fact with surprise, but as the culprit on the floor was beginning to stir, he found other things to occupy his mind.

"Toby, why don't you and some of the others entertain the gentleman on the floor for a while? I'd recommend a gag and rope, myself, but suit yourselves. I need to take Faith out of here."

Edward watched with mild interest as the patrons of the taproom seemed to stir as one upon this command. Nothing could have more effectively indicated the danger he had been in while sitting in this room at the mercy of the Irish earl. His respect for the man rose another notch.

"Perhaps a private parlor . . . ?" he suggested questioningly.

Morgan nodded curtly, then gestured toward Miles. "You'll understand if my solicitor joins us?"

"Probably not, but I can see the choice is not mine to make. Let us proceed." Edward stalked toward the taproom door, leaving the room behind him in a buzz of speculation.

"Perhaps I should ask Bess to take George . . . ?" Faith hurried after the two men, each of whom seemed determined to out-arrogance the other. She had seen Morgan in chains and with sword in hand and knew his pride, but never had she seen this coldly haughty expression. Anyone who had ever doubted the noble blood in his veins would not do so now. Even the formal Edward had met his match.

Edward was the one to answer. Turning more quickly than his size should allow, he offered his arm. "Certainly not. The heir to two fortunes deserves better than a tavern keeper. Bring him here and let me have a look at him."

Wrapping both arms protectively around her son, Faith warily regarded this stranger who would bestow fortunes upon a child he had never seen. He was either mad or wicked, but upon studying his face, she could find no sign of either madness or evil. Edward's gaze was keen and almost amused by her defensive posture. Reluctantly she held George aloft for his perusal.

Amazingly, he raised a quizzing glass to inspect the latest addition to the family. Morgan grinned at Faith's outraged expression. A man who would not hold her infant son was no man at all in her eyes. Morgan chuckled and lifted the bundle from her arms.

"Your credibility has just plummeted irreparably, my lord. Let us go inside and see if we can restore it." He

356 • *Patricia Rice*

nodded toward the open door to the side room that served as private parlor for the inn.

Once inside with the door closed, Morgan offered the infant to the big man to hold. "He's quite tame. I won't promise how long that will last, so you had best take advantage of it while you can."

Edward gingerly accepted the wide-eyed infant, clutching the blankets as if he feared the creature within would escape at a moment's notice. George solemnly eyed his massive great-uncle, waved a tiny fist, and popped it into his mouth. Awestruck, Edward managed a paternal smile.

"He is quite handsome, so far as these things go. You will, of course, want what is best for him."

That struck the mode for the remainder of their brief conversation. Faith indignantly removed her son and moved closer to Morgan's side. "Indeed, I will. He will fare much better than I did, thank you."

Morgan circled her shoulders and rubbed his hand up and down her arm. He was less certain that the question could be easily answered, and he regarded the Sassenach lord with misgiving. He knew all the arguments in advance. He had used them all on himself already. His place at Faith's side was precarious at best, and too newly won to hold with certainty. He waited for the blows to follow.

Miles brought out a chair and offered it to Faith. When she reluctantly took a seat, the men joined her at the table. Edward gave Morgan a brisk look, then returned his gaze to his niece. "I am here to offer recompense for past misunderstandings. My father, your grandfather, regrets heartily his treatment of your family. Unfortunately, it is too late for your parents, but it is not too late for you and your son. He wishes to be reconciled with you. As he has been increasingly ill of late, the matter has become of great importance to him. If for no other reason, I beg that you return with me."

Faith looked badly rattled by this approach. Morgan watched her with sympathy. It was one thing for a father to irrationally write off a son out of pride and ignorance, but to ask a warmhearted woman like Faith to turn her back on her only living relations was a strain to the imagination. Faith had learned much in this past year and a half, but cynicism wasn't a lesson that she had taken to. He reached over and squeezed her hand.

Faith sent him a grateful look and answered simply, "That would be most difficult. I will need time to consider it."

Edward nodded and went on. "I understand perfectly. However, you might not understand entirely what I am saying to you. You also have a grandmother, your mother's mother, who grieves mightily over the loss of her daughter. She has been heartbroken in her search for you. She had been under the impression that my father was looking for you after she learned of your mother's death. When she discovered he was not, she took it upon herself to begin the search. The worry has been detrimental to her health. I believe she lives only to see you again. Surely you must see that you cannot deny her that simple request. She had nothing to do with your parents' banishment. She has never ceased in her efforts to bring them home."

Tears had sprang to Faith's eyes, but she shook her head. "I am sorry it has taken so long for me to learn of my family, but it is too late. My life is here now. A journey such as you suggest should not be undertaken lightly, especially with a small child. Perhaps when George is older, we might return for just a little while, just to make amends. I cannot promise more than that."

Morgan watched her proudly, knowing what it took to say these words. They could not last, of course, but she had tried. The quiet, shy child who had swept his hearth had become a woman of her own, and he was proud to think she had consented to be his wife. If only matters could be otherwise . . .

Edward scratched his chair backward impatiently. "I do not think you understand, my dear. I am offering you a home with your family, not a visit to make amends. Your son will grow up with the finest tutors, knowing the finest society, going to the best schools. You will be gowned according to your station in life, never having to lift a hand to work again. Even if you can deny yourself all that, you cannot deny George the family and wealth he deserves."

The pampered heir squirmed restlessly in Faith's arms and sucked his fist a little louder. Faith gave him an absent smile and turned to Morgan. "Talk to the man, Morgan. You know perfectly well that I would be bored silly with such a life, but if you think it is necessary for George to have that kind of upbringing, perhaps something can be arranged a little later. I really will have to go visit my family sometime, and perhaps by then you will be ready to bring over more stock. I think it best if I take your son upstairs for the moment.''

All three men rose as Faith did, but Morgan caught her arm, holding her back a second longer. ''The decision to return is yours, Faith, I'll not make it for you. But if you give me your permission, I will try to decide what is best for George.''

Faith stood on tiptoe and pressed a kiss to his cheek. ''You are a worthless, conniving scoundrel, Morgan de Lacy, but I love you. Remember, I will not be parted from either of you, so make your decision accordingly.''

Smiling confidently, she left the men to their games of push-and-pull.

Glaring at the other man, Morgan returned himself to the chair. ''You heard her. Now what do you suggest?''

Edward indolently stretched his legs out before him and regarded his toes. ''I suggest you persuade her otherwise. You know as well as I do that you are a blackguard and a wanted criminal. Your marriage is on shaky ground, at best. I would not see the child declared bastard, but a convenient death certificate for one James O'Neill can be arranged. You will have your lands back in Ireland, reclaim your title, take an annual stipend for your silence, and Faith and the boy will be returned to the luxury that Faith has been denied for too long. You know yourself that you cannot provide what I can provide for them.''

Morgan stifled his anger as best he was able. ''And you think you can provide what they need? A family that would throw out one of its own, ignore his pleas, turn its back on the needs of a child—you would have me consign my wife and child to that?''

Edward threw his head back and returned the glare. ''And just what precisely were you doing not nine months ago? You fancy yourself better than us? I've had you investigated, de Lacy. I know precisely what you are, and I know my niece deserves better than that. I will see you hanged should you ever set foot in England again.''

''Then we shall remain here, shan't we? I don't need your bribes, Stepney. I can provide for them. I'm not entirely without means. Do yourself and your family a favor, accept Faith and our son as they are, allow them to visit, then let them go. You cannot possibly make them happy.''

Edward grimaced and set his fists on the table, staring at them rather than the man across from him. "You don't know the half of it, yet. I am the heir not only to the Montague fortunes but also to the title. I have no objection to Faith inheriting half that fortune. She will also have her grandmother's money in time. That will happen regardless of anyone's decision. My concern is for the title. When I am gone, it will go to Thomas unless other arrangements are made."

Morgan shrugged. "I can see reason for concern. The man belongs in either Bedlam or Newgate, but I'm sure you can see that arranged. You need only marry and produce the requisite heir in the meantime. I see that as of no consequence to me."

Edward drew his brows down into a fierce frown and lifted his gaze to the arrogant Irish highwayman. "You'd damned well better see the consequences. I'm incapable of having children. I have mistresses strung across half the damned town. I've been swiving women since I was fourteen. Not one of them has ever produced a child. Not one. It is a family trait. It has happened in the past. That is why there is an act of Parliament allowing the marquessate of Mountjoy to pass through the female line. As a direct descendant of the current marquess, Faith can pass on the title to her son. Your son will be named my heir and known as the Viscount Montague as soon as the paperwork has been completed. You see, he must return with me."

Morgan sat in stunned disbelief as he allowed the far-reaching implications of this statement to sink into his soul. To keep Faith selfishly to himself would be to deny his son the power that came with wealth and nobility. He was a selfish man. He could easily choose to believe that he was better for Faith than any arrogant Sassenach. At the same time, he was honest enough to know that he had not brought Faith happiness, nor offered her what she deserved. Should they stay here with him, struggling to make something of themselves, she would be worn out with work and worry long before she was thirty. He loved her too much to wish that fate on her. But that was what he had planned on doing. Until this. His need for Faith cried out in protest, howled malevolently at the thought of such a separation ever again, but the man before him held all the cards. Once again, the bloody British had won. He could not deny his son the

360 • Patricia Rice

chance to take better than what had been wrongfully denied him in the first place.

Morgan growled a furious protest, shoved his chair back, and stood up abruptly. Without looking at the earl, he strode toward the door, throwing back over his shoulder, "My man, Golden, will go with you. I'll see them protected by better than you. Miles, you make the arrangements."

Edward slumped forward with a sigh of relief and didn't look up as Morgan walked out.

36

MORGAN STOOD in the doorway and watched the tableau within as he had once before. Then he had thought of himself as an outsider, an intruder into the warm family scene of mother and child. Since then he had dared to believe they would accept him, faults and all, and he had been filled with the most miraculous joy at the thought of it.

He clung to the hope for just a little while longer. Faith lifted the swaddled infant into the air and smiled lovingly at his sleepy, contented face, then cuddled him in her arms again as she crossed the room to lay him in his cradle. Morgan knew she would turn soon and find him here, and the smile would grow to include him. She would open her arms and take him in, and he could lift her into his embrace, feel her gentle curves pressed against him, touch her with his kisses. She would run her fingers through his hair, tell him of her love—God, just the thought of that made tears come to his eyes. Morgan gripped the doorframe convulsively and reached for the mask he had worn for so long it had become second nature to him.

"We must talk, Faith." He strode into the room as if he hadn't a care in the world.

Faith spun around and gave a crow of delight at his appearance. As Morgan had known she would, she laid the child down and held out her arms in welcome. Instead of going to her, he took a seat on the one battered chair the room possessed. He gave the attic closet a disparaging look, taking in the ruffled but mended curtains at the window, the narrow, unprepossessing bed, and the uncarpeted floor, letting his gaze drift back to Faith's puzzled face.

Faith took a step forward trustingly, then, at his forbidding expression, settled for a seat on the bed. "Was he awful? He didn't seem half so bad as I expected. I suppose he must love his father very much to come all this way to plead his case. Do you think we might go back for a little while sometime?''

Morgan tightened the steel bands encasing his heart. ''I think that would be best, yes. The weather should hold good for quite some time, and George is a healthy lad. It would be best if you sailed when your uncle does. I'll see that your cousin is held back. He's the dangerous one.''

Faith tilted her head and tried to probe behind the unnatural calm of Morgan's voice. Morgan laughed or screamed or argued or ordered or teased. Morgan did not calmly discuss an impending journey of this magnitude. ''I cannot see the hurry, unless you prefer to live in England. I thought you might wish to stay here awhile and look around. I truly think we have a much better chance of a good life here, Morgan. You just have to give it a try.''

Morgan ground his conscience into dust and faced her squarely. ''I must return to my lands in Ireland, my dear. It will be a long time before they are habitable again, but I owe it to my friends there. You will have to return to England with your uncle. He can provide for you much better than I can.''

Faith clasped her hands nervously. ''Don't be ridiculous. You know I can live anywhere. We'll go to England together, then travel on to Ireland. Or we can go to Ireland first, if you wish. It does not matter to me. I do not care where or how we live, just so long as we are together. Isn't that what you want?''

He could see the hurt forming in her eyes, but it was much better now than later. She was used to being on her own now. He should never have come here in the first place. This time she would know him for the bastard he was and never take him back again. This was his final farewell. He wished there were some way to do it gently.

''That isn't how it works, Faith. If I go to England, your uncle will see me hanged. If you go to England, he will buy back my lands. This is good-bye, my love, for your own good, and for George's.''

Fury flashed briefly across silvered eyes; then she rose with a wicked swish of her skirts and walked toward the door. ''Oh, that is grand, Morgan de Lacy. That is grand indeed. Well, you and my uncle may go hand in hand to any hell you desire. I am staying here.''

With that she stalked out, leaving Morgan to stare disconsolately at the cradle where his son slept. He didn't care about Ireland anymore, he discovered. He didn't care about England either. He didn't give a flying damn for wealth or society. What he wanted was here, in this little room, and with the woman who had just walked out the door. But he would only make them miserable for his own selfish reasons. What he wanted had nothing to do with anything. What they deserved was more important. That was what love did to a man, he supposed. Stupid, bloody emotion, anyway. He was better off without it. Resolutely he rose from the chair, ran his finger over his son's soft cheek, and departed.

He found Edward sitting in the private parlor, critically examining a plate of roast lamb and green peas. At Morgan's entrance, the earl glanced up with irritation.

"Well, is she coming?"

"She has just effectively told us both to go to hell. She is quite accustomed to my leaving her. She has made up her mind to make her home here, with or without me. Perhaps you had best explain the details to her."

Edward lifted his head long enough to study the quiet agony in the man's eyes before nodding and wiping his mouth with his napkin. "Very well. I can see you are selfishly hoping she will stay. I thought you a better man than that. Go tend your horses or whatever it is you do. I will see to her."

Faith looked up with impatience and a trace of fear as Lord Stepney approached with what ought to be lumbering gait. He was so large that she had reason to doubt that they came from the same family, but her father had been tall and the family features were similar, just larger. She didn't like the look in his eye, but he couldn't harm her here. Bess was in the next room, and the taproom wasn't so noisy at this hour that they would not hear her screams. She was among friends here. She tilted her chin defiantly and hid her quivering nerves.

Edward eyed the linen she was folding with disfavor. "You are a Montague. Servants should be seeing to that. Your son cannot grow up watching his mother sully her hands like a common laborer. I mean to make him my heir, you know. He will be the Marquess of Mountjoy one day."

Faith held back the tears of anger and hurt as she glared

at this man who had destroyed her life with his promises of wealth and fame. "He is my son. You cannot take him away from me."

"But I can, my dear," he answered softly, not meeting her eyes. "I have it in my power to do as I wish with my heir. It would be much simpler if you went along with me. I do not mean to harm you, only offer you all that you have been denied before. But you must see that a future marquess cannot grow up over here, outside society's bounds. He will have all that a boy deserves, and a future that none other can equal. Can you in all honesty deny him that?"

"He will not have a father. Can you in all honesty deny him that?" Faith retorted, so angry that she could turn her back on any number of fortunes or titles. Uncle he might be, but in this moment she hated him.

Edward shrugged and lifted his gaze to her furious one. "There are men out there who would weep at a chance to have you for wife. Or I can serve in the place of the boy's father. I would be delighted for the opportunity. You see, I cannot have children of my own."

There was pain in his admission, and at any other time Faith might have felt sorrow for him, but she was suffering herself, and she had no room for his problems. Morgan would have her give up everything so he might go back to Ireland and their son have a title. Did her love mean so little to him, then? Of course. He had proved that before. Why should she doubt it now?

"Go away. Leave me alone. Haven't you ruined enough for one day?"

The tears breaking her voice took some of the sting from Faith's fury. Awkwardly Edward reached to take her in his arms and hug her against his shoulder. "He isn't worth your tears, my dear. Cry, if you like, but then forget him and think of your son. It will come out all right in the end."

It would never be right again, but the warmth comforting her was solid and dependable and had never been there to turn to before. Faith wept, and when she was done, she listened to his persuasive arguments and silently returned upstairs to pack her meager wardrobe. What difference did it make where she lived if Morgan didn't want her?

Faith half-hoped, half-feared that Morgan would come to her when night fell, but he didn't. He had said his farewells, carried out his obligation, and was probably now making his plans for his triumphant return to Ireland. He had sold her for a piece of land. She knew there were other factors involved, but that was what it boiled down to. Morgan didn't love her enough to stand up to her bully of an uncle and tell him they didn't want what he had to offer, that they had everything they needed right here, together. She and their son weren't enough for him. Tears burned her eyelids, but she refused to let them fall.

She had thought the pain terrible enough when she first had to make the decision to leave him. How could it be even worse this time? She had known he didn't love her. Why, then, had she taken him back? What kind of a fool would open herself to such punishment twice?

A fool who wanted to be loved. Sadly Faith folded up the lovely gown Morgan had given to her all those months ago and returned it to the trunk that had carried it to this land of hope and promise. She had worn it once, and then it hadn't been for Morgan. She would never wear another gown for Morgan. She must quit thinking like that. She had a family in England, a family eager to take her back into their arms. She and George would have a family again. That should be enough for anyone.

A tear spotted the yellow satin, but she tucked the gown away and reached for the next. Perhaps having a family again would be enough. It had been enough before her father died. Morgan had never really been her family. He had just been a substitute, and a poor one at that. She didn't even know why he had come all this way to find her. Had he grown bored in England and looked for new ways to expand his wealth? Obviously he had been up to his old criminal activities or her uncle couldn't threaten him with arrest. Perhaps he had left one step ahead of the law. The fact that he had come looking for her didn't mean anything. It couldn't mean anything. He had proved that this day.

She tucked the last article into her trunk of meager belongings. Her entire life could be packed into one box. She closed the lid and rose to check on the sleeping babe. He had recently begun to sleep through the night, but she wished he would wake up to keep her company. She needed a warm body in her arms right now, some proof that she was loved, if just for a little while.

Stroking George's dark hair, remembering a time when

she had run her hands through Morgan's thick locks, she sighed and turned away. The lonely bed offered no comfort, but she would have to sleep if they were to leave on the morrow. She didn't think she would ever sleep again. The picture of Morgan's dark head lying on that pillow made her heart grind with pain, and she tried not to think about it. If she tried hard enough, she might never have to think about anything again. That would be the simplest solution. Her uncle would be more than happy to think for her. He could take the place of her father, telling her what to do and when. She could mindlessly obey, and everything would be taken care of for her. It should rather be like being kept in a box of cotton, protected from the rest of the world. It would be nice to be wrapped in cotton again. As it was, one more blow and she might shatter completely.

By the time dawn came, Faith felt brittle enough to shatter without need of a blow. Stiffly she made her bed one last time. A boy came to the door to carry down her trunk, and she watched it go with a silent protest that should have sailed to the heavens. She glanced around the little room that had been her home for less than a year. Her son had been born here. Morgan had made love to her here. It wasn't the same as the cottage, but it had been a home for a while. Would she ever know a home of her own again?

Gathering her son up in her arms, she thrust that thought aside. She wasn't at all certain why she was succumbing to her uncle's pleas, but Morgan's defection had broken something inside of her. She knew she could make a life of her own here, but it didn't seem important anymore. It didn't seem important where she lived, or with whom. If it made her family happy for her to return, let someone enjoy a little happiness. There was little enough in this world as it was.

Faith allowed Bess to hug her and kiss the wide-awake infant, but the cotton was already wrapping around her, numbing the pain. Lord Stepney waited to take her arm, but she preferred to carry George and walk alone. It was too early for anyone to be about, but then, farewells were always senseless. She had come into their lives for a few brief months and would disappear the same way she had come. They lived without her before. They would live without her again. She missed Toby, but he was happy here.

Faith glanced up as she was helped into the wagon and found Miles uncomfortably sitting a swaybacked pony. She gave him a faint smile. At least she would have one friend with her. That was a comforting thought. He looked solemn and didn't return her smile, but that was his way. She liked the thought of having Miles at her back. Lord Stepney, after all, was a complete stranger.

He climbed up on the wagon seat beside her, tilting the bed ominously, but the ancient oak held, and the driver gave a sigh of relief as the equipment righted itself once Stepney was in place. The driver clucked his team into movement, and they jerked forward. No one came out to watch the little procession depart.

Faith fought back images of Morgan wildly riding after them, swearing his love and refusing to let her go. For whatever reason, he had decided she was better off with her family than with him. It made no sense to her, but men had an odd view of the world. He wouldn't change his mind. She could change her mind, however. She could stay, refuse to leave. What would Morgan do then?

She played with the thought, letting her hopes rise. If she stayed, would he? Was that what he was waiting for her to do? Was it his damnable pride that let her go with her uncle? Could she really have been so wrong about his love? He had said he loved her. Would he lie about a thing like that?

The horses traveled inexorably onward. Before long, it would be too late. She had to decide quickly. Stay here, work at the inn, take her chance at having to bring her son up without knowing family or father, or go to England, where she could raise George in wealth and society. If it were only herself, she would stay. She didn't need wealth or society. If the money were in her control, she might do some good for the Wesleyan cause, but she didn't fool herself into believing her family would allow that. She was much better off here leading a simple life and trying to carry out Wesley's methods on her own. But George . . . What right did she have to deny her son all that?

Faith glanced nervously upward to her forbidding uncle. He was frowning at the horizon and seemed to visibly push the wagon forward with his own energy. He was an enigmatic man, and she couldn't label him one way or another. She wanted to care for him, but it was much too soon. She wanted Morgan here to say it was all right.

Remembering another problem on the horizon, Faith

forced her tongue to work. "Cousin Thomas? Is he all right? Will he be returning with us?"

Edward's wide brow momentarily cleared and a trace of a smile turned his lips. "He will be staying here awhile. I have persuaded him that it would be beneficial to his health and to his pocketbook to remain outside of England for some time to come." He did not mention that it would be safer for all concerned if Thomas were to disappear entirely from their lives. The thought of protecting a fragile female and a helpless infant from Thomas' vicious schemes had been worrying. He had to thank the highwayman for providing the answer to that problem. But he rather thought it best not to tell Faith that. He smiled to himself and turned the subject.

Meanwhile, the object of Faith's curiosity cursed and wriggled in the confounded straw bed where he had spent the night. His hands were practically numb behind him where they had been tied for hours, but fury overrode his physical well-being. He had heard the first guard leave not long ago. He didn't know yet if another had replaced him, but it was time to get out of here. He'd be damned if he would let the ship sail without him.

Thomas scrambled to his feet and pounded his shoulder against the heavy stall door. The splintery wood gave slightly against the leather latches, but not sufficient to free him. He cursed and slammed against the wood again.

"Eh, Bill, what you keeping in here, a wild 'un?" The voice resounded with amusement not far from the stall door.

The question sparked a moment of hope. This one didn't know who he was. Thomas gave the door one more pound for good measure, then yelled, "Help me out of here!" Inspiration came almost at once at the shocked silence from beyond the door. "They've stolen my wife! Help me, hurry!"

The top latch slid open and the half-door swung out, revealing two young men in leather jerkins and homespun shirts. Thomas gave them a disgusted look and decided they only lacked the hayseed between their teeth, but beggars couldn't be choosers. His own once-immaculate coat was covered in straw dust, and bits of straw clung to his wig, which sat askew over his ear. Managing a desperate look didn't require much acting.

"Get me out of here! They've got my wife and son and they're heading for the harbor. They'll kill them! For the love of God, help me out of here!"

The stranger's panic was compelling, and one of the two swung open the bottom door and stepped forward with a knife to cut at Thomas' bindings while the other looked on eagerly. Little of interest happened in this town. This sounded to be the best adventure yet, one they could brag over for months to come at the tavern. From the looks of the stranger's clothes, there might even be a reward. Both young men waited anxiously for orders as the rope fell to the ground.

Fearing the return of his guard at any moment, Thomas only thought of fleeing before he could be spotted. Brushing off his coat and returning feeling to his hands, he glanced desperately about for some means of transportation. Two saddled horses in the yard outside caught his attention.

"I've got to go after them! Have you guns? Give me a horse and a gun. I don't know how much of a head start they've got."

The lads took the well-clothed gentleman at his word. One of them led an unsaddled horse out of a stall while the other raced to the mounts in the paddock. He pulled a long-barreled rifle from the saddle strap and threw it in Thomas' direction, then checked the loading of a second gun in his bag. Thomas grabbed the second horse, caught the rifle, and before anyone could stop him, led his newly acquired friends on a gallop out of town.

37

ARMS PILLOWING HIS head on the table, Morgan groaned and closed his eyes against the light sifting in through the shuttered window. With all the beds in town taken, and denied the comfort of Faith's, he had taken the easy way out. This morning his choice didn't seem quite as intelligent as he had imagined.

Pain shot through his head as Morgan attempted to raise it. What in hell had he done last night, drunk the barrel dry? Flashes of memory pierced his brain, and he shuddered, preferring not to think of it. He lowered his head again to the relative security of his arms and wished himself back to sleep, but some urgency gnawed at his innards, denying him that escape.

He rubbed his fingers over blurry eyes and tried to concentrate his wandering thoughts on the warning shrieking inside of him. He had spent years honing his instincts and listening to their mindless shrieks. He had never regretted it before, but he was regretting it now. At the moment, he would rather die than raise his head. Let them put a bullet through his brain and get it over with.

The shrieks grew worse, however, and Morgan forced his head upward one more time. The darkened tavern was not a pleasant sight to see or smell. The gorge rose in his throat, and he staggered to his feet in search of a basin. He hadn't disgraced himself since he was a lad first in service. This was no time to start.

Reaching his feet, Morgan staggered toward the door. The shrieks of warning were satisfied with this direction, so he propelled himself forward, catching at the jamb and swinging out into the brightly sunlit street on unsteady feet. The fresh air nearly bowled him over, and he leaned back against the building, gasping at this new assault. Water. He needed water.

Every tavern yard had a pump somewhere. He gingerly carried himself down the alley to find the pump and pail, and liberally applied the cold water to his disheveled hair and unshaven face. The splash liberated his eyes, and he gasped with relief as he doused the remainder of the pail over his head. This would teach him to indulge in excess again. By all the saints, how had his father stood himself the next day?

That question dislodged the panic that had woken him. Father. Faith. His son. He was going back to Ireland. Without Faith.

He was letting her get away. He was letting the one woman he had ever loved walk out of his life. For what? For a demolished castle on barren, bog-filled lands? For the people who had once lived in those lands? They were there no longer. No one was there. His family was dead. His friends and neighbors no longer knew him or cared. He had worked all these years for what? To rescue a memory?

But Faith deserved better. If he stayed behind, Faith and his son could have wealth and respect and the family they would never know otherwise. He was doing it for her. Why did the thought sound so hollow in the morning light?

If he loved her, he should be willing to sacrifice himself for her sake. That was what he was doing—making the world better for his family. That thought jarred Morgan's logic off its pedestal. That was how it had all started. He had left Ireland to make things better for his family. He had left behind all he had known and loved, and they had died because of it, because he hadn't been there to protect them, to help them, to love them.

Cursing, Morgan strode swiftly toward the street. He was an arrogant monster. Faith's family could take care of her. She didn't need him. How could he protect her better than they could? It wasn't the same thing at all. His family had no one. Faith had a grandfather and grandmother. A grandfather and a grandmother. Jesus, Mary, and Joseph, whom was he fooling? A grandfather who had disowned her father and a grandmother who had taken twenty years to find her. What in hell kind of protection would they be? And what kind of love would she find there?

The image of Faith's stunned expression as he had told her he was leaving sprang swiftly to mind, and Morgan groaned aloud. How could any one man be such a fool? She *loved* him. She had told him so, and he had no reason to doubt it. Why, then, did he do all in his power to destroy her love? She loved him, and she was willing to give up everything for him. Why had he thrown it all back in her face?

Because he was an arrogant, proud fool. Morgan's feet carried him in the direction of the stables housing his stallion. He had to be mad. This wasn't going to work at all. She would never forgive him. She was better off without him. If he couldn't live without her, he deserved to die. But his feet kept moving determinedly down the street.

Somewhere in his unconscious he recognized the figure hurrying down the street, but Morgan had his thoughts elsewhere. The stable loomed before him, and the cry of his restless stallion loosed an equal cry inside his soul. Without bothering to saddle the beast, he slid the bit into the horse's mouth and threw himself onto its back. Were he the hero type, he would call the horse Lancelot, but somehow, Mordred seemed more fitting. With that bitter thought, Morgan reared the horse backward and then gave him his head.

The black beast stormed out of the stable as if the devil were on its tail, as it might have been. Toby stepped backward just in time to avoid being trampled by flailing hooves, and he gazed in astonishment at the sight of the disheveled highwayman clinging to the animal's back. Never had he seen Jack ride out without cloak and ruffled linen, the picture of immaculate elegance. This stranger in his place sported the dark shadow of a beard, wild black hair escaping the ribbon on his queue, shirt opened to reveal an equally barbaric wedge of curls, coat and waistcoat gone, and shirt sleeves billowing with the force of the wind. But the eyes were the worst. They gleamed like emerald lanterns, fiery mad in a dark face of fury. Faced with a visage like that on a dark night, Toby would have surrendered his valuables too. But in the broad light of day, he kept his courage. Without hesitation, he dashed into the stable to help himself to the most likely-looking nag available.

"Lord Stepney—"

"Edward. Call me Edward. We're family, you'll remember."

Faith couldn't bring herself to call this imposing man

anything so familiar, so she nodded and continued before her courage failed her. "I don't think I can go through with this. It is very kind of you to come all this way to find me, and I truly wish to meet my family, but it would be better if you just conveyed my appreciation for now and left me here. Please ask the driver to let me down. I can find my own way back."

Edward stared at the tiny female beside him with amazement. She was no bigger than a twig, with a face of the same pristine beauty as fragile porcelain. The thick, rich beauty of her russet curls was hidden beneath the silk hood she had insisted on wearing despite the day's heat, and she didn't look strong enough to hold the child in her arms, much less carry herself and the babe the distance back to town. Not that he intended to let her do any such thing. Edward smiled genially.

"It is something like wedding-night dithers, is it not? One does not know what to expect of this stranger you must spend the rest of your life with. Do not let your fears rule you, Faith. We will do all in our power to make you happy."

Faith shook her head fiercely. "It is not the same. I felt no fear in marrying Morgan. I *wanted* to marry Morgan. I don't want to go to England. There is no earthly way you can make me happy. You can't be Morgan, and I can't be happy without him. Let me go, I beg of you. I must find him. He's doing this out of pride; I know he is."

The urgency and panic in her voice startled him, but Edward's swift look at his diminutive companion was interrupted by a frightened cry from the driver.

"The crazy fool—!" The driver jerked on the reins to bring the ambling horses to a halt.

Faith's heart jumped at the sight of the cloud of dust billowing around a trio of horses, but it took only a glance to realize none of the riders was Morgan. Miles reined his pony to stand beside the wagon, glancing nervously down at Faith and the infant and back to the disreputable strangers blocking their path. Faith sent him a questioning glance, and he shook his head.

The man in the forefront raised a long-barreled pistol, and as the dust settled, his features became recognizable, if not his bedraggled raiment.

Edward grunted in dissatisfaction and muttered, "Your

husband doesn't keep his bargains very well, if this is any indication.''

Faith stared at the stranger a little more closely, finally recognizing him as the man Morgan had knocked to the floor the day before. She shivered at the malevolent look of triumph on his face, but oddly, she felt no fear, only curiosity. ''Cousin Thomas?'' she inquired mildly.

The men on horses looked startled by her question, but Thomas merely gestured with his gun. ''I would suggest that you step down, dear Faith. I have a quarrel to settle, and there is no need for you to come between.''

Miles leaned over to help her, but Faith didn't move. She merely eyed the intruder with disfavor. ''You cannot settle a quarrel at the point of a gun, Thomas. My father died by a bullet, but it did not halt his work from going on.''

Thomas sneered. ''No, it did not. That convenient little tome helped us to find you. But it was not his work that I wished ended; it was his life. Now, step down, dear Faith, and let me put period to the only other obstacle in my way.''

Edward cursed beneath his breath, then gave Miles a quick look. ''Get her out of here, at once.''

Not a horseman by nature, Miles glanced nervously at his placid mount, then back to Faith's obdurate figure on the wagon seat. Morgan would have swooped down and hauled her out of the seat and ridden off into the sunset, or the dawn, or whatever. Miles would do well to climb from the saddle, tug Faith to the ground, and assist her up by herself. Get her out of here, indeed. Hiding his doubts, he leaned over again. ''Give me George.''

Stunned by her cousin's revelation, Faith did not listen to Miles but questioned Thomas disbelievingly. ''You killed him? You killed my father?''

The men behind Thomas were beginning to look exceedingly skeptical as the kidnapped ''wife'' turned furious, accusing eyes on her ''husband.'' With his quarry in sight, Thomas ignored their impending defection. ''Not I, my dear. What would I do in a bloody awful place like Cornwall? But there were those willing to accept my encouragement. Money has so many uses, does it not, Edward? But now is not the time to discuss it. Get down, fair cousin, or I will not be responsible for what happens.''

Fury blazed brightly in gray eyes once iced with despair. Had she a gun in her hand, Faith would have used it. As it was, Edward shoved her from the seat and Miles reached for her just as Thomas raised his weapon and cocked the pin.

Morgan, riding like a madman through the brush, had time only to see the weapon raised in Faith's direction and to realize his sword and pistol could not save her in time. Terror and despair and self-loathing filling him, he kicked his stallion into a flight directly between the wagon and the weapon.

Faith screamed at the sight of the coatless rider careening toward them. Despite the dust clouds forming beneath the horse's hooves, she had no doubt as to his identity, and when his raised sword flashed in the sun's light, her screams of protest froze every man there save one. The madman with the pistol already cocked merely grinned and pulled the trigger.

The explosion of sound and sulfur polluted the early-morning calm, sending noiseless pigeons flapping into the air and gulls into squawking flight. The smoke and dust combined to choke eyes and noses, but one pair of eyes saw the bright splash of red against white, and her cries answered for all.

Astonished, Edward found himself grasping a bundle of wailing, flailing legs and arms while the petite figure beside him fled over the side of the wagon. Miles grabbed desperately at the reins of his panicky horse, trying to keep it from trampling the woman heedlessly running between the wagon and his mount to the crumpled figure in the dusty road. Behind them, another horse galloped closer, and in front of them, the two miscreants who had stood behind Thomas now turned their mounts in chase after his fleeing figure.

Ignoring the confusion, Faith knelt beside the man in the road, tears streaming down her face as she pulled his head into her lap. "Morgan! Morgan, don't go! You can't die. Please, Morgan, I'll do whatever you say. I'll never quarrel with you again. You can't go like this. I love you. I'll always love you. Can't you see? Oh, Morgan, damn you, where's your coat? Why aren't you wearing your coat? Of all the times . . ." She lifted her head and cried to the men nervously clattering to the ground, "Give me your handkerchiefs, your cravats, something! He's bleeding!"

As she bent to apply the linen handed to her to the growing splash of red in Morgan's shoulder, black lashes fluttered briefly, then lifted, revealing a glittering green and gold. As gentle hands applied the compress, a quirk turned sensuous lips upward before opening to allow a whiskey-smooth voice to escape. "Anything? You'll do anything I say?"

Faith gave a cry of relief, and before the amazed gazes of their audience, began to rain kisses on his unworthy head. "Anything. You're a madman, but you're my madman, and I dare you to deny it."

"Oh, I'll not deny it, lass. 'Tis yours I am. Let me hear that part about love again, just to be certain 'twas you and not the angels singing in my ears."

"Angels, my foot and eye! If anything, 'twas the devil breathing in your ear. Damn you, Morgan, if you ever do this to me again . . ."

A brown hand reached up to pull her head closer, and for a moment russet curls mixed with black against the dust-caked road.

"I need to teach you a few new swear words, my *cailin*," Morgan whispered against her lips. "You'd think in all this time you'd have learned something more original. But it's a start."

There was nothing weak about his kiss, and Faith succumbed to the power of it, reveling in the touch of his lips against hers one more time. But then, hiccuping, wrenching back her sobs of joy and fear, she pushed away and wiped at her eyes. "Bloody, blithering idiot," she managed incoherently. "Miserable, rotten, scoundrelly, mangy cur. I'll never forgive you for this. Never!"

By this time Miles and Edward had positioned themselves near enough to hear this exchange, and they stared in bewilderment as Morgan's lips parted in a broad grin, revealing a flash of white against his bearded skin. With none of the weakness of a dying man, he grabbed a handful of his wife's curls and dragged her closer, until the heat of his breath seared her cheek.

"You always were a quick student, *cailin alainn*. Never is a long time, but I'm willing to accept the challenge. Give me a lifetime to teach you to love me again, and I'll rest easy."

His eyes closed, and she felt him slipping away. Panicky, Faith cried, "I'll not ever forgive you if you die on me, Morgan de Lacy!"

Dark lashes lifted once again, and a soft smile formed across his mouth as he watched the beauty of molten silver glitter in her eyes. "I love you, Faith, and I'll always love you from wherever I go. You needn't fear for me, lass. That's all I need."

Hot tears rolled down her face and splashed against his dark chest as his eyes closed again. As the men reached to lift Morgan from her arms, Faith whispered for his ears alone, "I go whither thou goest, my love. Keep that in mind."

Miles grunted at the soft smile on his client's face as he helped lift him into the wagon. It was the first time he had ever seen a gunshot man go grinning into the next world.

38

THE LATE-AFTERNOON SUN didn't reach the wine-velvet-draped room with its gilded trimmings, marbled mantel, and luxuriously carpeted floor. Upholstery in gold brocade and elaborate tapestry adorned heavily carved walnut furniture. The crystal glass enclosing unlit lamps shimmered briefly when someone pulled back a curtain, allowing a glitter of light into the room. The light danced over the ornate marquetry of a writing cabinet in the corner and glimmered along the baroque gilt console table against the wall.

The bewigged gentleman in the wide chair beside the mantel looked singularly at one with this richly garnished environment. Deep eyes glared from a face adorned with the crevasses of time and the carved angles of a beaked nose and square, obstinate chin. The thick glossiness of his wine-colored coat and gold brocaded waistcoat seemed chosen just to match the interior of this chamber, but he appeared totally oblivious of his own person as he glared in fascination at the delicate female occupying the room's center.

Russet curls pulled simply to the back of her head and held by combs, blue silk fitting neatly to a sweetly curved bosom enclosed in lavish lace, the object of his attention stood steadfastly with hands clasped in front of her, silver eyes returning his glare. "Your offer is very welcome, my lord, and I thank you, but I cannot accept it."

"Cannot accept it! You cannot refuse, you little twit! The child will be named my son's heir. He has a place in society to uphold." The man in the chair was slowly turning purple at this obstacle to his plans.

"He will uphold it elsewhere, my lord," Faith insisted adamantly. "I cannot accept your hospitality and I will not leave my child. It is unfortunate that our families were separated, and I would heal the breach were it in my power, but not at the cost of my child's happiness. We will be returning to the colonies as soon as practicable."

Mountjoy turned to another occupant of the room. "Tell her she can't leave. Explain this the way women do."

The slight woman on the only delicate piece of furniture in the room smiled faintly at her beleaguered granddaughter. "You are quite right to wish your child's happiness, my dear. I only wish I had considered your mother's more, and possibly none of this would have happened. But what's done is done. Can you not think of any circumstance that might persuade you to find happiness here among us?"

The man leaning against the draped windows did not need to see the rebellious look in Faith's eyes to know what she was thinking. Crossing his arms over his chest, wincing only a little at the movement, he intruded for the first time in this argument. "Do you really wish to number an Irish highwayman among your family? I think not. Faith, you needn't be polite with these people. They'll not listen to anything but their own wishes."

Mountjoy pushed up from his chair, brandishing his fist before falling back with a grimace of pain from his bandaged foot. The curse he emitted caused the woman in the corner to blanch, but Faith only smiled briefly at this almost-human reaction from the gargoyle she called grandfather.

"Damn your moldering Irish hide to hell, de Lacy!" he roared, frustration only increasing his ire. "Were it not for you, she'd be happy to stay here."

The flash of fury in Faith's eyes was easily detected, but before she could reply, still another voice intruded. The languid figure lounging across the settee lifted a hand of dismissal. "Were it not for him, you'd have neither granddaughter nor heir. He took the bullet meant for me. He took Faith in when no one else would. And he is the father of young George, if you've not forgotten. I'd say you were obliged to listen to the man."

Mountjoy settled back into his chair, growling. "I still cannot believe Thomas—"

Edward spoke more sharply. "Believe it. Your handsome nephew had the soul of Satan. Had he succeeded in removing me, he would have hurried your demise too. And do you think he would have allowed Faith to walk off with half the wealth? I cannot be sorry he broke his fool neck falling from that horse. It saved us all a great deal of trouble."

While this argument ensued and attention was drawn away, Faith's shoulders slumped a little. Before she could give in to despair at this continual bickering, Morgan was at her side, strengthening her with his arm, leading her to a seat near her grandmother. Lady Carlisle sent him a grateful look and patted her granddaughter's hand comfortingly.

"They do this all the time, my dear. It is their way of showing affection, I suppose. They cannot live together, but they cannot live apart either. They really are not very bad men, just thoughtless. Can you ever see it in your heart to forgive them?"

Faith gave Lady Carlisle a weary smile. Of all the people she had met since returning to London, this woman was the warmest and most honest. She would be delighted to keep her company and claim her as family if it were not for the querulous Montagues. In the weeks of their voyage, she had learned to admire Edward's intelligence and feel sympathy for his lonely state, but he was not the kind of man one warmed to. And his father . . . She shook her head and returned her attention to the loud voices on the other side of the room.

"So he's an earl! Why should I waste good money on some Irish bog just so he can call himself lord? By Jove, Edward, I think you've lost your wits this time. Did you not hear him say it? He's a blamed highwayman! Let him go back to the colonies and raise his bloody horses. There's nothing but thieves and doxies over there anyway."

Faith drew a scandalized breath, but once more Edward overrode her fury. "In that case, I think I'll buy some land over there myself. I was quite struck by the fertility of the soil. There's a fortune to be made over there. You won't object should I take an extended leave to see the property properly placed into production?"

"Bigawd, and where do you think you'll get the money from? You'll not see a single cent until I'm dead!"

Edward buffed his nails idly against his coat and admired them. "Oh, I think I shall be quite all right in that. Gambling is rather a boring pastime, really, but when the proceeds are invested wisely . . . It's quite amazing what one can do with the funds. Morgan, we've talked of this before. Do you not think I have sufficient to adequately establish a plantation over there?"

Standing protectively over Faith's chair, Morgan gave a

wicked grin. "Indeed, I would, Stepney. And I have a couple of animals over there I would be delighted to see set to breeding stock. It's a damned good place for horses, from what I've seen, almost as good as the emerald shores of home."

Mountjoy was turning purple again as he looked from one man to the other. "You wouldn't. You'll all be scalped and in your graves before the year is out. I'll not have it. Indeed, I will not. You will stay here and look after what is yours already. There is no need to go gallivanting around the world."

Edward looked bored again, but the smile didn't leave Morgan's face. "I do intend to look after what is mine." He placed a possessive hand on Faith's shoulder. "I understand Wesley is not averse to having Faith lend a hand with his writings. It will be a bit touch and go for a while, but I'm not a man to be idle long. We'll get along comfortably enough, though I must agree with Faith, it will be easier once we return to Virginia. She'll not lack for anything, I assure you. You may keep your coins, Mountjoy. We have no need of them."

Faith sent him a glancing smile. "I've already told Miles to give that trust fund to the Wesleyans, Morgan. Don't be too smug."

Morgan choked a little, and Edward coughed into his hand at the sight of the highwayman's face at this revelation, but the love that passed between these two was impossible to overlook. They were grinning at each other like demented lovebirds, and he twitched uncomfortably on the hard settee. "I think that quite settles it, then, Pater. If de Lacy prefers the colonies, I will send them over there to see to my purchase. I believe he will make an excellent partner, if I do not mistake. You can always look to Thomas' child for an heir, if you like. He doesn't seem to have inherited the Montague disability to produce a son. You have not forgotten Thomas had a wife and child, have you?"

Cornered, Mountjoy continued to glare at his offspring. "She's a whore, for deuce's sake! Who's to say the brat is even a Montague?"

Edward shrugged. "Who's to say I am? Or George? It's a nasty world we live in, Pater. Don't muddy it any more. Faith bears our name, and so does Sarah. Be content that they are alive and well and have both produced male children to carry on this accursed title. I do not foresee my imminent demise. There will be time to decide which should carry the name of Mountjoy. Let them be happy until the time comes.''

Faith relaxed and gave Edward a grateful smile. Morgan's hand caressed her cheek, and she leaned into it. It was a rough hand, browned and hardened by years of weather and work, but it was still gentle where he touched her. It was always gentle when he touched her. Remembering the nights of lovemaking they'd enjoyed on their journey here—after a hasty shipboard wedding to guarantee the legality of their marriage—Faith blushed faintly and turned a heated gaze toward Morgan's bold silhouette. He caught her look and returned it, and the air around them crackled with the tension that had sprung up.

Mountjoy turned to take in this little scene and grunted in irritation. The damned Irishman was a handsome devil, and women were fools for a pretty face. His granddaughter was no exception. Well, it was too late to change things otherwise. She'd already bred one pup and would probably be well on her way to breeding another, since Edward hadn't had the sense to keep them apart. He'd only held the babe once since he had arrived, but he was a lively enough brat. A second one wouldn't be unpleasant. And there was Sarah's whelp to consider. Edward might be right there. He'd have to bring that one into the nursery too. The thought of two babes in the nursery and another one on the way made his heart swell with pride. With any luck at all, he would have Northampton beat in another year or two. Then let them say Montagues didn't have it in them to procreate. He sent Edward a speculative look.

''Nobody's going anywhere,'' the marquess snorted, rising with the use of his cane. ''I'll disinherit the lot of you if you try.'' At the rebellious look forming on the faces around him, he waved the cane daringly. ''You can have your bloody Irish bogs and Virginia plantations, I don't care. You can bury your noses in books and gnash your teeth with the Wesleyans—but if I catch you lighting candles to any damned statues, I'll have your heads.'' Mountjoy glared deliberately at Morgan. ''But you'll conduct your affairs from here. I'll not let those children out of my sight, eh, Lettice?''

His audience looked vaguely startled at the mention of

"children," as there was only one inhabitant of the nursery at the moment, but the frail woman in the corner nodded understandingly and rose to lay a gentle hand on his arm. "You are quite right, Harry. We've lost enough time with our children. We'll not have any more of these ugly quarrels."

The marquess nodded vigorously, glared at his offspring, and stomped from the room. Uncertain as to how the argument had been resolved, Faith turned questioningly to her uncle. He smiled benevolently and rose gracefully from his seat.

"I'll have the papers drawn up immediately, if I have to keep a bevy of solicitors up all night. He's tired of managing the estate, has been for years, but he's been too proud to admit it. Let him think he's teaching us, and he'll come around. Well, de Lacy, do you think you can adopt a family of Sassenachs if you can help run the show?"

At the earl's use of the Gaelic imprecation, Morgan looked suspicious, but he had come to understand the man well enough. He nodded slowly. "I'll raise my son as I see fit. And if I don't like what's happening here, I'll take my family and go where I wish. I'll not be hobbled and tied for any man."

Edward shrugged his lofty shoulders. "I'm not one for travel. I'll leave that up to you. Between us, we can manage. Is that land in Ireland really a bog, or does it have potential?"

Faith watched Morgan's eyes light with eagerness and knew the decision made. Perhaps they would live in Ireland for a while. And she knew they both wanted that land in Virginia. London would never hold Morgan for long. But that suited her quite well. She fully intended to follow where he went, and perhaps she could take a little bit of her beliefs with her. There was work enough for two in any case.

She stood and took Morgan's hand, and his attention was instantly diverted. "Remember you left Mordred and Dolly with Toby. He'd be a fine one to ask to look around for a place over there. He already knows the best property around Williamsburg, and was talking of going farther west, where they're opening up those new lands."

She looked relaxed and confident, a woman capable of standing on her own and taking on the world's troubles—a far cry from the battered, half-starved child who had fallen at his doorstep. Morgan lifted a hand to Faith's tumbled curls, crushing their silken texture between his fingers as he smiled into her shining eyes. He wanted her like this always, a woman who could stand up to him and give as good as she got. He had no confidence in himself as a protector, but with Faith . . . Anything was possible. He had never seen himself married to a Sassenach, either.

"I'll not forget the lad and what he's done for us, *cailin*. But it's you we must think of now. It will take me time to make a place for us. Will you be happy here? Or shall I have Miles look for a wee place for us, whatever we can make out of what's left?"

Faith touched the linen cravat at Morgan's throat, wishing it gone. He looked so handsome in his midnight-blue silk, just like the earl he purported to be. Amusement crinkled her lips at the thought. "Shall I be Lady de Lacy, then? And what do we call George?" She slid her hands higher, almost encircling his neck, and he caught her waist with both his strong hands and smiled that heavenly smile down on her. "We could have a wee cottage in Ireland if that is where you go next. Or a cabin in Virginia. Or the dower house in Essex. Or we can take the fourth floor and climb out the windows when you wish to prowl about London. It makes no difference to me. Just take me with you, and I'll be happy."

"*Bean sídhe*," Morgan muttered against her hair. Then, remembering their company, he turned to Faith's uncle, only to find the room mysteriously empty. Grinning at the haughty earl's discretion, he turned back to the faerie-woman in his arms and lifted her clear of the floor. "We'll ride together, my *cailin*, have no fear of that."

Faith laughed as he swung her high in his arms and strode boldly toward the door. She would rather be kidnapped by a black highwayman any day then be rescued by a white knight. Flinging her arms gladly about his neck, she buried her lips against his throat and proceeded to show him just how much she feared his forward ways.